# PRAISE FOR DANIEL POLANSKY

*"Daniel Polansky is one of my favorite new writers. Again and again, he manages to reinvent and invert well-worn genres."*
David S. Goyer, screenwriter and director

*"Polansky is his own genre."*
Delilah S. Dawson, New York Times-bestselling author of *Star Wars: Phasma*

*"Surges like a revelation."*
Matt Fraction, Eisner Award-winning comic book writer

*"This f\*cking guy. He's too good to live…"*
John Hornor Jacobs, author of *Southern Gods*

*Daniel Polansky*

# MARCH'S END

**ANGRY ROBOT**

ANGRY ROBOT
An imprint of Watkins Media Ltd

Unit 11, Shepperton House
89 Shepperton Road
London N1 3DF
UK

*angryrobotbooks.com*
*twitter.com/angryrobotbooks*
March 31st

An Angry Robot paperback original, 2023

Cover by Sarah O'Flaherty
Edited by Paul Simpson and Andrew Hook
Set in Meridien

ISBN 978 1 91520 245 1
Ebook ISBN 978 1 91520 250 5

Printed and bound in the United Kingdom by TJ Books Ltd.

9 8 7 6 5 4 3 2 1

MIX
Paper from
responsible sources
FSC   FSC® C013056
www.fsc.org

*For my family, past and present.*

# BOOK ONE

## 2000

# ONE

The children were in the attic. Mary Ann and John sat on the bed, with Constance in the big rocking chair beside them, flipping through the book. Watching through the window overlooking the old oak tree you would have thought she was reading them a story, but she was not.

"T is for the Tower," said Mary Ann. She was eleven, with red hair and a recently fastened set of braces. "From where the March is ruled with strength and wisdom."

"Good," said Constance, turning the page, "keep going."

"U is for Under the Mountain, the kingdom of the petrousian, carved from rock and stone."

The book was bound with something like leather and lacked title, author, or colophon. The pages were ancient but neither yellowed nor brittle, shades of colored ink depicting a vast subterranean city, gravelly humanoids smelting ore and carrying iron and carving stalagmite.

"From earth and stone," she corrected. Constance was thirteen, big for her age, frowsy haired and friendly.

"What's the difference?"

Constance wasn't sure, but as the eldest she couldn't say that. "It's in the book."

"From earth and stone," Mary Ann repeated unenthusiastically.

Constance turned a page to reveal a troupe of knights – fox knights and owl knights and clockwork knights and knights that looked like jellyfish but with fewer tendrils – all marching or riding or flying in spotless armor, carrying shining weapons and fluttering banners.

"V is for…" Mary Ann began but did not finish. "Oh, hell, I never remember this one. Can't we just go to the party?"

"Don't say hell," said Constance, "and not until we're done with the book."

"Hell," Mary Ann said again, "and who cares about the book? Why do we have to do homework on a holiday?"

"Because we're Harrow," said Constance, wearing what was Mary Ann's least favorite expression. "We're special. Go again."

"V is for very boring," said Mary Ann, "for vexing and for vile."

"You should know this by now. I memorized it when I was still in third grade."

"Of course, you did, you're perfect." Mary Ann crossed her arms.

"Mother says–"

"You're *not* our Mother."

"No, Mother is our mother, and she said we had to finish with the book before we went to the party. Do you think I wouldn't prefer being downstairs, rather than babysitting the two of you?"

"I think you *love it*. I think it's your absolute favorite thing."

"V is for the Valiant, who defend the March from evil," said John, turning from the window. John was eight; you could tell by his height and his baby face and the children's suit he had been forced to wear – but not always by his eyes, which were bright blue and strangely serious. "W is for the widdershins, nomads and wanderers, who walk with their hands and eat with their feet. X is for the xerophiles, lords of the western wastes, monarchs of the endless sand. Y is for the yearlings, the mounts of the mighty, who will not see a second spring. Z is for the zoaea, who guard the Southern oceans in argosy and galleass."

Constance turned to the final page of the book, which was black from margin to margin with something darker than ink. "What comes last?" she asked, with more than her usual seriousness.

Even Mary Ann knew this one. "The End," she said, matching her sister's tone.

Constance shut the book with a snap. "Now we can go to the party."

Which was already in full swing below, festive music echoing up the stairwell, the landing packed with revelers. Strings of colored lights twinkled over the mantle, a fire crackled in its corner, mistletoe hung hopeful over doorways, wine mulled, dips congealed. The Harrow's Christmas party was an institution across the neighborhood. The living room and the dining room and the fancy room in the back where no one ever went were busy with friends and acquaintances, people who worked with Father and people Mother had once gone to school with and everyone fortunate enough to live in their development; except for the Wolfes who were out of town, and Mr Crowley who never came to anything and turned his lights off on Halloween.

In the center of it, wearing a long evening dress with her hair up in a high crown, stood their mother. Sophia Harrow was a tall woman, with skin the color of fresh snow and the same blue eyes as her son. With effortless grace she greeted new arrivals, charmed strangers, filled cups, disposed of plates, always with a smile by turns welcoming and gracious, the very model of a genial host.

'It must be a terrible thing to grow up with a mother who isn't beautiful,' thought Constance.

'I'll never be so pretty,' thought Mary Ann.

It was hard to tell what John thought.

Sophia was busy but she broke away as soon as she saw her children, bending down to kiss them one by one, even Mary Ann who usually objected.

"Did you finish with your homework?"

"Yes, Mother," said Constance.

"Yes, Mother," said Mary Ann, an instant later.

John didn't say anything.

"There's food in the kitchen, and you can have some Coke if you want, but not too much or it will keep you up." Sophia patted Constance and rubbed Mary Ann's shoulder and fixed little John's little tie. "What did I ever do to deserve such lovely children?" she asked, not rhetorically but as if waiting for the answer.

There were fifty people at the party but when Sophia spoke it was like she was speaking just to you, and Constance beamed and John strutted and even Mary Ann looked pleased. Then Sophia was called away to deal with some minor crisis involving a chafing dish and the children were left to the interference of their elders. They congratulated Constance on her height, made John tell them his age and complimented Mary Ann on the dress which she hated, before – in the fashion of adults – forgetting about them completely, leaving the Harrow children finally free to go their separate ways.

Constance found her father in the kitchen, standing over a sudsy sink, hands sheathed in orange rubber gloves. Constance took a towel and started to dry a serving plate.

"Wouldn't you rather be enjoying yourself?" Michael asked. Michael had taken off his suit jacket to wash the dishes, and the muscles in his back and shoulders, and his stout gut, stood taut in his dress shirt. He shared the same genially unruly hair as his daughter. Sophia sometimes joked that it was the wildest thing about him.

"I don't mind," said Constance.

Her father smiled and Constance smiled back.

Mary Ann slipped out onto the porch to where Uncle Aaron leaned in the chilly shade of the December evening.

"Done with your lessons?" he asked.

Uncle Aaron was Mary Ann's favorite person in the world.

He was terribly handsome, thin and dark with bright, striking eyes. He had lived in Europe for a while. He was also the only person Mary Ann knew besides their cafeteria lunch lady who smoked cigarettes, which was why he was outside, by himself, instead of inside, at the party.

Or so Mary Ann assumed. "Finally finished," she said. "Constance is such an apple-polisher – say 'a' instead of 'the' and you've practically got to start over."

"I used to hate the book when I was your age," said Aaron. "I could never get the V right."

"That's the one I missed!"

"Your mother could roll it off her tongue, of course," said Aaron, looking through the window at where Sophie stood over a tray of appetizers, pointing out various delectables to Mr Hoban.

Mary Ann took a firmer grasp on her uncle's arm. "I'm so glad you're back for Christmas this year."

"Yeah? Me too, Mule," said Aaron.

Mule was his special name for her, from when she was six and had refused to eat her broccoli even after the rest of the family had finished dinner and dessert and gone upstairs to wash up.

"Do you think you'll stick around after the holidays?" Mary Ann asked.

"Maybe," said Uncle Aaron, though he was staring at Sophia and did not look down.

John took a gingerbread reindeer from off a tray and went to stand in front of the Christmas tree, an overabundant Fraser Fir capped by a star which scraped the high ceiling. The base was bare, but in a few days it would be unapproachable with gifts delivered by an ageless Teutonic deity, tasked with dispensing punishment and reward among all the world's children. For John this remained a point of certainty; not once had he thought of poking around in upstairs cabinets for hopes of forbidden treasure. At eight, John still believed in magic.

"Finished with the book?" asked his grandmother, who sat by the fire with a quiet half smile on her face.

John took a seat on her lap. "Yeah," he said, "but it took *forever.*"

"Forever?"

"Constance and Mary Ann fight *all the time,*" said John. John had only recently been introduced to hyperbole and was losing no opportunity for practice.

"All the time?"

"Almost," he said, "Constance has to know better, and Mary Ann has to know best."

"It's part of having siblings," John's grandmother explained, "big table, lots of voices."

John swallowed this with his iced gingerbread.

Back in the kitchen Michael and Constance fought a desperate rear-guard action against the dishes, an endless horde of *hors d'oeuvre* plates, crystal glasses, serving trays and silverware. They fell into an easy, wordless rhythm, like dancing a tango or turning a double play in baseball. Constance would have preferred the second analogy.

"My loyal little soldier," said Michael.

Constance flushed proudly. "Somebody needs to help."

"Someone does," Michael agreed, "not everyone will."

Mary Ann had come in from the porch, and she watched as Sophia charmed Ms Alexievich and the Trevors with some or other sparkling observation, Mr Trevor smirking and Mrs Trevor giggling and Ms Alexievich laughing so hard that she coughed up most of her wine. Mary Ann wondered at how her mother had learned to hold her neck in that certain way, and to talk just loud enough that everyone had to lean closer to hear, and whether these were things that Mary Ann herself might learn with time and patience or if, like her blue eyes, they were a characteristic of her mother she could never acquire.

The fire in the great stone hearth – in previous years, reliably roaring – had burned down to hot coals. John's grandmother sighed.

"Do you miss him?" John asked.

"Of course," said his grandmother. "Every day."

This made John feel better. John missed his grandfather terribly – when Constance watched sports news, anytime he went swimming, sometimes for no reason that he could tell. Dead in his sleep earlier that summer, in John's mind he would remain forever a smiling, bushy-bearded giant, associated with the smell of wood smoke and motor oil, with a faded leather comfy chair, with a certain superficial severity, with safety and with home.

"No one loved the holidays like your grandfather," said his widow in the faded firelight. "He was like one of the kids, it was exhausting. Everything had to be exactly the same, every year – if you left out some tinsel or a plaster Santa he always noticed." She gazed into the dining room, where Aaron had come to join his sister as she held court around their makeshift bar. "He would have been so happy to see all of us together again."

Beginning as it did only a few years prior, John's sense of time was somewhat unreliable. Even still, he understood Uncle Aaron had not been to the house in a long time, a very long time, so long that John could only distantly recall having met him – at an outing to a fair, or someone's birthday. Too young likewise to be told anything, still John could piece together from the occasional strained silence and slammed door that however his dead grandfather might have felt on the matter, Aaron's return had not proved entirely easy for anyone.

"How come Aaron lives in Denver?" John asked.

"I guess he must like it there."

"It's far away, though."

Joan – this was the name of John's grandmother, though John was only dimly aware of this, her existence in his mind so entirely constrained by their relationship – sighed again and squeezed John tight. "Very far," she agreed.

So far that evening Mary Ann had eaten three buttered rolls and the crispy top off the creamed potatoes, and she was heading into the kitchen for another plate when she caught Uncle Aaron and her Mother engaged in the sort of conversation which children are not supposed to hear. She set herself against the wall and perked up her ears.

"I'm just suggesting you pace yourself," said Sophia.

"Thank you, sister," said Uncle Aaron, though not like he meant it, "but this isn't my first experience with alcohol."

"Yes, I think I recollect some of your earlier adventures. There was that Thanksgiving when you put most of Mother's turkey into the rose bush."

"Do you have these written down somewhere? Aaron's big book of failures? You could give it to the kids to memorize. 'C is for catatonic, a state of inebriation which Aaron reached just before we were supposed to take the family photo.'"

Against herself, Sophia broke into a slow chuckle. "You're such an asshole, Aaron, it's fucking unbelievable."

From the hallway beyond, Mary Ann's eyes went very wide.

"Don't let the kids hear you talk like that," Aaron warned.

"I never curse in front of the children," said Mary Ann's mother, "you entitled little cuntbag."

Uncle Aaron shook his head in confused dismay. "What would you even carry in that?"

"It's a portmanteau."

"I can't see it catching on."

Sophia laughed again, then drew closer to her brother, lowering her voice. "I'm glad you're back," said Sophia. "It's been...with Dad gone, I'll need your help."

Aaron set aside his towel, though there were still dishes wet on the drying rack. "We're on that again?"

"I can't be everywhere, and neither can Michael. Constance's young, and Mom's old."

"You think this was easier back in the day, when everyone had ten kids to help out with the harvest?"

"I think a lot of them died of cholera," Sophia pointed out.

Mary Ann tip-toed out of the kitchen and back to the living room. It was *very* late, at least by Mary Ann's reckoning. Mr Isherwood, who was partner at her father's firm, snored unabashedly on their couch. Beneath a sprig of mistletoe Mr Trevor was whispering something to Ms Alexievich which she either did not like or did, it was hard for Mary Ann to tell. The Endos were arguing about something in the corner, quietly though not subtly. Mary Ann felt like when she had ridden the Tilt-a-Whirl at the spring carnival and gotten very sick, but like with the Tilt-a-Whirl she did not want to stop. The Rat Pack crooned dated carols from the stereo and Mary Ann began to dance, an arrhythmic shuffle which missed the beat while taking up a lot of space in the room.

This expression of merriment was, of course, Constance's queue to ruin everything. "You're acting like a child," she said, putting one hand on Mary Ann's arm.

Mary Ann pulled away. "Just because you can't dance."

"You can't dance either, you just don't know it."

"What does this look like?"

But executing a fancy two-step Mary Ann caught the corner of a side table, spilling a glass of wine. With the preternatural sensitivity gifted to parents of young children, Sophia arrived from the kitchen a moment later, pursing her lips unhappily.

"Good job," said Constance.

"Shut up!"

"Constance," said Sophia, "will you grab some paper towels and clean up that spill? And Mary Ann, why don't you help your brother off to bed, it's late."

Ms Alexievich had disappeared, but Mr Trevor was smirking, and the Endos had set aside their quarrel to bear witness to another.

"But, Mom, it wasn't my fault," Mary Ann hissed, conscious of the eyes on her.

"It's not a question of fault, darling, but John needs to get to bed."

Mary Ann swatted aside this olive branch like a hovering mosquito. "It's not late for Constance!"

"Constance is thirteen, when you're thirteen you can–"

"I'm almost as old as she is, and anyway it was her fault! You didn't see, she grabbed me!"

Sophia offered a quick smile to the too-curious Mr Trevor, then leaned down to scowl at her second child. "Don't raise your voice."

"Sorry," said Mary Ann, not really meaning it, a feigned retreat to marshal her resources.

"Now, we've had a lovely evening," said Sophia, "but all good things come to an end. Forget about the mess, I'll clean it. Just go to bed, you're tired."

Mary Ann wasn't tired, she was furious, her face flushed, every muscle in her small body tensed. The sheer *injustice* of it! If Constance had just left her alone, everything would have been fine, Constance who had to tell everyone everything, and who thought the two measly years between them meant everything in all the world. "But Mom–"

Bowing her head to meet her daughter Sophia Harrow resembled a whip crack or a lightning bolt. "You're embarrassing yourself," she said.

Cowed, red-faced, eyes flashing swift death on her tyrannical mother and sniveling sister and the sniggering guests, Mary Ann fled to the safety of the upstairs bathroom.

We begin as independent anchors of all reality, growing later to allow the introduction of a caretaker existing exclusively to service our own immediate needs, our perception expanding beyond that in time to encompass fathers, siblings, next door neighbors, so on and so forth. But the process is piecemeal and imperfect, and even the best of us regresses in moments of stress. Mary Ann was no more ruthless a sociopath than any other adolescent, and yet in her mind just then being sent upstairs early ranked high if not foremost in the grim and tedious annals of humanity's crimes.

A knock at the door did not improve her mood. "Go away!" she yelled.

"I need to brush my teeth," said John.

"Go away!" yelled Mary Ann, "I'm peeing!"

"No, you're not," said John.

The door to the bathroom locked but if you jiggled the handle the right way it would open, and John started jiggling it just then, one final indignity which Mary Ann was forced to suffer, lemon juice on her paper cut, salt in her wound. She wanted to scream but she couldn't so instead she did this thing which was like screaming but did not come out of her mouth, gathering up all her energy with her chest and her head and her throat, with her lungs, with something that was deeper than her lungs and for which she didn't know the name, wanting to go away, anywhere, it didn't matter, just away, screaming silently until she couldn't breathe and her vision was streaked with dots of color, John coming through the door just then, little brothers surely the curse of the devil himself–

–They were in a kitchen. Not *their* kitchen. Their kitchen only had one stove with four burners and an oven beneath, and this kitchen had many dozens of stoves running along the wall, and whereas their stoves ran on gas these stoves were kept hot by thick cords of sweet-smelling wood. Speaking of fires, their kitchen did not have a very large one in the center of it, nor had it ever been used to cook the skinned body of a cow, or perhaps it was a deer, or perhaps it was something altogether different. In fact, there were many ways one could tell that *this* kitchen was not *their* kitchen, not the least of them being the cook, who wore a chef's hat and a dirty apron and possessed a super-abundance of hands.

"Well?" he snapped two fingers at them, and with two more he tweaked his handlebar mustache, and with a hand he stirred thin soup, and with yet another he pulled a loaf of bread out from the oven and set it on the counter, and with another he cut the loaf, and with the rest he attended to the myriad of other duties required of him. "What are you waiting for? The fig aspic needs to get taken to the ambassador from the Faunae Palatinate, and this krill is nearly ready for the hydronese." The Man-With-Many-Hands sipped a tasting spoon of his stew. "Just needs some garum." He snatched up a bottle and added a few dashes of a thick brown sauce into the cloudy brine.

John gaped. Mary Ann gawked.

The Man-With-Many-Hands managed to find one to massage the sore spot which had formed around his temples. "Don't tell me – today is your first day?"

"We're new here," Mary Ann admitted.

"Of course you are! Why wouldn't you be?" The Man-With-Many-Hands threw himself back into his work, stirring a mix of indigo cake batter, thinly slicing a bit of beetroot, grinding an array of spices with a mortar and pestle. "I don't have enough to do feeding half the March, now I'm supposed to break in two new servers! On today, of all days!"

"What's today?" Mary Ann asked.

For a moment, albeit a brief one, all of the Man-With-Many-Hands's hands stopped what they were doing, so shocking was this question. "What's today? *What's today?* Don't they tell you anything in – wait, what are you?"

"Humans."

"Don't they tell you anything in Humanland?"

"Not a lot," Mary Ann admitted.

"Today is the Coronation. Why do you think the Tower is filled with guests? Why do you think we're cooking enough food to feed an army? Why do you think we were so desperate for help that we, apparently, hired the two dullest creatures in the March as servers?" Their conversation had interrupted the clockwork machinery of his kitchen, and the Man-With-Many-Hands had to rush to make up for it, limbs darting off in all directions. "Just fall in line and ask directions once you get to the throne room," he advised. "But hurry along – the faunae are friendly enough, but the hydronese get testy when they don't get their krill."

Not knowing what else to do, John picked up the tureen filled with tiny, listless, sour-smelling shrimp, and Mary Ann collected a gooey cube of brown, and then the Man-With-Many-Hands opened and ushered them out the door and into a great stone hallway. There they joined a menagerie of strange creatures carrying stranger dishes of food; an opossum with a vast brick of brie, a shambling, animate slow-cooker heating fondue on its back, four fluttering songbirds each holding a corner of a bread loaf wrapped in cloth. The Harrow children found themselves following the cavalcade down the corridor and into a stairwell which seemed to go up forever and down the same distance and packed into line there was nothing to do but follow the general ascent. Mary Ann had never in her life climbed so many stairs – then again, she had never smelled krill soup before, or met a man with more than one pair of arms, and so perhaps this was not the most noteworthy of the evening's novelties. Up and up and up they went, John and Mary Ann following along behind an elephantine sock puppet – another first – whose gray cloth exterior obscured their view of what lay ahead.

Mary Ann had begun to wonder if they would continue their climb forever, something which seemed less impossible just then than it might have earlier in the evening, when without warning the steady procession of servers reached the top of the staircase and entered a many-tiered hall. It reminded Mary Ann of the time her father had taken her and Constance to a baseball game, except that the walls were blue stone and the distant ceiling an elaborate dome of some substance clearer than glass which bathed the room in starlight. Also, in place of the baseball fans there were all manner of unlikely if vaguely familiar beings; awkward, strutting clockwork creatures; animals who were larger than animals were supposed to be and who also wore clothes, which animals generally do not;

spindly humanoids in gigantic, impeccably painted masks;
robed bipeds with polychrome wings and vivid coxcombs and
sharp beaks; a cluster of upside down people with hands for
feet and feet for hands and heads that nearly clipped the floor,
dressed in colored caftans and burbling water pipes. Mary Ann
had the strange sensation of seeing an old playmate or a distant
relative she'd only known through pictures.

"We're in the March!" Mary Ann exclaimed suddenly.

"*Obviously*," John said. "I figured that out like a million years
ago."

Then it was like seeing the reveal in an optical illusion
or discovering yourself fluent in a language you have
never spoken. There was no need to ask directions, Mary
Ann recognized the embassy of the hydronese, diaphanous
sylphs lounging in pools of tepid water impatiently awaiting
their krill; and the gaggle of woodland creatures dressed in
Renaissance silks which could only be the fabled faunae,
sleek-furred lords and down-feathered ladies gathered in one
corner of the terraced amphitheater. Their chief emissary, a
severe looking sparrow, was just then returning to his perch
after paying homage to the cathedra which filled the center
of the room.

The chair was immense and fettered by a network of chains
hung taught from the ceiling, like the struts of a suspension
bridge. Each link was thicker around than a grown man and
made of a myriad of materials – graceful argent, untarnished
aurichalcum, grisly and misshapen iron, adamantine darker
than ebony, luminescent crystal, a dense tangle of colored
twine. The throne itself was enormous, so large and so grand
that it ought to have dwarfed its single occupant, though in
fact it served only to enhance her majesty. The Queen was
tall and willowy and wore a long dress which seemed to be
made not of cotton or silk but of the late evening sky, just
before night has fully fallen. She wore a silver diadem which
imprisoned a fallen star – the Bauble – and somehow, it was

no shock to Mary Ann discerning her mother's face in it's cold, perfect light.

Standing beside Sophia, dressed in a suit of red and black armor, stood Mary Ann's father. Michael was bigger than Mary Ann could remember ever seeing him, hulking, as big as he had seemed when she was still a small child and he used to hang her upside down by her ankles. He leaned against a single-edged sword which was larger than he was, sheathed in a scabbard sealed by seven heavy locks. A ring of keys hung conspicuously from around his neck.

Uncle Aaron sat on a chair perched just below his sister, dressed all in gold and trying hard to look serious. Joan, their grandmother, sat beside him in a black mourning dress. Rounding out the three, wearing the same insignia as their father, was–

"What the hell is Constance doing here?" Mary Ann asked.

"*Shhhhh…*" John shooshed.

But it *was* Constance, the same wild hair, the same superior look. She sat primly, straight-backed, her gaze set on the creature then performing obeisance to their mother, a bipedal salamander wearing a headdress of maroon and cyan which contrasted starkly with her banana yellow skin. There were many thousands of – well, not people, but creatures of some sort – between Mary Ann and the proceedings, but by some strange artifice she could hear the supplicant's voice as clear as her morning alarm clock.

"The molluschites swear fealty to the Harrow, who keep the March at peace, and safe from what waits outside of it."

"In the name of the Throne, and of the Harrow, we accept your loyalty," said Sophia, in the same voice that she had used to welcome Ms Dermout to their Christmas party, "and we swear to uphold the ancient pacts, to protect and defend you until the last of our line."

"May that day never come," said the ambassador, who rose and shuffled her way back to her deputation.

"The new Queen is terribly beautiful," said an off-white mouse in checkered livery in the dense crowd beside them.

"She's too young," disputed an orange octopus through dangling chin-tentacles, "who can trust a Harrow without gray in their hair? Now, her father, that was a ruler. Great big chap, with a beard that ran all down his chest."

"Age isn't everything," said the mouse.

"Say that twice," muttered Mary Ann.

Back on the main stage a bullfrog in golden robes with a golden chapeau and a golden rod flared his neckflaps and bellowed an introduction. "Aetheling Calyx is called before the Gyven Throne."

The Aetheling was nearly, though not quite, a man. His skin was mossy green, his hair were tendrils of root curled into a tight chignon atop his head. He was dressed entirely in skins and furs of various sorts; a nubuck coat, a fine pair of smilodon breeches, a rug from an ice bear around his shoulders, a crown of antler horns atop his proud forehead. Alone among all the nations present, he had arrived without coterie or attendants. When called he rose from an empty suite of leather couches and approached the throne with the sharp, controlled steps of a dancer.

"The Kingdom of the Thorned Rose is in attendance," he announced.

"Has the Aetheling come to offer fealty?" the herald asked.

There was a brief pause, then the lord shook his head slowly. "He has not."

There was a sudden lulling from the vast assemblage; the hydronese stilled in their pools, the faunae cased their chatter, the molluschite ambassador, still returning to her seat, gasped and looked nervous. Drinks were set down, haunches of meat returned uneaten to their plates.

Sophia maintained her implacable smile. Michael pulled his key ring from off his neck and undid the first lock on his sheath, the *chink* echoing with strange clarity throughout the crowd.

"Much is told of the Kingdom of the Thorned Rose," began Sophia, in the same tone with which she had reminded Mary Ann to clean her bedroom earlier that afternoon, "not yet have I heard them called oathbreakers."

"The word of a verdurite is more certain than the tallest redwood, or the growth of nettle come spring."

"And yet? When the End plagued your boundaries, warped the wood and corrupted your groves, did your pleas for help go unanswered?"

The Aetheling's face was hardwood but not unreadable, and Mary Ann saw him tense in indignation at the slight. "The wise reed bends to the storm, while the proud oak is uprooted."

"Fealty was the cost of that salvation – allegiance to the Harrow and to the laws of the Thousand Peoples."

"The verdurite have not forgotten their oaths," said the Aetheling, tossing a pointed look behind him, "alas that not all here can say the same."

"I object!" shouted the leader of the stony petrousian from where he waited to offer submission. Tall and stooped and crumbling, worn as a cliff face, he was assisted by two stout, stern looking children, rough and rigid as boulders. "If the north is in ferment, Under the Mountain is not responsible. The verdurites press our borders and harry our trade."

"What need has a tree for a cave? When we swore fealty to the Harrow we laid down our leather lassos and our spears of bone. For long years the Heartwood has thirsted, and our warriors lay awake in shame." The Aetheling turned squarely to face Sophia, his dark eyes stern and unbending. "But our faith has not been repaid. If the Tower cannot keep the peace, then the Kingdom of the Thorned Rose will be forced to make its own."

Sophia said nothing. Michael released another lock on his sheath. The mouse next to Mary Ann gasped. The cephalopod crossed its tendrils around its oblong eyes.

Mary Ann's grandmother, or perhaps only a woman who

looked and spoke and acted like Mary Ann's grandmother, Mary Ann was not yet sure, rose from her chair. She wore a dress of shot silk and leaned upon an opalescent staff. "We have met, have we not, Aetheling Calyx? When I visited the north, in the days when your anther was newly blossomed."

"I am surprised you still remember, Queen Mother," said the Aetheling respectfully.

"I am not so old as to have forgotten my time beneath your boughs. I have hunted horned serpent and eaten flesh unblemished by salt. When your thanes went north I rode in the vanguard, fought the End beside your houscarls and great heroes, planted our fallen in the Heartwood." She took on a wounded, disappointed look. "I had not imagined their sacrifice would be so quickly dismissed."

For the first time the Aetheling seemed pressed. Mary Ann felt a peculiar pang of sympathy, having been on the receiving end of so many of her grandmother's chidings. "The name of the Queen Mother will be known among my people so long as seed takes root," he assured her, "but we cannot sit idle while our lands are occupied by these…these…tunnel dwellers!"

The petrousian bristled and would have argued if Joan had not continued on swiftly.

"Trust us now, as you did then," said Joan. "If there is a grievance between you and the sons of stone, it can be relieved; harms mended, injuries healed."

"You would come north once more, Queen Mother?" asked the Aetheling, with the faint trace of a smile.

"My journeys have ended," said Joan, "only the last remains to me, and I hope to put it off for some years yet. But I am not the only Harrow – and my son, newly returned to the March, might serve in my stead."

Aaron sat up uncomfortably, looking like Mary Ann when she was called to the board in math class. Sophia threw a quick, worried glance at her brother, then her mother, then turned back to face her subjects.

"A delegation from the High Prince," Joan continued, "to inspect the boundaries, and ensure peace in the north. Would that satisfy?"

The Aetheling thought this over for a moment. In his silence Mary Ann could hear, or perhaps feel, the crowd grow anxious around her; shuffling hooves, paws pressed together, serpentine throats cleared. The Coronation, a rote if ebullient ceremony, had turned pregnant with the potential for violence.

"It would be a start," said the Aetheling.

Joan nodded, and Aaron fidgeted, and the crowd calmed slightly. Sophia leaned forward from her throne, the Bauble in her crown like the gleam of a lighthouse. "Aaron will be sent north, to adjudicate any disputes between the Kingdom of the Thorned Rose and Under the Mountain, and the Harrow will do everything we can to ensure harmony between your peoples. We do not yet know each other, Aetheling, but you will find me as amicable as my mother." Sophia's face turned suddenly hard. "And as fierce as my father. The oath your people swore to my family does not require revisiting, and this coronation is a mere formality – but a necessary one. Refusal to bend knee to the Tower is treason, and jeopardizes the safety of our land, and that I will not abide, not from you nor anyone. Against such madness I would gather all the loyal forces of the Thousand Peoples and send them north, to hew your trees to stumps and turn your scared groves to charcoal. The Harrow set peace above everything save honor. Swear fealty or find yourself an enemy of the Throne."

Mary Ann's father wore a look of grim ferocity which she could not ever remember seeing before. Three locks hung loose off his sheathed sword, and the room, vast as it was, seemed to have grown warmer. Mary Ann did not realize she had been holding her breath until after a long moment the Aetheling dropped to one knee, and the Thousand People broke into rapturous applause.

And then another page – a sneering tin clown with a wind-up key in the back of his neck – pressed Mary Ann to her task, and the evening passed in a whirlwind of quotidian tasks in impossible surroundings. It was hours before the two Harrow siblings slept, amid the ranks of a towering bunkbed shared by the lower staff, each rung a small platform with a cheval glass and dewdrop wash basin, twisting chutes leading to the ground – but she woke in her regular bed, below the framed Joni Mitchell poster, with the morning light shining in through her window.

*2023*

# TWO

Mary Ann first noticed her phone buzzing on the bedstand while Jeffrey knelt between her legs, and she consciously resisted the urge to check it. It rang again a few minutes later, but by then they were busy with something else, and so it was only later, when he got up to flush the condom, that Mary Ann saw Constance's missed call in condemnatory red.

"My sister is the only person under 50 who won't send a goddamn text," she said.

Jeffrey had come back to the bedroom and took Mary Ann's complaint as being other than rhetorical. "What does she want?"

"I haven't checked yet."

Jeffrey laid down beside Mary Ann and Mary Ann got up to open the window, the sticky scent of their comingled bodies replaced by the evening air. It was chilly for December in Los Angeles, which meant it was warm for most of the rest of the world. But weather, like misery, is a localized concern, and Mary Ann shivered even though it was much colder in Pittsburgh or Siberia. She undid the child's lock on her pill bottle and swallowed an olanzapine while gazing at the reservoir and the houses which twinkled with fairy lights in the hills below.

"Are you going to?" Jeffrey asked.

"What?"

"Listen to your message."

"At some point."

"You know they've got this voice to text thing now, it'll just type it out for you."

"I know."

Jeffrey rolled over to face her with a smile he was sure was charming. "Have you told them about me?"

"Should I have?"

"We've been dating for six months."

Though Mary Ann couldn't remember any specific conversation to this effect, Jeffrey introducing her as his girlfriend at a work party one evening the summer previous, a *fait accompli,* nothing to do but accept it or sprint off screaming. "I don't talk to my sister much about that sort of thing," she said.

"What do you talk to her about?"

"I don't talk to my sister much."

Jeffrey looked skeptical. Jeffrey's father was in Florida and his mother was in Arizona and their wide-spread, loose-knit family was held together by a vague sense of good-will, an attitude which Jeffrey assumed universal. There was some part of Jeffrey which seemed secretly to reject the idea that other people were *other* people, different altogether than he was, and not just shamming in some pointless effort of rebellion. "What's so bad about your sister?"

"Nothing, we're just different."

"How do you mean different?"

"Constance was always…she knew what she wanted to be. What she was supposed to be. Everything was always clear for her. She's got cute kids and she's on track to make partner and her house is always clean."

"And you're the black sheep?"

"John might have claim on that," Mary Ann admitted.

She closed the window, careful not to catch the senecio dangling above it. Mary Ann's apartment consisted of books and plants and a drawing table and not much else. Her plywood shelving groaned from the weight of haphazardly arranged paperbacks, and the greenery was likewise distributed absent any seeming order; a wandering Jew trailing from the ceiling, a prickly pear set on the bedside table, close enough to skewer an outstretched hand. It sometimes occurred to Mary Ann that at thirty-three she ought really to have acquired at least a few pieces of decent furniture; sculptured Scandinavian stools which were uncomfortable to sit in, a coffee table made out of an old butcher's block, but the truth was most of the time she didn't care. Anyway, she couldn't afford it—she could barely afford the apartment on her salary as an underemployed graphic artist, freelancing slow and none of the firms hiring.

"All of which is to say, you're not heading home for Christmas?" Jeffrey asked.

"No."

"You didn't tell me that."

"If I started telling you things I'm not going to do, I'd never stop. I'm not planning on taking up fly-fishing. I have no intention of voting Republican. I'm not going to spin class tomorrow."

"But you bought that class pack."

"I know. But it's so early."

"It's just as well anyway. Christmas in LA is the shit. It takes twenty minutes to get from Downtown to Santa Monica, and you can walk in to any restaurant without a reservation."

There were times when Mary Ann looked at Jeffrey and couldn't help seeing his cliché; a Hollywood shark in (or out of) an expensive suit, the too-toned body, the foodie aspirations, a creature of that uncomfortable intersection between money and genuine creativity. Then again, she supposed he could do the same thing with Mary Ann – a slightly past her prime manic-pixie dream girl, bobbed scarlet hair and a vaguely Bohemian affect. Except that Mary Ann got the sense that Jeffrey was doing this all the time, more or less, and didn't mind what he saw, that he preferred the image to Mary Ann as she was in her raw and warty flesh.

Jeffrey got up from the couch and looked at himself in the mirror, dropped down and broke off a dozen pushups, then got back up and looked at himself in the mirror again. "You should really move in with me," he said.

"I don't want to live in West Hollywood. I like it in the hills. It's cooler up here."

"Cooler like weather, or cooler like James Dean?"

"Both."

Jeffrey turned away from his reflection and waved a hand at Mary Ann's apartment. "You know you're too good for this, Mary Ann. You deserve better. I want to give you that."

The only light in the bedroom came from the flickering LED clock and the moon, and this last was obscured by her plants, and Mary Ann hoped it was too dim for Jeffrey to see her frown.

"What are you doing tomorrow?" he asked, returning to bed, "I'm meeting some people at the Roosevelt, you should come along. Six-thirty OK?"

"Sure," said Mary Ann, happy her indiscretion had gone unobserved.

"And wear that blue skirt I like," he added.

They rolled around a bit to see if Jeffrey would get hard again, after which Mary Ann had to spend a while pretending she wanted him to stay even though she knew he would not and anyway didn't want him to, and by the time this was finished it was very late and she had nearly forgotten her sister's call.

# THREE

John took his phone out and saw Constance was calling.

"You want this last line?" asked Billy.

The bathrooms at the Lady had a pansexual silhouette on the front and faded urinals and a sink with a wide countertop. John put the phone back into his pocket. "Sure," he said.

Walking out, Billy was his best friend and they were going to conquer the world. "– I mean you're such a fucking good cook, man, and with all my connections–"

"No doubt," said John.

Billy talked his way out the front door, heading uptown to pick up this actor chick that he knew, hadn't been in anything big yet but you could tell she was destined, you know, just one of those faces. John went back to the bar and took a seat beside Kiki.

"I hate that guy," she said.

"What can I say? He's always got coke."

"That's because he sells coke," said Kiki. Kiki looked like a chef, which is to say that she had too many tattoos and wore a more or less permanent expression of muted hostility. Depending on his mood, she was John's best or only friend.

"Only to subsidize his budding career as a restaurateur."

"Don't just say it like, 'he's always got coke', as if it was some sort of coincidence."

"Fair enough."

"It doesn't fall out of the sky. It doesn't magically appear in his pockets every morning. He's a drug dealer."

John called for the tab. "Do you want to argue nomenclature, or do you want to do the rest of this coke?"

"Begrudgingly," said Kiki.

Kiki was sort of seeing a guy who was DJing a set at a club just north of Chinatown. They came up the stairs at Grand Street Station into the fragrant smell of Canaan fir and white pine, warm and resinous despite the fading nasal drip. Rows of conifer laid against the chain link fence of Roosevelt Park, and a white girl in her late twenties sat in a fold-out chair beside them, wearing a ski cap and warm mittens and drinking from a thermos. It was one of who knew how many corner store Christmas tree dealers dotted the island, evergreen forests sprouting up the day after Thanksgiving to disappear come the 26th.

"Where do you think they go the rest of the year?" Kiki asked.

"Treeland," John explained.

"Treeland?"

"It's north of Vermont."

"Canada is north of Vermont."

"Not quite that far north. Why do you think she's wearing that ski cap?"

"Because it's cold?"

John snorted. "Not to her kind. You check under there, you'll see she's got little nubs like fawn horns, or ears that point up like a raccoon."

"Cause she's from Treeland?"

"They all are."

"And what's Treeland like?"

"It's nice, it's aptly named."

"So why leave?"

"There are some things you can't get in Treeland. Music instruments. White Widow. Spices of various sorts. So, they cut a few trees and haul them down here for the month." From his right, John looked like much of gentrified Brooklyn, thin and sallow though he had his mother's bright blue eyes. He smiled at the girl in the ski cap and she smiled back at him. "It's dangerous, though. They have to return home before the month ends, and they don't have calendars or clocks in Treeland, so it's hard for them to adapt. Sometimes they meet a dude or get really into a TV show and forget to go back."

"What happens then?"

John fingered the needles on a Douglas fir, exposing the left side of his face, which was broken from his jaw to just below his eye socket, his mouth contorted into a crooked half-sneer. The girl looked away.

"Best not to ask," said John.

Kiki's sort of guy's party sort of sucked, half-assed holiday décor strung around an unfinished basement attached to a speakeasy attached to a Chinese restaurant, but they'd come all the way into the city and there was nothing to do but drink until it improved. John's phone buzzed again, a notification from a delivery app on the screen above the message from Constance which he assumed was intended to pressure him about coming home for Christmas. It was a holiday tradition, like hanging stockings over the mantle, a pointless and awkward ritual but then, his sister was the ultimate lost-causer. John put the phone back into his pocket.

Kiki's guy finished his set and came over and introduced them to a bunch of his friends, who were part of some sort of loose noise collective or something. One of them had a tab of either MDMA or 2C-I but he couldn't remember which and so he and John each took half of it before the start of the next set. John wasn't exactly clear on what 2C-I was or did; later, when he was outside sharing a cigarette, and noticed a giant lizard come crawling out of a dumpster, he assumed it was a psychedelic.

The guy he was smoking a cigarette with was either named Tom or Tim, and either way didn't seem to see it. "It's just not realistic to pretend that people are going to be able to play the same role in your life forever."

"Sure."

"People change."

"They do that," agreed John. The lizard was the size of a large dog and its tail was much too long for its body, stretching back into the dumpster like some reverse diver's house.

"You have to be able to accept that, and not get stuck into dated patterns of behavior."

"I agree," said John. The lizard locked eyes with John for a long moment, as if the two were sharing a joke, then sauntered out of the alleyway towards Delancey Street, dragging its extended tail behind him.

"Anyway," said Tim or Tom, "that's why I've decided to become polyamorous."

"Appreciate you keeping me in the loop," said John, flicking away his cigarette.

It was nearing midnight on a Tuesday and the city that never slept was at least winding down. Whatever Kiki had wanted to happen with the DJ hadn't, and she looked cold and tired.

"You ready to go?" she asked.

"Tom's friend has an after-hours thing in Bushwick."

"Who?"

"Tom?"

"Tim?"

"Probably."

"You really trying to get me to go out to Bushwick? I've got work tomorrow."

"Yeah."

"You've also got to work tomorrow."

"Yeah."

So Kiki peeled off, leaving John to share an uber with Tim and Tim's friends. Crossing the Manhattan bridge apace with a half-empty Q train was like flowing through an artery, you could pretend you were part of something vast enough to be important. The bar in Bushwick was like every bar in Bushwick, unfinished wood and cheap bottled beer. It was loud though, and busy, and just then for John that was enough. He drank some of the beer and did the last of his reserve coke and the night dissolved into a series of moments like frames in a film reel. John on the dancefloor. John feigning a heartfelt conversation with a stranger who was buying him a shot. John watching a long-limbed silhouette watch him from across the bar, a spindly giant standing corpse-still against the speakers.

John in the alleyway outside, ejecting the contents of his stomach against a brick wall, making sure to keep his feet clear of the vomit. The moon was bright between the buildings. John was cold without his coat. He wiped his face and remembered a night long ago in another world when Mary Ann had performed a similar act of semi-public regurgitation. He remembered the message from Constance. He fished around in his pocket until he found a stick of gum, chewed through the remainder of the packet, then spat it into the puddle of his excreta.

"You OK?" Tim asked when he walked back inside.

"Fabulous," said John, rallying once more, "where to next?"

# FOUR

At first it had been scary, then it had been exciting, but mostly being at the hospital was boring, two hours in the waiting room with all the other sick people and the people who were waiting for other sick people. The children's section was all incomplete puzzles and picture books with the pages ripped out, and they'd left in such a rush that Julian hadn't even had time to pack his Nintendo Switch and so now he was reduced to playing LEGOS with his little sister, not even LEGOS with Star Wars characters or spinning ninjas but just regular LEGOS.

"These chairs are scratchy," said Evie. Evie was five, or five and three quarters if you were to ask her. She had her grandmother's blue eyes and teeth that were sometimes too big for her mouth.

"Yeah," said Julian.

"We've been here *forever,*" said Evie, who had received the Harrow penchant for hyperbole.

"No, we haven't," said Julian, heir to an equally characteristic pedantry.

"It feels like forever."

"Time is weird sometimes. Like, if you're in school time is slow, but during your birthday it goes very fast."

"Yeah," agreed Evie. She looked up from the tower she was building. "Do you think she'll be OK?"

"Sure, she'll be OK," said Julian, "Grandma's tough. Like Mom."

"Am I tough?" asked Evie.

35

"Of course you're tough. You're a Harrow."

Evie nodded firmly, reminding herself, then went back to her tower.

Constance sat nearby, one eye on the door they had taken her mother through, the other on her two children. At thirty-five she looked like a larger version of thirteen, the same wide face and big shoulders and short, thick limbs. Her hair was particularly frazzled that evening, but then she had a good excuse.

She checked her phone, more as something to do with her hands than because she thought she had missed a call. She tried to remember the last time she had spoken with John – a couple of months, some harried conversation while he was running to his job. He had seemed fine, not that that meant anything. John would step off a cliff smiling – but he'd still fall. As for Mary Ann, Constance recalled the circumstances of their last meeting with unhappy clarity, a cup of coffee when she'd come back east for a friend's wedding, small talk punctured by occasional interruptions of belligerence, an awkward hug and silence since.

She looked down to find Evie at her ankles.

"It'll be OK, Mom," said Evie. "Grandma's tough."

"The toughest," Constance agreed.

Adeline came into the lobby, looking slender and well-kept despite the hour. Julian leaped up from his LEGOs and ran to embrace her, and Evie scramble to join him. Constance had to consciously stop herself from doing the same.

Adeline gave the two children a less than usually thorough greeting, then hurried over. "I'm sorry it took so long."

"That's OK."

"I must have slept right through your phone call – you know how I get."

"Yeah," said Constance.

They smiled awkwardly. It was a little bit like being on a first date, except it was the exact opposite.

"How's she doing?" Adeline asked.

"I can't get a straight answer out of anyone. She's in intensive care right now, they said they're working on her."

"Jesus, that's horrible. I'm so sorry."

Constance tried not to enjoy the sympathy, the widening of Adeline's dark eyes, the way she set her hand against her chest as if to keep her heart from fleeing. "It's all right."

"Mom," said Julian, "Mom, Grandma Sophia got sick."

"I know, baby," said Adeline.

"But she's going to be OK," said Julian. At eight, Julian resembled Adeline in shape and Constance in personality. He was dark skinned and dark haired and was possessed of the keen confidence that there was a right thing to do in every situation, even if this was often to ask one of his mothers.

"Of course she will," Adeline agreed. She pulled a dollar bill out from her purse. "Which of my favorites is going to get a candy bar?"

"I am!" said Evie.

"Me too!"

"Two dollars? Well, I wasn't thinking of spending *two dollars*, but I suppose…" Adeline found a second single in her bag and gave one to each child. "If you come back with spearmint gum or jujubees or something, you're never going to eat dessert again."

"Mom's just kidding," Julian promised his sister, taking her by the hand and leading her to a vending machine in the corner of the room. Adeline waited until they were out of earshot before continuing.

"How you holding up?"

"I'm OK," said Constance, "I mean…you know."

"Yeah."

"I called John and Mary Ann, but…"

Adeline managed not to fill the end of this sentence, which Constance thought was kind of her. John had been *persona non grata* since coming to Julian's third birthday party drunk and present-less, and Adeline and Mary Ann had disliked each other from the start.

"What happened?"

There was a small pause, and then Constance said, "We were heading up to bed, and Mom collapsed."

Adeline asked, crossing her eyes. "You're a terrible liar. It really jumped a generation with you."

Constance seethed. "Do you think you could stop shitting on my mother while she's maybe dying in a hospital bed?" Constance had the most unpleasant sense of *deja vu*, a hundred conversations that had gone just exactly this way, half-heartedly defending her family against her new family, more on instinct than out of any real disagreement. Of course, her mother was a good liar, she was the best liar Constance had ever met, except maybe for John.

"You're right," said Adeline, "that was a horrible thing to say."

"It's all right."

"I'm not... it isn't easy seeing you."

"It isn't easy for me either," said Constance.

Constance might have said more; that the bed was always cold, that she had heard Julian crying alone in the bathroom the day before, that Evie had stopped eating anything but breakfast cereal and taken to scowling like a teenager; but the Doctor came out from the back just then, looking tired and somber. Constance found herself struggling to pay attention to their conversation, individual words – sedation, biopsy – obstructing the general flow like boulders in a river. Or fat in an artery.

The Doctor excused himself and left, and Constance and Adeline stood awkwardly for a while longer, watching Julian and Evie trade bites of chocolate.

"They'll never get to sleep, with all that sugar in them," said Adeline.

"Speaking of which," Constance began, "do you think you could take the kids for tonight?"

"Of course."

"I know you've got class tomorrow, I can make it up to you this weekend."

"Don't worry about it. As long as you need."

"Thanks."

"Constance?"

"Yeah."

"Be careful, OK? You don't have to tell me about it, I know you won't, but just...be careful. The kids need both their mothers. And you're all alone now."

Constance nodded sadly and went to say goodbye to her children.

# FIVE

To the Tower they came.

Choking the roads in uncountable numbers, carrying the last of their meager possessions, exhausted, mud-rutted, babes weeping and elders gasping, they came. In all direction they came, clogging the roads and eating from whatever was planted beside. Bands of molluschites clustered around the motile, house-sized shells of their sachems, constant vagabonds but still unused to such a trek. Anima with broken shafts and bent wheels rumbled through overturned murk, engines sputtering, clockwork eyes as desperate as their fleshy counterparts. Parched and withered hydronese passed listlessly, the dull mist of the late afternoon no substitute for their springs and rivers. Flocks of heron and swallow kept pace, some managing a graceless flight, others so exhausted they had been forced to the indignity of perambulation. Many others. Endless others.

Constance rode alone among them, in dark armor upon a pale yearling, with her father's weapon strapped across her back. On another day the sight of her high on her horned ungulate would have been enough to provoke hope in those she passed, or at least interest – but the refugees had eyes only for the road in front of them, and barely seemed to notice her presence.

Constance made for a molluschite elder, still sprightly by their standards, the size of a tractor-trailer or a blue whale, wiggling his way through the mud. His massive body was fuchsia and atop and around his great white shell hung pouches for supplies and for his descendants to rest in during the long journey, baby molluschite peeking up with brightly colored heads and wide, sad eyes.

Constance dismounted, trudging beside the elder for a few silent steps.

"Hello again, Constance."

"Pink."

"The last I saw you, your hair was all black."

"And you could still fit inside a building."

Pink smiled radula the width of Constance's arm. "Much has changed."

The line of refugees had slowed to near stasis, as somewhere far ahead servants tried desperately to find places to put them. Already the Tower was nearly at its limit, the rooms all occupied, the parks turned to tent cities, exiles sleeping among the orchards.

"Did you see it?" Constance asked.

"Only the start," said Pink. "We were in the far west, near the Wastes. The widdershin are wary people when you can even make sense of them, but something had changed. They were frightened. They'd heard rumors of…"

"Yes."

"They said the xerophiles were desperately arming, and those that could had already fled. At night you couldn't see the stars, or even the moon. The rivers turned murky, and then they turned black. The crops around them died or…worse than died. Grew sick and hungry, swayed against the breeze. The morning before we took to the roads, we found one of our pups dead in a thicket, strangled by the grass."

"I'm sorry."

"You will find similar stories among the rest," said Pink, stretching his neck out of his shell to gaze at the miserable crowd that surrounded them. "They say that it was worse further west. That all of Cactacathay has been swallowed up."

Constance thought of Cactacathay, the living city of the

xerophiles, clustered shrub castles bowing in greeting, garden pathways opening silently, the marketplaces fruiting nopales and prickly pear upon request.

"It can't be true," added Pink, "can it?"

Constance did not have an answer. Constance had long ago stopped imagining anything was impossible, bad things in particular.

Held up at the distant gates of the Tower, the refugees called a halt, collapsed into the mud or against one another. A family of mice in homespun cotton passed around a rind of hard cheese. A petrousian sat motionless, eyes closed, looking like a boulder lodged in the murky track. An oothecan curled up in a prickly ball beside him, feelers bent around its thorax. An aurochi, one horn broken and sickly with murrain, stared bleary at the horizon, eyes clouded and black.

"The anima greeted us with armed guard," said Pink. "Told us to keep marching, even their own kind. Wouldn't part with so much as a drop of oil, watched their kin clank and crumble along the roads. Said they had nothing to give."

They had little enough in the Tower either – autumn's crop almost finished, the weather-witches desperately trying to coax a warm spell from the south. Constance did not expect them to be successful. Constance could not remember the last time she had seen the sun shine over the Tower. Every day now was a dull drizzle threatening to turn to hard rain.

"They raided us when we passed the Toybox," said Pink.

"The merriling attacked you?" Constance asked aghast.

"Robbed, more like. There were none of us thought of fighting. There were none of us had anything to steal."

"To think of the merriling, sunk so low…"

"These are desperate times," said Pink, "and in desperate times, people look to their own. Their clan, their kin, their family."

"And then them alone, and everything else be damned."

"I did not say it was right," said Pink, "I just said it was."

The mice had finished off what was left of their cheese, though the smallest pup still howled for suck. Pink's descendants lay against their sachem's shell, taking what rest they could find. The petrousian had not moved in so long that Constance nearly thought him dead. The aurochi began to scratch at his raw and blistered coat. Giving in finally to her youngest, the mother mouse undid the front of her dress and offered her dry, useless pap. The aurochi, still scratching, erupted in sudden sternutation.

"The End is not all they speak of, on the roads."

"Oh?"

"They say your mother has taken ill."

"Do they?"

"Actually, the way I heard it she went into convulsions and vomited up a serpent that prophesied doom for all the March."

"It was a scorpion."

Pink did not smile.

"My mother is fine, Pink," Constance said. "She was feeling feverish, but will recover swiftly."

"One hopes soon."

"One does."

Pink swiveled its head towards Constance, reached out knobby antennae in an act of intimacy. "There must be a Harrow in the Tower."

"There is."

"Now, more than ever."

"There *is* a Harrow in the Tower, Pink, and soon she will call the rebellious lords to account and lead them against the End."

"I will hope for that as well," Pink said.

Constance was listening but she had her eyes on the aurochi, product of a veteran caution, that sixth sense which develops only after surviving the consequences of ignoring it. Her suspicion was rewarded or at least confirmed when the beast began to shake and shudder, as if each of its constituent bits, the leg and croup and dewlap, the hoof and mouth and hump, had taken independent offense against the rest.

"Stone in the craw!" it lowed in a voice which was not its voice, "hole in the cloth!"

The aurochi snapped upright, black bile bursting from its mouth and through its ringed nostrils and out its eyes, dripping slick over its muzzle. With one jerking, frantic motion it crushed the slumbering oothecan, plunging its hoof through exoskeleton and abdomen, coming out a sick green into the mud beneath. The family of mice screamed and tried to flee, father mouse pulling at his children, mother mouse carrying her babe, the aurochi wailing in its desperate monotone and hurrying after them.

There wasn't time for Constance to unsheathe her father's blade, held fast as it was by seven locks, the first named Folly and the last Necessity. This was its point, that it could not be released with impunity, that its cost was nearly not worth bearing. She snatched up a carrying pole from where it lay in the mud and brought it fast against the aurochi's skull, but it did not scream and it certainly did not die, knocking Constance aside and turning upon the fleeing mice. The crowd screamed and trampled one another in their fear, fur against feather against wood against pig iron. By the time Constance could force her way upright the aurochi had torn apart a screaming hydronese, drops of living water flung careless in the mud, and was turning to gore an anima when Constance got her hands on its tail. One great heave and she managed to arrest its motion before falling on it furiously, a flurrying concatenation from her mailed fists, shattering an eye socket, deep-denting its muzzle. Strong as Constance was, the aurochi was stronger and felt no pain, seemed unaware even of injury, the black still boiling thick from every orifice, spouting from its wounds and covering Constance's armor with fetid rot.

"Flies on the meat!" it howled as they rolled back and forth through the mud, "cracks in the bone!"

Constance came up on top and offered no quarter, battering the creature until its fur was mashed against bone, and that bone had been likewise split, cavities opened to the air, pink brain leaking and still it raged, each individual hate-maddened component, a jerk of a fibula, a shudder of a hoof.

Not dead but at least ruined, and Constance stood finally, careful to avoid its last spasms. "Bring fire," she ordered. Her fists had swelled against the hard steel of her gauntlets; she would need to get a smith to cut them off. A shallow cut wept from her forehead, and she blinked away blood. "It's the only way to finish it."

Because it would not quiet, the thing that had been an aurochi and was now only the End, some fragment or tendril or spy of that force or creature which had sent half the March fleeing from the borders. From out its split muzzle, forced by punctured lungs through a ruined trachea, it continued its desperate, plaintive cry. "Filth in the water! Fissure in the stone! Flaw in the grain! Flaw in the grain!"

# Six

In the hour just before dawn Sophia Harrow woke from sleep. She could not remember where she was, or how she had gotten there.

"G is for the Gyved Throne," she said, "from which the Queen is bound to her people." Her blue eyes were dull from the drugs, and her mouth was parched. "H is for the Harrow, rulers just and wise, who keep the March at peace."

She lay silent amid the disharmonious counterpoint of heart monitors, coughing patients and muttering staff. A child screamed. Sophia began to weep softly.

"Oh God," she asked, "what have I done?"

*2001*

# SEVEN

"The trick with skinning a jubjub bird," said the Man-With-Many-Hands, "is you've got to cut against the grain. Go straight in and you'll ruin it."

A section of the kitchens had been kitted out for the use of the Tower's more diminutive denizens, mice and saprophyte and the like, and John stood over a low table wearing a puffy white chef's hat and eviscerating an avian the size of a deer. Getting to use real knives was one of the many things that John could do in the March that he was not allowed to do at home.

"That's better," said the Man-With-Many-Hands, "you're going to want to reach into the gullet and pull out the tonsil stones, they're sweeter than rhubarb pudding. But cut out the uvula first, it's terrible poison – one touch and your skin turns a permanent maroon."

John dutifully removed the pudge of flesh, then continued on with the dismemberment.

"You really never plucked a jubjub bird before?" asked the Man-With-Many-Hands. In addition to overseeing John, the Man-With-Many-Hands was dicing daikon, chopping cucumber, grating garnish and checking a tray of meat pies which browned in a neighboring oven.

"We don't have jubjub birds in Humanland."

"Humanland sounds like an awfully boring place," said the Man-With-Many-Hands.

"You're not wrong," said John.

48

In a small herb garden outside the kitchen, Mary Ann and Ababab and Jolly Bones chewed sprigs of mint and watched the afternoon sunlight caress the Tower's stone. After her first, forced journey, Mary Ann had found subsequent passage between the worlds far easier, no longer requiring whatever power she had called upon the night of the Christmas party. The March seemed to have accustomed itself to their presence and would carry her and her brother off most evenings.

"So, you don't have parents?" asked Mary Ann, incredulous.

"Nope." Ababab was a nonesuch, a single-shot creation sprung from the magic of the March, some peculiar and ungainly amalgamation of the dreams and fears of the inhabitants. He was part cobweb and part daddy long legs and a little bit of the evening sky. When he was laughing or got too excited, he would sometimes forget himself and be carried along with the wind for a few seconds, before anchoring himself to the ground once more.

"Not even a mom?"

"Nope."

"Huh," said Mary Ann. She thought about this for a while. "But what about when you were born?"

"I dunno," said Ababab. "What about when you were born?"

"I can't remember it," admitted Mary Ann.

"Neither can I. I wasn't, then I was. And so was everything else! The sun and the sky and the air and the trees. And dirt! You ever think about how amazing dirt is?"

"Rarely," admitted Mary Ann.

"There are so many different kinds! Stony dirt and fine dirt and, whattayacallit, wet dirt."

"Mud?"

"That's the stuff! Anyway, after I came to be, I wandered around a while, looking at the sky and the dirt, and then I ended up at the Tower."

"Better dead in the Tower than bored in the provinces," agreed Jolly Bones. Jolly Bones was a tin clown with bright green hair and an oil-stain smile which never changed. He wound absently at the wind-up key in his neck, as much a nervous tic as mechanical necessity. "When I think of spending the rest of my days in the Toybox, surrounded by stuffed animals and wooden trains…"

"What's so awful about the Toybox?" asked Mary Ann.

"You know there's nothing there to eat but candy?"

"I love candy."

"Forever? All the time? Bubblegum for breakfast and pixie sticks for lunch?"

"I guess I'd start to miss pizza."

"You came to the Tower because you got sick of dessert?" Ababab asked.

"Not *just* that," said Jolly Bones. "Nothing ever changes in the Toybox. Everyone works in the toffee mines or the bottle rocket factories, punching their clock, wasting their lives away. The Tower is where it's at. All the Thousand People stuffed up against one another, trading and arguing and fighting. A place like this, a clever clown can make his fortune."

"You're a scullion," Mary Ann pointed out.

"For now!" snapped Jolly Bones, "but not forever."

Really Mary Ann was in no position to judge, being herself a scullion – which, so far as she was concerned, was basically the best job ever, traveling throughout the breadth of the Tower, carrying messages and trays of food which she could usually pick from without anyone noticing, peering at all the strange wonders to be found. It had turned out the Tower was not a tower at all, but a city with who knew how many creatures living inside its ring of walls. It had its own neighborhoods and boroughs, its own parks and gardens, its own granaries, orchards, apiaries, grazing pens, chicken hutches, taverns, restaurants and theaters, its own smiths and leatherworkers, a mail service carried by inchworm and butterfly, troops of guardsmen to maintain order. From across the length and breadth of the March the Thousand Peoples had come to serve the Harrowed, a riot of color and form, an endlessly diverse cast of creatures living in something which nearly resembled harmony.

John came outside, no longer wearing his puffy white chef's hat.

"What's your brother doing here?" asked Jolly Bones.

Mary Ann shrugged her shoulders, embarrassed, as older sisters tend to be, by the inconvenient existence of younger brothers.

In contrast to the wind-up clown, Ababab seemed as please to see John as he would have anyone else, brimming over with innocent enthusiasm. "Hello, John! How'd it go with the jubjub bird?"

"The Man-With-Many-Hand's is going to make it into a pie."

"Why don't you go back and watch him, then?" asked Jolly Bones. "This is where the scullions hang out, and you aren't a scullion."

"No, I'm a cook, which is better," said John, sticking out his tongue.

"Cook isn't better than scullion," Mary Ann objected.

"Cook is like *a million times better* than scullion. I get to use a knife, I get to put things in ovens–"

"Chained next to it is more like," countered Jolly Bones, "getting yelled at by a know-it-all with more fingers than brains."

"You carry things," said John, "a robot could do it."

"Hey! Some of our best scullions are anima!" objected Ababab.

"Sorry," said John, "but still."

Jolly Bones pressed out his tin chest. "We don't just carry things – we carry things everywhere."

"*Anywhere*," agreed Ababab.

"From the outermost battlement to the Harrow's hidden chamber at the top of the spire–"

"–there is no hidden chamber at the top of the spire," John attempted to interrupt.

"A scullion sees it all. We know all the Tower's secrets."

"I think you're a big brag," said John.

"Mary Ann, tell your brother to get out of here. For that matter, you should go with him, seeing as you're not a real scullion either."

"Hell I'm not!" snapped Mary Ann.

"You're only an apprentice scullion. You haven't taken the test yet."

"What test? I never heard anything about a test."

"That's cause it's secret," said Jolly Bones. His face was more than usually sneery. "You can't be considered a proper scullion until you've visited the tomb of the first Harrow."

The Tower went sideways for a long time, but it went up forever, and to go up like that it had to go down as far, or nearly. The top of the basement was used for mushroom farms and homes for those of the Thousand People who could not bear the touch of sunlight, but below that were who knew how many more levels, storage chambers given over to mildew, dark dungeons, crooked catacombs, and odious oubliettes.

"What's the tomb of the first Harrow?" Mary Ann asked.

Jolly Bones assumed a peremptory air. "After the first Harrow came to the March, and conquered the Thousand Peoples–"

"Conquered?" John objected.

"How do you think you get to rule something, then? You think they just ask you to sit on the throne? The Harrow are here because they were meaner than whatever was here before the Harrow, and meaner than anything come since, and if that ain't how you like to hear it you suck eggs." Jolly Bones turned back to Mary Ann. "Anyway, after the first Harrow came to the March, and conquered the Thousand Peoples, he started to get bored. He already owned the west, and the east, and the rest of the directions likewise, and he didn't have nothing left to do, just sit on the Throne getting old and bored. So, he decided he'd go down."

"Down?" Mary Ann asked.

"Into the ground," explained Jolly Bones, "along with all his lords and ladies, his champions, his bodyguards and his war machines."

"Like in an elevator?"

"Tell your brother if he wants to listen, he has to shut up," said Jolly Bones.

"Be quiet, John," said Mary Ann.

John retreated into a glowering silence.

"I don't know about the elevator," said Jolly Bones, "but I know that he went down into the ground, to see what was underneath everything. Below the dirt, and the stone, and whatever was below the stone. Down as far as he could go. Down to the very bottom."

"What did he find?" Mary Ann asked.

Jolly Bones shook his harlequin head back and forth. "Nobody knows. But whatever it was, it ate up his whole army, and it ate up most of the First Harrow likewise. But not all the way – the Harrow was too tough to die, and he fled back up to the light. Or tried to, anyway, because when he got back he was so ugly that no one could stand to look at him, he was too awful. His children and his grandchildren, all the rest of the Harrow, they didn't know what to do. They couldn't kill him, see, on account of he was still a Harrow, but they couldn't let him into the light neither. So, they walled up the hole he had made, and they built the Tower on top of it, to make sure that he could never get out again. But there's a hidden room in the basement that nobody but us scullions know about – and if you go down there, and you sit quietly, and wait a while, you can still hear the First Harrow begging to come back home."

It seemed to Mary Ann that the afternoon had grown suddenly cold, gray clouds passing over the sun, the courtyard chilly despite the great fires baking out from the kitchen.

"But *you've* been down there?" John asked.

"You have to, if you want to be a proper scullion," said Jolly Bones.

"I'm a cook, though," said John, "which is better than being a scullion."

Jolly Bones blew a stannic raspberry. "You're too scared to go anyway."

"Call me a cow, I won't milk," which was something that his grandmother liked to say.

"*I'm* not afraid to go to the tomb," said Mary Ann, "or anywhere else in the Tower."

"We'll find out about that," said Jolly Bones, smirking. "Head down the stairs till you come to the bottom basement–"

"–not the top basement," Ababab interrupted, "where the bugs live, below that."

"Head down the corridor, then take a right–"

"–no, a right–"

"–that's what I said!"

"Oh, OK. Keeping going."

"Take a right and then a left and then another left, but like a *long* left, and then it'll be on your right. No, left."

"Right," said Ababab.

"You have to take a kitchen candle with you," Jolly Bones added, "and stay there until the wick burns down. If you come up before then, it doesn't count."

"Don't wait for me," said Mary Ann, with a proud shake of her red hair, "maybe I'll get tired and have a nap." She made a point of not looking behind her until she was back in the kitchens, on the way to the basement, at which point she noticed John padding along behind her.

"What are you doing?"

John shrugged.

"I didn't ask you to come along."

"But you didn't say I couldn't."

Nor did she then. In truth, Mary Anne *was* a little bit scared of going down into the basement and didn't mind having a sibling along – even a younger one.

The east stairwell was busy with oothecan retreating to

their underground chambers and saprophytes hauling up the afternoon's mycelium harvest, but soon the traffic trickled away and John and Mary Ann were left alone. They passed a young molluschite struggling his way up the steps, and then they passed a very old mouse, his eyes rheumy and white, but after that they saw no one. The door to the basement was closed with a thick iron lock, but the wood around it had warped and sogged and sagged away. Its hinges groaned when Mary Ann pushed it open.

Inside it was very dark. Mary Ann removed a beeswax candle from a neighboring wall sconce. By its light Mary Ann could make out damp, unfinished walls, and old containers left rotting in corners, a musty sense of things forgotten. They followed the directions they'd been given deeper into the catacombs. Mary Ann had the distinct and uncomfortable sense of the endless weight above her, as if the whole Tower was a headstone, and she beneath it.

"Why did you let Jolly Bones bully you into this?"

"I didn't," said Mary Anne, although she knew she had.

"He's a big jerk."

"He isn't," said Mary Ann, although really, she thought he kind of was.

Not that it mattered. John was too young to understand that just because someone was a jerk didn't mean that their opinion didn't matter – but Mary Ann was in her second year of middle school, surrounded by pubescent sadists, and had come to understand that power in most situations is held by the person most willing to use a whip, whether it was Jolly Bones bragging about being a proper scullion, or Rachel Swaner making fun of Becca Calanesi's Halloween costume. Something else that middle school had taught Mary Ann was that you were either in, or you were out, and that this distinction, if unfair, was all important.

They had come to a fork in the tunnels which, according to their directions, did not exist; a split in the path, two gloomy passageways leading down with nothing to recommend either.

"What do we do now?" Mary Ann asked.

John brushed some dust off his tunic. "We go back."

"But we haven't reached the tomb yet!"

John groaned as if stabbed. "*Obviously* it's a trick."

"What's that supposed to mean?"

"There is no tomb. They sent us on a wild goose chase."

Mary Ann knew he was right as soon as he said it. It was part of what made John so frustrating, that he could believe in Santa Claus and like Disney movies and also be entirely, a hundred percent right about things. "Hell," said Mary Ann, turning around.

Mary Ann never was sure how they got lost on the way back, only that at some point she looked up to discover they were in a subterranean stretch which did not look like the rest of the Tower, with its perfect, endless blocks of blue stone, but seemed rather to be some natural network of caves, ancient and unknowable. Phlegmy droplets exuded from the walls and dripped down from the ceiling. A stewy funk in the air seemed to strangle the light from Mary Ann's candle. They heard sounds for which they could not account, a high-pitched chirrup, then something like a laugh, and then a voice speaking.

"You're late."

Mary Ann was thinking that it was good luck that they had stumbled on someone else down there, and was about to answer, when she felt a sharp blow to her ribs, turned to see John's finger over his mouth.

"There's much to do to prepare for his coming," said a dry, deep, not altogether unpleasant rasp.

"Let's get this over with, then." This voice was still and smooth as well water. "We'd best not be down here any longer than we have to."

"Frightened of the dark?"

The conversation came, Mary Ann realized now, from some neighboring sprawl of caves, the sound carried by a quirk in the stone. John was hunched tight, eyes squinting, as if by doing so he might hear more clearly.

"I don't like being this close to the heart of the Tower. There could be guards anywhere."

"Be easy, my friend. The Harrow have grown arrogant in their evils and have no thought of rebellion."

There was the sound of wood scraping against metal, as of something opening, a chest or crate. The dry voice hooted.

"Pikes, knives, arbalests, the whole kit and caboodle," said the wet voice, "not that they'll be much good without someone to use them."

"Worry not. His promise spreads like wildfire. His name is written on bathroom walls and carried on scraps of paper given to the wind. The Thousand People mutter it in their sleep, a silent army soon to wake."

"By the Tower, you've got a way of talking."

"By the Tower?" repeated the dry voice, grown suddenly fierce. "By the Tower?"

The watery voice didn't answer, and Mary Ann could feel fear grow in the silence.

"Swear by shattered glass and shards of porcelain, swear by broken chains, swear by the very dust of the road," the dry voice began again, "but do not swear by the Tower – it will not stand much longer. The King in Rags is coming. Father to the orphaned, redeemer of the dispossessed. In his wake he carries the vengeance of a thousand years. He will snap the heavy fetters of the Gyved Throne, he will shatter the Tower, he will free us from the tyranny of the Harrow. The future is coming, my friend. Make sure you're on the right side of it."

# EIGHT

They woke that morning in a warm house with fat, fluffy clouds of white wafting past their windows. Over a breakfast of hot cocoa and colored cereal the children watched the local news with rapt attention, erupting in excitement when their formal reprieve was announced. Between the end of December and the start of spring the days had little to recommend them, except that every so often you could skip one.

When they were finished eating, Sophia helped the children into scarves and sweaters and snow boots and mittens then sent them outside to play. The best hill in the neighborhood was at the other end of the court, on an undeveloped thicket just past where the Endos lived, and Sophia watched from the window, a cup of coffee in hand, as her three children, carrying plastic sleds and an inflated inner tube, trundled off.

The rising banks of snow and brief absence of children gave the Harrow household a rare stillness. Michael napped in a comfy chair, a paperback dog-eared beside him. Joan made a pie. Sophia did the laundry, cleaned the kitchen and two of the bathrooms, and spent an hour on the phone changing their car insurance – there are, of course, no off-days for mothers.

By mid-afternoon the snow had stopped, the weather turned gray and cold, and Sophia and Joan set out to find the children.

"I can still remember when your father used to take you and Aaron sledding down here," said Joan. She was dressed in her heaviest coat but shivered as she walked, and her skin seemed faint covering for her bones. "He had that big wooden toboggan he used to set you off on."

"I remember," said Sophia.

"Do you remember the time that Aaron hit his head against a tree, and we had to take him to the emergency room?"

"I can still see Dad sprinting back to the car."

They continued on up the hill, past a patch of black ice outside of the Winthrop's.

"Have you heard anything?" Joan asked.

By unspoken agreement, the Harrows rarely discussed the March outside of its borders. Not a strict prohibition, carrying no force of law, still it was a useful practicality, for in the daylight hours the events of the other world could only be recollected with difficulty, distance and time become matters of dispute. For instance; how long had it been since Aaron had set out on his mission to the north? Here it had been three weeks since Christmas and they were still deep in the January doldrums, but as to the March? Where the seasons shifted with the collective mood, where time was marked by adventures, pageants and crusades, rather than according to any standardized calendar? Who could say?

"Under the Mountain sent a message when he left their borders," said Sophia.

Joan frowned. "But nothing since?"

"No," said Sophia, "nothing." Saying it she felt that tremor of pleasure that she had always felt when reporting her brother's failure, and likewise the shame that accompanied that pride, an old ache, constant since childhood.

"It was a good idea," said Joan.

"We won't know that yet."

"A good idea isn't a guarantee of success, it's just a good idea. And it *was* a good idea. Aaron's problem is that he doesn't trust himself to do anything, and so he never tries. He's stronger than he thinks. Than you think."

"I hope you're right," said Sophia, knowing that she ought to be more supportive, if not of her brother than of her mother's hopes for him.

To which she was barely clinging. "Perhaps it *was* too early," Joan added nervously.

It would always be early for Aaron, was what Sophia thought. There was something about him which had never moved beyond youth So bright, so sweet, so full of a promise which wasn't quite met. Sophia could never figure out whether she loved her brother too little, or too much.

Such considerations, as well as any further conversation, were mooted when Sophia heard a scream which she knew, the way a mother knows, was John's. She broke into a run, arriving at the top of the hill to see a circle of children at the bottom, and in the center Constance squaring off against the youngest Hambry boy, Sophia couldn't remember his name. The snow around them was sparkled with red and by the time Sophia arrived it was over, Constance's arm locked around the boy's neck, the mob of children chanting in excitement.

"Enough of that!" Sophia shouted.

The crowd dispersed like pigeons flushed by a terrier. Constance released her adversary, who pulled away gasping and snarling.

"What's going on here?"

"He hit John," Constance said flatly.

"You're a liar," said the Hambry boy, still wheezing, "I wasn't doing nothing."

"Then why is John's nose bleeding then, huh?" Mary Ann asked.

The back door of the neighboring house opened, and Mrs Hambry came hurrying out, looking thick and slovenly. She wore stained sweatpants and an autumn jacket. She was angry. "What's all this?"

"I'm trying to figure that out," said Sophia calmly.

"He asked to borrow my sled," said John, "only I was using it and–"

"Your sled sucks, who'd want to borrow it?"

"He's always doing this stuff, Mom," said Mary Ann. "I swear he's just trying to get attention–"

"Like I'd even care!"

"So then he pushed me–"

"–he tripped and he fell over and then his crazy sister came over and smacked me when I wasn't looking."

"You were looking fine," said Mary Ann, "you're just angry that you got beat up by a girl."

Sophia turned to her eldest. "Well?"

Constance shrugged. She was breathing heavy, but her eyes were cool and hard. "He shouldn't have hit John."

"The three of yours, ganging up on my Louis!" said Mrs Hambry, having deduced what she wished from the cacophony. "You ought to be ashamed!"

"That's not how it sounds to me," said Sophia.

"I don't want them sledding down here anymore!" Mrs Hambry shrieked. "You all need to get off my property!"

"It isn't your property," Sophia explained calmly. "It's next to your property. That's not the same thing."

"You fucking Harrow, you think you own everything, always did."

"There's no need for that sort of language," said Sophia.

Mrs Hambry had tobacco stains on her fingers and whiskey on her breath. She pointed at Constance. "And that one! Running around like some kind of gorilla. Ought to put a skirt on her. They've got names for little girls like that."

Sophia rarely quarreled, and never raised her voice. She betrayed her loss of temper with a slight squint to her blue eyes, and a flutter of her long fingers – still enough to give the impression of a great power barely restrained, like standing below a cracked floodwall. "Watch what you say about my kid," she hissed.

Mrs Hambry lowered her gaze and muttered unhappily. Louis had disappeared behind her skirts. The other children watched with excitement and quiet awe. Sophia stood indomitable for a moment longer, then turned and started back towards the house, her children following in a proud line behind her.

# NINE

A week on the road had taken Michael and his daughter far
from the Tower and deep into the pastoral splendor of the
Harvestlands, verdant with perpetual spring and lush in its
unending foison. Accompanied by an escort of valiant they
rode beneath past endless rows of maize, brown and purple
and black and sometimes just corn colored. A farmer who was
either dressed in husks or formed from them gaped in awe at
their passing, though he managed, after a long moment, to
return Michael's wave, and even to blush red as a ripe tomato
with joy at the acknowledgment.

"Remember that most of those you meet have never met a
Valiant, or seen a Harrow, and will remember this moment for
the rest of their lives, and tell their children about it, and their
children will tell theirs," said Michael. His armor was stowed,
but his blade, sheathed and locked, hung across his back. He
rode an easy seat atop his aging yearling, corkscrew horns solid
as the flat of a hammer. "It's the only chance he'll ever have to
feel a way about you, and so you'd best make him feel good.
He won't know that you're tired, or sad, or have a stone in
your boot that's driving you crazy. All he'll remember is that
you passed him once and did not bother to wave – and even a
small wound can fester."

Constance waved vigorously at the farmer in response,
though he did not seem to notice.

Sir Floppy pulled beside them, matching pace with their
mounts on four padded paws. Sir Floppy was the second-in-

command of the Valiant, a long-limbed, off-white hare. He wore a black leather cuirass and an eye-patch made of the same. He was stern and serious and acclaimed as the greatest fencer in the March, and Constance was rather afraid of him.

"There's a clearing ahead which should serve as a campsite," he said.

"Near the river?"

"Just before."

"As you think best, Sir Floppy."

Sir Floppy nodded, turning his one good eye onto Constance. "How does it feel to be riding with your father for the first time?"

"It's an honor I hope to prove worthy of," said Constance.

"Too young to be always on about honor and duty," Sir Reginald Fitzwillow called out from behind them in his rich, highland brogue. Sir Reginald Fitzwillow was a bear. Not a bear the way Sir Floppy was a hare, not a kodiak or a grizzly, but a teddy bear, though still very large, a giant of felt and plush and soft cotton. A sparr ax was strapped to his back and his fur was brown mottled with colored strips of cloth – it was Sir Reginald Fitzwillow's boast that he had forgotten all the wounds he had taken in service of the Harrows. "When I was your age, I was the worst rowdy in all the Toybox, there wasn't a ballerina or a drummer boy that didn't know my name! A little wildness, that's what's needed in the young."

"A little wildness?" asked Dame Delta, fluttering along above. "Is that what got you facing five years mining sugar?" Dame Delta was an anima, one of the clockwork people. She looked something like a kite and something like a pocket watch and was said to know every town, hamlet and village within the points of the compass. Her patagium was yellow silk and her talons were bent brass, and Constance had not yet accustomed to the rust-colored gears which served her for eyes.

"A misunderstanding," insisted Sir Reginald Fitzwillow, "I've told you that a thousand times–"

"The judge gave him a choice – gaol, or the guard," explained Dame Delta. "If he wasn't a knight he'd be rotting away in prison."

Of course, Constance knew Sir Reginald Fitzwillow's history, as she knew the stories of all of her father's companions, as she knew what Sandy Koufax's E.R.A. was the year the Dodgers had won the pennant and that Bill Russell was the best basketball player of all time. Since she was old enough to want a thing, she had wanted to be where she was just then, riding through the March with her father and his companions. She felt proud and happy and anxious.

The Valiant traveled light and made camp quickly. Those who had mounts tended to them, those who didn't gathered firewood and set up the tents. Constance unsaddled and brushed her yearling, then gave it a feedbag of blood sausage and salted jerky. She left it untethered after, for no yearling will accept a restraint—their obedience can be earned but never compelled.

She found her father and Sir Floppy making plans for the next day's journey, looming over her father's partway-unfolded map of the March – you could never unfold her father's pocket map of the March completely, not unless you had all of the March to unfold it upon – when Dame Delta interrupted, alighting on a neighboring branch.

"There's an arcimboldi here who would like a word."

Her father put aside the map and waved their guest forward. It might have been the farmer from earlier, or it might have been another like him, Constance wasn't sure. He looked thin and wiry and in awe at his own bravery. He wore shabby pants and no shirt and a hat made of knotted husk. His eyes were walnuts, his lips were cherries and his nose looked like an ungleaned corncob.

He was one of who knew how many serfs, small farmers and planters in the March, and seeing him her father folded up his map and rose respectfully, greeting him with the same courtesy he would have any landsgrave or bey. "May the day shine bright on your crops," Michael said, "and the evenings be warm and short."

"May you get no more rain than you need," said the farmer. He managed to return the blessing by rote instinct, but afterward, gazing at her father and the rest of the Valiant, fell silent.

"Well?" said Sir Reginald Fitzwillow, towering over the vegetal visitor, "Out with it. The Champion doesn't have all day."

"Beggin' your pardon, sirs. Ladies. Sirs and ladies."

"No pardon required," said Michael. "The Valiant serve the Thousand People. How can we help you?"

"Thing is...there's this thing...this thing in the river."

Michael nodded, as if expecting to hear this. "Which river?"

"Down a ways. By the ford."

"What sort of thing?" asked Sir Reginald Fitzwillow.

"Dunno, sir. We just call it the thing in the river."

"What's it look like?" asked Dame Delta.

"Green," said the farmer, "and slimy."

"And what's it doing?"

"It perches by the river, and it won't let no one across. In front of the ford. Yells at you if you try and come near it. Can't use it anymore. The ford, I mean. On account of the thing. In the river. Have to walk all the way round to the bridge if I want to go to town. Takes twice as long. Anyway, I was hoping that, maybe..."

"You want us to salt your slug, eh?" supplied Sir Reginald Fitzwillow.

The arcimboldi were staunch pacifists and obligatory vegans, and the farmer shuddered at this suggestion like dry leaves before their final abscissions. "Oh, no, sir! Nothing like that. Just... maybe... ask it to stop?"

"Ask it to stop?"

"Or get rid of it? Take it to another part of the river? Tell it to stop yelling and throwing stones when we try and cross?"

"How about we bring it a root beer, while we're there?" asked Sir Reginald Fitzwillow.

Michael silenced the bear with a quick look, then turned back to the farmer. "It is well that you brought this to our attention. The Valiant keep the peace."

"The Valiant keep the peace," Sir Floppy agreed.

Constance managed her affirmation an instant later.

"We'll make sure to take care of your problem. Sir Floppy, give this fellow something for his bravery in coming to speak with us. Sir Reginald Fitzwillow, Dame Delta, perhaps an evening's tussle will make room for your dinner?"

"Sir Reginald Fitzwillow *always* has room for dinner," said Sir Reginald Fitzwillow, "but my lord's word is my command."

"Fine," grumbled Dame Delta, "but I won't get into the water."

"You could use a bath," said Sir Reginald Fitzwillow, ambling over to where he had set his sparr ax, "you smell like clock oil."

"Wait," said Sir Floppy, then leaned in and whispered something to Michael.

He looked at a suddenly anxious Constance, then back at his aide. "You think?"

"She'd best learn some time."

Michael chewed this over a moment, then nodded. "What do you say, Constance? Up for a bit of work?"

Constance's heart bruised her rib cage. "At your command, Sir."

"See? See? This is what I'm talking about," lilted Sir Reginald Fitzwillow, "all this Sir and Ma'am business. Fine for a knight, but for a girl?"

"You'll remember," said her father, "that she is one, and to keep her out of any danger."

A gear turned and Dame Delta extended her gliders and bowed with creaking dignity to Michael. "We will place her safety above our own."

"Of course we will!" said Sir Reginald Fitzwillow. "Did I even need to say that? Sir Reginald Fitzwillow, the Harrow's most loyal servant? Sir Reginald Fitzwillow, who has lost count of the wounds sustained in their service?"

"You shouldn't brag so of your weakness for arithmetic," said Dame Delta.

Michael turned to Constance. "You're not going along to fight; you're going along to watch. Keep your eyes open and do everything either one says."

"Everything Dame Delta says," amended Sir Floppy.

Dame Delta led the way, flitting from tree branch to tree branch, occasionally riding an air current into the sky. Constance followed Sir Reginald Fitzwillow as he ambled on below, singing a Toybox tune about a gumball man and a princess, and the troubles inspired by their love.

Dame Delta returned from scouting to take up a perch on Sir Reginald Fitzwillow's shoulder. "Green and slimy, he said."

"Doesn't narrow it down," said Sir Reginald Fitzwillow.

"Could be a slubberdegullion."

"Could be a tatterdemalion."

"Could be a lot of things."

"Doesn't matter," said Sir Reginald Fitzwillow. "There isn't a creature been hatched, built, born or brewed mean enough to unsew my stuffing."

"He'll be thinking that up until we put his ashes in their tomb," Dame Delta told Constance.

"And why shouldn't I be? Take a piece of advice from your old uncle Sir Reginald Fitzwillow – you walk into everything like the odds on overdog, and everyone else brought in to fill out the cards. Fearless!" he roared. "That's the only way to be. Half the battles you fight are won because you're sure you've already won them."

"The other half are won because you've planned them out in advance," added Dame Delta.

"What's planning, but a complicated sort of worrying?" asked Sir Reginald Fitzwillow. "I leave that to those better suited for it. That farmer to his crop, you and Sir Floppy to your plans, myself to mead and valor."

Closer to the river the woods had turned to bog. Strange

swamp trees twisted out of the murk, and Constance's boots squelched with every step.

"It'll take forever to get this out of my fur," Sir Reginald Fitzwillow complained.

"What happened to all that talk of valor?" Dame Delta mocked.

"Death is one thing," said Sir Reginald Fitzwillow, "and mud quite another. Just because you can fly doesn't mean you have to rub it in."

Constance was thinking that this would indeed be a useful ability when the trunk of rotted wood on which she had been unknowingly standing gave way, and she fell into the darkness below.

She came to lying on her back, covered in grime. A few flickers of sunlight leaked from above, outlining a small underground chamber formed from the vast remains of a dead willow. She could hear Sir Reginald Fitzwillow howling for her, but she could not see him.

Constance forced herself upright. She was scared. She knew she shouldn't be scared, but she was.

She was also not alone. Something rustled in the far corner of the cave, though it took a few seconds before Constance could make it out.

"My roof!" it hissed, "that was my roof!" The creature was indeed green, and slimy, as the farmer had promised, but it was also scaly and yellow-eyed and had several rows of crooked teeth, a subterranean eremite with dim notions of hospitality. "Not asking, never asking, just tramping across, and now look at it! Ruined! Ruined!"

"I'm sorry about your roof," Constance began.

"Sorry don't fix it! Sorry don't do nothing. What's sorry? I got half a mind to... I ought to..." the thing shook its squamous snout. "Go away!"

"I didn't do it on purpose–"

"It's done though, ain't it? My house but your hole?"

"If you'd just listen for a minute, I'd–"

"Just like the rest of them, tramping across the river without even a please or a fresh fish or a bit of silver!"

"It's rude to interrupt!" snapped Constance, "and the river isn't just yours!"

It was not the most eloquent retort, but it got to the heart of the matter, or at least it was enough to infuriate the creature, which shook its tail in a mad rage. "Breaks my roof, falls into my cave, then starts telling me what's what?" The creature had sulphite eyes and a turtle shell for its back. "Stupid little girl. Bad little girl. Should learn proper manners."

As it got closer Constance found it was smaller than she'd feared but larger than she wished. She remembered what Sir Reginald Fitzwillow had said, and that she was a Harrow, and she gave as nasty a sneer as she got. The thing went left, and Constance went right, and as they passed she gave it a kick in the shins which sent it stumbling and howling into the murky water beyond. It was up in a flash but once again Constance was quicker, slipping its clawed paw and barreling into it with her broad shoulders, the two tumbling through the rotted wood of the chamber and out into the sluggish, slow-moving river beyond. They wrestled back and forth, rolling through the mud, elbowing and clawing.

Hovering above the riverbank Dame Delta gave a cry of greeting, and while Constance was too busy fighting to pay it any attention Sir Reginald Fitzwillow came swiftly.

"A scamble!" he yelled, "Give it what for! What for!"

Dame Delta found a gust to ride and unfurled her talons, but Sir Reginald Fitzwillow waved her out of the air.

"Not yet."

"If something were to happen to her…"

"You'd deprive the girl of her first victory? You'd steal her day of glory?"

"That's the Queen's daughter!"

"Exactly," said Sir Reginald Fitzwillow.

The Dame retracted her claws and then settled on a branch; loud and coarse, still Sir Reginald Fitzwillow was no fool.

Down below Constance had the scamble on the run, a fierce series of hooks which sent it stumbling, and then swift into a headlock of the kind that had subdued Louis Hambry. Here there was no mother to interrupt the savage monomachy, no intruding figures of authority, only strength against strength and Constance proved stronger. "Do you yield?"

The Scamble scraped and struggled, it lashed its scaly tail, it pawed at Constance with its crooked claws, but did not answer.

Constance's face was covered in mud and her arms and shoulders inked with scratches and bite marks. She tightened her grip further around the sliggling, wriggling thing, until it gasped and went limp. "Say uncle!" she roared, and this time it was not a question but a command.

"Uncle!" the monster managed to cough, "Uncle!"

From the riverbank above Sir Reginald Fitzwillow beat his fuzzy hand against his furred chest, and Dame Delta hooted with all the air in her clothwork bellows.

"Blood runs true!"

"The cub!" roared Sir Reginald Fitzwillow, "as fierce as her father!"

It was the best moment of Constance's young life. It made up for a lot of what would come after.

*2023*

"Jeffrey? Fine, I suppose."

"But you aren't certain?"

"It's comfortable."

"Is that enough for you?"

"For now."

"How does Jeffrey feel about this…ambivalence?"

"I'm not sure he's noticed. Last night he was practically asking to come back to Baltimore for the holidays."

"Does that seem so absurd to you?"

"On many levels. Anyway, I'm doing him a favor. Any guy I bring home will be walking into a firing squad. You should have seen the hell my mom used to make for Constance's wife." Ex-wife? Had Constance and Adeline signed their papers? Mary Ann couldn't remember, although she knew that she should.

"Your mother sounds like she has a lot of control over the family."

"She's the center of the universe. A universe, anyway."

"I'm sorry?"

"Never mind. My mother isn't a bad person or anything, just…right too much of the time."

"That's a failing?"

"Can be. You start thinking you're right all the time, and then that you can't ever be wrong. When Dad was around, things were better. He could even her out a little. They were a good team. After he died, she got… harder."

"A heart attack, you said?"

"…that's right."

The Doctor took this down diligently, her pen in a neat, constant flow. "This was before you were institutionalized?"

A strong word, bringing up images of rotting Victorian prisons and lobotomized mooncalves in white straitjackets; in fact, it had only been seventy-two hours, just long enough for the scars on her wrists to scab over. "Yes."

"How did the rest of your family react to your father's death?"

"Constance took his place. John just kind of... drifted off. Look, could we stop talking about my family, please?"

"Actually, Mary Ann – I think you brought it up."

That fucking notepad. "Right."

"It must be a struggle to imagine such a strong woman as your mother incapacitated by illness. We grow up imagining that our parents are somehow superhuman, infallible–"

"Only the first."

"Excuse me?"

"I never thought my mother was infallible."

"No?"

"Quite the opposite – whatever she said, I did the opposite."

"You were the rebel?"

"Someone has to be, right? Constance was the golden girl, John was...John."

"We can get locked into early patterns of behavior. It's important to give yourself the space to grow out of them."

"I don't surf, and I never wanted to be an actress. I came to California because it was as far as I could go from Baltimore while still speaking English. Except for Australia, I guess, but who wants to go there? My point is, I took as much space as I could get."

"Retreating from a situation isn't the same as processing it."

"I processed it. I decided I'm better off alone. When you're with your family, you're not who you are, you're who you were when you knew them. And I don't want to be that person."

"Being connected to others helps provide a sense of continuity, grounds us in shared experience with a broader community. Without that, life would be very lonely."

"Life is lonely. That's true no matter how you live it."

Doctor Feranz's face was blank, and she scribbled furiously in her black leather notebook. "Then you aren't planning on going back to Baltimore?"

"I just don't see the point. I'd feel bad, they'd feel bad, we'd all feel guilty for feeling bad, and then I'd fly home. Why not spare everyone the trouble?"

"That's a pretty easy out. But then, you always were the weak one, weren't you, Mary Ann? Running away from anything that scared you. Maybe if you'd been a little stronger, your father would still be alive."

"…what did you say?"

"I said if you weren't such a coward your father might still be alive, instead of dead in the forest where you left him." Doctor Feranz had fallen into monotone, and her pen flew across the paper. "A heart attack? A broken heart, maybe, both of them. The worst most people get out of their first love is a case of herpes, but not you, Mary Ann, you're special. Do you think about him, ever? Your lover, I mean. Or your father. Do you think about either of them? Dying on the ground, pulled away into nothing. Which do you think about more?" Her eyes were dark. "And you haven't even started on John. Poor John! In the car – more like driving it! You were supposed to have protected him, that's what elder sisters are for. Constance would have managed it, Constance would have saved him, but you couldn't even get that right. Of course, you feel guilty, Mary Ann, of course you can't sleep and drown yourself in anti-psychotics. You're a paracide, a regicide, and soon you'll end the world–"

Doctor Feranz slapped a hand to her mouth and sprinted out of the office, a trickle of bile leaking onto the carpets. Mary Ann sat still for a long moment, listening to her doctor retch uncontrollably in the bathroom next door. Then she took the bottle of olanzapine out of her pocket and dry-swallowed the rest of what was inside. Doctor Feranz's notebook lay open on the floor, revealing the elaborate sketch she had created; a horde of steam-powered humanoids, cheerful rabbits, nimble plants, wide-eyed children's toys, anthropomorphic weather patterns, all smiling and waving, beckoning the viewer onward into the bright, happy land beyond.

# ELEVEN

"M is for the March," said Julian, "where the Thousand People live in harmony."

"I thought a march was like a walk," said Evie.

"It is like a walk," said Julian, "but it's also a place, I guess? At the edges of things."

"Oh," said Evie. "OK."

They sat on a swing on the front porch reading from the book and waiting for their grandmother to return from the hospital. It was unseasonably warm for late December, and next-door Hank Washington worked in his winter garden, dark and tightly muscled in a white t-shirt. In the kitchen Adeline cleaned up what remained of their early dinner, and kept a vague eye on her children outside.

Julian turned the page. "N are for the nonesuch," he read, "without parent, sibling, or heir, born from the dreams of the March." Below this line of doggerel were a crowd of uniformly dissimilar creatures, strange mixtures of animals and plants and minerals and meteorological conditions and abstract concepts.

"It must be sad not to have a mommy," said Evie.

"Or a brother."

"Or a sister!"

Julian laughed. "Or a sister."

Evie took off her glove and put her thumb in her mouth. There was a school of thought, held by both her mothers, her grandmother, and various other parental figures, that five and three quarters was too old to be sucking your thumb, but as yet this was a premise to which Evie assigned no particular merit. "Do you think Mommy A will stay over?"

"I don't know."

"But you think she might?"

"I don't *know*, Evie."

"She could stay in my bedroom, if she wanted. I could sleep in the attic with you. There's plenty of space."

This was impossible, but Julian could not clearly articulate why. At eight life was full of these mute truths, though Julian felt confident he would understand better as he got older. He turned the page to reveal the oothecan, chitinous and proud, but they were interrupted before he could introduce them.

"What are you reading?" asked Hank Washington, leaning over the wooden fence which divided their properties.

Hank Washington was fifteen or maybe sixteen or maybe eighteen – Julian was not very good with ages – but definitively in high school. He had moved next door last year, just after he and Evie and Mommy C had come to live with Nanny. He was tall and dark and had shaggy hair. He was often outside in his garden, which bloomed according to the season and sometimes a while after. He lived with his mother, who Julian had never seen and whom Mommy C said was unwell and whom Mommy A said was fond of a drop, whatever that meant.

"The book," said Julian.

"I can see that. What book?"

"It doesn't have a name," said Julian. "It's the book."

"It's our book," Evie corrected, pursing her lips and setting her blue eyes against the newcomer. "What do you want?"

"I heard the ambulance last night. I just wanted to make sure everything's all right."

"Nanny had to go to the hospital," Julian explained.

"She's OK, though," said Evie, "she's tough."

"I'm glad," said Hank Washington. "What kind of book is it, that doesn't have a name?"

Evie snatched the book out of her brother's hands and set it behind her back.

"That's not very nice," said Julian, although he knew that the book was secret, sacred, not to be shown or even discussed. If Mommy C or their grandmother had been home they would never have been allowed to take it out of the house. But it was just Mommy A, and Mommy A was not a Harrow.

A car turned into their driveway. Hank Washington smiled and headed into his garage. Julian and Evie sprinted down off the porch, swarming Sophia as she alighted slowly.

"Nanny!"

"Nanny!"

"Are you OK? What was the hospital like?"

"Were you scared?"

"I made you a picture!"

Constance left her mother to fend off the children's affections and went inside. She found Adeline finishing up in the kitchen, wiping the counter free of crumbs.

"How'd it go?" she asked.

"All right, I guess? They ran some tests, we'll have to wait for the results. How are the kids?"

"A little on edge, but they calmed down after lunch. Evie wouldn't eat my enchiladas, though. She said I didn't make them like you did. I told her I taught you to make them, but she didn't care. I had to make her a peanut butter sandwich."

"Mary Ann was the same."

"You've said."

Adeline set her rag down on the sink.

"It's strange to see you here," said Constance.

"It's strange to be here."

"How are things?"

"They're all right. Trying to use the holiday to finish an article."

"Are you coming to the Christmas party?"

"Are you having the Christmas party? I figured with everything…"

"Mom insists."

Adeline sucked a tooth. "I'm not sure that's a good idea, Connie."

"It would mean a lot to the kids."

"And your mother?"

"It'll be busy, I doubt she'll notice."

Adeline had the habit of raising her hand in front of her mouth when she was about to laugh, as if trying to hold off some impropriety. "The Harrows throw a good party," she admitted.

"Always did."

"Do you remember the first time you brought me?"

"Back when I was in law school?"

"That neighbor – what was his name?"

"Mr Trevor. He asked if we were in a sorority, and you said we were members of the Sapphic sisterhood."

"I was pretty funny, back then."

"I thought so."

Things might have gone in many directions from there, who could say, the point was mooted when Sophia came into the kitchen, stiffly and slowly but otherwise lacking any indication she had spent a night in critical care.

"Hello, Adeline."

"Hello, Sophia," Adeline said, pulling away from Constance, "I'm so sorry for your troubles."

"Thank you. And for you looking after the children, while we were gone."

"You don't need to thank me, I'm their mother. Mothers look out for their children. That's what we do."

"Yes, it is, isn't it? Protect what we have."

Adeline smiled thinly. "I'll leave you to it. Constance, call me about this weekend, I can come by to pick the kids up if that would help."

"I will," said Constance, wanting to say more, not knowing what it was. "Thanks."

"Swift recovery, Sophia," said Adeline.

"Happy holidays," Sophia responded.

Then Adeline was off, into the living room to say goodbye to Julian and Evie, who, wearying of their grandmother, had found something bright and stupid to watch on the television. Constance was tense and anxious and started to re-clean the kitchen.

"Do you want me to make you something to eat?" she asked.

"I'm fine," said Sophia, "I ate at the hospital. How long was I gone?"

Constance shrugged and wiped off a spot her almost ex-wife had missed. "You know how it is over there. Things change fast."

"Change how?"

"Mom, please, take the night off. Watch something with the kids, or–"

"Am I dead, Constance?"

"What?"

"Am I dead? Have I died? Am I in the grave, and experiencing a peculiarly banal afterlife?"

"No, Mom, you're not dead."

"Then I'm still the Harrow, aren't I?"

There was a part of Constance that was angry but there was another part, a part of which she was ashamed, that proved desperately relieved, because her mother was back now, and everything would be all right. "Yes," she said, "you're still the Harrow."

"What's going on?"

"The wards have failed. The End rises from all directions. The roads are clogged with refugees. The machines send polite equivocations, the bugs are arming, and all we hear from the toys are strange rumors of a new lord."

Sophia took the news of her kingdom's collapse with accustomed equanimity. "Have you spoken with your siblings?"

Constance wondered if they been left to second because they

were less important, or because her mother was frightened of the answer. It was hard to imagine her mother frightened of anything, but Constance knew this was only her own delusions. Everyone was afraid, all the time. "Mary Ann texted me this morning. I haven't heard from John."

"She *texted*?"

"That's what I said."

Sophia pursed her lips. "We'll have to do it ourselves then. Call the High Council – but first, contact the faunae, tell them to raise the banners and come to the Tower, knights and serfs and free-beasts, every one. And we need to get a message to the Proscenium, if the End is coming, they'll be next. As far as the Toybox goes..."

Constance wiped aimlessly at the countertop, seeing the spots Adeline had missed. She wondered how their old house was looking without her to take care of it. Her other merits aside, Adeline was an half-hearted menial and inept handyman, Constance wasn't sure she could so much as change a lightbulb. She wondered what Adeline did there, all alone at night, with her books and papers or sitting in front of the television with a bottle of bourbon, thinking about things like Constance thought about things, mistakes she had made, words badly chosen, that ill-considered series of follies which added up, somehow, to a life.

"–Constance? Constance? Are you listening?"

"Of course, mother," Constance said, snapping to attention, "I'll call the High Council. Whatever you want."

# TWELVE

"You look like shit," said Darinel.

Darinel was a chef at *Avi's*, and worked the line next to John. Avi's was the sort of establishment that printed its menus daily and in faintly old-fashioned font, and before distributing them the servers were instructed to ask if anyone at the table was gluten free.

"Worse than normal?" asked John.

"A little," said Darinel.

John's slumber, fitful and dream-wracked, had carried him through the morning and most of the afternoon, by which point it had been too late to call Constance, barely enough time to take a shower and put on pants and catch the 3 train into work.

"My Mom is sick," John said.

Darinel turned aghast. "I'm so sorry, man. What's happened?"

"I'm not sure, I have to talk to my sister."

Darinel had a mother in Oaxaca to whom he sent a non-negligible portion of his paycheck and found John's dispassion slightly unbelievable. "You haven't called her?"

"She's in the hospital."

"You should tell Avi. He'd let you go home."

"No, he wouldn't. Invertebrate tend to be lacking infilial piety."

"Avi?" asked Kiki. Her shortened nocturnal adventures had left her looking fresher than John, and she finished up her prep before coming late to the conversation. "Better be careful – I just saw him bitching out the fish guy."

84

"You notice he never stops squinting?" John asked.

"We have a word in Spanish for people like Avi," Darinel admitted.

"Yeah?"

"It's asshole."

John smiled and Kiki snickered and Avi, who had come into the kitchen just then, looked over with a scowl – not because he had overheard so much as an instinctive response to merriment. He was a handsome, gray-haired man in his early fifties who had recently underwent a very competent but still noticeable face lift. He clapped his hands unnecessarily and the staff turned to attend him.

"All right," he began, "we're a little short-handed with the holidays, so everyone needs to keep up their end. You may have heard the salmon is fucking garbage tonight, so servers should try to steer people towards the duck, and as for the rest of you–"

John tried to imagine his mother in the hospital but found something about the picture felt wrong to him, like in those children's books where you're supposed to spot the mistake – a schoolroom with a giraffe hidden in the coat closet, an office with a chair on the ceiling. To think of Sophia Harrow laid up in bed, zonked out on painkillers, her pale blue eyes (the same eyes that John had) roaming pointlessly –

"Are we boring you, Mr. Harrow?" Avi snapped.

"The salmon is dry, so we should paint it with miso," John said, "and we're low on truffle, so slice it thin. Thinner than usual."

Avi nodded stiffly. A wrong answer would have pleased him better, but he found something to argue about with the *sommelier* and that seemed to make up for it.

It should have been an easy evening, Tuesdays were slow, and it was nearly Christmas, but somehow the dinner service started bad and got only worse, two wrong orders that Darinel and Kiki both insisted were the others fault, a cut of prime that had to be returned because it was the wrong side of medium, although only barbarians and former Presidents ate burnt steak. The mood was tense, and John was feeling shaky from the night before and Avi had already bawled out the pastry chef when a pot banged to the floor and Kiki gasped in pain.

John pulled her towards the sink and ran cold water over her puckered pink wrist.

"Fuck," said Kiki, "fuck."

"What happened?"

"I thought I saw…" Kiki's eyes were white and wide, and she tried to stop them from peering at the parboiled flesh of her forearm, "at the window, I thought…"

Before she could finish Avi came bursting into the kitchen. He'd been primed for explosion but seeing Kiki's burn realized some demonstration of concern was necessary. He did his awkward best to split the baby. "Are you all right? What the fuck did you do?"

"I'm fine," said Kiki after a moment, "I got my sleeves caught on the pot handle."

"Fuck," Avi said, looking at Kiki's wound for a moment before telling a busboy to take her out the employee exit and to the nearest hospital.

The back of the house was frazzled; the *saucier* had stilled beside a simmering portion of glaze, the *boucher* stood aimless atop a haunch of beef. Several of the servers were standing in a corner, muttering, and John was peering through Kiki's window at an undistinguished stretch of alleyway, trying to determine what had so startled his best friend.

"What are you standing around for?" Avi snapped. "It's filling up outside." He took a quick glance at Kiki's empty station and swallowed hard. Avi had not worked the kitchen himself so long as John had been there, and John suspected he had never been any good at it, one of those culinary geniuses who can manage perfection with three hours and nine assistants but would go catatonic if you put him behind the fryer at a

Denny's. "Somebody get Fiorella on the phone," he said, "tell him it's an emergency, I'll pay him double."

"Fiorella is in Paris," said John.

"Denis, then, he's–"

"I'll take care of it," said John. He turned his ruptured face on Avi, begging an argument that never came. It was a virtue of hideousness that most people would agree to almost anything to stop looking at John's face.

John hustled back to his station, plating two orders of duck before turning to Kiki's queue. He freed a slice of beef Wellington from the oven, set it to cool, and finished off a mushroom risotto with slivers of upcharged, almost certainly artificial truffle. He double-checked the crust on a chunk of cauliflower cut to look like a t-bone steak and blessed a chicken breast with a few droplets of lemon juice before sending them both out to the floor. His hands moved of their own accord, his mind turning towards the next task, the next ingredient, one act following another implacably, like a stone rolling downhill. It was very close to thinking about nothing. It was very close to death, except there was a great deal of movement involved.

"You're killing it tonight," said Darinel.

"I knew a guy who could do ten times as much," John said.

Darinel laughed, because of course John was joking.

Depending on whether one is a rationalist or a pessimist, the odds of one very bad thing happening after another are no higher than normal or virtually certain. Personally, John felt no surprise when Guillermo, a short, scowling man with deep set eyes and a ruthless competence, cut off his thumb while trying to slice a loaf of bread.

"I'm not crazy," he insisted as they bundled up the wound and set him against a wall, "it crawled out of the fucking burner!"

"All right, all right–" Avi said, trying to quiet him.

"It smiled at me! It smiled right at me!"

For all his other merits, Darinel was sensitive to the sight of blood and had to go in the office to lie on the couch, and so they were down four people by the time they sent the busboy off on his second visit to the hospital. Avi's eyes were narrow and he was breathing heavily but before he could find someone to scream at John went to Guillermo's station, threw out his crimsoned potatoes and started on another batch. And now it was no longer easy, not a simple paradiddle but a frantic and improvised cadence, John finishing off the glaze on an order of duck and then moving to Guillermo's stove to double check the heat and then back to Kiki's station to get going on some salmon, the difference between a perfectly pink rib and a ruined order of fish a matter of ten or fifteen or at most twenty seconds. The orders piled up one after the next, half of Manhattan stopping by for a last dinner with a prospective lover or to cap off a work party or just see old friends before returning home for the holidays. John chopped, John diced, John fricasseed and fried, John garnished and John plated, John attended to every one of a thousand details without failure or interruption. John was on fucking fire.

And then it was eleven-fifteen and the last customers had been ushered out of *Avi's*, tipping a raw quarter and offering loud compliments to the chef, and John could finally set down his knife. He felt tired. He felt good. He hadn't thought about his mother or cocaine in nearly five hours. Resting from his labors John could see that the other cooks, not to mention the waiters and bus boys and even the dishwashers were all watching him with something between appreciation and awe.

"That was… not bad," said Avi.

John took off his apron, balled it into a corner and threw it in the linen basket.

"You are a raging asshole," John said, smiling, "and you over-season your meat."

And, with that, John waved goodbye to a shocked Darinel and headed out into the evening.

*2001*

# THIRTEEN

In the eastern quadrant of the Tower, past the peach orchards and the apiaries and the sugarcane fields, a spring had been diverted to create a low, murky bog. It was an unruly, little visited section of the city, far from the bustle of the central spire, where hydronese harvested crayfish and aging herons sat on the docks selling off the day's catch. Over a stone levy and past the damp *batture* the *Captain's Rest* lay forever moored in the shallows, a mothballed galleass recommissioned as a hostelry, masts naked to the sky. By the time Mary Ann and Jolly Bones ascended its slipway dusk had fallen, their arrival attended by a crepuscular orchestra of crickets and croaking frogs.

The boat was big, rotted, and low slung, listing slightly on a current strong enough to complicate movement, if a rich draft of cordial wasn't enough. It was crowded with all the creatures who called the quags their home; fisherfolk and netmenders, cranberry harvesters, scullers and clam-catchers. An orchestral anima played itself as a concertina, accompanied by a molluschite tooting a fife. A pair of strutting, smaragdine mallards tried to chat up a hydronese too drunk on salt water to pay them any attention. A one-eyed widdershin stood warily beside the window, holding a mug of ale between his toes. Taking up the better part of one corner was an exiled zoaea, his carapace a sickly, moss-covered green, inset eyes dull and despairing. He shared the table with a mottled, aging owl, its feathers damp and gray, one wing withered from some ancient injury.

Mary Ann and Jolly Bones forced their way to the counter.

"What do you want?" asked the bartender, a fat otter with a knife scar bisecting his lip and nose.

"Two cups of cordial," said Mary Ann.

"You got money?"

"Is that what you take here?" asked Jolly Bones. "I've been getting by on sheer charm."

"We've got money," Mary Ann said, placing a silver coin with her mother's head onto the hardwood. The bartender poured them two shorts of liquor the color of red Kool Aid, and when he handed it to Mary Ann she leaned in and whispered something to him.

"What?" said the bartender.

Mary Ann said it again, louder, but not loud enough to be heard over the music.

"What?" the bartender asked again.

"A new day dawns," Mary Ann half yelled.

"Shhh!" the bartender hushed. He glanced around warily, but the mallards were too busy preening to pay attention and the rest of the patrons were focused on their drinks. "Follow Strix," he suggested, offering the owl in the corner a long, lingering look, then went to serve his other customers.

All the tables were occupied, and so Mary Ann and her companion found themselves beside a grimy port window which overlooked the bog. The widdershin watched them suspiciously, inverted head peering up from the floor, drinking through a copper straw. The cordial was sickly sweet, but Mary Ann was that sort of girl who only ate the marshmallows out of her morning cereal, and she didn't mind, the liqueur leaving her warm and light and slightly nauseous.

"You think they can handle it?" asked Jolly Bones.

"You can count on John," said Mary Ann.

"You sure? You said by human standards he's just a little kid."

"He's older than he looks."

It was John after all who had found the location of the inn, long hours wandering around the Tower listening to rumors from the other scullions and messengers, hanging about in underlit stairwells and the dirtier corners of the bazaars. How long, exactly? Who knew? Time in the March was not time in the world, it was pointless to try and equalize them. To think about one while you were in the other was a frustrating task, like holding onto a dream through till afternoon, the details becoming fainter, the essential truth of the thing rubbed away to nothing. It worked the other way likewise, and sitting there drinking her cranberry cordial Mary Ann found it difficult to recall, or difficult to believe, that she had a math test the next morning and had been sent to bed early for fighting with Constance.

"I still don't understand why I'm here," said Jolly Bones.

"We're here to investigate the plot against the Tower."

"That's why *you're* here."

"You live in the Tower too."

Jolly Bones grunted disdainfully at this incontrovertible truth.

The owl in the corner stood upright and abstained from drink, though his cancriform assistant made up for it, dumping half-buckets of liquor into its mouthparts. Watching him Mary Ann saw that others within the bar, the hydronese and the mallards, were doing the same.

"This is it," said Mary Ann, "are you coming?"

Jolly Bones shrugged nervously and turned at his wind-up key but, in the end, he joined Mary Ann as she headed towards the back stairs. These led to a storage room below, crates of empty bottles and kegs of wine pushed up against the mildewed walls of the ship. By this time the room was crammed full, the hydronese and the mallards, the molluschite who had been playing the fife, several others Mary Ann had not noticed, followed at last by the zoaea, who closed the door behind them then folded his pincers and blocked the exit.

Below decks the list of the boat was more noticeable, and the stench of cranberry soured the air.

The owl waited for the room to quiet, then stretched his wings as wide as they could go, showing off his ruined left pinion. His eyes took up most of his face, jaundiced yellow saucers that seemed to stare straight at Mary Ann.

"We have been betrayed," he began.

A sharp instant when Mary Anne thought of frantic escape, but the owl continued on, and her heartbeat gradually returned to normal.

"Betrayed from the moment of our birth, and from a thousand years before. Betrayed by our princes, betrayed by our chiefs, betrayed by our parents and theirs. I weep to look upon the map, to the four corners of the compass! In the Hive the oothecan are caste slaves, drones acting as servile fodder for their queens. In the Toybox the masters sup on marzipan while their servants make do with stale licorice. The great among the faunae oppress the low, and Under the Mountain the children of stone waste their youths as chattel to their elders. And above it all, looming in mockery, sit the Harrow." Strix shook his head fierce from side to side, one-hundred and eighty degrees of condemnation. "Damn the Harrow! Damn them and thrice damn them and a hundred times damn them! No punishment could be sufficient for their evils! An eternity of penance could not purify them of their crimes!"

"What do I care about the Toybox, or Under the Mountain, or any of it?" asked one of the mallards. "I'm no crofter or peasant. I catch my fish, and I sell them. I am free as anything in the March."

"Then you are not free at all," Strix retorted, "for who would speak of freedom so long as the Tower stands? So long as the eyes of the Harrow are upon you, judging your crimes or what they say are your crimes?"

"What about the End?" asked one of the hydronese.

"What about it? Have you seen it? Has anyone? It lives in

your closet and beneath your bed, and it will eat you if you don't fall in line! We are kept in bondage by fear, my friends, nothing more."

This was not true, Mary Ann knew, or could not be true, but around her she could feel the crowd agreeing, the mallards bobbing their heads and even Jolly Bones leaning in closer.

"And yet all is not lost! The King in Rags is on his way! Walls cannot stop him; no moat can keep him out. He is without crown or title, he has neither land nor castle, but he has an army all the same! His voice is carried by the wind, and an endless horde serves his cause. For now, we speak in whispers, and walk in the shadows. But soon the last lord will throw off his cloak and reveal himself, to lead us to an undreamed of tomorrow."

"So we replace the queen with a king?" asked the molluschite. "What good is that?"

"Not replace! The King in Rags is the throne-breaker, who will tear the Tower down to its foundations and return the March to what it was before the Harrows made it their plaything. For generations uncounted we have known only slavery, but the day is coming when the Thousand People will take what has so long been stolen. When the masters will be forced to the plow and learn of the whip. When their hands will crack and mottle, their brows bead sweat, their shoulders ache from hard labor. Tomorrow is fast on its way, my friends – will you be a part of it?"

The crowd roared, the crowd clamored, the crowd clapped their claws and stomped their hooves and rock the ship with their enthusiasm. The conventicle concluded, Strix slipped out of the room, escorted by his crustacean protector. In the sky far above them Ababab drifted silently along with the wind, a little dark spot among the night clouds, waiting to follow the King in Rags's prophet as he continued about his treason.

# FOURTEEN

The table was set, the red sauce simmered neatly on the stove, the pasta was cued up in a colander beside a pot of boiling water. Joan sat at the island counter drinking a glass of white wine with ice cubes in it. Constance and Michael were in the basement, trying to fix the washing machine, and Mary Ann and John were in the living room, watching cartoons.

"Enjoy it," said Joan.

"I try," said Sophia.

"But not hard enough."

"How do you know?" asked Sophia, as she made a quick pot of cream sauce for Mary Ann. At eleven, Mary Ann still steadfastly refused to eat 'things that tasted like other things', by which she meant any admixture of flavors, and Sophia was left to make her peanut butter sandwiches or cheeseburgers without ketchup.

"No one does. You can't, really. There's some part of us that never really believes things will change. We know they will, but we don't *believe* it."

"You should put more ice cubes in your wine," said Sophia.

"Don't be rude."

Sophia tossed the pasta into the pot of water, then went into the living room. John sat on the couch, hands wrapped around his legs, and Mary Ann knelt beside the coffee table, sketching something with a set of colored pencils. Sophia took her mother's advice and watched them from the doorway, trying to savor this rare moment of amity, a happy interlude between the constant low-level bickering which was the steady state of familial existence.

"–disappears into the warrens," said John, "and he can't follow him in there."

"*He* can't," said Mary Ann, "but maybe *we* could."

"Maybe," said John, "maybe not."

She and Aaron had been like that, once upon a time, making up games, talking in their own shared shorthand, inseparable when they weren't screaming at one another. The thought of her brother curdled through Sophia's gaiety. She wondered where he was, if he had gotten lost somewhere in the March or if he had come back but not come home, just decided to step off somewhere. It wouldn't be the first time, a collect call in three months from New York or Boston or Barcelona saying he was sick or broke or just terribly sad.

"Hi, Mom," said John.

Mary Ann startled. "Hi, Mom."

Sophia crossed into the family room, folded a blanket, and set it on a chair. "What are you two talking about?"

"It's for a story she's illustrating," John said quickly, "about two kids in a castle."

"She's a princess," Mary Ann smirked, "and he's her errand boy."

"He keeps trying to stop her from making bad decisions, but she doesn't like to listen."

Sophia was only half paying attention. "Well, dinner is in five minutes, go on and wash up."

"Yes, Mom."

"Yes, Mom."

They waited until their mother had headed towards the basement before continuing.

"Nothing's changed," said Mary Ann, "if we come clean now, we'll just be little kids who got in over our heads, and it'll be years before they let us go back."

"What do you think will happen if that owl caught us following him?"

"He won't," Mary Ann promised, "that's not how it works."

"How what works?"

"Things. You know."

"It's not a story," said John.

"Isn't it?" Mary Ann asked, finishing off a last bit of shading. "Do you want to tell Mom?"

"No," John admitted.

"All right, then." Mary Ann slid off the couch and headed to the bathroom to wash her hands. "It's settled."

The Harrow's basement was unfinished, damp concrete filled with cardboard boxes of books and discarded toys, a two-year-old washing machine which rarely fulfilled its intended function but had, at least, proved an engaging project for Sophia's husband and eldest daughter. She arrived to find it pulled away from the wall and partially disassembled, Michael knelt beside its opened back, Constance standing beside him with the toolbox.

"Do you think it's the rotor?" she asked.

"Could be, kiddo. We'll have to take the rest of it apart to find out."

"You could just call someone," Sophia pointed out.

"If you own something, you should be able to take care of it," Constance explained, "calling someone every time you need something fixed is irresponsible."

"You are too young to be talking like that," said Sophia. She leaned down and gave her husband a kiss on his grimy cheek. "It's only cute when your father does it."

Michael smiled shyly and Constance blushed and then they both went to clean themselves up. By the time they made it to the dinner table the rest of the family was already waiting, Mary Ann and John jostling about in their seats, Joan almost done her glass of wine. Sophia served Michael first, and Mary Ann put cream sauce on her naked pasta. Joan asked Michael about his day at work, and he answered between bites of food in his dry, faintly distracted fashion. It was nothing special, really, but in years to come would grow jumbled about with other dinners in Sophia's mind until it began to serve for all of them, the platonic ideal of what was once her family, content, healthy, rich with the promises of tomorrow.

# FIFTEEN

Queen Lavender greeted them as they entered the high hall, a scarred, imperious monarch. Her carapace was the deep brown of polished teak, her antennae crested nobly and her wings, useless with age, hung behind her like a cloak. In her lower arms she held a scepter, but with her topmost pair she waved her guests forward.

"The children of the Hive greet the Harrow's champion," she began, nodding her head to her thorax, "may his foraging bear fruit, and his line breed female."

"Queen Lavender," said Michael, likewise bowing.

"This must be your eldest." The Queen turned her glittering, compound eyes, like thousand-faced carbuncles, onto Constance. "May you bear true to your mother's line."

Constance wore a long dress that Sophia had packed for her, but her hair remained its usual disorderly self, frizzed further from the damp of the Hive. She felt foolish, but she managed her bow nimbly. "The strength of the Harrow is the love of the people," she said.

"May they never lose it," added Queen Lavender.

After leaving the Harvestlands, Constance and the rest of the Valiant cut a path to the Low Mountains, towards a great black splotch in the gray stone which ultimately revealed itself as a vast warren occupied by the scuttling subject oothecan. Some vestigial prejudice had carried over into the March – the memory of things disappearing behind fridges, a vacation to Cape Cod when their cottage bathroom had been infested with dark dots – but Constance was pleasantly surprised to find the Hive was a clean and orderly place. Freed from threat of footfall or pesticide the oothecan proved quiet and meticulous, moving about rapidly but with order and even a strange grace. Among themselves they communicated only by scent, and the tunnels were rich with incongruous odors like thick perfume; a summer breeze, an apple pie cooling on a window sill, sheets fresh from the drier. Most of the Hive was a senseless-seeming maze of narrow passageways, but the guest quarters adhered to hominid specifications. True, everything was composed of calcified excrete, not only the walls and ceilings and floors but the tables and the chairs and the cookware and everything else, but so long as you didn't make a point of thinking about this it wasn't so bad.

Their official greetings finished, the Valiant were led towards a low feast table at which waited the Queen's handmaidens, younger, paler, smaller iterations of their monarch. Bustling about as waitstaff were dozens of male drones, half the size of their female counterparts and lacking in any humanoid pretensions, multi-limbed, faceless figures. They worked with an endless, unhurried efficiency, bringing plates and refilling glasses. The oothecan ate lying on small, hard pillows, but low chairs were provided for their guests, finely wrought if not quite correct, the arms too long and the legs too short. The food itself proved more of a puzzle, half a dozen slicks of colored paste along a serving dish, a thin black spoon waiting beside.

"It's actually pretty good, once you get in your mouth," said Sir Reginald Fitzwillow. Out of the field, away from his ax, the bear seemed anxious and uncertain – but at least, Constance thought, he didn't have to wear a dress. "Just don't concern yourself about where it came from."

"Food is pretty weird any way you think about it," said Dame Delta, perched on the rail of the chair beside her best friend. "How is this any different than buttermilk?"

"I'm not usually staring at the cow while I drink it," Sir Reginald Fitzwillow pointed out.

Conscious of her duties as ambassador and not wanting to seem like a child, Constance brought a spoonful of canary-yellow goop to her mouth. It had the consistency of toothpaste and the taste of ripe fruit drizzled with salted honey, and Constance found herself finished with it all too quickly. A fulvous streak proved to be buttered popcorn, a neat line of cyan akin to a country-fried steak Constance had tried two summers before when they had gone to visit cousins in North Carolina.

It was amazing, though you would not have known it from the Queen's handmaidens, snuffling up their portions with curled black palps and no particular indication of enjoyment. Teams of male drones hovered nearby in anticipation of a command. Michael, with Sir Floppy beside him, quietly related the events of their journey to the Queen, who lay on a raised settee.

"The Harvestlands bloom once more," said Michael. "The roads are quiet, and the Gales have blown kind. They have hopes for summer again soon."

"The arcimboldi are fortunate to enjoy the protection of the Harrow," said the Queen, "to be watched over like larvae, their errors pardoned, their injuries ameliorated, their path marked wide and clear."

"No more fortunate than any of the other peoples," said Sir Floppy.

The feast hall was hung with small lanthorn, each emitting a foggy light and a faint smell of cinnamon. Like the rest of the Hive, the walls and ceiling had been engraved in twisting patterns, like a maze or a labyrinth. Constance tried to follow one through to the end but grew nauseous and had to turn back to her plate.

"You're just jealous," said Sir Reginald Fitzwillow to Dame Delta. "All the things we get to eat – peaches, bacon, chocolate popovers – and you're stuck with oil."

"Stuck with it? Stuck with it? There's nothing finer than a drop of oil. A thousand different types, and each sweeter than the last!"

"Ah, you're pokin' bogey!"

"You've got coal, lamp, rapeseed, whale, leviathan–"

"–and how is the princess finding her time away from the Tower?" asked the Queen, from where she lay prone at the head of the table.

It took Constance a moment to realize that she was the princess in question. "It's been instructive."

"She's a quick study," promised Sir Floppy. "On the way here, she wrestled a scamble into submission."

Constance blushed a bright red, thinking it contrasted unkindly with her dress and feeling grateful for the dim light.

"One more bondsman added to the Harrow's count," said the Queen, in what might have taken as a compliment, "your daughter starts on her family's business early."

"I was defending the arcimboldi," said Constance.

"It amounts to something very similar, does it not? Because to help one, you must injure another. And neighbors bicker. There is always some new injury to revenge, and the borders spread accordingly."

"The Harrow have never sought conflict," said Sir Floppy, "only met it when it came."

Her father sat quietly, spooning his pap with courtesy if no excess of relish. But Sir Floppy ate nothing, his arms folded around his chest, his mouth a thin line below his white whiskers. Relations between the Hive and the rest of the March had not always been easy, the oothecan having a sinister reputation as much for their shape as for the strange flesh magics they were said to practice far below ground.

"In any case, it seems to have been a productive journey," said the Queen, "the Hive can only hope that your uncle is enjoying as much success on his own mission."

Michael set his spoon beside the bright streaks of mush on his plate.

"And how does it go with the High Prince?" the Queen continued, "we've heard no word from the North."

Nor had anyone else, at least so far as Constance could guess, though she was smart enough to know how little her parents actually told her.

"The North is a very long way away," said Michael noncommittally.

"The Champion speaks true," said Queen Lavender. "Let us hope that he meets with no difficulty among the verdurite. The Kingdom of the Thorned Rose are ever factious. They have only known the yoke of the Harrow for a generation and may still chafe beneath its weight."

"Not yoke," said Sir Floppy.

"Once more?"

"The verdurite enjoy the protection of the Harrow," said the rabbit knight. His good eye was blank and flat as the stretch of black cloth which mirrored it. "They do not labor beneath its yoke."

"Pardon – it is not often that the children of the Hive communicate with speech."

"I think you speak very well," said Michael. "Perhaps it's time to tell more of your own troubles. Your message was vague. Something terrible must have happened, for the Hive to beg the assistance of the Tower."

The Queen's antennae fluttered above her head, perhaps an expression of annoyance, perhaps because she smelled or detected some foreign odor, perhaps for no reason whatsoever. "War is unknown between oothecan. Among ourselves we shed no ichor, and our legs are never raised in anger."

"Among yourselves," Sir Floppy muttered.

"When our numbers outgrow a settlement, a new queen is chosen, and she leads her drones further into the mountain, to find a new colony. It has been a fecund season, and the Hive nearly full. A month ago, we began the process of expansion. Three missions were sent to find a suitable spot for a nest, led by my mightiest handmaidens, battle-hardened veterans. None returned."

"The End?" asked her father.

The oothecan betrayed no feeling on their faces, mandibles and clypeus unrepresentative of joy or sorrow, but still Constance gathered some sense of unease spread across the table.

"Perhaps," said the Queen, "though we've seen none of the other signs. In days of old we would have dealt with it ourselves, my knights gathered beneath our standard, a great host to march into the dark. But today is not yesterday, and the oothecan are the faithful servants of the Tower. When there is trouble, we know better than to tend to it ourselves." The Queen spoke in a buzzing monotone, but the mockery was unmissable.

Constance could not remember her father ever yelling at her. In the Harrow household, discipline was left to her mother's icy ferocity. It was Sophia who stood you in a corner, sent you to your room, kept you away from the television or a tub of ice cream, and Michael who called you back down, comforted you, kept aside a portion of the chocolate mint he knew you liked. Even genuine misbehavior only earned from him a saddened confusion, as if he had never quite accustomed himself to the reality of cruelty or cowardice.

Though this, in Constance's mind, was far worse. Her father turned his wearied countenance off the Queen and towards his Valiant. "Sir Reginald," he said, "how many of us were lost when last we came to the Hive?"

"–trying to tell me that you think a glass of coal oil is the same as a dram of whisky?"

"Sir Reginald!" Michael piped.

"What? Sorry? What?"

"When last the Valiant came to the Hive, to put down the thing that had come from the depths. How many were lost?"

The fuzzy bear turned from arguing with Dame Delta and lost all trace of his usual smile. "Five met their weird that day. Dame Talon, Sir Cinnabar, the Knight of the Bedraggled Seat. Sir Gneiss. Dame Caterwaul, who taught me the sparr ax."

"May their names be remembered," said Sir Floppy.

"Till the coming of the End," added Dame Delta.

The feast hall had grown still, the only sound the constant buzzing of the drones.

"I have journeyed a very long way from my home to defend the children of the Hive," said Michael. "Fight we will, and die if we must, every one of us, and my daughter as well, whom I love more than life itself. Not for treasure, and not for power, but because the Harrow swore an oath to defend the March, an oath from the first of their line to the last, may that day never come. And the Harrow keep their word, whatever the cost."

The Queen dipped her antennae and returned to her plate. Her knights and handmaidens mimicked her. The drones hummed senselessly. Constance had never been so proud to be her father's daughter.

*2023*

# Sixteen

John left the restaurant feeling tall enough to duck power lines but by the time he got off the subway he had shrunk to human size or even smaller. Shivering on the walk home he passed a guy sleeping behind a trashcan windbreak and a mother screaming at two young children. There was broken glass at the bottom of his stoop and the stairwell was rank with winter damp. His studio apartment was no cleaner than he remembered. He removed his overcoat, and his boots. He went to the toilet, washed his hands, threw some water on his face, and opened a beer. Then he took the handgun from the back of his sock drawer and set it on the night table beside the window.

John was not a very good son, according to the world's estimation or his own. He forgot birthdays, his phone calls were rare and brief, he had once moved to Sao Paulo for six months and not bothered to tell anyone. But years ago he had promised himself that, whatever his other failings, he would not force his mother to attend his funeral, a silent oath which he held to like a crook on endless evenings spent staring out at the Brooklyn skyline, sucking over bad memories like a sore tooth.

In very black moods he liked to think of the gun as his pension; and so, when he had finally gotten around to listening to Constance's message earlier that afternoon, his first thought had been that he was nearly vested. It was rather a selfish consideration, but then, people are complicated, and, as was mentioned, John was not a very good son.

He pulled a chair over from where his dinner table sat in the center of the room and set it beside the window and the night table and the gun. He drank his beer in steady, smooth, even motions, almost continuously. Accustomed to assuming the worst outcome in every situation, John figured his mother was dying, and that he would have to return home. Mary Ann too, most likely. Constance and her kids were already there, John belatedly remembered. That had been a surprise, Constance throwing in the towel on her perfect modern family, Constance who never gave up on anything. Where would he even sleep? They'd have to cram him onto an air mattress or something. Julian was – six? Seven? Which would make Evie – four? Five? They probably wouldn't even remember him. Something else to feel shame over. He finished his beer and got another.

Mom would make them have a party; John was as sure of that as he was the gun on the table. All those awful old leches and cheap neighborhood drunks. He'd have to buy the kids presents, and he'd have to be on his best behavior, lying through his teeth about every aspect of his life and tip-toeing across the endless mind field of family history. Which was fine for him and Mom, but Constance and Mary Ann couldn't pass a hill without trying for a last stand, they'd be at each other's throats by dinner time. Smile for the camera phone in front of the stockings, whip up a quick Christmas feast, be back by New Years. Earlier, maybe? Depended on how long Mary Ann stuck around. John got another beer.

And after that, what? Constance would take the house, and the throne too for that matter, lacking any rival claimant. Mary Ann would return to California and whatever fuzzy existence she occupied, fuzzy in both the sense that John was vague on its details and that Mary Ann, to the best of his impressions, seemed largely indifferent to it. Disappointment had taught Mary Ann that there was no point in going for what you wanted. He supposed it had taught him that there was no point in wanting anything. He wondered idly how long he should wait after his mother's death before joining her in the ground. Better to tough it out a few years, and give the others a chance to heal? Or condense the tragedy it into one horrible late winter? It was a cruel irony that one's existence could simultaneously be an intolerable burden while also supporting the existence of beloved others. Nor was John capable of pretending the physical and emotional distance between him and his siblings would lessen the pain of his removal. John would only lie to others; at least, that was the lie he told himself.

Out of beer now and he knew when it came it would not be planned or the result of any rational calculus. It would be a night like any other, like this one, when the required concoction of despair and bravery and liquor finally ignited into self-murder. John caressed his fractured face. It wasn't his fault. It wasn't anyone's fault. It was just how it was. There was something wrong with it all, some fundamental imperfection. A crooked thing. A lack uncountable.

John shook his head, put the gun in his pocket, moved aside the bed table, opened the window and climbed out onto the fire escape. A very light snow had started to fall, not enough to stick to asphalt or cancel school but sufficient to slick the metal staircase and to quiet the din of the city. Abnormally quiet, in fact; reaching the roof, John couldn't hear cars honking or people talking or the screech of the L shuttle but only the low hum of the heating unit and the voice that had been in his head.

"Taint to the marrow," it said. "Rats in the stores."

It squatted on the precipice of his building, a begrimed emaciate wound in filthy cloth. It might have been human. In this city, in this age, there were people that looked like that.

But John, who had seen worse things still, knew it was not. "Evening," he said.

"Always," the thing agreed.

"How'd you get here?" John asked.

"Born to suffer."

"But how'd you get *here*?"

"Cracks in the foundations," it said. It picked at a pustule with an ingrown fingernail. "Holes in the walls."

The snow had picked up. John was freezing. He had completely forgotten that he had ever wanted to die. "What comes next?"

It had strange, sharp movements, jerking its head like a bird. "Locusts at harvest," it said. "Gasoline on a trash fire."

"Why?" John asked, coming closer. "What do you want?"

Its smile was dazzling, teeth expanding to fill a mouth expanding to accommodate the teeth, a checkerboard pattern of green and off-white wide as a regulation board. "A crooked thing," it reminded him. "A lack uncountable."

It howled and tensed suddenly upright. John stumbled and pulled the gun out of his pocket but instead of coming forward it dropped back, stepping neatly off the ledge. John was still expecting to see it come soaring back up when he felt the shudder from the ground below and heard the screams of passerby.

He hurried out the back stairwell five minutes later, carrying a duffel bag and heading towards the subway stop on Franklin. At Penn Station he bought a ticket heading south. Just before getting on the train, he texted Constance to tell her he was coming home.

# SEVENTEEN

The Harrow looked old. Sir Floppy could see it and so, he thought, could the rest of the High Council. Though the Bauble still shone transcendent from crown, Sophia seemed shriveled beneath it; her shoulders withered, her face lined with care.

"You sure she's up for this?" Sir Floppy whispered to Constance.

"I strongly suspect she isn't," Constance whispered back.

"Then why–"

"You think I tell my mother what to do?"

Sir Floppy had no answer to that.

The council table was wrought in living metal, a map of the March with every land and city blossoming atop its surface. There were eight spots around its edges. Only six were occupied; one chair sat forever empty in memory of the Kingdom of the Thorned Rose, blighted for its sins; another, reserved for the petrousian, was likewise unused, Under the Mountain closed off since the coming of the End; Sir Floppy himself held the chair of the Faunae Palatinate, and spoke on behalf of his animal kin; Wisdom, representative of the Proscenium, sat to his left, his mask painted into an expression of somber thoughtfulness; Queen Myrrh of the oothecan followed, prone on an upraised pillow; Citizen Anemometer likewise made no use of a chair, his body a complex adding machine with a roller in place of legs or feet, but he occupied the Clockwork Republic's spot at the table; finally, in place of their usual representative the merrilings had sent Springheel the jack-in-the-box, a garish painted face attached to a bobbing coil.

The head of the table was, of course, reserved for the Harrow, and after a moment to build anticipation, Sophia spoke. "It does my heart good to see old allies in these times of darkness."

A gear creaked within Citizen Anemometer. Queen Myrrh wiggled her antennae. From inside Springheel's box came a jaunty tune which he could not or would not mute completely.

"The End has come," Sophia continued, after it was clear there would be no response, "the wards have fallen. The first of their outriders are already upon us. We hear nothing from the xerophile and must assume the wastes are lost. The zoaea report that the southern sea is flooded with water which is not water, and their beaches awash with carrion."

"Discommoding rumors, no doubt," said Citizen Anemometer. "Though surely no cause for disquietude."

"More than rumors," said Wisdom. "The Proscenium is hard pressed. The End is only a few days from our borders."

"We have met the End before," said Citizen Anemometer.

"It has never been this bad," said Sophia, "not in all the long history of the Tower."

"In desperate times," said Wisdom, "the need for action grows only greater."

"And who would you call to arms?" asked Citizen Anemometer. "The mob of refugees we had to force our way through to get to the Tower?"

Constance felt compelled to respond. "That mob, as you call them, are your neighbors, laid low by a misfortune that is none of their making."

Springheel let out a little giggle but said nothing more. He was a far cry from the previous ambassador, a wise, comforting creature made of faded felt named Binky. But rumor spoke of strange changes in the Toybox, of a cruel mayor, of black jokes and wild games, and it seemed Springheel was an agent of this new power.

"If a herd of strangers came to tramp through your bedroom, would you offer them passage?" asked Citizen Anemometer rhetorically.

"In such circumstances," added Queen Myrrh, "there is no difference between refugees and invaders."

"Refugees tend to be thinner," Constance said flatly.

"The Harrow do not turn away those of our children in need," said Sophia, "though we hear that there is different custom among your own lands."

Queen Myrrh wiggled her top arm at the chair where the Kingdom of the Thorned Rose had once sat. "Ask the verdurite of the kindness of the Harrow."

Constance's hands tightened furiously around the table, but Sophia only smiled. "By all means, ask the verdurite of the consequences of disloyalty – should you be able to find one."

"Surely there is no warrant for such captiousness," said Citizen Anemometer nervously. "Nor the situation so teratical."

"The situation is as the Harrow presents it, though as always she draws her own conclusions." said Queen Myrrh.

"Conclude, brood, delude!" chirruped Springheel. "Pick your poison and chase it down with soda pop!"

The rest of council went silent, awaiting some explanation for this nonsense, but Springheel only rocked silently on his corkscrew, his face a cheery, maddened leer.

Sophia continued. "You think to face the End alone? To wall up your gates and close off your borders? To defeat it by sheer denial? By yourselves, you are doomed. Unity is our only hope."

"At present, we have no evidence of calamity, and no cause for panic," said Citizen Anemometer.

"Fear the End, obey the Harrow!" added Queen Myrrh, "we have heard this song for generations."

"They're classics for a reason," said Constance.

Springheel laughed again, but no one paid him any attention.

Sir Floppy was a knight, a soldier, often a killer, but never a diplomat. "You're a fool if you think to stand against the End alone," he said to Queen Myrrh. "You're a fool and your people are good as dead."

"The Palatinate may enjoy its status as running dogs of the Harrow, but the Children of the Hive are not content. If the End has arrived, we would meet it on our own terms."

Springheel bobbed into the conversation once more. "Squirms, worms, rhymes with germs!"

"If the ambassador cannot offer coherence, he ought at least manage silence," snapped Citizen Anemometer.

"The Toybox have been the faithful allies of the Tower for time immemorial," said Constance, though she was not sure who she was reminding, "and have as much right to a seat at council as any."

"High seat, booster seat, toilet seat, they're all touching your bum!" Springheel informed the council.

"Why have you invited this lunatic to the table?" asked Citizen Anemometer, exasperated.

"This is no time for jokes," agreed Queen Myrrh.

"It's always time for a joke!" responded Springheel. "So long as it's not on you! But what if it is? The End is here, the End is now, the End is everything. Nothing left but to laugh and play! The Smiling Man points the way! Anything for a laugh! Anything for a laugh!"

With this last bit of madness Springheel returned to his box, leaving the rest of the high council to stare at one another in astonishment, a state of confusion which lasted only a moment, and which turned swiftly to fear as Springheel erupted out once more, carrying a round, black ball with the word "BOOM!" painted across it. The wick was a thin fingernail from detonation, Constance up from her chair and Sir Floppy bounding forward though he knew it was too late, anticipating the brisance which would tear his fur from his flesh and his flesh from his bones, which would paint the council chamber red and black and pink and white.

It did not come. A spread of something like steam surrounded Springheel, except that steam is hot and this was not hot at all but terribly cold, so cold that it froze Sir Floppy's whiskers from yards away, so cold that it cracked the wood in Springheel's box, warped his spring, extinguished the fuse on his bomb and left the ambassador encased in a thick block of ice, his mad face trapped forever in its final grin.

Sophia remained standing a moment longer as the energies she had summoned dissipated slowly from her body, leaking back into the ether. Wisdom sat stunned, Citizen Anemometer had fallen flat on his back while trying to retreat, and Queen Myrrh was scuttled halfway towards the door, an impressive feat though it would have done nothing to save her had the bomb gone off.

"Fear not, my children," said Sophia, "I am here to protect you. The End will be driven back, the wards reworked. The maltreated will be succored, the guilty will be punished." The Bauble was blinding bright, and the high lords of the Thousand People looked aside in awe. "The line remains, and the old oaths still hold. There is a Harrow in the Tower, and fate help any who would stand against us."

# EIGHTEEN

It was rush hour by the time Mary Ann left her psychiatrist's office, a period which in Los Angeles lasts from roughly just before dawn to twenty minutes after you get home. There was an accident on the 10 and Mary Ann ended up on the surface roads along with everyone else, Fountain clogged as a stopped toilet and Sunset no better. Hollywood was filled with lunatics, suited men in expensive cars honking at streetlights, costumed superheroes drinking iced coffee, hawkers selling celebrity star tours and sightseers fool enough to purchase them, a gaunt man with rabbit ears tucked below a Dodgers hat, an unshod transient pushing an overfilled shopping cart up Gower Avenue, eyes brimming with tears. By the time she made it back to Silver Lake happy hour was over and Mary Ann had to pay full price at the hipster dive bar that she stopped into, drinking one gin and tonic after another, doing her best to think about nothing or as little as possible. Leaving she discovered that night had fallen, and she was thoroughly sotted. She walked the five blocks home rather than risk the unlikely humiliation of a DUI, coming through the front door to find Jeffrey sitting at the kitchen table.

"Where the fuck were you?" he asked.

Mary Ann set her purse on the counter and put her keys beside them. She felt she was due a reward for making it all the way from the bar without running into anything, and she went to the fridge and poured herself a glass of white wine. "What?"

"I was waiting at the *Roosevelt* for two hours. My boss was there, I looked like a fucking asshole."

"I'm sorry," said Mary Ann, "it's been a crazy day, I had this thing happen at my therapist, and–"

"You weren't answering your phone," said Jeffrey, as if he had not heard her. It occurred to Mary Ann that the light had been off before she had come inside, and thus that he had been sitting in darkness.

"I had it on silent," she said, "I didn't want to talk to anyone for a while."

"That's all you've got to say? You didn't want to talk to anyone? You need to grow up, Mary Ann, start acting like a fucking adult."

Mary Ann found she was having trouble paying attention to Jeffrey, her mind drawn back to the odd events of the afternoon and long before, of foreign lands and strange adventures and the girl who had survived them, a girl she found she had half-forgotten. "Jeffrey," she began, "who are you talking to? How are you even in my house?"

"You gave me a key."

"I gave you a key in case I got locked out, not so that you could camp out in my kitchen like a psycho."

"I was worried," Jeffrey hissed.

"You don't sound worried, you sound angry. And I don't like being yelled at."

"I'm just trying to figure out where you were today."

"I told you, I got distracted after my appointment. I needed some time to decompress."

"What are we, Mary Ann?" Jeffrey asked, his eyes hooded and dark. "What am I to you?"

"The way you're acting right now, I'd say not very much."

"Not very much? Not very much?"

"Jeffrey, I don't have the energy for this. Like I said, it's been a very long day, and I need to book a flight."

"A flight? Where?"

"Back to Baltimore."

"I thought you weren't going home?"

"I changed my mind. I do that sometimes, I told you that. Like I'm changing my mind about your key, which I'd like back before you leave."

"Leave?"

"I'll give you a call after the holidays. I think we need time to think about our relationship. What we are to each other, like you said."

"Are you fucking someone else?" he asked.

Mary Ann laughed despite herself. "Jesus Christ."

"So that's it, then?" Jeffrey's nose had started to bleed, black in the dim light. "Who is it? That guy at the coffee shop who's always smiling at you? Your yoga teacher?"

"My yoga teacher is gay. Everyone's yoga teacher is gay. And not to get all Bechdel test on you, but my life doesn't revolve around dick."

"You think this is funny, Mary Ann? You think my feelings are some kind of joke?"

Her friends had stories of college stalkers and online predators and drunken bros and leering uncles but somehow Mary Ann had slid into adulthood without her share of the misfortunes to which her gender were commonly subjected. She was not as scared as she should have been and wasn't sure if this was the olanzapine or the liquor or only that she had been in far worse situations. "You know what, I don't need any time to think about our relationship, you just put a period on it. Give me my keys and get the hell out of my apartment."

It was only when he stood up from the table that Mary Ann remembered just how big Jeffrey was, muscles thick from CrossFit or boot camp or some other contemporary fitness trend, supermen in dark rooms screaming for you to sweat. "You're a selfish little cunt, you know that? Everything I do for you, and this is what I get?"

It only takes that instant for the floorboards to rot below us, for the façade to tear, for the world to shift. It wasn't just the bad lighting, whatever was leaking out of Jeffrey's nose was black, not a color at all but the absence of one. He was coming towards her, hands raised, eyes dark and maddened, when Mary Ann struck him in the head with her mostly empty bottle of chardonnay.

It shattered and he dropped down to one knee as if about to propose marriage but he did not scream, though the blood ran through his hair and down a day's worth of stubble. Mary Ann sprinted into the bathroom and locked the door, knowing as soon as she was inside that she had made a mistake, a terrible mistake, the window above the toilet was narrow enough to squeeze through but beyond was a three story drop and Mary Ann didn't like her odds. She scanned desperately for a weapon, her pink lady's razor, a bottle of perfume someone had given her as a gift, the plastic plunger beside her toilet. Jeffrey hurled himself against the door, the cheap lock bending, wood splintering, another push certain to tear it from its hinges, Mary Ann screaming soundless angry terrified needing to escape and–

–She stood amid an endless plain below a too-bright moon. Around her a vast horde was on the march, so huge and so numerous that it seemed as if the entire valley was moving and yet the night was silent, not only of conversation or breath but of those noises which even the stillest evening would expect, night birds singing and crickets chirruping and the wind passing through the trees; yes, even the wind. Mary Ann knew with certainty that she was worse off here than she had been alone in her house with Jeffrey, knew it even as the infinite-seeming host noticed her with whatever singular mind possessed it and turned a thousand neighboring heads in her direction. She began to scream once more–

–And then she was under an overpass, the 5 or maybe the 2, cars rolling over the highway above her. A line of ragged tents ran along the sidewalk. A grimy, grim-eyed man worked on a bicycle.

"You all right, lady?" he asked, setting aside his wrench. "You look like you've seen the devil."

*2001*

# NINETEEN

The fight started over a piece of pizza. More has begun over less. Michael and Sophia were on their weekly date, with Joan taking on responsibility for the children. It was impossible to agree on a movie and John would only bowl if they used the kid's lanes, with their wide rubber shoulders (something which Mary Ann felt far too old to do) and so Joan had punted and taken them to the mall. John had bought a plastic figurine that shot a plastic fireball and Mary Ann had bought some new sketching paper and Constance hadn't bought anything, saving up for a new bicycle, and then they had headed to the food court for an early dinner. Joan had ordered two slices of pepperoni and two of cheese because John only liked cheese and Mary Ann had just that week begun experimenting with vegetarianism, but back at their table they discovered they were one short.

"We can cut it in half," said Joan.

"But I'm hungry!" said John. "And Mary Ann always eats pepperoni."

"Do you know how they make pepperoni?" Mary Ann asked. "Do you have any idea what they do to the pig?"

"You've been a vegetarian for like, three hours," said Constance, "just pretend it's still last Tuesday."

"Maybe you could pull them off?" suggested Joan.

"When you pull them off, the cheese comes off too," Mary Ann pointed out. "It ruins the whole thing."

Joan did her best to divide the pizza with a plastic knife, but it came out crooked and in the end no one was happy. Which, though the definition of justice according to many sources, did nothing to reconcile her tired band of savages.

"You're both such babies," said Constance, satisfied with her extra slice and several years of seniority, "it's only pizza."

"All right, now," Joan interrupted, "everyone eat their food and be nice."

"Just give your half to John," said Constance, "you can eat something when we get home."

"You're always taking his side!"

"He's only eight."

"And you're only thirteen, and you pretend you know everything. I'll be thirteen eventually," said Mary Ann, "and when I am I won't be such a jerk."

"But will you be a vegetarian?"

"Shut up!"

"Mary Ann, lower your voice–"

"But she said I was a–"

"So what? Who cares what she says? She could call you a cow but it wouldn't make you milk, would it? Can't the three of you just eat your food in silence for two minutes?" Joan said it with a snap, and by her standards rather cruelly – but even grandparents are occasionally allowed to lose their tempers.

The children turned to glum silence. John chewed over his reheated pizza with a tragedian grimace. Constance, likewise, did not allow her sense of insult to interrupt her feeding. Mary Ann, however, left her half-slice untouched and had turned her chair away in mute defiance.

Joan couldn't help but laugh. "You are so much like your uncle, it's uncanny. Put an Orioles hat on your head you could be Aaron."

"Me?" asked Mary Ann.

"Yeah, you. Your uncle had a very strong sense of fairness. It wasn't always accurate, but he felt it very intensely. Not your mother. She got what she thought was hers. If it was her sitting here, she'd have choked down that slice of pizza before I got a chance to cut it in half."

"Mom?" Constance asked, shocked.

"You think she was always your Mom? You think she was born knowing exactly what she was supposed to be doing every minute she did it? You think she never pooped her pants? Let me tell you something, everybody in the world has pooped their pants at some point. It's why you should never be too impressed by anyone, or too proud of yourself."

"What was Aaron like?" John asked.

"Aaron also pooped his pants."

Mary Ann snickered.

"Did they fight?" asked Constance.

"Oh, God, did they fight. They fought all the time. It was like they thought there was some kind of prize at the end. There wasn't though. And your Granddaddy, rest his soul, he wasn't blessed with any exaggerated sense of patience. The two of them missed more dinners than a starveling. Your mother used to threaten to call child services."

John had looked up from the remnants of his pizza, and Mary Ann had turned back to the table.

"This one time," Joan continued, seeing that she had them on the hook, "I'd taken both of them to the zoo, but we had to leave early for some reason, I can't remember. Anyway, your uncle wanted to go to see the monkeys, and your Mom wanted to go see the lions."

"They don't have lions in the zoo anymore."

"No, but they used to, before they realized it was inhumane to put them in tiny cages until they died."

"What's inhumane mean?"

"It means cruel," Mary Ann explained.

"What happened then?"

"We flipped a coin, and it came up lion, and your uncle wouldn't have it. He and your mom started screaming at each other in front of this poor peanut seller. I was so mortified,

I thought I was going to die. Anyway, I finally calmed them down, or thought I did, and we started walking off to see the lion, and I looked around, and your uncle was gone."

"Gone?"

"Gone." Joan could still remember the moment, a busy crowd full of tall boys and short boys and fat boys and boys eating ice cream but no sign of Aaron, her own Aaron, flesh of her flesh.

"Where was he?" Constance asked.

"He was in the monkey cage."

John laughed.

"No, he wasn't!" said Mary Ann.

"Playing on one of the tire swings. The zookeepers were *not pleased*, I can tell you that much. He never was quite right after. Lived off bananas for a whole year."

"He wasn't in the monkey cage, Grandma," said John.

"No, he wasn't. He'd gotten lost trying to find it, ended up crying by the bathrooms. Your mother saw him, ran over and gave him such a hug I thought she was going to break his ribs. Then we went to see the monkeys." Joan looked to Mary Ann. "Because that's the other thing about your mother – she knew when to put family first."

And after a moment, Mary Ann sighed and handed her younger brother her half slice of pizza.

# TWENTY

The hunt began early the next morning, the Valiant and the oothecan leaving the safety of the Hive for the endless caverns below. Queen Lavender and her handmaidens were ready for battle, exoskeletons like heavy plate, carrying curved swords in doubled-hands. Constance marched beside her father and Sir Reginald Fitzwillow, button eyes taking in the caves with wary disgust.

"Ochone!" he lamented, "but I'll never get used to this damp. The bright sun in a blue sky, that's the place for a bear."

Dame Delta, wings useless in the narrow passageway, agreed with him. "Gliders don't do much good in these caves."

Constance felt herself sweating through her heavy plate.

"Don't worry," said Sir Reginald Fitzwillow. "There's nothing down here the Valiant can't handle. And they might be preening dobbers, but those bugs know which end of their swords to carry."

"Don't call them bugs," said Sir Floppy, "or that other thing you called them. And don't let your guard down." Unlike her father and the rest of the Valiant he was not dressed in a steel panoply, wearing only light black leathers and carrying an elegant saber at his hip. "Anything happens, stay close to Sir Reginald Fitzwillow."

For every Valiant and soldier there seemed half a dozen drones carrying provender and extra weapons, holding aloft torches made, like everything else the oothecan used, of dried spit. These sizzled and gave off a strange sort of smell but they were plenty bright and marching with so great a host Constance felt more than safe, she felt powerful.

The passage broke into an underground cave large enough that the drone's torches could not illuminate its extent. Tapestries of lichen covered the walls, squamulose growths, spiky and slick. Something breathed heavily in the distant dark, and the Queen's guard moved swiftly to form a cordon around their monarch, buttressed by their scuttling, obedient servants. Thus arraigned they moved slowly forward, the drones leading the way, expendable servants of the Hive, their sole purpose lying in anonymous sacrifice.

"By the Tower!" said Dame Delta.

"That's a muckle beast," agreed Sir Reginald Fitzwillow.

Indeed, it was so large that Constance had difficulty seeing it, the way you would have difficulty recognizing a skyscraper standing at its entryway. There was too much of the thing – a tail, a trunk, pincers, spines, a beak above a mouth, another tail, eyes where eyes should be and where eyes shouldn't, claws, quills–

"A gallimaufry!" said Sir Reginald Fitzwillow. "I'll get a fine trophy today!"

"You'll have plenty to pick from," said Dame Delta.

–Rams horns, a narwhal horn, a rhinoceros horn, claws, fangs, cloven hooves, too much and too many, an immiscible agglomerate. It stretched across the back of the cave, making piteous, contradictory sounds and trying to stay in the shadow.

"Keep your torches steady," Michael ordered, "it hates the light."

"Can't stand to see itself," added Sir Reginald Fitzwillow, "hardly blame the walloper."

It was huge and terrible and hideous beyond imagining, but still they were the Valiant, the crusaders of the Tower, victors of more battles than the March had peoples, and they outnumbered the gallimaufry a hundred to one. Constance was frightened and excited but more excited than she was frightened. The Queen's handmaidens pressed ahead of the drones, each of their hands and the swords in those hands at the ready. Sir Reginald Fitzwillow unslung his sparr ax, a long pole capped by blades the size of airplane propellers. Dame Delta took flight in the open expanse of the cave, extending her talons-like-knives.

Only Sir Floppy remained wary, his hand on the hilt of his weapon, his single eye grim. "Gallimaufry never come this close to the surface," he said, "never. Something must have drawn it here."

"Or someone," said her father.

But before he could go any further a drone – one of the nameless horde of which, even in her short time in the Hive, Constance had grown used to ignoring, as one ignores a wall heater or a running fridge, because it is useful and never talks back – began to scream. "An end to the chains! Freedom from the masters! All hail the King in Rags!"

"All hail the King in Rags!" echoed the drones, the chorus filling the cave, the gallimaufry going wild in fear or excitement, lashing out with a tail, hooting a torso-trunk. Then, single-minded as a clock hand, the drones extinguished their torches, and the cave was plunged into darkness.

Queen Lavender and her knights screeched in fear and fury and were echoed by the chitterings of the accompanying drones, for their act of defiance was suicidal, the maddened multifarious monster knew no allies and ate of all sorts of flesh. To this harsh melody was added the sounds of battle, the clank of heavy armor, the whistle of blades, Sir Reginald Fitzwillow's bellow, Dame Delta's squawk.

Constance thought to fight, but she could see nothing to fight. She thought to run, but the path was black before her. And so she cowered, blindly, until a sudden spark illuminated her father's face huge and bright in front of her. "Train the light on me," he said, setting the match in her hands, "and keep it steady."

Around them the gallimaufry went about its terrible business and her father did the same, pulling his ring of keys from off his neck and fitting one into the top lock of his sheath. Folly, Madness, Cruelty, Suffering, Despair, Regret, and finally Necessity were the seven wards that held back the power of her father's weapon, and with steady fingers he opened one after the next. Her back turned, Constance could only hear the fight rage around her, the *thwack* of metal against flesh, the *crunch* of a shattered carapace. The high-pitched war song of the oothecan was eclipsed by the wounded cry of "ochone, ochone!" and despite herself Constance turned to look, her lambent match revealing Sir Reginald Fitzwillow dragging a life trail of white fuzz along the stone floor, Dame Delta fluttering above him, dodging the gallimaufry's tentacles and screaming in rage.

Her father grabbed Constance roughly by the shoulder. "Keep the light on me!" he yelled.

His fear was the most frightening thing she had seen that day, the most frightening thing she had ever seen, and something shifted inside Constance, the loss of that false certainty that things would be all right. She realized her father was no god but only a man, holding things together as best he was able, and that she would need to do the same. She turned away from the death screams of her friends and held the light on her father's weapon.

He was through Folly, Madness, Cruelty, Suffering, Despair, and despite everything his hands were swift and sure, finding a long, bronze key from his key ring and matching it to its accompanying aperture. The screaming had dulled to an occasional bright burst of agony as the gallimaufry went about its slaughter. Constance thought she could hear Lord Floppy cursing, and Queen Lavender hissing, though it was hard to tell one oothecan from the next, and she was quite sure that the soft rustling, growing louder, was the beast itself, its thick, mucousy trunk, its hundred arms and dozen befanged maws–

The last lock clicked. Michael drew his sword.

It was not a sword. It was not anything, a simmering spread of absence which unraveled whatever it touched, be it air or flesh or stone. By its flat and colorless illumination Constance could see that their force was broken, the Valiant scattered, the Queen and her knights splattered and dying; and that the thing which had done this would soon be joining them in death.

For the gallimaufry could not stand against her father, his not-sword sawing a serpentine neck smooth as sharp scissors through wrapping paper even as he ducked beneath the darting maxilliped which came as counter. "For the Tower, for the Harrow!" Michael yelled, cleaving through cuticle and chitin and scale, receiving for his efforts a burst of multicolored ichor which painted the cave prismatic. The thing shrieked its polyphonous scream, turned to escape, feelers twisting and hips swiveling, but it was too late now, her father upon it, *flicker-flash* and one head was gone, *flicker-flash* and another. With its last it sang its dirge in a thousand voices, the cry of a nightingale, the pain-maddened bark of a dog, the desperate low of the bovine, each voice offering futile protest.

And then it was over, the weapon back in its sheath, her father gasping for air beside it, as if he had run a marathon or spent a long time weeping. Someone had gotten a torch going, revealing the sad horrors left behind. Sir Floppy knelt beside the upper half of Sir Reginald Fitzwillow, covering the bear's button eyes. Above him Dame Delta fluttered about furiously, wailing for her lost comrade. The Queen was nowhere visible, her knights broken and wounded or begun the remorseless slaughter of their brothers. Michael carefully refastened each of the locks on his sheath, shielding its terrible power once more.

It did not feel like victory.

# TWENTY-ONE

Sophia was just about to start on the chicken when she heard a soft wrap at the kitchen window and turned to see Aaron standing there with one finger to his lips, urging her to silence and gesturing for her to come outside. He looked gaunt and worried. His coat was too thin for March, and he shivered beneath it.

Sophia peeked into the family room, saw the children watching television while their grandmother drowsed in the corner, then joined her brother on the porch outside.

"Did you know?" he asked without preamble.

Sophia was set to lie, as she did often and with perfect fluency, but coming to the moment she could see there was no point. "Yes."

"Does Mom know?"

"I suspect she suspects."

Aaron pulled a box of cigarettes from his jacket and lit one with thin fingers, trembling, one could only assume, from the cold. The first hit of nicotine steadied him. "Did Dad tell you, or did you just figure it out?"

"There are things that only the head of the Harrows should know."

"That's convenient."

"How did you learn?"

"There was something wrong in the north, that much was true. I could smell it as soon as I got up there. Something in the wind, that mustiness, like opening the door to a room that no one goes in anymore. You know what I mean."

131

"Yes."

"It had gotten into the soil, and into these things that lived beneath the soil. They aren't in the book. We don't have a name for them. They were like worms, but they had hands, little baby hands. Vestigial, I guess. Or maybe the opposite, maybe they were growing into them. It doesn't matter, there aren't any left. They were almost gone by the time we got there, driven mad by the End. They had this city they had built beneath the ground, cathedrals and bridges that looked like they'd been made of sugar. Beautiful. Like nothing else I'd ever seen..." He fell silent a moment, then shook his head and continued. "They'd gone mad and ruined it, gnawed away at the foundations when they'd run out of flesh. That's when they started coming up out of the dirt." The ash on the end of Aaron's cigarette had grown long and gray. He tapped it off and continued. "We took care of them. That is to say, we killed them, all of them, and burned them after, the way you have to. By then it was just me, the rest were dead or... worse. Sir Lallydaddle got infected, begged to be sent home, tried to kill me with his mace. Dame Alabaster wandered off into the woods weeping, wouldn't answer however long I called." The cigarette was down to its nub, and Aaron went to end the butt against the porch.

"Don't do that," Sophia said, reflexively. Then she flushed. "I mean, I can get you an ashtray."

Aaron put the cigarette out on the sole of his shoe. "I decided to keep heading north, to see if the wards still held. I'm not sure how far I went. Far enough that the light started to last for only a few hours each day. It's smaller than Earth, have you ever noticed? A few hundred miles is enough to reach the end."

Though in fact Sophia thought that this was a false equivalency, that it was more likely that the March was flat or that it was convex or that there were simply certain portions of it which the sun, for its own indecipherable reasons, disdained to visit.

"Things up there aren't solid. It's hard to know what is and what isn't, if what you think you see is real, or..." he shrugged. "I can't explain it. I walked until the day didn't come, and it was always dark. And then I went farther."

Aaron fell silent once more. It was that sort of early spring evening where one could be forgiven the blasphemy of supposing winter might never leave, cold and dark. Dirty slicks of slush gathered on gray curbs and beneath the boughs of hibernating trees. The wind picked up.

"What did you find?"

"More darkness," said Aaron. He lit another cigarette and coughed out the exhaust. "We don't deserve it."

"But we have it," said Sophia, "and who would take it if we gave it up? Power isn't a reward, it's an obligation. It belongs to whomever will wield it best."

"And that's always us, isn't it? It's a neat bit of arithmetic you have there."

"I was always better than you at math."

"I never bothered to study," said Aaron.

"What will you do?"

"I'm doing it. It's nearly done. Our time has passed, Sophia. They have to be left to figure it out on their own. To try and fix the wound we caused. It needs to end."

"And you'll end it?"

"If I have to," said Aaron.

There was, of course, a part of Sophia which hated her brother, as there is a part of everyone that hates anyone they love. There was so much between them, history dense as a labyrinth or a thicket. Looking at him she saw both a gaunt, haunted man one step away from a transient and a bright-eyed child, handsome and always nervous.

Mary Ann came out onto the porch. "Uncle Aaron? What are you doing here? Did you come for dinner?"

"Go back inside," said her mother.

"Listen to your mother, Mule," said Uncle Aaron.

"Where have you been? Mom's been worried."

"I said go inside!" Sophia snapped.

Her Mother sometimes lost her temper but rarely yelled, and Mary Ann blanched back, even as Aaron pulled up the edges of his jacket and walked swiftly off the porch.

"Uncle Aaron?" Mary Ann called as he disappeared down the block, "Uncle Aaron! Come back!"

# TWENTY-TWO

The Mushroom Market was the central exchange for those of the Thousand People who lived below the ground; stony petrousian, saprophytes with their billed caps, purblind moldwarp and colonies of reremice. It took up a sizable if half-forgotten portion of the Tower's sub-structure, a maze of stalls and thin tents lit by carbide lamps affixed to the lower stalactites. In wicker baskets and on wooden tables could be found every conceivable variety of the eponymous fungi, morel and cremeni, portobello and lion's mane, not to mention fresh packed loam, living portraits in colored moss, gemstones of every type and quality, copper ingots, iron bars, and endless crates of truffles. It was an array of splendors rarely enjoyed by those occupying more rarefied positions within the Tower – all loyal servants of the Harrow, no doubt, but there would always be a divide between those who loved the sun and those who feared it.

"Can you see him?" Jolly Bones asked.

"No," said John, "but I can see Mary Ann."

From a hundred yards ahead, hidden in the shadows of an awning, Mary Ann watched Strix wobble through the bazaar. The old owl made no attempt at stealth, moving with an awkward, rolling gate, his talons *clip-clip-clipping* against the stone floor, his broken wing bent around him. Mary Ann was in disguise, a hooded cape pulled over her head, Ababab concealed beneath, curled around her body with his spidery tendrils.

Strix went into a dram shop and so as not to be conspicuous Mary Ann turned to the nearest table and began looking through a collection of black trumpets.

"A silver will get you as many as you can fit in your hands," promised the vendor, an ancient petrousian, her skin pitted as a sea cliff.

"They're very nice," Mary Ann agreed, though in fact she detested mushroom, a particularity she had come to mourn since giving up meat.

"I've never had black trumpet mushrooms," whispered Ababab, peering up from underneath her hood, "what do they taste like?"

"I dunno, they're kind of… funky."

"Sweet as a peach!" corrected the petrousian. "They've been growing in dung for months, I cut them fresh this morning."

"Growing off what now?" Ababab asked.

"Shhhh," hissed Mary Ann.

Strix came out from the dram shop and lolloped deeper into the bazaar. Mary Ann made what she hoped was a natural seeming gesture with her hand and John and Jolly Bones took point, shuffling past them and after the owl.

"What do you think he's doing?" asked Jolly Bones.

"That's what we're trying to find out."

"What happens when we catch him?"

"We'll give him up to the guards."

"And then?"

"I dunno. They'll probably give us a medal."

"I am metal," Jolly Bones pointed out.

They switched places again, John and Jolly Bones waiting as Mary Ann went ahead. The owl shuffled down a lane reserved for mongers of taproot, past wicker baskets of poppy mallow and sugar beets, coming finally to a busy carrefour where a crowd bet on a pair of dog-sized mantis. The owl whispered something to a grotty hydronese dressed in long rags, his hair clotted with murk. Mary Ann tried to keep her attention on them but kept being pulled back to duel, the fierce staccato movements of the combatants, the occasional bright burst of verdant blood. Ababab snuck cautiously above her collar but seeing the fracas he grew nervous and buried himself back below.

From where they stood, John and Jolly Bones could see none of this, or only that Mary Ann was busy in a crowd. They waited beneath the awning of a gem wholesaler, beside a broke down anima begging for oil money.

"I better get more than a pat on the head for all this work I'm doing," said Jolly Bones.

"What do you want?"

"Money? Titles? A great big carriage to ride around in?"

"You'd be defending the Tower. That's not enough for you?"

"The Tower isn't going anywhere, just maybe the Harrow. And what do I care about the Harrow?"

"Shouldn't talk that way," said the anima from where he sat on the floor, his hinges bent, his gearwheels busted. "The Harrow protect us. The Harrow keep the March at peace."

"What have the Harrow ever done for you? Sitting there on the hard stone, begging strangers for silver?"

"That's not nice," said John.

"Nice things aren't always true," said Jolly Bones, "and true things aren't usually nice."

John noticed his sister leaving, and tossing the beggar a coin he hurried after her.

They came to the outskirts of the market, where the poorest vendors worked, a saprophyte with a clutch of withered shiitake, a rat selling tarnished candelabras and toothless combs. Mary Ann continued, and John kept after her until the bazaar finally ended, and the rest of the basement began. John could hear a low, rumbling torrent as they got closer to the great underground spring which kept the Tower supplied with water, growing louder as they turned down a side corridor.

"Maybe you were listening to that owl too long," said John.

Jolly Bones blew a raspberry. He was very good at it. "New king the same as the old king. What do I care who's in charge? Just so long as I get mine."

"That's all you think about?"

"You're too young to understand," said Jolly Bones, tromping ahead airily. "You need to look out for yourself in this world, John. There's no one else around to do it."

John did not think this was true, or did not want to think this was true, but before he could argue they came around a turn in the tunnel to find a muddied hydronese holding Mary Ann tight in its grip, Strix close beside.

"My wing may be ruined," he said, "but my eyes are as keen as ever."

A clatter against the stone and John turned to see the owl's bodyguard blocking their retreat, a hulking zoaea, eyestalks cruel and wary. John could not ever remember being so frightened, not even when his father had taken him to a haunted house the previous Halloween.

"Foolish creatures," said Strix, "to have heard the truth and not to have listened."

"Kill them and be done with it," said the hydronese.

"Death is a permanent solution," the owl pointed, "and premature. The King in Rags does not come to destroy, but to liberate, to free his children from their false loyalty to the Harrow, from their lies and their cruelties."

"You're the liar!" shouted Mary Ann, wriggling in the hydronese's long arms. "The Harrow protect us!"

"You would say that, wouldn't you?"

John's heart was beating fast and hard and heavy in his chest, so heavy that he thought he could feel its imprint in the air around him, in the walls of the Tower and the torchlight shadows.

"What's that supposed to mean?" asked Jolly Bones.

"How many of their kind have you seen in the Tower? That pink skin, those grubby little fingers?"

"I'm...not sure."

"Think harder," said the owl, "think as though your life depended on it."

Behind his painted face, Jolly Bones seemed to wince. "What are you saying?"

"These two are scions of the Harrow, future tyrants sent to strangle freedom in its cradle. They are not your friends, merriling. You are a pawn in their game."

Ababab twisted beneath Mary Ann's cloak and Jolly Bones looked startled, or as best as he was able with his mouth formed to a permanent grin. John could feel something building around him and retreated into his silhouette.

"But..." Jolly Bones began, "but..."

"So young, and already so much like her mother." The owl turned towards Mary Ann and her captor. "Perhaps your solution is best, after all."

But before he could obey his master's command Ababab struck, launching himself from beneath Mary Ann's cowl and wrapping the pliable taffy of his impossible body around the face and throat of the shocked hydronese. He dropped Mary Ann and began to beat at his head, imprinting his fist through Ababab and into his own aqueous form. Mary Ann was stunned and Jolly Bones uncertain and the zoaea slow and only Strix moved with certainty, a swift slash with its talon and Ababab screamed and dropped to the ground. The owl hovered over him a moment, then pecked twice through his elastic torso and Ababab groaned piteous and went still.

"You killed him!" Jolly Bones gasped, in confusion as much as horror.

"A pity," said Strix, and he seemed to mean it, even as Ababab's viscous blood dripped off his beak. "Another benighted soul, dead on behalf of the Harrow. But at least he will not make his passage alone."

John's back was against the wall and his body cloaked in

shadow. Only his eyes, bright and blue, remained visible. "Stay away from my sister," he said.

The hydronese pulled a long knife from his worn coat. "She won't get nothing you don't."

John hurled himself forward, dragging the darkness along with him, shadows like tendrils, talons, tails, blades. The hydronese dropped his knife and began to scream, a thousand shallow cuts tearing through his clothes, flinging droplets of living water against the wall.

"For the Harrow and the Tower!" John roared.

Jolly Bones fled, sprinting back towards the bazaar, and Mary Ann watched her brother with some mix of awe and excitement and jealousy at this strange new thing of which he was somehow capable, Strix retreating in a whirl of bloody feathers, John tearing through his enemies like a weed-cutter, certain to emerge triumphant until the zoaea, moving with unexpected speed, grabbed him in one pincer. John's penumbra gnashed and lashed at its shell, flayed the blue scales red, the great crab emitting a strange sound which might have been a scream and flinging John face first against the stone walls of the tower.

There was a crack which was the most terrible thing that Mary Ann had ever heard, but John did not scream.

Mary Ann did, however, as she had at that night after the Christmas Party but this time with her voice as well, her body tense and fierce and furious, all her muscles against one another, wanting to be away, gone, back home, somewhere where nothing bad like this could ever happen and then–

–They were in their bedroom, everything exactly as it had been except that John was on the floor and gasping shallowly. Mary Ann ran over to him then flinched back, his face a mess of scarlet and pulped pink.

"Oh my God, John, oh my God."

John felt for his wound, trembling fingers coming away bloodied. Then, like any other eight year-old, he cried for his mother.

# TWENTY-THREE

The March was at war.

In the Palatinate cruel stoat and starveling sparrow warred with white mice carrying silver swords, with proud badger and fat-fed squirrel. The Toybox had seen violent uprisings in the toffee mines and gumball plantations, ragtag bands of ragdolls thronging the roads, the porcelain ballerinas and velveteen rabbits shut tight in their gingerbread houses. Post-regicide, the Hive's new queen acted with swift violence, putting entire nests to the torch, immolating future generations rather than risk the spread of rebellion. Under the Mountain the youths had grown restive, flint-skinned adolescents and their denser younger siblings refusing, for the first time in the memory of that ordered and ancient people, to do their chores. In the Prosopon the understudies roared for higher billing, the garden cities of the xerophile had been turned to armed camps, the widdershin swore oaths of amity even as they committed bloody fratricide, piratical zoeae raided their coastbound brethren. Across the length and breadth of the March, from one compass point to the next, the Thousand People turned against themselves in violent convulsions, internecine warfare as terrible as anything the March had yet known.

High atop the Tower, in the secret room of which only the Harrow knew, Sophia waited for her baby brother. She was dressed as she had been during the coronation, a long gown of deep blue, the Bauble perched atop her head. She carried neither artifact nor weapon, as if disdaining their use.

Joan sat stooped in a chair behind her daughter. Once upon a time Joan had climbed trees, kissed boys, and danced the jitterbug finer than any of her companions; once she had led the Harrow against their enemies; once she had met a man that she had loved, and born that man's children, and loved and raised those children, and thought to watch them continue that cycle.

Now she was old. "They'll be all right," she said. "Children are resilient."

Sophia's eyes were the same fierce blue as her mother and son but clearer somehow, colder. "You think time is going to fix John's face?"

"That's not your brother's fault."

"I disagree," Sophia said flatly.

The top of the Tower stood above the trees and the mountains and the clouds themselves, the moon alone higher. The wind howled hateful, bellowing through the open window, guttering the torchlight, and then that wind was Aaron, and Aaron came inside.

He was tall and thin and stooped, dressed in a patchwork cloak composed of every conceivable sort of fabric; faded cloth, mottled wool, rank fur and torn hide. He was gaunt, thinner even than when he had come to see Sophia, the magic of the March having elevated this particularity, his hunger and his sadness, into some quintessential aspect of his being. Like his sister, he was unarmed.

His eyes went wide when he saw Joan.

"You shouldn't have brought her," he said.

"I told her not to come," said Sophia.

"Brought me?" Joan objected. "Who the hell do you think you're talking to?"

"This is between you and me, Sophia," said Aaron.

"You and me and my kids."

Aaron seemed to shrink. "What does that mean?"

"John is in the hospital right now. They're going to operate on his eye tomorrow morning. One of your followers beat his head against a wall."

"How did they even get here?"

"We don't know yet," said Joan, "we think Mary Ann... we don't know."

"Did you imagine your little rebellion would come without blood?" Sophia asked.

"Would you believe I barely had anything to do with it?" Aaron asked. "A few words to a drunk in a wayside tavern, a song I hummed to the wind, suddenly half the March is up in arms. They even came up with the name – I was hearing about the King in Rags for weeks before I realized who they meant," Aaron smiled sadly. "Drop a pebble in the water, and downstream a city floods. We warp the place by our very presence. We don't belong here, Sophia. It's not our story."

"And this is better?"

"No – but what comes next might be."

Sophia's face was a furious sneer, and she seemed barely to hear what her brother was saying. "The King in Rags – they got the last part right. The first you'll have to fight for."

"I told you; I've never used that name. I don't want to be king. I want to break the crown."

"I think you're jealous."

"Jealous?" Aaron repeated, as if having never heard the word.

"Dad picked me for a reason. You can't hang onto a job; you can't pay your rent. How many times have I had to come drag you out of the gutter? And now this." Sophia shook her head. "Break the crown! Free the March! Are you sure you're not doing this because you couldn't stand a lifetime of being second best?"

"No," Aaron admitted, "I'm not sure. I've never been sure of anything in my life, not like you and Dad always seemed to manage. I look out and all I see are questions. Perhaps a bit less certainty mightn't be such a bad thing."

"You think that because you've never been a parent."

"They're not children, Sophia."

"They're all my children," she hissed.

The wind had picked up again, thick with detritus, pollen and dead leaves, scraps of lost paper, and it blew throughout the room, against the walls and the blue light which spread out from Sophia. They were in the Tower and then they were down by the sledding hill, tussling in the high snow, and then they were at the dinner table, pointing fingers while their parents watched on, and then they were in high school or perhaps college, shouting furiously. Every argument and feud renewed and always the same, notes in a song played out over long decades of distrust, disagreement and injury. Around them the Tower roared with strange colors and broken sounds, and Joan wept. With Aaron incarnated across the firmament Sophia could see he was stronger than she had credited, that some of the things she had thought were selfishness were not that, or not only that, could see that core of innocence which he had somehow maintained against a cruel and bitter world. She loved him in that moment, but she did not weaken.

And in the end, the contest was never in doubt. Aaron fought only for himself, or for the truth, or for some dream or hope that he had; and Sophia fought for her family. There was a crack like thunder or a snapped spine or a splintered chair or a broken heart and Aaron screamed, and all of the Aaron expressed in the air around him burned off like a sparkler. Sophia's withering indanthrene light flared brighter, until the whole room filled with it, every nook and dark corner, the shadows erased, the Tower and the March itself turned to a weapon, a cocked fist, a whip crack.

But it was not Aaron the blow landed against, it was Joan, spreading out her essence, putting herself between her son and her daughter in a final act of conciliation. She gasped and collapsed out of her chair and onto the floor. What remained of Aaron fled out the open window and into the night beyond.

Sophia stood alone.

# BOOK TWO

## 2005

# TWENTY-FOUR

At first glance the Harrow's Christmas party looked as festive as ever. Stockings hung over the mantle, the noble fir was brightly lit, and long dead Motown stars sang jingles from a newly installed stereo system. In the dining room the adults gossiped and chatted and ate finger food and drank mulled wine. In the hallways the adolescents milled about awkwardly, making eyes at one another and joking about the mistletoe. It was only with careful attention that the cracks could be seen; the slightly too frantic attempt at merriment, an empty chair by the fire.

John wore a green jumper with a reindeer knitted on the front. It was awful and stupid looking, but John knew it didn't really matter. He could walk through the party stark naked, chestnuts dangling, and they would still stare at his face.

"You OK?" Constance asked.

"Fine."

"Eat some gingerbread, it'll cheer you up."

"I'm fine," said John again.

"You look miserable."

"I always look like this," said John, which was true but not really an answer.

Mary Ann stood by the drinks table, waiting to sneak a glass of eggnog. It had been five years since her first taste of cherry cordial, in a waterside bar in an impossible land, and since then all she'd managed was kegger beer served in dixie cups at high school gatherings, flat and watery. But eggnog was mostly sugar, and Mary Ann imagined she might cultivate a taste for it. Her mother was in the parlor being charming and her father had found work to do in the kitchen and left alone she poured half a glass and went into the hallway with the rest of the teenagers.

"I fucking told coach, I'm not going to play if I can't play attack," said Scott Callick, wearing a hemp necklace outside his dress shirt, "but he said that Joe is a Senior, and that I had to pay my dues, and all that crap. Which is bullshit, cause I'm the best player on that shitty team."

"Damn right," said Tim Schorr, who was like Scott Callick except less so.

"Wow," said Mary Ann, sitting on the chair across from Scott, "lacrosse. Cool. That's cool stuff."

"Whatever," he huffed.

"No, really, I think lacrosse is super cool. Getting to walk around all day, holding your stick."

Scott Callick blushed. "It's better than being in the fucking drama club. You think you're going to end up in Hollywood, just because you got to play Emily in *Our Town*?"

"I think I've got a better chance of making it as an actress than you do as a professional lax bro."

Tim Schorr snorted but Scott Callick just smiled and stared at Mary Ann's legs. Someone would have said something if Constance hadn't pulled Mary Ann aside.

"What are you drinking?"

"Lemonade," said Mary Ann. "I pressed it fresh this morning."

"If Mom and Dad—"

"You going to tell them?"

"They won't need me to tell them if you puke onto the fruitcake. You need to pace yourself," Constance said sanctimoniously, "it's going to be a long night."

"Relax, Constance," said Mary Ann, smiling at Scott Callick, "it's a party."

Michael was in the kitchen, gloved and sudsy. He had taken off his tie, but globs of soapy water stained his white shirt. The work went slowly, cleaned dishware piling up in need of drying. The bald spot on the crown of his head stood out.

Sophia arrived carrying a handful of wine glasses. "Were you just going to leave me out there all night?"

"Someone needs to clean up," said Michael.

"Don't do that."

"What?"

"Do the thing you want to do and then act like it's a thing you're doing for everyone else."

"If you're trying to suggest that I'd rather attend to a sink full of dirty dishes than have to listen to Mr Gass update me on his prostate developments..."

"It's tradition. I thought you were excited for this."

"Tradition isn't always enough. It's been a long year, I'm tired. I don't feel like talking to these people."

"Maybe you should have said that before we sent out the invitations."

Michael set a serving dish onto the drying rack. "Would it have mattered?"

Constance found herself pinned down outside of the bathroom, making awkward conversation with Ms Dermout, who looked the same as she had five years prior, as if her body had grown so withered as to allow for no further deterioration.

"And do you know where you're going next year?"

"I applied early admission to University of Maryland," said Constance, "but I won't hear back until January."

"I'm sure you'll get in," said Ms Dermout, "a clever girl like you."

Constance would get in. There wasn't a school on the east coast that wouldn't have lined up to admit Constance to its hallowed halls, the president of two clubs and the star of her varsity softball team and proud possessor of a 3.77 GPA discounting honors courses. She was a serious, devoted, mature young woman, who did everything she was supposed to and mostly did not seem to suffer from this obedience.

"It's good of you to stay close to home," said Ms Dermout. She was drinking a glass of whiskey and eating a slice of peppermint bark. Little flecks of white chocolate were caught along her thin mustache. "So many children these days don't understand the importance of family."

"I've noticed," said Constance, looking at Mary Ann and Scott Callick standing in the hallway, Scott flexing desperately in his too loose dress shirt, Mary Ann pretending she didn't care.

John had sat at his spot by the fire all night, except twice when he had gotten up for a piece of gingerbread. The evening had grown loud and long, and John had been largely forgotten amid the excitement – the best of what he could hope for, all things considered.

Mrs Rhys and Mr Trevor, at least, seemed blissfully unaware of his existence from where they stood drinking beside the neighboring stairwell.

"Just tragic, all that's happened to them," said Mrs Rhys.

"Heartbreaking," agreed Mr Trevor. Mr Trevor had come with his second wife, a too thin woman with an orange spray tan who left early, pleading of a headache, though Mr Trevor had remained behind to drink the Harrow's liquor.

"Poor Joan."

"She was such a presence."

"Not to mention little John…"

"A car accident, wasn't it?"

"That's what they said."

"Tragic," Mrs Rhys said once more.

Though John could tell she didn't really mean it, or only meant it part ways. John did not wonder that a person might enjoy the misfortunes of other people, even other people they said were their friends, even other people that they genuinely thought of as friends. John was a precocious twelve year-old. John had learned plenty.

Mary Ann was on her third glass of eggnog, each taken less stealthily than the last but the way the party was going no one had noticed. Amazing that as a child she hadn't realized how much of the festivities were driven by the over-consumption of alcohol; why Mr Gass once arrived in his Benz but left in a taxi, that Christmas when Mr Trevor had to be escorted outside by her scowling father, most of the years that Uncle Aaron had chosen to spend with them.

"The holidays are so boring," said Mary Ann, not so much because she thought it but because she needed a thing to say, "like, who even cares about presents, you know?"

"Totally," said Scott Callick.

"Stuck at home for two weeks, having to listen to Christmas carols and pretend I like whatever dress Mom picked out for me."

"Tell me about it. We're supposed to go to Harrisburg to see my grandmother, which, like, is literally the worst thing ever. She's got a television so old it doesn't even have an a/v port. I'll be stuck playing Gameboy."

"How would anyone even survive if it wasn't for video games?"

Scott Callick smiled a little. There was probably not much to recommend Scott Callick, in the grand scheme of things, but he could take a joke. "Tim's cousin is having a New Year's party," he said. "We're going to get a keg. You should come by."

"I'll see if I can make it," said Mary Ann, playing with her hair.

The party was still going strong when John slipped upstairs and brushed his teeth and went to bed. No one noticed him leave. It took a long while to fall asleep, the bottom half of the house loud with merriment, or at least its external manifestations. John stared up at the shadows on the ceiling, forcing them into patterns, a few slivers of silhouette making up a face, a wolf, a castle.

Coming to the March was like arriving in a dream. In dreams you never stop to wonder why you are standing in the middle of Central Park or your father has a potato for a head, you accept the unreality without struggle, reconciling each ill-fitting piece into a seamless whole. John was in his bed and then he was in the great hall, amid a fanciful crowd of revelers carousing beneath the fettered auspice of the Gyved Throne. Tables were laid with all manner of sumptuous delights, roasted jubjub bird, collops glazed with mince, brightly colored syllabubs and freshly shucked oyster. Everyone else was already there, Sophia in her blue robes, Michael and Constance in the armor of the Valiant, Mary Ann picking at her ballgown. In attendance likewise John could see Sir Floppy and Dame Delta and a handful of the Tower's bedels and seneschals, not to mention representatives of all the Thousand People, ambassadors from the Proscenium and the Hive and the Clockwork Republic, trying to look important.

John gave his mother a wave that she didn't notice, busy as she was in conversation with the xerophile envoy, a formidable bulk of spiny green come from his far western wastes. The servers and waitstaff hustled about in inconspicuous order, clearing cups, replacing trays of food. John had not been back to the kitchens since the day Ababab had died and his face was ruined. He thought about asking someone if the Man-With-Many-Hands still held court, and if Jolly Bones had returned to his position as scullion, but he did not. It would only have confused whatever poor server he questioned, the gap between them so vast as to make conversation impossibly awkward. There was no turning back the clock. That some something else which, young as he was, John had already learned.

Constance broke away from receiving the plaudits of a pistachio-hued molluschite to check on her little brother. "You doing all right?"

"Fine," said John, then added a belated "congratulations."

The Thousand Peoples knew no gods and celebrated no

holidays, which would have been difficult to observe anyway, given the unreliability of the seasons, but the anniversary of the coronation was always occasion for merriment. This year's commemoration was particularly important, marking as it did Constance's official ordination into the ranks of the Valiant, the first step, or so popular wisdom supposed, in her ascent to the Gyved Throne.

"Thanks," said Constance, trying to look humble and sort of succeeding. "It's just a silly little ritual."

In fact, this was what John thought also, though he knew better than to agree.

"You should eat something," said Constance.

"We had this conversation already."

"Did we?" It was always a struggle to recall home when you were in the March, everything, even the best things, were faded and bedraggled by comparison.

"Yeah," said John, but he went to get some dessert all the same.

Like John, Sir Floppy felt out of place at the great gathering, more comfortable in the field than the Tower. He stood by the windows, drinking slowly from a glass of carrot liqueur, happy to find a moment alone with Constance. "The armor fits you," he said.

Constance tried not to blush. "Thanks."

"You've earned it," he added. "I never had a student who learned her arms so quickly."

This time, Constance could not help herself, a rose hue rising to her chubby cheeks.

"Are you ready for what comes next?" asked Sir Floppy.

"More than ready," Constance promised.

"It's a heavy responsibility. Fighting is one thing, diplomacy another. It will be the first most of the March has seen of the next generation of Harrow. The Thousand People need to know they're in safe hands, that the Tower will continue to protect them, come what may."

"It'll just be a bunch of dull ceremonies and cocktails parties," said Constance. "Are you worried I'm going to start a war?"

"I'm not worried about you at all," said Sir Floppy, casting his long brown eyes to where Mary Ann sat laughing.

The elite of the Thousand People gadded about, amused by their own machinations and a small orchestra of prosopon and several troupes of merriling engaged as jesters. On the dance floor a strutting aurochi kept a stately pavane with a supple hydronese, and fresh from similar exertions Mary Ann rested along the walls, surrounded by a tight net of courtiers.

"A whole season wandering around the provinces," she said, her voice dripping with contempt, "can you imagine anything more boring?"

The Gravinate Vixen wiggled her pointed nose and covered up a laugh with a wave of her fan. Flattery clapped her hands in characteristic appreciation of Mary Ann's joke.

"At least the faunae shall show you a fine time," said the Gravinate, parochial to the end. "The nests and cities of the Palatinate are a wonder. We can go hunting, and there will be tea parties and balls every night in honor of your arrival."

"That's the easy part," said Mary Ann, "but after you, we're supposed to go to the Harvestlands–"

"Ugh! Judging vegetable competitions, no doubt."

"The arcimboldi do try so very hard," admired Flattery falsely, "though they are about as interesting as watching wheat grow."

"Tell me about it. And after I've put a blue ribbon on the largest potato, or whatever, we'll head north to the Kingdom of the Thorned Rose."

The Gravinate choked her vulpine face in disgust. "To think of our Princess forced into such an indignity! Appalling!"

"Sleeping in the dirt and forced to eat raw meat!"

"Absolutely barbaric!" added the Gravinate, popping a bit of sweetbread into her snout.

Flattery swiveled her mask back and forth, cautious before

continuing – though the verdurite, whose relations with the rest of the March remained cool if no longer sanguinary, had neglected to send an emissary. "They're cannibals, you know," she said, in a hushed voice.

"Flattery, really!"

"It's true!"

The Gravinate Vixen gave a charming, horrified titter, though Mary Ann tossed her head, indifferent. "I don't think it counts if you're eating a different species."

Citizen Anemometer, ambassador of the Clockwork Republic, wheeled himself into the conversation, offering a creaking bow by way of greeting. "In point of fact, the verdurite never went so far as to consume the flesh of their captives, though it is true that before your grandfather received their submission, they would drain the blood of captured soldiers to their ancient trees – some sort of religious ritual. The petrousian, the arcimboldi, they all lived in constant perturbation of abduction. But I see your drink is empty." He snapped mechanical fingers at a passing server. "A taste of something sweet, for the Harrow."

"Really, I shouldn't–"

"Nonsense," Citizen Anemometer interrupted, "festivities are best lubricated with libation, whether it be distillate of grape or the viscous press of good oil. And is tonight not a festive occasion? Your sister's ascension to the noble ranks of the Valiant, our lands graced with so brave an heir?"

Mary Ann pursed her lips and shrugged and was happy when the server arrived with her wine.

It was Constance's night, but Sophia was still the center of it, as she was of every room she occupied. The lords and ladies and ungendered elite of the Thousand Peoples vied for her attention, charmed her with compliments, asked quiet favors which she dispersed or withheld according to her own counsel. Michael stood in her shadow, comfortable in that position, even preferring it, and Constance was doing her best to look deserving of the honor about to be bestowed upon her, nodding politely at everyone, answering each salutation with somber self-seriousness.

John was perhaps the only person in the Great Hall failing to enjoy himself, and this despite a sustained assault on the dessert tray, working through an *alexandertorte* and a fistful of benne balls and two long snakes of jalebi and half a bearclaw before turning finally to several gelatinous cubes stuffed with almond and rose petal. "What's this?" he asked a prosopon *patissier*, who remained standing behind his creations.

"Turkish delight."

"Huh," said John, his lips white from powdered sugar, "I thought that was just something in storybooks." He took a bite and chewed a while. "It's kind of gooey."

The servants went about dimming the lights and the orchestra drew to a quiet close. The Queen had assumed her position atop the Gyved Throne, the countless weight of chain hanging above her, each link the unique legacy of an ancestor, every life trammeling the Harrow further to the March. Sophia sat stiff-backed and regal, her eyes deep set, the Bauble luminous from her forehead. Sheathed on her lap was a slender, silvery saber.

"Constance of the Harrow," announced the anuran herald from his place at the foot of the throne, "you may approach the Gyved Throne."

From the end of a long, crimson carpet Constance took steady steps towards her mother's seat. Mary Ann watched from the crowd which had turned silent in anticipation, standing on tip toes for a better view.

"A signal honor, for one so young," Citizen Anemometer whispered from her shoulder.

And one Mary Ann did not begrudge her sister for in the slightest. Who would want to be a knight, have to practice with your sword every day, lift weights and muck out stalls? And as for being Queen, well, who even cared? It was like in school – anyone could get straight As, so long as you didn't mind doing everything they told you to do whenever they told you to do it. Mary Ann drank more of the wine that Citizen Anemometer had given her.

Constance knelt at the foot of the throne and Sophia rose gracefully, removing her ceremonial sword from its sheath. "Do you come before me clear of mind and honest of heart, prepared to speak the oaths of the Valiant?"

"Yes," Constance said proudly, from beneath the heavy shadow of her heritage.

"In full knowledge and acceptance of what those oaths entail?"

"I do."

Of course, not everyone was satisfied with a smile from the teacher and your name on the honor roll. *Some people* wanted more out of their lives. *Some people* valued a little thing called free-thinking. *Some people* weren't content to be their parents' smiling puppets. Mary Ann's goblet was empty.

"Do you swear to protect the Thousand People, and to uphold the laws of the Tower, even if it costs you your life?"

"I do so swear," said Constance.

"Do you swear to show mercy before the humbled, and courage before the strong?"

"I do so swear," Constance added.

'Do you promise to take the trash out, and never borrow the car without asking, and always come home before curfew?' And the worst part was Constance had to act like it was some kind of sacrifice, piling on obligations so she could feel superior. Mary Ann's head was spinning, and her stomach felt riotous.

"Constance Harrow," said the Queen, "in the name of the Tower, and the Thousand People, and the March, I dub thee–"

Sophia's sword was raised to deliver the *colée* when Mary Ann made a mad dash for the exit, better than puking onto Citizen Anemometer's clockwork but an indiscretion nonetheless and one she was sure that she would pay for later. Not that this was then her primary concern, stumbling through the hallway on legs which had gone idiot, shoving her way towards the privies even as her dinner made a bold play for escape. She managed to hold it down until she was over a basin, then spewed sick-sweet and scalding, curdled eggnog and roast chicken and wine. She finished. Then she started up again. Then she groaned and lay down on the floor, watching the room spin around her. She tasted wretched. It was just like last summer when she had played beer pong with Kristine Kopranos, except this time there was no one around to hold her hair.

Her mother was waiting when she finally came out of the stall, blue robes perfect, blue eyes hard. She wore a furious frown. The scent of bile hung thick between them.

"Mom–" Mary Ann began.

"Well talk about this tomorrow."

"But Mom–"

"Clean yourself up," Sophia snapped, "then come back to the throne room." She shook her head bitterly. "You're a Harrow. Learn to act like it."

*2023*

# TWENTY-FIVE

John stood outside the house, trying to figure out what had changed. The front siding was newly stained, and the porch somehow different, though it took him a while to see they'd added railings to the steps. Apart from that he might still have been a child, the morning light falling on the green grass, the front door an inviting red, the turret-like twist of the attic.

"Can I help you?" asked the boy working in the garden next door.

"Unlikely, but I'm open to suggestions."

"This is the Harrow's place."

"Yeah? You sure?"

"Why are you staring at it?"

"I'm in the market for a four-bedroom with a ratty upstairs bathroom and a basement that floods when it rains." John cracked a broken smile. "A little late in the year to be working on your tulips, don't you think?"

For most people a long stare from John was enough to send them scurrying – the way his eye flared in its junked socket, the ruined cradle of his smile – but the boy did not budge. "I've got a green thumb," he said. "Who are you exactly?"

"Who are you?"

"I'm Hank Washington. I'm the neighbor."

"I pieced that last bit together, thanks."

The front door opened, and a child hurried out of it, wearing a winter coat and an orioles cap pulled tight over his head. His sister came after, sucking her thumb, her hair pulled up in a ponytail.

"Hi Hank!" said Julian, coming down the driveway.

"How you doing, kid?"

"I'm doing OK," said Julian, stopping to stare at John. The last time they had seen one another Julian had been young enough to mewl but not much else.

Evie knew right off, however, from old pictures and because they shared the same blue eyes. "I know you."

"You do," John agreed.

"John!" yelled Sophia, from where she had appeared on the patio. "John! You're back!"

John gave Hank a superior sort of smile and then went to hug his mother.

"You look great, Mom," he said, holding his arms around her shrunken body and parchment thin skin.

"I feel fabulous," said Sophia.

They were the only ones left in the family who could tell a good lie, and gained a certain joy from the bold if pointless bluff against reality.

"You're my uncle!" said Julian, in astonishment. "You're Uncle John!"

"The one and only," said John, turning down to face his nephew. "You must be Evie."

"I'm Evie!" said Evie.

John sucked at his tooth. "That doesn't sound right."

"She is, though," said Constance, coming out to stand beside her mother.

"You sure?"

"Positive."

"Well, if your mom says, I guess it's probably so."

"How you been, John?" Constance asked.

"I been all right," said John.

With everyone watching Constance and John managed an embrace, though it didn't last long. Hank Washington at least was spared the embarrassment, waving a goodbye that no one noticed and retreating to his garden.

"No luggage?" Constance asked.

"I was in such a hurry, I must have plum forgot."

"Two days after I called."

"Hush, the both of you," said Sophia. "We're happy. This is a happy moment."

"If you didn't bring a bag," Evie asked, "then where are our presents?"

"I like this one," said John.

"Uncle John," said Julian, "do you want to go to the park with us? We're going to throw the ball around."

"I'm going to go on the slide," Evie disputed.

"Evie is going to go on the slide," Julian allowed. "Mom and I are going to throw the ball around."

"That sounds great," said John. "Maybe your mom could loan me one of her old gloves?"

Constance pursed her lips. "Let's see what we can find inside."

Leaving the children with their grandmother, Constance walked John into the mud room of his childhood home. They had repainted the walls and moved some furniture but there was still an indefinable sense of sameness, the smell of the wood or the faint accretion of all the bodies that had passed through in all the years – Harrow bodies, his ancestors and kin.

"You moved the coat rack," John observed.

"About three years ago."

"I hated that coat rack."

"I'm pleased to have brought you joy," said Constance, rooting around in the side closet, past heavy coats, woolen mittens, lacrosse sticks, fungo bats, and various aerodynamic throwing implements.

"How's it been, over here?"

"All right," said Constance, face obscured by shadow. "It could be nothing. Or, not nothing, but nothing bad. We're supposed to get some test results back soon. Of course, you know Mom, the world's worst patient, won't even take a day off to watch sitcoms or whatever. I mentioned canceling the party and she just about tore my head off."

"And over there?"

Constance found a battered mitt amid the various sporting equipment and handed it to John. "It's bad."

"Bad like what?"

"Bad like not good. It's back."

"It never left."

"You think I don't know that better than you, John? I've been here watching it."

"You're burning through your stock of sanctimony pretty quick."

"Don't worry, I got plenty in storage."

John stretched his borrowed baseball glove awkwardly over his hand. John had never gone in for sports, nor for that matter for any form of organized activity which required him to show up at a specific place at a specific time to accomplish some predetermined task. It was a predilection which he sometimes supposed had limited his professional opportunities.

"The borders have fallen," said Constance. "The crabs, the shrubs, most of the west...all lost."

"And how have our loyal subjects taken the reversal?"

"The masks are besieged; we're going to try to bring them into the tower. The bots and the bugs have decided now's the time to go rogue. There's some new mayor among the toys, sent a jack-in-the-box to the high council as a suicide bomber."

"The merriling?"

"That's what I said."

"So, the teddy bears went rabid," John said, smiling.

"This is funny to you? The future of our family is funny to you?"

"Everything is a little funny to me, Constance. That's why

I'm still alive. Anything else been happening? Anything...
strange?"

"Like what?" Constance asked, growing concerned, but
before she could get an answer Evie interrupted, coming inside
for a juice box.

"What are you talking about?" she asked.

"Boring stuff," said John.

"Adult stuff," said Constance.

"Taxes," John agreed, "investments. That sort of thing."

# TWENTY-SIX

Mary Ann drove east along route 40, all through the night and most of the morning, stopping only for coffee and to void herself of coffee. She had lived out west for years but never grown used to its endless inland wastes, its mounds of dust and rock that went up forever and on forever, which made the east coast seem like a frame from a stereoscope. A hundred miles out of Albuquerque Mary Ann's adrenaline started to give out. She rubbed her eyes and turned up the gospel music which was the only thing she could get on the radio and followed a painted sign off the highway reading "Food .6 miles".

It lived up to the billing, a glass square over faded pavement, tufts of wild grass breaking through. The booths were leather and the checkerboard floor was cracked. A few twists of tinsel and a cardboard Santa reminded patrons that Christmas came even to the desert. At the counter a man in a trucker hat wolfed down a plate of ham and eggs while a local drank tepid coffee beside him. The single server had been working there for a very long time. Mary Ann took a seat in the back.

"How you doing?" asked the waitress.

"Fine," said Mary Ann.

"Coffee?"

"Yeah."

In Los Angeles the diners were either hipster innovations or long-running establishments given over to kitsch, and in any case they all offered avocado and oak milk and egg-substitute. Below the single sheet of paper promising biscuits

165

and country-fried steak Mary Ann could see generations of graffiti scarred into the table, records of forgotten loves and half-remembered grudges, an intricate maze etched into the laminate with the edge of a knife. The men at the counter were arguing.

"Everything's going to hell," said the trucker.

"Maybe," said the local.

"Whole world on the move, it seems like. I came out from Amarillo, didn't hear one word of English the whole time."

"Maybe."

"Where they even come from, you figure?"

"Who knows? It's a strange world."

The waitress returned with Mary Ann's coffee. "Sugar?"

"Black is fine."

"You know what you want?"

"Eggs," said Mary Ann, because she couldn't think of anything else.

"What do you want with them? We got bacon, ham, sausage..."

"Toast is fine."

"Wheat, white, or a biscuit?"

"Wheat," Mary Ann said finally.

The waitress retreated to the kitchen.

"Where we supposed to put them all?" asked the trucker.

"Dunno," said the local. He was an old man, withered by sun and wind and carving a life out of the unforgiving dust.

"I'm as tolerant at the next fella," said the trucker, "but a thing gets set in a place for a reason, you know? Cause it's supposed to be there. You don't see me driving down to Sonora and trying to set up in someone's house."

"No, I don't see you doing that."

The window was grime streaked and outside the sun blanched against the asphalt and the blank sand. The tinny sound of a country song wafted out from the kitchen, along with the smell of frying meat. The incised maze stretched to the corner of the table, farther than Mary Ann had realized at first glance.

"Not that she cares about it," said the trucker, "hidden away in her tower with all her finery."

"Dunno about that," said the local.

"She's supposed to take care of things, ain't she? Supposed to keep us safe? But then, I guess the little fella never did matter much to those sorts."

"Should be careful how you talk. They've got ears everywhere, you know."

"Who cares? Whole thing's falling apart, what's she going to do to any of us now? Way I figure it, them bugs got the right idea. Build your walls high and damn whomever lies outside of them, that's their problem. Got to look after your own, when things get bad. No time to be playing martyr."

It wasn't a maze at all, it was a labyrinth, and any way you went you found yourself in the same place. Mary Ann looked up to see the man in the trucker hat was too big to sit on his stool, too big for his hat, too big for his big rig, even, adipose slouching out from his t-shirt and off his neck, Brobdingnagian flesh rolling nearly to the floor.

"What are you looking at?" he asked, noticing Mary Ann's attention.

The local turned to stare, a third eye blinking dully in his forehead. "Can we help you with something, Ma'am?"

Mary Ann threw a twenty on the table and sprinted back to her car.

# TWENTY-SEVEN

The Valiant were on the move, the hooves of their yearling thundering along packed earth, bands of exiles pulling themselves to the side of the road to offer passage. Dame Delta was a dark cloud against the clear sky, grown huge with the passing of the years. Far below Sir Intrepid came first in the vanguard, his painted veneer steadfast even as he rode to the aid of his desperate and besieged people. Sir Szyylstyx was next, the first nonesuch to be named Valiant in a generation, followed by Lady Scarlet of the molluschites, the Knight of the Veiled Countenance, the young Sir Shale, his skin harder than armor, Dame Whitecap with her trident and tangled tresses, a hundred others, the picked soldiers of the Tower, fearless warriors dedicated to the Harrow and the Gyved Throne.

"Not enough," said Constance quietly, "not nearly enough."

Sir Floppy had grown old in the Tower's service, his teeth longer than his ears, but he kept steady pace beside Constance, bounding forward on all fours. "It will have to be."

"Are we doing the right thing? Leaving the Tower at a time like this?"

"The prosopon are our allies," said Sir Floppy, "and need our help. Besides, your mother can handle herself."

Constance hoped this was still true. In the road ahead an enormous wagon sat stuck in the mud, a team of badger trying desperately to free it, their mouse driver screaming warning at the encroaching knights. It was an impassable impediment which Sir Intrepid diverted around without slowing, a feat matched by the following Valiant, Sir Cirrostratus the quetzal cruising over the top of the carriage with a beat of his feathered wings, Dame Saguaro of the xerophile veering neatly around on her gigantic, custom-made velocipede. A few terrifying seconds and the Valiant were past, their pennants fluttering bright in the afternoon breeze, the mouse left to gape open-mouthed in astonishment.

"Any word from the Toybox?" Sir Floppy asked.

"They took potshots at our emissary, which is word enough. We've still no idea who this Smiling Man is, or what he wants. Apart from blood, I suppose."

Sir Floppy grunted bitterly. "That's enough for some. What about the Hive?"

"Nothing since the council meeting, but the refugees tell strange stories, about flesh magics and drones sent out slaving. It will be a terrible thing if the Hive has turned traitor."

The path to the Proscenium split along the borders of the Clockwork Republic, a demarcation which in happier days had been largely nominal, the anima trading freely with the prosopon and the merriling and anyone else, offering their mechanical marvels for ore and scrap metal and coal and oil. From high above Dame Delta gave a steam-whistle of warning, and as they came around the next bend Constance could see an iron mob blocking their path.

"Right now, I'd think the Hive the least of our concerns," Sir Floppy observed, wiggling his white nose in worry.

The Valiant pulled into neat ranks, a perfect display of dressage, or aerobatics, or cycling, depending. Sir Intrepid stretched his hand along his heavy mace, Sir Szyylstyx looped fleshy tentacles around several of the half spears that hung across his scaly torso, and Dame Saguaro set the kick stand down on her bike, flexing the thousand spines protruding from her thick, green skin.

The anima bristled in reflection. They were forged for war, clanking engines and mechanical pincers, glaive blades for fingers, cannon grafted onto their broad backs and projecting from their cast-iron torsos. Constance rode slowly out to meet them, conscious, as ever, of her place as the Champion and her position as second Harrow.

Among the ranks of living weaponry Citizen Anemometer was an incongruity, developed not for combat but for assessment, discourse, and prevarication. Over the long years he had grown larger and more complex, all sorts of measuring and computational devices incorporated into his body. His voice was the same as ever, an unctuous, portentous thing, though in his defense it did come, quite literally, out of a bag of wind, the pump in his torso expanding and contracting as he spoke. "Allow me, on behalf of the citizens of the Clockwork Republic, to offer you the sincerest and most affectionate of greetings on this lustrous gloam, along with my personal wishes that your journey has been both felicitous and swift."

"A few moments ago, I could at least have said it was the last."

"I offer unalloyed apology if we have in any way impeded your progress. Had the citizens of the Clockwork Republic possessed foreknowledge of your intentions, rest assured we would have arranged some more appropriate reception."

"You seemed to have enough time to call out your tanks," Constance observed.

"Troubled times require constant vigilance, and the Republic has seen fit to garrison forces along its frontiers."

"If I didn't know better, I might think you were here to intimidate us."

"Perish the very suggestion! Our troop are only here to ensure the safe flow of commerce, and the stability of our borders."

"You mean prey on passersby and watch while my country is overrun?" interrupted Sir Intrepid.

"What business is it of ours, what happens to the masks?" asked one of the anima, a hulking brute with a mortar-like maw and arms that ended in ax blades. "Shifty things, anyway, swapping souls like hats."

"Now, now, Captain," Anemometer objected, "such aspersions get us nowhere. Though still I must, according to patriotic compulsion and no personal animus, query as to your purpose this afternoon, and the need to progress with so large a force?"

"My purpose is the safety of the March," said Constance, "and the wellbeing of its people, the same as always and ever. The Proscenium is besieged by the End, their walls all but fallen. We march to their aid."

A gear whirred inside Citizen Anemometer's skull, and his mouthpiece flipped to a sympathetic frown emblazoned on a plate of bronze. "Yes, we have heard similar speculation. Terrible, how swiftly rumor spreads."

"This is no rumor. The End has come."

"There are certainly those who think so."

"Why do you suppose half the March has fled their homes?"

"Fear itself has wrought more ruin than wildfire."

"Though not near so much as cowardice," said Constance.

Anemometer pulled at a carriage return, as if clearing his throat. "Of course, all are entitled to their own opinions – a lively debate allows for an active citizenry! – but the Clockwork Republic cannot afford to risk its stability for the sake of a few wild stories."

A shadow hung over them, growing larger until Dame Delta landed with a heavy thud in the road beside Constance. Like Anemometer, the years had seen Dame Delta refashion herself, and now the clothwork raptor Constance had known in her youth was caged in thick metal and sharpened pinions. Her beak was the size of a saber, and she stared at her kinfolk with undisguised fury. "Scrimshankers and gudgeons!" she cursed. "To see us fall so low. To think of what you fools have made of us."

"Best shutter that squawkbox," said one of the anima soldiers.

"May your gears rust," Dame Delta said, "and your rivets loosen."

"Keep on like that, you'll get your wings clipped."

Gears clicked and Dame Delta expanded, rows of iron spines bristling from off her body. "Your sire was shaped from scrap metal, and your dam was a rapeseed drunkard."

The anima snorted and sneered and his fellows joined in, fuses flaring to life, lances extending, rotating blades whirling. Sir Cirrostratus drew his obsidian warclub and Dame Scarlet notched an arrow and from beneath his heavy cloak the Knight of the Veiled Countenance pulled a hatchet and a long dagger. They were on the cusp of combat until Constance undid the first lock from her sheath, and then everyone went still.

"Each second wasted here is further tragedy for the prosopon," she said. "The anima are yet the allies of the Harrow, and I would cut my wrist before I broke a bond of loyalty." She let her ring of keys fall loose at her side once more. "You're here already. Ride out with us, see for your own eyes what fate befalls the Proscenium."

"Alas," said Anemometer, "the use of military force outside of our particular partitions would require the assignation of the Council of Seventeen, duly ratified by the quinquevirate and the appropriate hierarchies. To order reconnaissance on my own recognizance would be a flagrant breach of established policy. Lamentable though we find our neighbor's troubles, the Republic is sufficiently provided with its own not to go searching for more."

"There will be trouble soon enough, whether you meet it boldly or hide your heads."

Anemometer's gears spun once more, rotating his face inclement. "Ought we take that as a threat?"

"Is it a threat to observe that fire is hot, and known to spread?" Constance wheeled her mount, turning toward the left fork and the Proscenium which lay ahead. "The End is coming, and you cannot stop it from behind your walls of steel, no matter how many committees you create to study the matter. Your only hope lies with the Harrow," she said, spurring her yearling and shouting as she sped away, "as it ever was!"

# TWENTY-EIGHT

There is a silver lining to every cloud, and no gale so foul that it doesn't blow fair for someone. The Home Far from Home had been booming since the start of the troubles, the roads packed with refugees willing to sell all they owned for a night beside a warm fire and a bit of watery garbure. Bucktooth's back room was stuffed with the treasures and heirlooms of the Thousand People, bits of machinery from exiled anima, *objets d'art* of desperate prosopon, baskets of crops from fleeing arcimboldi. If Bucktooth had been a more thoughtful creature, he might have wondered what this endless procession of exiles portended, and how long his good fortune might run. But Bucktooth was not a thoughtful creature, and that evening at least his eponymous incisors stretched in broad greeting, the only one in the roadhouse managing a smile, at least until the man in black arrived.

Though his face was so ruined you could barely recognize it, an upward curl to the half of his mouth which still functioned properly, a little gleam in his good eye. He stood at the threshold for a moment, gazing at the crowded inn, his black cloak still caught in the night wind.

"Don't dally by the door!" said Bucktooth, cheerily. "The rooms are full, but you're welcome to find yourself a spot on the floor – so long as you have something to trade, that is."

The man in black approached, slipping past a family of hydronese and a prosopon with a scuffed mask. Up close he was taller and his face yet more awful, but Bucktooth, a long veteran of the hospitality trade, did not blanch.

174

The man in black placed a coin on the counter. "The Harrow herself," he said, "or her representation."

"Been a long time since we've seen any gold," admitted Bucktooth.

"I imagine you'll still take it."

"Oh sure, sure," said Bucktooth, though he bit the coin first, noted the satisfying toughness of the metal. "Have a seat wherever you'd like."

"I'll take a room."

"Like I said, all the rooms are full, but you're welcome–"

"You're welcome to throw whoever is in the best of them onto the floor. Might have to give them some of what I gave you, but I'm sure you can figure it out."

"All right," said the innkeeper, after a moment.

"You got any wine?"

"A keg from the harvest before the harvest before last."

"Send over a jug of that as well," said the man in black.

"Wine's an expensive item these days."

"I'm sure you've watered it down sufficiently to meet your costs. Of course, if that's not satisfactory, you can give me back my gold, and I can find somewhere to sleep along the road."

Now the man in black was the only one smiling. But Bucktooth chose not to argue, and after a moment the man in black worked his way back through the crowd once more, stepping over the prone body of a snoring nonesuch and around the prosopon. He found a spot in the corner of the room, an orphaned aurochi calf wiggling aside to allow him space. He put his back against the wall and spent a moment watching the exhausted, anxious, frightened crowd.

"It's good to be home," John said, though no one was listening.

*2006*

# TWENTY-NINE

Sometimes, when he was watching television or reading a book or helping his mother cook dinner, long hours would pass without John remembering he was hideous; but in public and in school especially that was impossible, each passing student and widened glance a constant reminder. It began promptly each morning at seven-thirty with the bus driver, a very nice woman who always asked about John's health and had with that kindness further ensured the general enmity of the rest of John's cohort. First period the kids were mostly too tired to bother him, but things picked up by physics, during which Chuck Perl would kick at John's chair when he wasn't looking, and Scott McDonald would sometimes pass cruel if inaccurate doodles of his warped face. At lunch he might have shared a table with Bobby Ricketts and Peter Backof and Mike Rubin and the other boys with whom no one else would sit – sallow, bespectacled youths whose unpopularity seemed, according to the middle-school mindset, potentially contagious – but he always ate alone. John suspected his scar had only made manifest what was already an essential quality within him, a feeling of isolation which he had carried out the womb.

English class came next, during which he was paired with Gwen Litt on a group assignment. It was the teacher's decision; left to their own devices John was inevitably the last man out, sitting on the sidelines in gym class, forced to make collages in a corner by himself. Gwen was the sort of dark-haired, bespectacled girl who took school with unbecoming seriousness, and following her lead John was forced into some simulacrum of interest.

"What are Grendel's motivations?" asked Gwen, reading from a question on their worksheet.

"He's the villain," said John.

"That's not a motivation."

"He's villainous?" John suggested.

Gwen Litt was too serious to smile.

"He's trying to kill Beowulf," said John, "and the book is called *Beowulf*. Therefore, he's the villain."

"All Beowulf does is get drunk and start fights," said Gwen Litt. Gwen was not pretty but one day she would be, when she had taken off her braces and grown into her big brown eyes. This was not as good as being pretty today, but it was better than anything John had to look forward to and he could not help but feel a little jealous.

"It doesn't matter," said John. "We're humans. He's still our guy."

"That's it? He's one of us, so we like him more?"

"Pretty much. Grendel is big and mean and Beowulf is bigger and meaner. Grendel dies and Beowulf wins and so we read stories about Beowulf. If Grendel had won, we'd be green and scaly and we'd read stories about him." John forgot himself and smiled. "But he didn't, so we don't."

Behind her glasses Gwen Litt's eyes swelled wide with pity.

Was it really worse, the pity?

Yes. Worse.

# THIRTY

They came to the Kingdom of the Thorned Rose by way of
the Faunae Palatinate and the Harvestlands, been feted and
celebrated in both, greeted by happy mobs of their subjects
and attended by perfumed courtiers. After a final celebration
among the arcimboldi, where a prodigious pumpkin had been
awarded seasonal honors and they had feasted on great vats
of boiled peanut and fried okra, Constance and Mary Ann
had journeyed north, along with Sir Floppy and a handful
of Valiant as escort. Three days seemed to have taken them a
million miles. The deep north was a barren place, and sparsely
populated. There was one road which led into the Kingdom of
the Thorned Rose, a rutty track rarely used by outsiders, for
the verdurite sold little and bought less, and were in any case
not renowned as the most hospitable of hosts – a reputation
they seemed to justify, the Harrow finally arriving to find no
onearound to greet them.

"Where the hell are they?" asked Mary Ann.

"Maybe they got lost," said Constance.

"In their own woods?"

"That was a joke, Mary Ann. I don't know where they are."

"They'll be here," said Sir Floppy. "Whatever else, the
verdurite keep their word."

The trees in the Kingdom of the Thorned Rose were less like
trees and more like skyscrapers. Staring carefully, Mary Ann
could just make out the boughs very high above, a verdant
canopy which captured the sun and sustained a perpetual

twilight. The forest floor was strangely barren, the towering topiary choking off their descendants' hope of growth. Still the forest seemed alive, with ground birds and butterflies and scurrying squirrels and the constant buzz of cicada.

"Are you the Harrow?" a voice asked.

Mary Ann looked up to see a boy sitting in a tree, looked again and saw that he was not quite that. His skin was the color of rosewood, and his hair curled thick and stalk-like down his back. His eyes were a deep, chestnut brown. He wore a snakeskin vest and stained leather pants.

"Obviously," said Mary Ann.

Constance cleared her throat. "I am Constance of the Harrow, daughter of Sophia and Michael, here to serve as ambassador to the verdurite."

"We had anticipated a reception," added Sir Floppy.

"You've found it," said the boy. He slipped neatly down from the tree, dropping the long distance to the ground and landing in a comfortable crouch. "I'm Thistle. You may come with me."

Without waiting to see if they would take him up on his offer he headed deeper into the woods, and Mary Ann and Constance and their escort of Valiant lead their yearling along after. The verdurite were nomadic, following game through their endless forests, bound only to their Heartwood groves, hidden copses of sacred trees which preserved the life and lineage of their clan. They had no settlements and erected no structures, content with the arboreal cover beneath which they lived and died. Heading deeper into the forest Mary Ann passed hyperion redwood and giant sequoia and trees which looked like baobab but were far, far too tall, along with verdurite that blended in so neatly with the surrounding foliage that Mary Ann had to look hard to tell them apart. The children of the Kingdom of the Thorned Rose showed no reaction to the Harrow's arrival, neither celebratory nor antagonistic, apparently indifferent to the presence of their nominal overlords.

The wind changed, and the pleasant, heavy scent of the forest was cut through with an iron tang. Mary Ann's yearling grew obstreperous, pawed and whinnied.

"What's wrong with your animals?" asked Thistle.

"They're carnivores," Constance explained, "they grow fierce at the smell of blood."

Thistle nodded in agreement. This he could understand. The other Valiant stayed behind to tend to the mounts, while Sir Floppy, Constance and Mary Ann headed through one final wall of trees and into a small clearing in the woods, where the source of their mount's excitement became quickly evident. The head and neck of an enormous serpent stared back at them, eyes the size of headlights, a hundred-pronged rack of antlers growing crownlike from its head. The verdurite had sawed through its enormous throat but the beast remained uncertain of its death, tongue lolling, jaws gnashing.

"Watch out for the teeth," said Thistle.

"Are teeth sharp?" Mary Ann asked, "I hadn't heard."

"It's poisonous," Thistle explained, "one touch is enough to keep you paralyzed for a week. We dip our arrows in it, and sometimes our spears."

"Good to know," said Constance, narrowing her eyes.

They followed the snake's trunk further into the clearing, the body held tight with leather lassos and pierced with arrows of barbed bone, coming finally to where the Aetheling Calyx and several of his followers butchered the beast. It had been five years since Mary Ann had seen him – five years as it was counted by the Harrow, though who would say what that mean in the March – but he looked much as he had, an imposing hardwood presence clad in fur and animal skin. He knelt beside the snake, decorticating its scales with a knife of long bone, and did not look up at their arrival.

"You would be the young Harrow," he said.

"Constance of the Tower," Constance said, "and Mary Ann of the same."

"Fortunate that we happened upon the crowned serpent while we were close to the meeting place."

"And if you hadn't?" asked Sir Floppy.

As answer the Aetheling reached into the beast's endless belly, grunted and pulled out a long string of entrails, blood spraying along with it, a bright crimson mist which leaked into the dirt. When he rose, his hands were red from the tips of their fingers to the hard, dark muscles of his forearms. "Dinner is at sunset," he said, "you may rest until then. My son will show you the way."

Thistle stood beside his father, arms crossed warily, as if thinking to disobey. Or perhaps this was only Mary Ann's impression, because an instant later and without any further objection he led Mary Ann and Constance toward a small clearing which been set out for their use.

"Arrogant little twerp," Mary Ann said.

"The verdurite have their own ways," said Sir Floppy, "it's not for us to judge them."

"Being rude is a custom?"

"They're not rude," said Sir Floppy, "they're just hard."

"We're the Harrow!" Mary Ann insisted. "The first to visit the Kingdom of the Thorned Rose in two generations. And in anticipation they're prepared what – snake barbecue and stream water?"

"You should try some stream water," said Constance, "it's not so sweet as you're used to, but it might help you keep down the snake."

"You'll get the same as the Aetheling or any of the rest of them," said Sir Floppy. "Don't let the title fool you – that's just a convention they use for outsiders. All verdurite are equal beneath the boughs. They have no respect for office, only action."

"I thought you didn't like them?"

"I don't like them," admitted Sir Floppy. "I hate them. I've hated them since the Conciliatory War, when my fur was pure white, and I had both my eyes."

"What happened?"

"They'd been taking captives from the petrousian and the arcimboldi, and we were sent to stop them."

"And?"

Sir Floppy had paused in his bathing, his scarred face lost in uncharacteristic nostalgia. "It was a stalemate. They wouldn't meet us on open ground, and we couldn't get into the forest, an archer in every tree and our yearling good as useless. They only swore fealty when the End came, poisoning their forests and threatening their Heartwood. That was a day. Your grandmother with shining staff, their thanes and houscarls sprinting out from the great trees..." He finished washing his long ears in the creek, got up and shook his fur dry. "I don't like the verdurite, but I respect them. They are dangerous allies – they'd be worse foes."

Dinner that night was, as predicted, a length of the great snake spitted over a bonfire made from fallen wood and dead brush, for the verdurite would not cut a tree even for kindling. Amid the gathering darkness their hosts sat quietly, repairing their bone tools, drinking from bladders of water, talking in low voices. An old man played a slow, sad tune on an instrument made from spine and gut-string, but apart from that and the crackling fire the forest was quiet. Even the children played their games in near silence, chasing each other from tree to tree, mute save for the patter of their feet against the branches.

When the serpent had finished cooking the Aetheling offered the first portion to the ancestors, standing now in their Heartwood, then began to serve out the rest. The Harrow received no priority of place, but then neither did the Aetheling himself, eating after the best part of the beast had already been disposed, coming unexpectedly to sit beside Constance.

He stared at her for a while, chewing at a hunk of gristle. "You have brown eyes."

"Yes," Constance agreed.

"Your grandmother's were blue."

"I remember."

"She lived among us for a time."

"I knew that also."

"She was a very wise woman, your grandmother. She saw more than she said."

"Let's hope I got that from her, at least."

"Yes," said the Aetheling Calyx, "let us hope."

Mary Ann knew, of course, that the verdurite considered everything which grew from the ground sacred and were prohibited from its use or consumption. Their clothes were fur or skin, their weapons bone and horn, their fare exclusively meat. But still to watch them as they supped on muscle and sinew and fatty chunks of marrow was enough to make her nauseous.

"You're not eating?" asked Thistle.

"I'm a vegetarian."

"Like the apostates?"

"The what?"

"The arcimboldi, you call them."

"Why do you call them apostates?"

"Because they have abandoned themselves," said Thistle, "chosen plow and hearth over the wind and rain. Because they have forgotten the scent of wildflowers. Because they are damned."

Mary Ann laughed.

"Why is that funny?"

"It's always funny to hear someone repeat something they've heard," said Mary Ann. "They have this weird sort of intonation, like they're singing a song."

It was hard to tell what Thistle was thinking, his face set serious and somber. "Your sister eats meat."

"My sister and I are different people," Mary Ann announced boldly, shaking her scarlet hair as if in reminder.

"And the rest of the Harrow?"

"I guess I'm different from them too."

After his first few sentences, the Aetheling had spent the dinner in silence, and Constance and Sir Floppy had not seen fit to interrupt, chewing over their thick, savory, not entirely unpleasant hunks of snake.

The Aetheling cracked the last bone between his hands, scooped out and swallowed the marrow, then threw it into the darkness. "Tomorrow, we roam west, towards the high woods. You are to accompany us?"

"That was my mother's command. We were sent here to learn more of your people," said Constance, "to understand their ways."

"So that you may rule us better when your day comes?"

"The verdurite owe fealty to the Harrow," said Sir Floppy, "and the line of Harrow remains unbroken."

The Aetheling turned his grim stare on the Valiant's leporine leader. "You were one of those they posted on the borders, in those days when the verdurite remained free?"

"I was. And you were on the other side of those borders?"

"I was."

Then it might have been one of your arrows took my eye?" Sir Floppy suggested with a low smile.

The Aetheling shook his head. "I wouldn't have missed."

Sir Floppy's long teeth glinted in the firelight. "I was still a kit when we rode against you, and my word held little weight – but if I'd had my way, we'd have burned you out, tree by tree, root by root, until there was nowhere left for you to run. Then we'd have rode you down like wheat grass."

The Aetheling considered the mass slaughter of his people without reaction. "Do you have anything to say to that, young Harrow?"

Constance spat a piece of gristle onto the ground in front of her. "I'm trying to take after my grandmother," she said.

Sir Floppy laughed. The Aetheling remained as inscrutable as ever.

Dinner ended abruptly and without ceremony, the verdurite finishing their meals and fading into the forest, to find rest cradled in some high curved bough. Thistle led Mary Ann and her companions through the caliginous woods, the new moon lost behind the high foliage.

"You honor us with your escort," said Constance politely.

"My father wasn't sure that you would know your way," Thistle explained. "Outsiders find our paths treacherous."

"Just your paths?" Mary Ann asked.

Thistle considered this as he took a neat leap over the small stream beside their camp. "My father says they tell stories of us, in the world beyond the forests."

"Are they true?" Mary Ann asked.

"Probably some of them," Thistle admitted. "Sleep well, Mary Ann Harrow. Tomorrow will be as long a day as any." Then, offering a perfunctory nod, he disappeared back into the looming forest.

Mary Ann could see her sister's smirk even in the dim light. "What?"

"Nothing, nothing."

"Stop smiling."

"I can smile."

"Is there something you want to say to me?"

"Scott Callick is going to be jealous."

"Shut up!"

"What is the rule for cheating on your boyfriend while you're in a different dimension? Is it like hooking up at summer camp?"

"Scott Callick is *not* my boyfriend," hissed Mary Ann. "I don't even like Scott Callick. He's eighty percent body spray."

"And what about Thistle?"

Mary Ann gave a demonstrative shudder. "What about him? He's disgusting. He's a conceited bully, and his breath stinks of meat."

But lying that night in her small tent, and even waking next morning in her bed at home, all Mary Ann could think of were his eyes.

# THIRTY-ONE

"You're too hard on her," Michael said.

"Who?" asked Sophia.

"Both of them, really, but Constance doesn't mind."

They were in the back corner of an Italian restaurant downtown, newly opened a few blocks over from the harbor. It was their weekly date, a tradition that they had maintained over the course of twenty-odd years and three children, while their friends and contemporaries were arguing over alimony and fighting messy custody battles. At forty-eight, Sophia remained a beautiful woman if a bit thin, her neck long and her face all angles. Michael was twenty pounds heavier than when they had first met, but the flesh hung well on him. His beard was still thick, and so were his arms.

"Constance has a sense of responsibility," Sophia said, "and broad shoulders, thank God. She gets that from you."

"Don't try and butter me up," said Michael, smiling. "You know what I'm talking about."

"You're talking about Mary Ann getting drunk after the Christmas party."

"You think she invented that?"

"Only took to it with aplomb."

"She made a bad decision. Kids need to make bad decisions so they can learn to make good ones."

"They only learn to make good ones when they've been punished for the bad."

There were no holiday parties in Michael's past, no

arguments across dinner tables, only the absent silhouette of a father and a mother who had always blamed him for that loss. A late convert to the notion of family, his devotion outshone those raised in the faith. "You think she doesn't feel ashamed? Having to come back to the party with puke on the hem of her dress?"

"She ruined her sister's moment."

"Constance has plenty of opportunities to feel good about herself."

"She's sixteen."

"Exactly."

"Sixteen is old enough to know right from wrong."

"It's also young enough to be forgiven a mistake."

"People have that rule backwards."

"How do you mean?"

"A mistake at forty is a mistake. A mistake at sixteen is the start of a pattern."

Marriage requires maintaining a nautical chart of your partner's subconscious, but Michael continued on, heedless of the shoals. "Mary Ann isn't your brother."

Sophia dabbed a corner of her mouth with her napkin, as if to hide her teeth. "Not yet."

"You think it helps, having her hate you?"

"Teenagers should hate their parents, that's the way of things."

"You hated Joan?"

Sophia softened. "Never," she admitted, "but there was a period when I would have dropped something heavy on my father's head if I had thought I'd get away with it."

The waiter arrived with their dinner, and they buried themselves in their plates.

"How's your salmon?" Michael asked.

"Overcooked."

"You always think that."

"I'm right."

"I know you're right, but you still say it every time."

"It's not my fault that the chef can't cook his fish," said Sophia.

Michael's steak was likewise slightly overdone, but he went at it with happy relish. Her husband's ability to pan joy from the frustrating dross of daily existence was a quality which Sophia adored as much as envied.

He lacked any capacity for subtlety, however, and setting aside his fork Sophia could tell he was nerving himself into something, and was even fairly certain what that would be.

"Did you think about what John's teacher said?" he asked.

"No."

"No, you haven't thought about it, or no, you won't do it?"

"There is no way in hell I'm sending my kid off to be educated in some special needs school."

"That's not what she said."

"It's what she meant."

"This isn't a Dickens novel; they're not going to chain him in a cell."

"My son is not going to school on the short bus. End of story."

"He's miserable where he is," said Michael. "He never says anything, you ask him a question and he just grunts. As soon as he comes home, he locks himself up in his room, if it wasn't for his music, you wouldn't even know he was there. Maybe a change of circumstance would—"

"Would what? Fix his eye? Make his face like it used to be?"

Michael was the only man Sophia had ever met who did not flinch when she snapped her voice. "That was a nasty thing to say."

"It's a cruel world."

"Then why be common?"

"You think I don't want to cry, every time I look at him? Every time I think about how everyone else looks at him? My poor little boy, having to carry that for the rest of his life…"

Sophia took a sip of her wine. "But they'll be looking at him like that forever. There's nothing anyone can do to stop that. He'll either learn to deal with it, or..."

"Or what?" Michael asked. "Finish the end of that sentence."

But Sophia wouldn't, taking another bite of her overcooked fish. "John will be fine," she said finally. "John's tough."

"He's smart. That's not the same thing."

"John will be fine," Sophia said again, an affirmation or a prayer but in any case, the end of the argument. She flagged down a passing server and flashing him a bright smile. "Excuse me," she said, "I'm afraid this fish is a bit too well done for my tastes."

Offering gestures of apology and the deference appropriate to a woman of Sophia's stature, the waiter took the plate and scurried away.

# Thirty-Two

John made it from a sprig of mandrake pulled from the graveyard at midnight and a tuft of hair that he had cut from his head with a pair of silver shears, and that morning while his sisters were in the far north and Sophia was listening to petitions and Michael was off investigating a disturbance among the xerophile he shared his secrets; their favorite breakfast cereal, their most recent nightmare, the name of the girl at school they had a crush on. Then he dressed it in the black doublet that he had been wearing, choosing for himself a hooded huke stolen from the servant's quarters and a backpack filled with dry rations.

"Are you ready?" asked John.

"I suppose so," said John. "I'm not sure how long I'll last, though."

"Not very long," John agreed, "but you don't have to. Just a couple of days."

"And then?"

"I don't know. I guess you'll go back to being what you were before you were me."

"What was I?"

"Nothing."

"Oh," said John.

"Does that sound so bad?" asked John.

John thought a moment. "Not to me."

Nor to John either.

John left John in John's room and headed quickly into the

191

corridor. With his cowl pulled up no one paid him a second glance, and descending through the Tower he thrilled to a pleasant anonymity which he would never enjoy in the real world, where he was distinct by virtue of his deformity. Five years and he knew the Tower as well as he did his own house, that there were seventeen steps leading down from the attic to the second floor, that the Bridge of Summer Sighs was the swiftest route to Lady Basalt's Barbizan. The weather-witches had done their job and it was a warm afternoon, something like late March except not so damp, and the great boughs of the damson trees fruited purple. All along the Western Viaduct the Thousand People promenaded, a family of smiling saprophyte on a rare visit above ground, a prosopon prosperously busking with a violin, a pair of hydronese lovers necking against the balustrade, melting into one another in amorous enthusiasm.

In the courtyard far below a small herd of yearling gamboled about a wide enclosure, too fierce to be stabled or even fettered. The colts were taller than men and their horns were spiraled and blunt as battering rams, newly foaled and already near to full grown. John wondered what it would be like to have all your life condensed into so brief a span. He decided it would not be so different, that the length of the thing did not matter so much as its universal end point. Descending from his chambers John had felt the tiniest rasp of uncertainty but as he reached the end of the viaduct and descended to the square below, he found it had disappeared completely.

The outer bailey was busy despite the hour, travelers come to gaze on the marvels of the Tower, bands of actors hoping to ply their trade before the Harrow's court, caravans carrying goods to all the distant corners of the March. An aurochi newly arrived from his distant province blinked at the array of peoples and pinched his dewlap as if in fear of dreaming. A pair of quetzal shared a bag of roasted nuts a hundred feet above the ground, their wings beating lazily. Troupes of friendly guardsfolk oversaw the amiable anarchy, directing visitors and occasionally intervening in some small dispute.

Near the main gate a clan of molluschite prepared to set off, packing goods onto the chipped white carapace of their elder. She rested in anticipation of the long journey ahead, as her descendants clambered about her massive body, tightening the straps on a sleeping basket, double-checking the cinch on a strongbox.

"Where are you off to?" John asked one of the molluschite youths, unshelled and still somewhat human-looking despite his short tail and blush-colored skin.

"West to the Proscenium, then out towards the Clockwork Republic. Always good haggling to be done with the anima."

"What's it like?"

"Which?"

"Either. Both."

"The Proscenium is all right. You know where you stand with the prosopon, even if it gets confusing when they change their masks. They're always desperate for an audience, though. Got to be careful where you walk, or you'll end up sitting through a dance recital."

"What about the Clockwork Republic?"

"Not for me. The air is filled with soot from all their factories. And if it's not soot, it's talk. No one talks like the anima; they stand on the corners shouting at each other all day."

"About what?"

"Whatever. Politics and such."

"It sounds marvelous," said John.

"You think?"

John gathered up his courage. To flee the Tower and leave a fetch in his place was one thing, but the possibility of rejection worried him as much as it would have any other unpopular adolescent. "Need another hand?"

The molluschite cocked a head which was the color of the eraser at the end of a number two pencil. "What's your name?"

"Will of the Dells," John lied.

"What's a dell, exactly? I've always wondered."

"I think it's like a valley."

"Shouldn't you know?"

"It's a family name, we've been in the Tower for generations."

"Oh," said the molluschite, considering, then set out a four-fingered paw. "Pink."

John smiled awkwardly. "Nice to meet you, Pink."

"Likewise. You'll have to ask our sachem if you can come along, but as far as I'm concerned, you'd be welcome."

The sachem listened to his request, inspecting him with eyes the size of trashcan lids, then swinging her stubby neck in agreement. Any other caravan would have charged him passage or at least given him a thorough interview, but for the molluschite the freedom of the road was an article of faith, and the goodwill of the other peoples their aim and chief protection. Friendly and useful, they wandered the breadth of the March, trading their wares in the peace offered by the long arm of the Harrow.

They started out at sunset, traveling west in the shadow of the Tower which silhouetted itself against the ground ahead for what seemed endless miles. The adults went first, energetic despite the hour, singing a merry traveling song. The youths walked behind or rested atop their plodding elder, who oozed her way along, taking up most of the road and leaving a slick of slime in her wake. John and Pink sat astride her great shell, eating from a bag of sunflower seeds Pink had brought for the journey. The last rays of the sun reflected off the battlements, its rich azure walls bright in the glowing gloom.

"Strange thing, leaving the Tower," said Pink, "something sad about it, but nice at the same time, you know?"

John didn't answer.

"Well," said Pink, cracking another seed, "I guess it'll be there when we get back."

"I'm never coming back," John promised, then turned to face the road ahead.

*2023*

# THIRTY-THREE

"It's me," said Mary Ann.

"I can tell," said Constance into the phone, wincing as soon as the words had left her lips, "I mean, it's good to hear your voice."

"Right. Where are you?"

"In a coffee shop, waiting for Mom's prescriptions to get filled." It was of the tawdry chain sort, busy with shoppers from the neighboring mall and offering gingerbread flavored drinks, but it was also next door to a pharmacy and halfway to Adeline's new apartment, and thus a convenient place to meet. "Where are you?"

"Near Bowling Green."

"Where is that?"

"Kentucky."

"You're driving?

"Yes, I'm driving."

"Why?"

Constance could hear her sister's frustration across two thousand miles. "Because I didn't want to fly."

"Are you all right? Did something happen?"

"Can we not get into this right now? How's Mom?"

"What do you think?"

"I think she's probably pretending everything is fine."

"Got it in one. John's here."

"Since when?"

"Yesterday morning. Showed up out of the blue, didn't even think to call."

"How's he doing?"

"You know John."

"And how are things... over there?"

Three boys came into the coffee shop just then, sallow and pockmarked, wearing white t-shirts which were far too large for them and carrying skateboards. One kept his headphones pulled over his ears as if to drown out his companions, and Constance could hear the music from halfway across the room, brutal and arrhythmic.

"Not good," said Constance, "very bad."

"How bad?"

"Just get home as quick as you can, all right? There aren't enough Harrows to go around."

"Is it the..."

"It's what you think it is," said Constance, "it's just worse."

One of the boys got a cup of water from the counter, then they sat down beside a mother and her child, plugging their phones into the communal chargers and laying their skateboards along the bench. The boy in the headphones stared at Constance. Constance stared back. There was a silence on the other end of the line, long enough that Constance was beginning to think the call was dropped until she heard Mary Ann sigh.

"Will you be home in time for the party?" Constance asked.

"You're not going to do that this year, are you?"

"It's tradition. Mom insisted."

"Jesus."

"She wanted to do it, Mary Ann. Who knows how much longer... I mean, it was her choice."

"It always is."

The boy finished his water and began to pick his nose as if it were a lock, forefinger swiveling, the surrounding customers watching in embarrassed horror. The boy in the headphones was still looking at Constance. Constance was still looking back at him. It was a dull sort of stalemate. "Did you call just to make trouble?"

"No. I called to tell you I'm coming home and...to see if everything else has been normal."

"What do you mean, everything else?"

"Has anything strange been happening? Not in the...here, I mean."

"John asked me the same thing. Strange like what? What are you asking about?" Constance felt a sudden flush of concern puncture the general annoyance she felt towards her sister.

The line crackled. "...seeing things...off my meds... bleeding..."

"I can't understand you," Constance said. "Mary Ann? Mary Ann?"

The signal was lost, but Adeline arrived just then and there was no time to call back. Rising simultaneously according to some mute signal the boys headed to the exit, passing Adeline who took the seat across from Constance.

"Sorry," she said, "my meeting went long."

"It's OK," said Constance, "I appreciate you making the time. The school says they need Evie's records before the start of next year."

"It's no problem," said Adeline, handing over a small folder.

"Do you want a coffee?" Constance asked.

"I've gotta get to work," Adeline said, with what might have been regret. "Everything goes crazy before the holidays. It's like they think the world will end before the start of January."

"Don't worry about it."

"Who was that on the phone?"

"Mary Ann."

"When does her flight get in?"

"She's driving."

"She's driving?" Adeline asked, shocked.

"That's what she said."

"Why the hell would she do that?"

From out the side window, past an old man watching YouTube clips on his battered smartphone, Constance could see the three boys lounging beside the trash bin. Not lounging, standing, still but watchful, like birds on a telephone wire, anticipating carrion.

"I don't know. You can take it up with her," said Constance, "she'll be home for the party."

"If I was going to start with something," said Adeline, "it wouldn't be that." Adeline was the issue of a once-popular novelist and a semi-renowned heart surgeon, a late life romance, without siblings, both parents long dead. She might have understood better if she had come from a family like Constance's own, the perpetual buzzing tension, loyalties towards people that you rarely spoke to and sometimes hated.

"Mary Ann hasn't had it easy," Constance said, "neither has John."

"It's amazing how you still stick up for them. It's genuinely amazing."

"They're not so bad," Constance said lamely.

"John is a self-obsessed junkie, and Mary Ann would rather chew a razor blade then come back to the east coast. Neither of them can be bothered to get to know their nephew and niece."

"Mary Ann sends presents."

"That's your best defense?"

"You've only ever seen my side of it," said Constance.

"Oh, believe me, I'm no stranger to your character flaws," said Adeline, half-jokingly.

"There's more to it than you know," said Constance. "You can't understand. Not really."

Adeline hunched her eyebrows. "Because I'm not part of the club?"

The boys had turned to stare at her, the one who had been staring at her before and the two others, dead eyed and unblinking, mouths open, looking practically identical in the cold light of the afternoon.

Constance snapped her head back to her soon to be ex-wife. "It's not like that."

"It's exactly like that. That's literally exactly what it's like. The wardrobe won't work for me, so my opinion doesn't matter."

Adeline had learned of the March and Constance's second existence while visiting the Harrow's one Christmas, rising from a midnight slumber to find her lover gone and the house empty. It was an impossible manifestation of what she had already come to recognize was an impassable divide between her and the other Harrows, Constance included. Their tangle of shared history was too dense, too many in-jokes and half-faded scars, an ancient and prickly growth onto which she would never be grafted.

"You know that wasn't my choice," said Constance.

"No, it was your mother's choice. It was your choice to stand by while she made it."

"What did you want me to do, Adeline? Leave her to take on everything? John was gone, Mary Ann was never coming back. There was no one but me."

"That's an easy out."

"I don't want to do this again," said Constance, sighing.

"Neither do I," said Adeline. "I guess that's why we're getting a divorce."

"I guess so."

"I'll stop by the party to pick up the kids," Adeline said, rising to leave, "I hope your mother's tests come back OK."

It was fairly gallant, as last words went. Adeline returned to her car. The boys were gone from the parking lot. Constance sat and listened to the corny Christmas music and watched a fat man eat a scone and felt sad and wretched, drinking her cold coffee in a pointless act of penance until it was time to pick up her mother's prescriptions.

# THIRTY-FOUR

"P is for the prosopon," Julian said, "who wear their truth for all to see."

Evie ran her fingers over the stiff paper of the book, along a group of masked figures, each visage its own perfect articulation of some essential passion, the characters smiling, frowning, snarling in fury, gasping in fear. "If they're so honest, why don't they show their faces?"

"Their masks *are* their faces," Julian explained, though he didn't really understand either.

"Everyone wears a mask," John explained, "but at least with the prosopon, you know that the mask is the truth."

They were on the front patio, the children in their usual spot on the porch swing, John leaning against the railing and drinking a cup of black coffee.

"How do you know so much about the prosopon, Uncle John?" asked Julian.

"That was my book, back when I was your age. Or our book. Actually, your mother never really let me touch it, and by the time it was my turn I'd already memorized the thing, so in practice it was mostly *their* book. But the point remains."

Julian was a good-natured child who liked to smile and was slow to anger and had cheerily accepted his long-lost-Uncle's return. Evie, though some three years his junior, was a tougher sell. "What's C for, then?" she asked.

"Cthulhu."

Julian giggled. "That's not right!"

"Are you sure? Double check."

But Julian set aside the book, more interested in his uncle than he was in his homework. "What's New York like?"

"It's like living inside of a gigantic castle, with moats and bridges, where everyone looks different and talks different and eats different things. Also, it smells."

"Yeah?"

"Yeah. Especially in the summer."

Julian thought hard on this. "I don't think I could ever live in a place like that."

"You'd get used to it," John promised with a smile.

"What do you do?" Evie asked.

"I cook."

"Mom cooks," said Evie.

"Yeah," said Julian, "but you never eat it."

"Shut up!" said Evie.

"It's true – you only eat pasta with butter on it and chicken nuggets, but I eat salmon and arugula and last week I even tried some of Mommy A's pesto."

"Your mother's a pretty good cook," interrupted John, "but I'm better."

"Really?"

"Yup. Even better than your grandmother."

"No one's a better cook than Nanny," corrected Julian with the sublime self-certainty of childhood, the boundaries of which are perfect and absolute and extend just beyond the walls of one's house.

Sophia appeared out the front door just then to settle the matter in John's favor. "Your Uncle John is the best cook in the family. He's had special training. He attended a very prestigious cooking academy when he was only nineteen."

"But I didn't graduate."

"So?"

"It doesn't count if you don't graduate."

"No darling, it counts if you learn."

"I might be the best cook," John said, "but your grandmother still knows everything."

Sophia was summoning a clever retort when her phone rang from her pocket. She took it out, saw who was calling, swallowed a frown, then went inside. John watched her retreat even as Julian turned to the next page of the book. "Q is for the quetzal," he began, but did not get to finish, Evie taking her grandmother's exit as the moment to interrupt.

"Did you always want to be a cook?" Evie asked.

"A chef," Julian corrected.

"A chef."

"Not always. When I was your age, I wanted to be in charge."

"Of what?"

John shrugged. "Everything."

"How come?"

"I thought I'd be good at it," John admitted.

"Then what happened?"

"I got a little older."

"What happened to your face?" Evie asked.

Julian turned aghast. "Evie, hush!"

"I was in a car crash," said John.

"Did it hurt?"

"Yup."

"Sorry," said Julian.

"That's OK. It doesn't hurt anymore," John lied.

"How come you never come to see us?" asked Evie.

"Evie, stop!" Julian insisted, "you're being rude!"

"That's all right," said John. He knelt down beside his niece. "I'm not sure, Evie. Life gets weirder when you're an adult. Things pile up on top of one another and suddenly you're thirty. You plan on doing one thing, and then another thing happens instead. Does that make sense?"

"No," said Evie.

"Not really," Julian admitted.

"Do you always have a reason for the things you do?" asked John.

"Of course!" said Julian.

"Do you?" asked John again.

Julian pondered the question with the earnest self-seriousness of a child, looking at a thing for the first time and trying to fit his brain around it. "I think I do, usually, but sometimes after my reasons don't seem very good. Like, at camp last summer, Justin Knipp said that we should sneak into the gardener's shed to see what was there, and then we got caught and had to go talk to the head counselor. And there wasn't even anything in the gardener's shed, just some rakes and stuff. Plus, I don't even like Justin Knipp."

"Exactly," said John.

Sophia watched from the kitchen window as the Washington boy made his way up their steps, dark and handsome and smiling warily.

"Yes," she said into the phone, "I understand."

Sophia liked and pitied Hank Washington, with his mother who never left her house and no siblings and this preoccupation with gardening, which surely must seem as alien and unhip as the Electric Slide to his generation of budding internet influencers. With her shrewd and pitiless glance she could detect nothing perverse in his affection for her grandson and granddaughter, only an abiding loneliness and hope for a remedy. That loneliness can be found as often, and far more sharply, in the company of others and especially of those closest to us, was a truth he had not yet had the opportunity to learn.

"Thank you," Sophia said, "I'll set up the appointment."

"I was thinking I could bring some flowers by before the party tomorrow," Hank Washington was telling John, "for decoration."

"I wouldn't want you to dig up the bulbs," said John, waving at Washington's fallow garden.

"I grow some in the garage."

"Aren't you the budding horticulturist."

"I guess."

"Get it? Budding?"

"I got it," said Hank Washington.

Sophia opened the kitchen window and called the children in for lunch. Julian slipped off the bench and put the book in his backpack.

"Bye, Hank!" he said. "See you tomorrow!"

Evie sucked her thumb and scowled and then followed her brother inside. John let an awkward silence build around him for a while before continuing.

"When I was a kid the Gaddis lived next door," John said. "They were pretty weird. One time the dad tried to get me to go to his garage, said he had some photos he wanted to show me."

"I'm sorry to hear that."

"It's OK, I didn't go. Anyway. Who was it that said that thing about fences and good neighbors?"

"Robert Frost," said Hank Washington.

"A florist and an honors student! Your mother must be pink with pride."

"I'll bring the arrangements by Tuesday morning."

"You go ahead and do that," said John, waving jauntily as Hank Washington went back to his garage. Inside the children were sitting at the kitchen counter and Sophia was cutting the crusts off four slices of white bread.

"What did he want?" Sophia asked.

"Just being friendly," said John. "Who was that on the phone?"

"Solicitors," said Sophia, setting aside her knife. "You want me to make you a sandwich?"

# THIRTY-FIVE

The lights were off in Hank Washington's house. The lights were often off in Hank Washington's house, a silent, dusty place too large for its two occupants, like an old manor gone to rot, abandoned wings and rooms which never saw use. He had no siblings and no father and barely even a mother, a quiet woman who seemed to disappear even as you stared at her, like the fade out of a film. Had he another existence to compare it to, Hank Washington might have thought himself lonely; though of course, he did not.

Hank's bedroom was a stark exception to the uniform gray of the rest of the house, green with foliage, plants sprouting from pots on the floor, rising in planters on the walls and dangling thick from each window. A hydroponic growhouse cast its beneficent glow on chard and artichoke and a handsome sprout of sativa. He misted some hanging tillandsia, then he went to the window and stared at the Harrow's front porch, now empty.

In one corner of the room, nearly overgrown by a dangle of burro's tail and strings of pearl, was Hank Washington's desk. On a bulletin board hanging above it the Harrow family had been recreated, photographs of Julian and Evie climbing aboard the bus and sitting on their porch, Constance and Sophia talking, even one of Adeline dropping the children off from school. In the center of the collage was a loose sketch of a woman that he had never met, with long hair and bright eyes and a sad smile.

# Thirty-Six

Jeffrey sat on his couch in his apartment off Sunset. The curtains were drawn. Outside, Los Angeles continued about its holiday idyll, half the city fled, the rest taking advantage of their absence. On Jeffrey's table was an empty bottle of Japanese whiskey and a dozen dented cans of microbrewed beer. He hadn't slept in a long time. A bandage around his forehead had grown grotty.

"Christmas isn't about *things*!" proclaimed the father from Jeffrey's flat screen, imparting this realization to his family after two hours of miserliness. Jeffrey had been watching Christmas movies for the better part of forty-eight hours, since driving home bloody from Mary Ann's house, and they had begun to run together. The men were mostly handsome, and the woman were always beautiful. The children were precocious and wide-eyed. The disagreements were clean and clear and not all that serious and ended in easy amity. Everything fit, everyone knew their place.

Jeffrey went into his bathroom and looked at himself in the mirror. He took off his shirt. He tightened the muscles in his chest and sucked back his belly fat. He curled a bicep. He reached up to where Mary Ann had struck a bottle against his forehead and slowly unwound the bandage. The skin beneath was raw and pulped and red, and where it was not red it was the black of something long dead. Love was like that, an open wound and not somewhere easy like your forehead but between your fingers or on the sole of your foot, where no matter what you did you were sure to brush against it. Jeffrey had loved Mary Ann from the day they had met, in a cocktail bar in downtown LA that had to be entered through a secret door in the back of a pizza shop. She'd been sitting in the corner drinking something pink out of a rocks glass, looking cool and sexy and exactly like what Jeffrey had always wanted – pretty but not too pretty, just human pretty, and clever but not like she had to show it off all the time. They were going to move in together and she'd help him redecorate his apartment and learn to bake and grow her hair out. It was perfect. He had it all planned out.

"It doesn't matter if you don't have an expensive car, or a big house! What matters is family!" the father announced from the living room.

"Even Uncle Tommy?" asked his buck-toothed, tow-headed progeny.

Jeffrey pushed his finger into his mangled flesh, watching puss and bile and something that wasn't either of those leak out. He wiggled his finger deeper, through the rent in his numb flesh, tapping slowly against his frontal bone, feeling the vibrations through the pink beneath. It did not hurt. It did not hurt like his thoughts of Mary Ann.

"Christmas is about being with the ones you love!" said the father.

"Yes," Jeffrey agreed to his reflection, "exactly."

# THIRTY-SEVEN

Mary Ann was driving along a one lane highway in southern Kentucky and trying not to get angry at her sister. She had managed a few hours of sleep the night before, curling up at a rest step in the back corner of her car, but the first light of morning had pulled her from a fretful slumber and she had been on the road ever since, speeding east in her aging compact.

"What do you mean, everything else?" Constance asked.

"I mean has anything strange been happening? Not in the... here, I mean."

"John asked me the same thing. Strange like what? What are you asking about?"

A tractor-trailer cruised at a safe, which was to say tedious, speed in the lane ahead. Mary Ann crossed the median and accelerated passed. "I've been seeing things," she admitted. "At first, I thought it was just me, I'm off my meds and... well, it's not just me. Things are bleeding into one another. There were these two men in the diner yesterday, and then back in LA Jeffrey – that's the guy I'm dating – he went crazy, or something, it was like he'd been poisoned, or...Constance? Constance? Are you still there?"

Mary Ann wasn't sure if Kentucky had laws against talking on your phone while you were driving – her impression was a state where you could bring a gun into a bar was unlikely to insist on "hands free" usage – but between rule and wisdom is a wide gap, and coming around the corner Mary Ann saw a creamsicle-colored snail wider than the eighteen-wheeler she had just passed stretched out over the double lines of the highway. There was no time for shock but only movement, dropping her phone and jerking the wheel and sending her car over the rumble strip and onto a stretch of mud, a tree looming fast ahead and needing to be gone to not be there not to die not to die–

–The car rolled forward another hundred feet by sheer momentum, squelching through tufts of grass and splashing thick ruts of mud into the air even as Mary Ann depressed the brake to the floor, coming finally to a slow stop. The lack of expected impact and the sudden freedom from death left her at first not giddy but nauseous, opening the car door and puking up what little remained in her stomach. When she had finished, she rinsed her mouth with a half-empty bottle of water she'd bought at a gas station the evening prior and, careful of the puddle of vomit, alighted from her car.

Mary Ann had not seen the March for nearly twenty years, since that horrible day in the Heartwoods. The months after that were vague and bleak and miserable, and she could only recall them through a gray sedative haze. Whether it was the medication, or if the March had withdrawn itself from her in disapproval or sympathy, Mary Ann had spent enduring the banal tranquility of mundane existence.

Still, there was no question that this was, in fact, the March. The land here was not altogether different from where she had been, rolling grasslands and scrub trees, but the air was cleaner, sharper, free of the taint of chemical and carcinogen so constant as to be forgotten except when in abeyance. In the Kentucky she had been driving through it was morning and the light was cold and bright but here it was late afternoon, and the foothills hung with brume so thick Mary Ann could barely see a hundred feet ahead.

"And not a tow truck around for miles," she said.

It wasn't a funny joke but it was good to be alive and so she laughed anyway, a manic expulsion of energy which had built up over her long journey east, two largely sleepless days and the horrors which had led her to flee LA. She thought of Dr Feranz, wondering at what her humorless therapist would have said if she could see her patient just then, giggling like a lunatic.

"She'd probably have me committed," Mary Ann said to no one, then stopped smiling suddenly. Between her doctor's compulsive visions and the full-scale intrusion of the March into her world had been barely forty-eight hours. Something was wrong here, terribly wrong. The levees cracked and weakening, the breech threatening to flood reality itself.

They slipped out of the mist as if called by her unhinged good humor, a dozen or perhaps more, it was hard to tell when they scuttled so close together, one limb much the same as an antenna or a thorax and Mary Ann no entomologist. They were half her size and faceless, maggoty things, carrying shillelagh and spider-silk nets. Mary Ann had heard stories of the Hive but never been there, her only familiarity with the oothecan the knights and courtiers who came to visit the Tower; decorous, oddly-beautiful creatures that smelled of expensive scents. Of their hideous male inferiors, she had no experience, and after so long away from the March she had lost the easy habit of ignoring impossible things and not finding the fantastical horrifying.

She forced on her best smile, wondering even as she spoke if the drones could understand her. "Hi! Nice of you show up so quick. My...chariot went off the road, and I'm a little banged up."

They gathered cautiously around her but did not answer or did not answer in any fashion that Mary Ann could understand. One wandered over to her car, leaned down to smell her sick, then gave the door a careful push. Discovering it would not fight back the drone grew bold and wrapped the chassis with his club, denting the aluminum.

"Don't do that!" Mary Ann shouted, and they backed away

for an instant. "Or, actually," she considered, "do whatever you want. I don't think I'll manage to get it out of here anyway."

But the drones had already lost interest, returning to circle Mary Ann. It was like in that movie, Mary Ann thought, except that they were larvae and not little people in bear suits.

"I'm a princess lost in a strange world," she explained, half-jokingly. "I need to get to the Tower. The Tower? My mother lives there, she's the Queen. It's a thing."

The drones came up only to her waist but as they crowded around her Mary Ann could not help but flinch backward, a reflexive disgust inspired by their serrated legs and wiggling antennae and rapid, discomfiting movements. She felt a sharp pain below her knee and dropped to the ground, staring into their compound eyes and chittering mandibles and then was swallowed up by darkness.

# THIRTY-EIGHT

The party in the Toybox had been going now for weeks, months, it was hard to remember anymore, a twenty-four-hour bacchanal stretching from the Gumball Palace all the way to Butterscotch Square. The malt shops were thronged with customers and the novelty stores had been ransacked, crates of itching powder and whoopee cushions torn open and tossed in the thoroughfare. The sky was forever being rent with great scintillations of fireworks, exploding throughout the night and most of the day likewise, for the Smiling Man's party was both perpetual and mandatory. Below posters admonishing passersby that "A Jolly Merriling is a Loyal Merriling!", and to "Laugh Last, Laugh Best!" a wheeled wooden chicken, buzzed on giggle-juice, turned in tight circles. On the steps of a confectionery a band of wind-up monkeys clashed cymbals in an uneven cadence as, a callithumpian parade of dress-up dolls and toy cars and googly-eyed slinkies snaking down the avenue. Against the broken display windows of a ruined patisserie a stuffed giraffe cavorted with raggedy Andy, frottering sexless felt bodies. A ballerina pirouetted passed them and down a dark alleyway, pointe shoes skipping nimbly over a puddle of sugary excreta.

Reaching the shadow of the side street the ballerina's mouth turned to a hard line, and her mincing steps grew swift. She wore a soft blue shawl over a pink tutu but shivered beneath it, for away from the packed mess of bodies the evening was cold. With her forced smiled abandoned she looked harried and nervous, even before she came around a corner and ran smack into a squad of sentries, newly-cast sentinels of the Smiling Man's regime.

"What's your hurry?" one asked.

"Don't you know there's a party going on?"

"A jolly merriling is a loyal merriling!"

"I just needed a bit of rest," the ballerina said.

"A rest?"

"You mean a break?"

"From the party?"

"But it's a party!"

"It's the *last* party."

"Don't you want to see the finale?"

"Of course!" insisted the ballerina, affecting an awkward enthusiasm. "I wouldn't miss it for the world."

"You can't miss it!"

"It can't be missed!"

"Everyone's going to be there!"

"Who laughs last, laughs best!" the tin soldier reminded her.

"Maybe she doesn't like to laugh."

"Doesn't like to laugh? What sort of a merriling doesn't like to laugh?"

"I love to laugh," the ballerina assured them, "it's just that I–"

"A jolly merriling is a loyal merriling!" the tin soldier said again.

"Aren't you a loyal merriling?"

"Show us your smile," one of the soldiers demanded.

The ballerina did her very best, stitching a crooked grin across her face, though the tin soldiers seemed unimpressed and were closing closer when a voice interrupted their cruelty.

"Hey, sorry, I was wondering if you could give me some directions?"

A start, a shout, and the soldiers turned to face the newcomer. He stood against the wall of the alleyway, dressed all in black, his face wan and ruined. "I was looking for the palace, but I think I got turned around by the chocolate water fountain."

"You ain't no merriling," said one of the soldiers, unlimbering his pop-gun.

"No, it's cool, I'm a collectible."

"A what?"

"It's like an action figure, but more expensive. I've got thirty-four points of articulation," the man in black wiggled a long finger in demonstration of his flexibility, "and retail at a hundred and twenty-nine, ninety-nine."

"Stay where you are," said one of the soldiers, aiming his weapon.

"Actually, while I've got you, maybe you could help me with something else. I've got this nephew I need to buy a toy for. What's in with the young folk these days? Are Furbys still big? No, I guess not. But there's probably something like a Furby, right?"

"Lunatic," said one of the soldiers.

"Crazy or not, he shouldn't be out alone."

"Dangerous thing, being out alone at night."

The man in black smiled his crooked smile. "I am the night," he explained, which in evidence grew suddenly darker, the moon obscured behind a cover of shadow, the alleyway turned to pitch, all the evening coming to reside within the narrow confines of the street. John pulled the ballerina free even as the air filled with the retort of pop-guns and the screams of the incautious soldiers, both soon lost amid the general celebratory clamor. Like frantic lovers they hurried hand-in-cloth-hand through the city, until John felt confident they had escaped pursuit.

He turned to look at the creature he had just saved. She was beautiful, in the fashion of toy ballerinas. She had lost her shawl in the escape, but her eyes were threads of rich blue, almost the same colors as John's own. She stood reflexively in first position, feet turned, arms slightly outstretched, mouth open nervously.

"Well?" John asked, "wherever you were heading, it has to be safer than staying on the street. For both of us."

"Thank you for your help, kind sir," said the ballerina, dipping her head guilelessly, "but I need to get home. Mother and father will be terribly worried, not to mention my various aunts, uncles, cousins and–"

"You can save the damsel-in-distress bit. You look the part, but you don't act it."

The ballerina turned her head back and forth, as if wary of being overheard. "Did the Harrow send you?" she whispered.

"Let's just say I'm a friend," said John. "I'd think you'd have few enough of those to question my origin."

The ballerina stared at John for a moment longer, then came to a decision, taking his hand once more. Wearing false smiles, they returned to the packed boulevard, toys on balconies tossing candy and confetti and plastic beads to the mass below. A textile mermaid crooned in an off-key soprano, board game pieces waved sparklers, a nutcracker waited open-jawed to prove his strength upon anything anyone thought to thrust into his mouth. It was like Bourbon Street during *Mardi Gras*, or Rio anytime of the year, the merriling gorging and drinking and laughing and puking and then coming upright to gorge and drink and laugh once more.

But a long few blocks from the main streets the lights began to dim and the gaiety to fade. Here the businesses were closed, and the schools shuttered, every merriling in the Toybox given over to debauchery or quarantining themselves away in their houses. Past toy train tracks the city turned grotty and grim, closing into a crooked maze of streets abutted by dollhouses partitioned away into tenements, dozens of unfortunate merriling packed inside, anthropomorphic trucks left idle and jack-in-the-box without room to spring. They crossed a marzipan bridge over a sickly stream choked with confetti and corn syrup, continuing warily through a tent city of forgotten toys, stuffed animals with matted fur and exposed fluff eating sticks of chocolate beside trash can fires. Catching sight of the newcomers they forced their miserable maws into empty grins, for the Smiling Man's spies reached even to the bitterest ends of his domain. The slum spread long out into the night, but the ballerina led the way with swift familiarity, coming finally to a chain link fence surrounding an abandoned amusement park, a rotting Ferris wheel looming high above.

"A safehouse?" John asked.

"One of the last," said the ballerina. "The Smiling Man has spies everywhere. Rubber duckies patrol the river, and the paper airplanes keep watch on us from above. We've heard nothing for months and had all but given up hope of the Harrow's return."

"We?" John asked.

"You'll see," said the ballerina.

She contorted herself neatly through a hole in the fence, but John had to pry the metal loose with his tendrils of shadow. Inside the fairground lay forgotten, the concessions grown tumbledown, wheels of fortune unspun and plush prizes unclaimed. Abandoned tickets and empty boxes of popcorn lay scattered in the muck. Vandals had been at work, defacing the tilt-a-whirl and wrecking the carriages on the merry-go-round, gouging out the eyes of an ostrich and breaking the tip off a plaster yearling.

"It's been forsaken since the Smiling Man took power," the ballerina explained sadly, "these days we merriling pursue darker pleasures."

"Yeah, what the hell happened to you guys? You used to be so fun. I mean, personally I always thought it was a little tacky, but still it beat this Orwell-on-ecstasy thing you've got going on now."

"It all changed so fast," the ballerina said. "First the rumors of the End, and then the fear of it. Do they know of fear, where you are from?"

"We've got a casual acquaintance."

"The merriling did not. We knew only sunny days and cloudless skies, cotton candy and marshmallow. Our pits were filled with balls, our edges child-proofed. It was such a terrible thing, being scared."

"And that was it? A few days of ennui and you all lost your fucking minds?"

The ballerina stopped at a stand advertising funnel cake, pulled a key out from a secret pocket in her unitard and unlocked the shutter. Inside were crates of powdered sugar and cans of chocolate sauce and a set of secret stairs. The ballerina found a glowstick hidden among the supplies and cracked it, then led John down the steps and into a sewer below. The underground river reeked of saccharine, and the water was thick with sludgy fudge. John followed the ballerina along the embankment and farther into the gloom.

"At first there were some that tried to stop him," she said, "our old mayor Binky, some of the plush elephants, the wisest among the rocking horses. But soon they were bullied into silence or disappeared. It was better to dance and to sing than to think about the End awaiting us."

John could understand this better than he might have wished.

"I think perhaps we just needed an excuse," said the ballerina. In the green light of the glowstick her face had taken on a sickly cast. "The Smiling Man gave us one."

She came to an access door set into the rock and rapped on the peephole. It opened for a moment, then shut once more. There was the sound of a bar being undone and the door opened, and the ballerina ushered John inside. The room was brightly lit and coming from the deep darkness of the sewer John was blinded, had to rub at his eyes before he could see the dozen tin soldiers waiting to meet him.

The ballerina slammed the door shut. "A scream is very

much like a laugh, after all," she said through the bars of the Judas hole.

John had time only to summon up a faint cushion of shadow before the pop guns exploded around him.

*2006*

# THIRTY-NINE

They had been in the Kingdom of the Thorned Rose for a month; or perhaps for more than a month, or perhaps for less, it was even harder to tell time in the forests than in the rest of the March, one day giving seamless to the next. Sir Floppy and the other Valiant had been called back to the Tower some weeks earlier, leaving Constance and Mary Ann embedded among Calyx's clan. Without crops to tend or jobs to work, without money or articles of trade, the verdurite were free to give time to any passing peculiarity which caught their attention, entire afternoons lost following a trickle of water back to its source or inspecting some particularly vibrant epiphyte. Their only concern was food, though this was a constant one, for lacking salt and eating only flesh the verdurite wavered always between feast and famine. The previous week had been mostly the latter, the clan forced to eke by on tree grubs and thrush, and there had been rejoicing when a scout found trace of giant beetle, or as much rejoicing as the verdurite, a somber and serious people, could manage.

They woke just before dawn, the great trees girdled with morning mist, the verdurite busy about their work, sharpening their spears and tightening their leather lariats. There were no distinctions of sex among the verdurite, and all but the youngest and eldest were to take part in the day's hunt. After breakfasting on rainwater and crushed ant and bird marrow the clan broke off into small groups and headed out to their assigned positions. The verdurite had no mounts and kept no dogs, their hunting all done by stealth or, when this was impossible, by battue, driving their prey into waiting ambush.

This last was the part that Mary Ann and Constance and Thistle were to play, sitting in in the lower boughs of a hardwood, waiting for the hunt to begin.

"How about that?" asked Thistle.

"No, that's bark."

"So?"

"You can't eat it," said Mary Ann. "I mean, I can't eat it."

Along among the group that day Mary Ann struggled to maintain interest, personally indifferent as she was to the outcome of the hunt. The time she had spent in the forest watching her sister and new companions feast on burnt intestine and tree termite had done nothing to change her committed conviction towards vegetarianism, although it was admittedly somewhat touch and go finding produce that wouldn't leave her poisoned, for all that Thistle tried to help.

He pointed at a glut of fungi growing off the tree. "How about that?"

"You never know with mushrooms," said Mary Ann, "best to be careful."

Thistle tugged at a long tendril of his dark hair. "What's the worst that could happen?"

"I'd die miserably," said Mary Ann.

"Just try a little bit."

"You're such a jerk."

"How much noise were the two of you planning to make?" asked Constance.

"This much noise," said Mary Ann. "No, wait – this much. Exactly this much."

Thistle did not laugh – Thistle never seemed to laugh – and obviously Constance didn't find the joke amusing, but Mary Ann thought it was funny, and that was generally enough for Mary Ann. Their time in the Kingdom of the Thorned Rose had gone no way towards ameliorating the growing divide between the two sisters, with Constance diligently learning the customs of the verdurite and Mary Ann spending most of her days with Thistle. Unlike her sister, Constance had committed to the obligate carnivorousness of her adopted people, and after days picking the flesh off bird bones and squelching bugs between her teeth, she was hungry and ill-tempered.

"We'll hear the call before they start," Thistle promised. He carried a lasso and a bone knife in a leather sheath along his chest. "It will be a long morning, I suspect. The beetle is a fierce beast and must be harried before it dies. Aim for the chinks in its armor, or the mouth if it offers a shot – though that's a dangerous cast, and a miss will leave you in peril."

Constance had long since stowed away her armor, assuming the dress of the verdurite as she had their diet, clad in animal leathers and carrying a long spear carved from the bone of a massive quadruped. "I suppose we'll see," she said, confident enough to remain silent. She had not become a Valiant by virtue of her name alone, long years spent with Sir Floppy learning the tools of war, the *estoc* and the *misericord,* the *pernach* and the *bec de corbin.*

The false call of a finch turned Thistle to sudden silence, enough to make clear the game had begun. Constance readied her spear and even with all her PETA posters Mary Ann felt her heart beat faster. The world teetered on the edge of stillness, a surreal hypersensitivity rendering the thick scent of the wood more fragrant and brightening the brown and green of the endless forest.

And then that stillness broke into a wild cacophony, the distant verdurite erupting in hooting hunting cries, a terrible corresponding bellow which could only be the beast itself. The woods were alive with motion, warblers and kinglet exploding upward in a sudden rush of color, Thistle twirling his lariat, the ground itself thunderous with the footfalls of the galloping beast. Entering their clearing the beetle proved the size of a passenger van, with a glimmering, kaleidoscopic carapace.

Its mandibles were half the size of its body, a flat curving ax blade large enough to separate a sequoia with a single stroke. A creature so massive should not have been capable of moving so fast, tarsi clattering as it sprinted down the forest path, upending a sapling in its frantic escape. The first group of waiting hunters failed to bring it down, a loop of leather falling short of the creature's legs, a shower of arrows breaking against its prismatic integument.

Constance remained still as a cocked pistol, waiting as she had been taught for her single perfect moment to throw. Thistle was not so cautious, managing a cast with his lariat which caught one of the beetle's legs tight round the tibia though he was not able to hold it for long, the beetle's momentum pulling him off his perch and the lasso from out of his hands. The beast careened passed and Thistle, getting up quickly from his fall, hurried after it, joining the pack of hunters in swift pursuit of their quarry.

Mary Ann followed him an instant later, down from the tree and trying to match his perfect, nimble steps. The beetle outpaced them in its desperate rush for escape, Mary Ann and Thistle running along after, the path narrowing atop a small gully, the rest of the verdurite ahead or behind them.

"They'll turn him back, you'll see!" Thistle said. "Be ready!"

The beetle was fast and the beetle was strong but the verdurite worked like a pack of wolves or a good house band, in skillful and perfect unison. Mary Ann heard the beast bellow, then the sound of its footfalls growing nearer once more, realizing the danger only when it was too late as the tortured creature careened back toward them, shafts of bone driven through its rainbow exoskeleton, bleeding black from a dozen wounds, pain-maddened, lowering its billed head as it charged. An instant before oblivion Mary Ann grabbed Thistle by the shoulders and hurled them both down the ravine and out of the way of the beetle's charge, which carried it back down the path and toward Constance, alone now beneath the trees.

It bore down on her, frantic and terrified, wanting only to end its suffering, Constance wanting the same but still waiting, waiting, the bone spear loose in her hand, the beetle growing larger in her vision until it filled full the frame and only then throwing, like a football through a tire swing, the spear driving past the mandible and through the palp and into the soft brain, the beetle dropping instantaneous though sheer momentum furrowed its corpse through the dirt, leaving it to rest finally a few short feet from Constance herself.

From the bottom of the ravine Thistle and Mary Ann heard the cheering of the verdurite and knew the hunt was over. They were bruised and battered, and Thistle had a shallow cut along his cheek, but other than that they remained miraculously unharmed.

"You saved my life," Thistle said, as if he still could not believe it.

Mary Ann pulled him close and kissed him.

# FORTY

"You're spending too much time together," Constance said.

"Isn't that why we're up there," Mary Ann joked, "to make new friends?"

"We're up there to remind them the oaths they took still hold and will whichever Harrow reigns in the Tower."

"Right, whichever," Mary Ann said, mockingly, "could be me, could be John, could be a long, lost cousin."

"You know what I mean."

It was early evening, and they were in the living room watching the Orioles lose to the Red Sox. Constance was watching, at least, Mary Ann was doodling vaguely in her sketchbook but mostly thinking about Thistle.

"I thought you hated him."

Mary Ann had hated him, right up until she had become obsessed with him, and strangely, it was due to the same qualities which initially repelled her. His odd quiet, his sense of sobriety which verged on superiority, his adamant refusal to bend to her will. "What else am I supposed to do? Eat grubs and look at trees? He's the only one up there you can talk to."

"Just keep it at that," said Constance.

Mary Ann laughed uproariously, falsely, a little nugget of fear at the core. "Are you going to give me the talk now, Constance? Sometimes boys expect certain things? You're not Mom, even though you like to forget it."

"We're not talking about giving a blow job at Homecoming," snapped Constance. "There are consequences to things.

stupid."

Sophia came into the living room then, interrupting their conversation. "Have either of you seen John? He was supposed to be home from school an hour ago."

"No," said Mary Ann.

"Not since last night," said Constance.

The bus to John's middle school came at seven-fifteen, and Constance and Mary Ann did not generally leave until the house until eight, Constance driving in the second-hand Camry she had received as a birthday present the year before, so most days the girls did not see their little brother before arriving home in the afternoon.

Sophia found Michael in the basement, tinkering away with the washing machine. Not the old washing machine, a new one, though it suffered from a similar plague of ailments.

"Do you know where John is?"

"No. Is he up in his room?"

"Wouldn't I check there first?"

"Probably."

"When was the last time you saw him?"

"Last night, before he went to bed." A wrinkle spread across Michael's forehead. "You know what, I think he told me that he was going to be late today – something about baseball tryouts?"

You could hear Sophia purse her lips from across the room. Michael set aside his toolbox and got up from behind the washing machine.

"He told you what?" Sophia asked.

"He said he was thinking of trying out for the baseball team."

"John hates sports."

"He's eleven, he doesn't know what he hates," said Michael. "I thought it was a good thing, he's been so lonely lately. Maybe he'll make some new friends."

Sophia bit down into a grimace and tensed her hands

together. "Sometimes, I think I married the dumbest fucking man in all of existence."

Back in the TV room the Orioles struggled through the eighth, a man on first and third and the pitcher in an anxious impromptu with his catcher.

"All I'm saying is, you need to be careful," said Constance.

"What?" asked Mary Ann, who was thinking about something funny that Thistle had said the day before, or the night before, or however you wanted to describe time spent in a place where time did not make any sense.

"You need to be careful," Constance repeated. "All that stuff about watering the Heartwood, you know that's not a metaphor? Before Grandpa stopped them, they used to give blood sacrifices to their sacred trees."

"That was a long time ago."

"It really wasn't. They're half-savage at best, Mary Ann. What if something happened?"

"Like what?"

"I don't know, something. What if Thistle gets it into his head there's more to things than there are? Than there should be. Or what if his father decides he doesn't like how close you're getting with his heir? If anything happened, if things turned bad...we're all alone up there, Mary Ann. It's just the two of us."

Their father came bolting into the room, looking anxious and flustered. "Have you seen your brother?" Michael asked.

"No," said Mary Ann crossly, "Mom already asked us."

"Why?" Constance asked.

But Michael didn't answer, his eyes clouded, and after a moment he hurried back into the kitchen. Mary Ann looked at Constance and Constance looked at Mary Ann and then they both followed to where their mother spoke anxiously into the phone.

"Hi, Jane? This is Sophia Harrow calling, how are you? Yeah. Actually, I was wondering if you'd seen John today? My husband thinks that he was trying out for the baseball team, and I thought maybe he and Bobby... No, don't worry about it. Must have gotten our wires crossed."

Sophia hung the phone back on its cradle. Then she sat down at the kitchen table and set her hands against her forehead.

"Nothing?" Michael asked.

"You heard," said Sophia.

Michael took a seat across from his wife. "I'm sure he's fine."

Sophia didn't say anything. Constance was worried. Mary Ann was mostly just confused.

"Should we call the cops?" Michael asked.

Sophia laughed bitterly. "And say what exactly? You know damn well where he is, Michael, and you know the cops won't be of any help."

# FORTY-ONE

"You're a little flat," said Chartreuse, "it's rain we're looking for, not thunder. You have to build up to it, start low. Like this…" He broke into a brief aria.

John listened carefully, then attempted imitation. "How's that?"

"Too high," said Chartreuse. "You keep going like that you're going to make it hail."

Chartreuse was a middle-aged molluschite, fat and well-respected. Soon he would be an elder, and would find a shell and split off into his own clan to trod the endless roads of the March. Already you could see his body growing into its next form, his tail getting thicker and longer, his legs withering away into uselessness. His fingers could no longer manage spool and thread, and soon he would not even be able to hold a fork or stand fully upright, but he remained the clan's best weather-witch, with a stunning countertenor and an uncanny knack for charming the gales.

Together they stood atop a peak in the foothills above Under the Mountain, overlooking white capped cliffs and verdant valleys and a sky which, despite their better efforts, remained sunny and bright. Chartreuse demonstrated his technique once more, John listening a moment then pitching his voice low and sending his song out towards the open air.

"Better," said Chartreuse, "but make sure you're not clipping your syllables. Rain hates that, you've got to keep it fluid."

On a small plateau some quarter mile down the path the

molluschites had set up their market, stands of brightly colored cloth with their sachem resting in the center. The petrousian had come to meet them, trading ore and metalwork for rough wool and glass beads and other things considered treasures among the children of stone. The arrival of the molluschite was a source of joy to the sedentary denizens of the March, their prices reasonable and word inviolate, honest merchants and weather-workers without peer. As a rule, the petrousian cared little for this last, living as they did beneath the ground; but a long, soft rain would swell the rivers that powered their subterranean grinders, and for the better part of the morning John and Chartreuse had attempted to coax distant stratonimbus into the clear sky.

"It's not just about the tone," Chartreuse explained, "it's about the feel."

"What do you mean?"

"You have to think about the rain while you sing. Not the rain so much as what the rain feels like."

"It's water, it feels wet."

"How you feel about the rain – how it makes you feel when you feel it."

John turned once more to his song, recalling the sound of a summer storm against the windows of the bedroom which he hoped to never again see, and the time he had got caught in a cloudburst while walking home from the playground, wet despair giving way to shameless glee as he accepted his thorough soaking, jumping in puddles, splashing mud on his pants.

"Good," said Chartreuse, "you're getting it!"

John swelled with pride as the clouds gathered tighter around the peak, dimming the afternoon sun. A wind picked up along with it, whipping at John's cloak, and he turned to see Pink coming up the trail. John waved, but Pink did not wave back.

"You're a quick study, Will," said Chartreuse, "how long have you been with us now?"

"A month," said John.

"You've got a knack for it – the gales like you. Soon you'll know enough to find welcome anywhere in the March."

John smiled brightly. John could do anything. Anything could be done. His time journeying with the molluschite had been the happiest of John's life, he had nothing to compare it to but those dim memories of early childhood in which every experience was novelty and every new day a wonder. Beside an underground lake in the Riverlands he had traded tales with an albino hydronese, blind and beautiful, fair skin untainted by the touch of sunlight. In the Proscenium he had played a bit part as a tiger in a stage play, roaring his one line majestically, and in the Clockwork Republic he had gambled with a living slot machine and come away victorious.

Better even than the adventures was having someone to share them, John and Pink finding themselves fast friends, joined in the sudden camaraderie of mutual adolescence. The rest of the molluschite had likewise embraced him unreservedly, sharing their food and their knowledge and their stories. If they were aware that his ruined face was a deformity and not the normal state of his race, they had never mentioned it, and among them he was not ugly John to be mocked and pitied or Prince John to be honored and ignored but just plain Will, to be judged by what he said and what he did rather than what he was or what people thought he was. John had never known friendship before, not really, and it was only from this new perspective that he had grown to recognize the full scope of his loneliness, that gnawing despair which he had supposed the constant state of mankind and not his own unhappy burden. It made him sad, sometimes, to think of how he had been, but only for a minute and even then with some trace of joy, for all that was gone now, the wound closed, the bone healed, his dark days behind him.

Except that when Pink finally reached them at the top of the peak his face was set in an uncharacteristic frown, and his eyes were frightened. "There are soldiers here looking for you," he said.

"What?"

"Knights on yearlings. A rabbit and a couple of others."

Chartreuse cleared his throat. The rain clouds drew closer.

"It's not what it looks like," said John.

"It looks pretty bad," said Chartreuse.

"I haven't done anything wrong."

"Be that as it may," said Chartreuse, "the molluschite are faithful servants of the Harrow."

John laughed at that, a bitter laugh, a laugh that should not have come from a child. "Which ones?"

Chartreuse did not know what that meant, and neither did Pink.

"Where are they?" John asked.

"Searching the market," said Pink. "Sachem sent me up here."

"To do what?" John asked, though he knew the answer.

"The wellbeing of the clan comes first," said Chartreuse. "It has to."

"Of course," said John.

"If there's been some sort of a misunderstanding, I'm sure it can be resolved. The Harrow are just."

But it was not justice John wanted, it was freedom. "I understand. It's OK. Thanks for..." There was something in John's throat. "Thanks for everything. It was..." but he found he could no longer speak.

Pink looked at Chartreuse. Chartreuse looked at John. Then he sighed. Then he turned back towards the edge of the peak and began to sing, a low dirge which made John think of fog choked cities and vast alluvial plains, of flooding streets and rivers overflowing their levees.

"Go," said Chartreuse between notes, "we'll keep them off as long as we can."

John and Pink hurried back down the peak, skirting away

from market when they came to the first fork. Their path led deeper into the crags which rose above Under the Mountain, towards a narrow crevice sheering through the rockface.

"It's not anything bad," John promised.

"It probably isn't that good, though, or they wouldn't have sent the Valiant."

"Do you want me to tell you?"

Not having shoulders, the molluschite did not exactly shrug, but they had a similar sort of shrugging motion and it was one that Pink performed just then. "It would just confuse things. The less I know, the less I'll have to lie about."

"I'm sorry," said John. He thought of the consequences of his capture, carried home on the back of some yearling to whatever banal punishment awaited him – extra chores, a month without dessert, being cut off from everything bright and rich that he had found in a short life with more than its share of misery.

They came to the mouth of the crevice, a chink in the wall of slate that surrounded them.

"We'll try and throw them off your trail," said Pink, "but I'm not sure how long that will work. If you can get down below, the petrousian might hide you for a while."

"OK."

"Good luck."

"It wasn't a lie," said John. He blushed. "I mean, some of it was, but nothing important. You're the only friend I ever had, besides my sisters, and they don't really count. You and the rest of you. Some of the things I said were lies, but that was true."

Pink smiled sadly. "Can you tell me your name, before you go?"

John looked down at his feet and swallowed hard. "John," he said.

"Goodbye, John."

"Farewell, Pink."

John watched Pink head back to the market, rain beating against his saurian head, the rising wind picking at the ends of his cloak. Then John was alone, and then he was in motion, scurrying through the fissure and deeper into the mountain, trying not to slip on the dampening gravel. After a few moments he could hear them in pursuit, screaming his name through the narrowing crevice, which had grown so tight that John had to turn sideways to pass.

"John!" roared Sir Floppy from not so far behind him, "John! Come back!"

But John ignored him, slipping out from the narrow pathway of rock, scratching a line of red on his cheek – not the ruined one, the normal one – and finding himself high atop a narrow ledge above a roaring river. For a vertiginous instant he thought he might stumble, but instead he set his back against the mountain wall and hurried ahead as best as he was able, mincing along the rain-slicked stone. The ledge was barely wide enough to place his shuffling feet, and it took every bit of concentration to keep himself steady, blind to Dame Delta until she appeared in the air beside him, fluttering her cloth wings.

"You need to come home now, John," she said.

John screamed and nearly fell, and Dame Delta retreated into the sky. "Careful! Careful!" she shouted.

Sir Floppy had managed his pursuit with predictable speed, standing at the start of the narrow projection on his hind paws, nimble despite the slippery path and the now driving rain. "It's enough now, John," he said. "It's time to come home."

"Leave me alone!" John shouted. "I don't need your help!"

"The Queen is worried."

"Let them worry!"

"You don't really mean that."

"I'm not going home," said John.

"You're not in any trouble," said Sir Floppy, "she just wants you safe."

Dame Delta perched on a jut of stone above them, gazing down with sad clockwork eyes. The storm had picked up, fat droplets of water beating against her cloth wings and on John's forehead and on the river far below.

"Get back from the ledge," said Sir Floppy, "Please. Something bad could happen."

"Something bad did happen," said John, turning towards the rabbit knight, noting with a bitter sort of pleasure that this veteran of a hundred bloody battles, feared across the March for his sharp blade and savagery, could not look at John's face without blanching. "It happened five years ago."

"I'm a Valiant," Sir Floppy tried once more. "I've sworn an oath to the Harrow and the Tower. I won't leave you here."

"Come on, John," said Dame Delta, "there's nowhere left to go."

But of course, she was wrong. John closed his eyes and leaped from the edge of the cliff.

*2023*

# Forty-Two

Nearing midnight and still there were a million things yet to do. They'd put the tree up the week before, a little trimming party with Julian and Evie, but the rest of the decorations still required unpacking, colored lights strung over the mantle, souvenir Santas set in their assigned niches. They needed to carry the extra tables up from the basement, and the dozen-odd folding chairs that gathered dust the other three-hundred and sixty-four days of the year. There were cookies to bake and food to prepare to go along with the genuinely absurd amount of booze which they had purchased. Adeline had Julian and Evie, so it was just Constance and her mother preparing for tomorrow's Christmas party, the fact niggling at Constance like a sore tooth.

"Butterballs, or sugar cookies?" Sophia asked, digging through a box of old recipes indexed on note cards, some recent creations, others hand-me downs grown faded with age.

"Evie thinks butterballs taste sticky."

"You daughter has terrible taste in sweets," Sophia lamented.

"Don't you think I know that?" Constance asked. "I watched her eat a pane of fondant off a holiday cake last week."

"Mary Ann was like that," Sophia said, smiling. "She ate nothing but processed sugar, I'm still not sure how she stayed so thin. You remember she used to dip her toast in maple syrup?"

"I remember," said Constance, though in truth her siblings' youthful vices did not seem so charming to her as they did to her mother; her sister only ate dessert, and her brother never cleaned his room. Speaking of which; "Where is John, exactly?"

"He said he was tired."

"He's tired? From what? Having two children and a full-time job? Wait, no, that's me."

"And you manage it with such grace," teased Sophia, turning back to her recipes.

"How the hell I'm going to get the tables up by myself?"

"I can help."

"You're not in a fit state to be carrying things."

"I'm fine, Constance."

"Is that what the doctor said?"

"He said I do anything I feel like doing," said Sophia, "and right now, I feel like baking cookies and helping you carry a table up from the basement."

"What else did he say?"

Sophia pulled a note card out from her box, narrowed her eyes at the inset scribble. "My mother had the worst handwriting. Absolute chicken-scratch. Do you think this is a three, or a five?"

Constance looked over. "I think it's a six."

"Shit," said Sophia, but smiling as she said it. "I've been using her recipes for twenty years now, and I still can't get them right."

"Your cookies are great."

"My cookies *are* great, but they're not as good as my mother's."

"I'm sure that's just your memory. Everything seems better when you're a kid."

"No," said Sophia, thinking of Joan, whose eyes she shared though she was not sure how much else, a softer woman, sweeter and more forgiving. "She was just a better a baker than I am." Sophia set the recipe aside and reached for another. "What the hell, I'll make both."

"Mom," Constance tried again, "what did the Doctor say?"

"He said that they're still waiting to hear back about some tests."

"I thought we were supposed to have those by now."

Sophia shrugged. "It's the holidays, Constance, even for doctors. I'm sure whatever it is, we can wait till after Christmas to hear about it." She got up from the counter and took a baking bowl out from a cupboard. "Have you heard from Mary Ann?"

"Not since yesterday," said Constance. "She said she'd be back in time for the party."

"Do you think we should call her?"

"I've been a little bit busy, Mom, maybe you noticed?"

"What do you want, Constance, a medal?"

"A word of thanks, maybe? Or at least a little help from John."

"We should be happy to have him back home."

"I should be happy? He should be happy I'm letting him stay in my house."

Sophia narrowed her eyes.

"In our house, I mean."

"This is a good thing, Constance," said Sophia. "The whole family together again. How long has that been?"

"I dunno. Not since Evie was born." Even with the recent plague as an excuse Constance knew this to be shameful, her siblings become near strangers. But the days were long and busy and almost more than you could take, and at night who had the energy even to compose a text message, and anyway they didn't bother either, Constance was still waiting on a birthday call from Mary Ann and as for John, well, he might have been dead before turning up the day prior.

"And in time for the party," Sophia smiled once more, lost in the days when the house had thronged with people, and there was light and laughter in every room. "It'll be great. It'll be just like old times."

But Constance, who could remember these better, felt less certain.

# FORTY-THREE

The Proscenium had been a kingdom of artists, of musicians and poets, of composers and sculptors and the finest joiners in all the March. Sited precipitously atop a limestone hill, reached through a well-paved mountain road, its gates were always up, the freedom of the city open to any who could pay its penny fee. Its walls were painted backdrops to be disassembled and rearranged at will, and apart from an occasional spear carrier the prosopon wielded no weapons. Protected for untold generations by the strength of the Harrow they had wiled away their time in matinees and first showings, exchanging odes and pictures, swapping roles according to whim and fancy.

But the curtain falls on every play. Long weeks of hard rain had matted down their pleasure gardens and ruined their sets, turned their coulisses to mushy masses of cardboard and oil paint. Half the city had already fled, abandoning their orchestra pits and letter presses even as the slopes and valleys to the west filled up with the encroaching End. Before her arrival Constance had entertained some dim hope of saving the city, a sharp strike to drive back the enemy, but looking over their numbers, the slow spread of the faceless multitude, she had quickly abandoned that hope. The Proscenium was lost, though the prosopon might survive as refugees within the Tower.

All morning and throughout the afternoon Constance and the other Valiant had worked toward this goal, overseeing the prosopon as they vacated their ancestral homes, trying desperately to decide what was worth taking amid crates of props and hand-bound manuscripts and half-filled sketch books. Even as the vanguard of the End reached the outskirts of the city the Valiant had remained to defend it, waiting until the last of their charges had left on the long road east towards the Tower. The End was terrible, and the End was near-certain, but the End was slow, stumble-staggering except when they neared untainted meat, then turning fierce and ravenous. Sir Snout had been lost in the fighting, and Dame Delta had taken an injury which had ruined her wing and left her all but flightless though she still hopped about, angrier than usual at being bound to the earth.

Their delaying action had not been without casualty, but it had at least been successful, the Valiant escorting the last of the Proscenium's inhabitants through a gap in the limestone cliffs and into the valley below. A low humming filled the air.

"Keep going," said Constance, waving on an old woman with a mask of abject innocence and a child with a leering death's head grin, "we can't stop yet."

Constance had never before thought about how much there was to feel; not just happy or sad, but joyous, ebullient, vivacious, despondent, melancholic and forlorn. As the fleeing prosopon passed her in train she had occasion to mull over each of these, the vast and potent slate of emotion made manifest in the masks of the refugees. For her part Constance could feel nothing but anxious and angry, a reasonable response to the circumstance if aggravated by the blade festering on her back, for since arriving in the Proscenium she had kept six locks on her sheath undone, and only Necessity remained to hold back the raw portion of annihilation caged within. Constance had eaten a chunk of hard tack for lunch but puked it up soon after, and she struggled to keep her mind on the task at hand, consumed by memories of old injuries and insults, small wounds festering in the dark corners of her psyche.

"We will return," said Dame Intrepid, riding past with

characteristic confidence. Earlier that afternoon Sir Intrepid had swapped his mask with another of his race, and the Intrepid who faced Constance had thick thighs and a full chest beneath the tight black weave of her unitard. Apart from these cosmetic changes she was identical to her predecessor, one hand on her great mace, painted face fearless despite the horrors on which it had peered.

Constance envied the knight's confidence but could not pretend to share it. Dame Intrepid continued on as escort, and Constance waited grimly atop her yearling as Sir Floppy came through the defile, escorting a straggler with a mask of boundless misery who carried an omnibus the size and weight of a cornerstone.

"Everyone out?" Constance asked. The hum had grown louder.

"Yes. This was the last of them."

"And the End?"

Sir Floppy shrugged his shoulders. What was there to say about the End, except that it was coming?

Constance watched the prosopon proceed east leaving countless treasures behind them, marble sculptures and unfinished bronzes and elaborate mosaics pasted on the city walls, a library so large the bookkeepers themselves often went astray. "So much gone," she lamented.

"Yes," said Sir Floppy.

"If we'd just gotten here earlier–"

"We didn't," said Sir Floppy, "and we did the best we could. A city can be rebuilt. At least the people who will rebuild it are safe."

"For how long? You've seen it. It's larger than any army that ever existed, larger than all of them put together. And more rise with every step, soon they'll swallow up the Hive and the Clockwork Republic and anyone else that thinks to stop them."

"We'll find a way. So long as the Tower stands, there's hope."

"Hope is in short supply these days," said Constance.

"Then it's grown more precious for its scarcity."

"And when it's gone?" Constance asked. In the distance a troupe of prosopon maneuvered a grand piano through the mud, four of them roped to a sledge like pack mules. "What do you have, when hope dies?"

Sir Floppy turned his one good eye on her, an eye which had watched countless squires turn to knights, and knights turned to heroes, and heroes turned to corpses, which had seen battles lost and battles won, which had looked long upon every form of suffering and not yet blinked. "Pride," he said.

The End might be anything, was everything, growing in strength and number as it had spread across the land, like termites or boll weevils except that these pests only consumed and the End corrupted. Among its number it now contained specimens from every one of the Thousand People and innumerable others besides, creatures and clans that had never made contact with the Harrow, which lived under the ground or in the trees or above the clouds or along the distant, half-known lands which met the borders. It was a clew of these which struck then, the hum growing louder and then suddenly much louder and then there were things coming out the cliff walls, faces full of blunt, chattering teeth and blind eyes, worms the size of motorcycles maddened by the taint of the End. They were ropy and long and waved with withered, infant arms and they seemed to be rotting as everything which the End touched rotted. Like some fetid fleshy flood they ran out the crevice and down towards the Valiant and the fleeing prosopon, intoning their hideous polyphonic cacophony through vermiculate pharynx, mouthpieces of the End offering their portion of its unholy hymn.

"Chink in the armor!"

"Burl in the grain!"

"Mold in the walls!"

"Tear in the eye!"

"Fault in our stars!"

Constance's yearling reared and it was all she could do to remain atop it, but earthbound Sir Floppy had no such handicap, his blade free in an instant, dodging neatly between and above and around the worms, sickly gusts of pus bursting out as his sword flashed among them. Hearing the commotion Dame Intrepid turned and spurred her mount back towards the melee, bellowing her war cry boldly, the weight of her flanged mace falling to either side, splattering the purulent bodies of the worms against the walls. Constance's yearling went down between the writhing mass, crushed between tautly muscled annuli, Constance flung to the ground. Sir Floppy was beside her in an instant, a whirl of fur and steel, hopping nimbly over every attack, his blade a shield around Constance, gaining her time to recover from her fall and to find the crooked black key on her ring and slip it into the final lock.

It was a terrible thing, the sword which was not a sword, every awful feeling, every shred of anger and bitterness and contempt and self-contempt flaring up all at once, like throwing water on an electrical fire; when she was in middle-school and she'd been called a dyke for the first time, Shauna Moze laughing and blushing as if she could not believe her own bravery; the day her father had died; the things she had said to her sister after her father had died; a fight she had had with Adeline outside of a bar just before she had realized that they were going to get divorced. It was a terrible thing to hold the sword but it was far worse to endure it, for the End was the End and not nothing, only nothing is nothing, only the sword which was not a sword was nothing. Constance sheared through the corrupted flesh of the worms, bi- and tri- and quadrisecting them till they lay like coins of flesh in the mud but still they came, Dame Intrepid lost beneath their wrangling legs, swinging her mace and roaring even as she fell. Sir Floppy continued his desperate dance, fur matted down with sweat and ichor and now blood, his own blood, red against his off-

white coat. They would not stop and Constance could not hold
the blade forever – putting her grandmother into the ground;
the hard edge her mother had worn after, every smile carrying
its hint of sneer; the day Mary Ann had come home from the
institution, bandages on her wrist, eyes vacant and dull. Sir
Floppy's broken arm stretched useless beside him and his good
eye was fading but still his sword was a fierce blur, screaming
"for the Harrow, for the Tower, for the March!" even as they
dragged him down. With the last of her strength Constance
allowed the sword which was not a sword to extend further,
an uncorked spasm of nothing with which she sheered apart
a wave of worms and through the stone impasse beyond, the
endless weight of the mountain collapsing in on itself, burying
the pathway to the ruined Proscenium and the still wriggling
corpses of countless End-ridden worms and the bodies of
Dame Intrepid and Sir Floppy Longshanks, the finest knight
the March had ever known.

# FORTY-FOUR

John woke chained against a wall, his hands and feet fettered, a thick iron collar fastened around his neck, his captors taking no chances. It was hard to call the room a dungeon, painted as it was in garish green and tacky crimson, but it was as close to a dungeon as the Toybox possessed. The baby doll who stood over John was likewise serving substitute as a soon-to-be-torturer, laying out lines of jagged metal on a gleaming instrument table with chubby plastic hands. Half a dozen tin-soldiers with pop guns waited in case their prisoner had any sudden yearning for freedom and to serve as bodyguard for their monarch, who sat on a three-legged stool, staring scornfully down at John while the ballerina knelt at his side, winding his key.

"Hello Jolly," said John, "it's been a long time."

"You will call the Lord by his proper name," said the baby doll, leering with his bright, lidless eyes, "or pay the consequences."

"Hello again, John," said Jolly Bones, who seemed not to stand on ceremony so much as his subordinates or was just enjoying the situation too much to mind. "Surprised to see me?"

"Actually, I kind of saw it coming."

"Quite a lot of foresight to end up in chains."

"Oh, I dunno. It can't be all sunshine. You need a little rain just for the sake of variety."

Jolly Bones motioned to the baby doll. With the collar stiff around his neck John did not see the blow arrive, his jaw swelling with sudden pain, a tintinnabulation in like he'd just walked out of a night club.

"A silent merriling is a cheery merriling," said one of the soldiers.

John spat blood onto the floor.

"Cleanliness is next to happiness," the soldier reprimanded.

"Am I going to have to hear that all night?"

"Not *all* night," Jolly Bones promised nastily.

"You wouldn't see your way to offering the condemned a cigarette, would you?"

"A what, now?"

"Never mind, I forgot that doesn't exist over here. It's crazy that with everything you've got here, no one ever figured on cultivating tobacco."

"I'm sorry our hospitality hasn't been up to your standards – but don't judge us too quickly, the real fun hasn't even started yet. You'll laugh, John. Everyone laughs, once we put the Tickler on them."

"The Tickler?" John asked the baby doll. "For real?"

"What's wrong with it?" asked the Tickler.

"It's a little on the nose. Then again, I am talking to Wally Wets Himself. You know, no one even plays with you guys anymore? It's 2023, children only want branded content and expensive electronics. This whole regency-era vibe makes me feel like I'm trapped in a cocktail bar on the Lower East Side."

"Once more, Tickler," said the Smiling Man, "with feeling."

This time John was expecting it, but it didn't make a difference, his vision gone cock-eyed and bile welling up in his throat. John managed a few second of silence and the Tickler returned to his preparations, pulling a feather duster from his bag and setting it down beside the rest of his instruments.

"Do you see now what the Smiling Man has saved you from?" asked Jolly Bones, lowering his tone of voice, playing to the tin soldiers and the ballerina as audience. "Do you understand the depths of their desperation? It is not enough to lock ourselves in the Toybox, still they search us out, covetous of our carefree ways, jealous of our joy! Born miserable, they think to steal our birthright of happiness. But no longer! No longer will we offer outsiders our googly eyes, plush tummies and snap-on accessories! Our days of servitude are over! The misfortune of the March is no concern of the merriling. Beneath the watchful eye of the Smiling Man, we are free! Free to tell our jokes and sing our songs and eat all the candy we want!"

The tin soldiers, obedient by their nature as a cat is subtle or a wasp cruel, bellowed in agreement. The ballerina looked up at the monarch, her eyes wide with adoration.

"Not to throw a hink in that otherwise absolutely fabulous plan," John admitted, "but aren't you kind of forgetting about that whole end of the world thing we got going on?"

"All things come to an end," said Jolly Bones, philosophically, "the question is, how do we spend the interim? In guilt and terror, screaming and bemoaning our lot, wishing for atonement? No! Never! Fear is for you outsiders, as are guilt and shame. For a merriling there is only joy."

"A joyful people are a mighty people!" said one of the soldiers.

"Frowns are forbidden!"

"The merriling laugh last!"

John considered this philosophically for a moment. "Well, you are fiddling while Rome burns, but I got to give it up for at least stealing the violin. How did you manage that, exactly?"

"You mean how did I become the first officer of the Toybox, generalissimo of the jovial people, magnificent monarch of the merriling?"

"Sure, all of that."

"Why, John – I owe it all to you."

"Me?"

"Not you, but your people at least."

"Maybe it's having been punched in the head a couple of times, but I don't follow."

"Power requires more than pop-guns and Catherine wheels – it requires a reason. Not a reason, even, just a story.

The Toybox for the merriling, dancing in the shadow of the apocalypse."

"And you calling the tune?"

"Someone has to," said Jolly Bones, "that's another thing the Harrow taught me."

The Tickler had finally unpacked his bag of torture devices; a crooked scalpel, a jar of itching powder, a thumbscrew, a choke pear, a malevolent looking whoopee cushion. Jolly Bones's gears, properly wound, *tic-tic-tocked* in the loud silence.

"Clever," said John.

"Thank you."

"There is one thing you've overlooked, however."

"Is there?"

"This isn't your story."

"Whose is it, then?"

"It's mine, obviously," said John. "You're a featured extra at best. Once upon a time a little bit of me and my sister imprinted on your fate. If we'd spent those weeks in the kitchen playing dominoes with a sock-puppet, it'd be him I'd be staring back at right now."

Jolly Bones seemed nonplussed, resting his hand on the still kneeling ballerina. "But you aren't, are you John? You're staring at me. At least until I take those pretty blue eyes of yours. What do you say, Tickler? Got something you think could manage that?"

Indeed the Tickler did, an instrument which looked a bit like a corkscrew and a bit like a hole punch. He held John's head with one knobby hand and leaned over him, crooked tool extended, looming large, his shadow fat and thick and recoiling suddenly, a tight black pulse of penumbra which struck below the Tickler's bulbous chin and sent the doll stumbling backward, forking off and darting around the room, swallowing a torch, striking a lantern against the ground. The light faded and the shadow grew stronger, extending swift talons in all directions until the room was plunged into darkness and that darkness was a living thing, that darkness was John itself. Someone moaned. Something screamed.

A match flickered, and John leaned down to light a candle. He stood freely, his chains shattered on the ground, smiling a grim smile even as the tin soldiers and the ballerina and the Tickler and Jolly Bones himself lay choking on the floor, mouths and noses covered tight with thick bands of shadow.

"You always had exaggerated ideas about yourself, Jolly."

John picked up one of the Tickler's knives from where it had been knocked onto the floor. He gave it a little flourish and leaned down over Jolly Bones, who stared up with painted eyes full of hate even as the shadow crushed his throat.

"I'm the fucking Harrow," said John, terrible in his wrath, "and you're just a Goddamned toy."

# FORTY-FIVE

Mary Ann was not sure how long she had been in the dungeon, the time passing in dark and anxious boredom with nothing to do but fret. They had been fed twice, so a day at least, drones delivering a gray paste which tasted of forced rations and gave the prisoners noxious gas. The smell was the thing Mary Ann minded most about being locked in an oubliette, dozens of them packed closely together, captive refugees from across the March; a mottled raven, chained so it could not fly, a pitiful, graying molluschite, several etiolated arcimboldi.

Mary Ann's arrival had inspired no particular interest among the other prisoners, who had grown used to the routine – the door opening, a stranger being shoved through, the door closing once more. Mary Ann had attempted conversation, but no one seemed to know anything and all were despondent, driven to the roads by the End, now captured by the oothecan for some unknown but surely insalubrious purpose. So, she had done as the rest of them had, taking up a spot on a moldy palliase and waiting in vain hope of freedom.

Next to her were a family of petrousian, dwellers from Under the Mountain. A fragile looking elder, wizened and eroded, sat beside a new mother, a child like a nub of obsidian crooked in her arm. Watching over them warily was a pyknic youth with granite biceps and a face smooth as a river stone. The child began to cry, and her brother, or father, Mary Ann was not certain then which he was, offered it the last bit of his paste.

"You're good to them," Mary Ann observed.

"They're family," said the petrousian, as if this explained everything.

"That's all there is to it?"

The petrousian shrugged shale shoulders. "Of course."

"Not everyone likes their family."

"Likes? I liked my pet mantis, but we had to let it go when we took to the roads. I liked my neighbor, but she fled before we did and I'll never see her again." He stated it as dispassionate fact, as if beyond sadness. "Our home is gone, and our village. The things we owned, the people we knew, all gone. Family is what remains when nothing else is left."

Mary Ann didn't know what to say to that.

The door opened but this time instead of shoving in some unfortunate captive several oothecan knights came through themselves, carrying hooked spears and bilboes. One hissed a command and when that was not followed with sufficient speed struck the nearest captive with the flat of her weapon, sending a wilting arcimboldi to the ground, and the rest of the prisoners made a hurried rush for the exit. Pushed forward by the crowd, Mary Ann discovered theirs was one of dozens of cells all being vacated like an expulsion of puss from a boil, a ragged mob of anima and merriling and faunae, of limping, broken-armed widdershin, two quetzal with their wings cruelly plucked, a pinkish-brown biped in torn jeans and a t-shirt whose eyes went wide and desperate when he saw Mary Ann.

"It's impossible!" he cried, grabbing her by the shoulders. "None of this is real!"

It wasn't John and it wasn't Constance and it wasn't her mother and it wasn't the ghost of her father but it was a human all the same, five fingers on his hands, thinning brown hair.

"You have to help me!" he cried again, but Mary Ann could not help him, could not help any of them, and an instant later the mad press pulled them apart, the oothecan hurrying their captives ever forward.

Outside it was night, the moon painfully bright after the long hours below ground and what it shone upon too terrible to stare at it for any length of time, imponderable in its awfulness. The path to the Hive had been lined with defensive positions, and shielding the entrance was an unfinished wall, the edifice made, like everything else among the oothecan, from their own distillate, a rippled cordon of hardened saliva which screamed which somehow screamed, a living wound towards which they were being pressed. There was a happy instant wherein Mary Ann imagined they were only to be used as forced labor but coming closer she could see the source of the sound were the living beings entombed within, ranks of faunae and anima and merriling kept motionless but alive by some hideous artifice. An oothecan forced a struggling arcimboldi into position within the wall, as above it a thing which looked like a bladder with eyes disgorged a waxy concentrate, intoning incantations as its plaster-like effluvia rose above the arcimboldi's shoulders and then his mouth and then his eyes, closing off his cell but somehow leaving him the capacity to express pain.

The petrousian boy roared and broke the chains which held him, falling on the oothecan, a spear shattering against his stone hide, snapping one insectoid arm as if it were a toothpick, screaming for his family to flee. But pressed as they were this was impossible and despite her powers Mary Ann found herself equally immobile, her powers nonfunctional, like trying to wiggle your ears or curl your tongue if you cannot wiggle your ears or curl your tongue, straining to find a muscle which isn't there. All she could feel was a fear so all-encompassing that it would not allow for thought, like a deer in headlights, stunned beyond capacity by the certain immanency of its own demise. A barbed spear found the soft meat of the petrousian's eye and he added his screams to the chorus which echoed throughout the valley, Mary Ann managing finally to focus all the energy tensed up within her on a single thought – home, home, home – then vanished in an instant, leaving the prisoners behind to meet their hideous awaiting fate.

# FORTY-SIX

The arrival of the prosopon had thrown the Tower into further chaos, harried sensechals and sleepless stewards trying to find space among an already overcrowded city. Long forgotten storerooms had been cleaned of dust and crammed with disparate exiles; furry faunae quartered with unshelled molluschites and brooding xerophile, silently pondering their garden-city, now lost to the blight. Against strong objections the grand apartments of the Lords and Ladies of the March had been divided and sub-divided and then sub-divided again, arcimboldi making their beds beside ivory tables and gilded music boxes and priceless *objets d'art*. Every ship on the bo which could be patched up and made to float if not to sail was crammed with refugees, waterfowl and hydronese crowded together on rotting hulks. In the basements the saprophyte worked day and night to expand their caves, offering refuge to those fossorial creatures who eschewed the touch of sunlight, badgers and blesmols, the few remaining petrousian, anyone else desperate to bed down amid the dark and damp.

And in their private room at the very top of the Tower, Sophia and Constance sat alone.

"He was a great warrior," said Sophia, "and a dear companion."

"The greatest," said Constance, "and the dearest."

"The old guard are all gone," Sophia said sadly. "I'm the only one left."

"You have me," said Constance.

255

"Yes," said Sophia, though it seemed to give her little comfort. "It's a terrible price to pay."

"He would have wanted to pay it," said Constance.

"We will miss his sword, when the End comes."

They would miss more than that, Constance thought. Sir Floppy who had taught her to be a knight, not only to fight but to abide by the rules of chivalry – to champion the weak, to challenge injustice wherever she saw it, to hold her life as cheap if in service to others. Foolish, faded notions, their chief virtue that they were all but impossible to uphold.

The candles in the girandole guttered, cast long shadows, sent silhouettes along the wall, and then one of those silhouettes was John and John was smiling. On the table in front of their mother he tossed a tarnished tin key, of the sort used to wind a clock.

At the first sign of trouble Constance had freed her poignard from its sheath, putting it aside only when she recognized her brother. But Sophia remained implacable as ever, even as she leaned down to inspect John's gift. "What's that?"

"Did you want the whole head?" John dropped into the chair beside Sophia, hanging his long legs over the support. "The Smiling Man is kaput," he announced, "and the Toybox turned loyal once more."

Sophia looked at the key for a long moment, then back up at John. "So that's where you've been."

"That and Christmas shopping. Is Julian too young for one of those flying plastic drones they sell at the mall?"

"Obviously," said Constance.

"He'll grow into it."

"You think killing the head of the Toybox will solve all our problems?"

"Probably not," John admitted. "The way I see it, the merriling are just more mouths to feed. But it puts the rest of them on notice. The anima, the oothecan...they had swords, last time I was here."

"And how long ago was that John?" Constance asked. "Back two days and you think you own the place."

"You'd rather I left tinpot Tito in charge of the Toybox? Two days was what I needed fix that problem, give me another week, I'll have the Thousand People lining up to do cheer routines."

"That simple?"

"Pretty much. The Toybox were terrified of the Smiling Man. Now they're terrified of us. I found the old mayor in a dungeon and left him in charge. He'll arrange for them to evacuate to the Tower, though someone else will have to figure out where they're going to sleep." A flagon of wine stood beside Sophia, and John poured himself a glass and quaffed it in one go. "Did I do good, Ma?" he asked, half-mockingly, or entirely mockingly, with John it was hard to be sure. "Are you proud?"

"You should have told us what you were planning."

"I wasn't planning it until it happened," John admitted. "I figured I'd take a look around the Toybox, see what there was to do. I found an opening, and I took advantage of it."

Sophia rolled Jolly Bones's wind-up key between her hands thoughtfully, then turned to face her son. "What do you want, John? What are you up to?"

John smiled his warped smile. "Isn't that obvious? I want to be king."

*2006*

# FORTY-SEVEN

"Are you scared?" asked Mary Ann.

"No," Thistle insisted, "I just don't want to."

They lay alone together in a deep corner of the endless wood, beside a small pond, a break in the forest canopy allowing a few traces of sunlight to reflect off the surface. Mary Ann ate from a vine of wild grapes, and was tempting Thistle with its pale, plump fruit.

"It's like... I dunno. If you were to cut your hair off and eat it."

"I like your hair," said Mary Ann.

"I like yours," said Thistle.

Mary Ann ran her hands through his tangled mane and kissed the corner of his neck. He returned the embrace half-heartedly, his mind stretching elsewhere.

"We'll arrive at the Heartwood tomorrow," he said. "No outsider has seen them in generations, not since your grandmother led us against the End."

"What's it like?"

"They."

"What?"

"What are *they* like. The Heartwood is alive. My grandmother and grandfather, and theirs, and theirs, all the way back to the first root."

"You can like... talk to them?"

"Not talk, not anymore. When we were a free people, and watered the copses with red, they would sometimes speak to us of the past. But these days they slumber too deeply to hear our calls."

"That's a lot of pressure, meeting your entire family line. I hope they like me."

Thistle pulled away from Mary Ann and rose to his seat. He was shirtless in the warm sun, his chest muscles stiff and proud. "What happens to us?" he asked.

"What do you mean?"

"You know what I mean."

Mary Ann knew. "Do we have to talk about it?"

"I suppose we don't."

"There's nothing really to say."

"Nothing," Thistle agreed.

"My parents would never…"

"My father would kill me."

Despite the time Mary Ann had spent among the verdurite she was not sure if this was a joke. She knew Thistle better then she had ever known anyone in the world, but she also sometimes did not really know him at all, the gap between them at once irrelevant and unbridgeable. Perhaps filicide was common custom among the verdurite, and they staked misbehaving adolescents atop swift growing shoots or roasted them over a fire like the horned snake.

It was an irremediable tragedy, but somehow Mary Ann could not feel sad about it. The moment weighed so heavy it was difficult to imagine another might arrive, as if time had come unstuck and it would forever remain this afternoon, with the sun warm and the flowers blooming and Mary Ann herself young and beautiful.

She ate another grape. "You should try one. It's good. It's sweet."

"It's forbidden."

"It's still sweet."

And slowly, hesitantly, as if he feared it might burn his hand, Thistle plucked a grape from the vine and rolled it between his fingers. Gathering his courage, he popped it into his mouth and chewed a moment, the juice running down his chin.

"It's not bad," he said.

Mary Ann kissed him, tasting the grape on his mouth and his tongue, sucking at the sweet even as with uncharacteristic awkwardness he undid the clasp on her dress and pulled it over her neck. She felt his chest tight against the buds of her breasts, his skin which was smooth and solid as polished ebony. She grew damp, flustered, frightened, pushed him down into the soft dirt and kissed him roughly, received his kisses in return. Somehow his trousers were off, and she took him in the palm of her hands, trembling even as he thickened to her touch. There was a moment like jumping off the high dive and then it was done, or starting, sitting astride him with a sharp ache inside her, biting back a scream even as the pain rose and then somehow lessened, not eased but added to by a growing swell of warmth. He gasped beneath her. She caught his breath in her mouth. It was strange and awkward, but it is strange and awkward for everyone the first time, whomever they are and whomever they accept. He was too rough at first and then he was too gentle, holding her body as if afraid it would break, as she thought it perhaps might, finding a growing rhythm, rocking back and forth, opening around him and–

–They were in her bedroom, his eyes gazing up at her, mouth open in shock, the sunlight coming in through her window, a framed Strokes poster on the wall. Below she could hear her mother and her father fighting over something, and then–

–They were beneath the trees once more, gasping in fear and triumph. Sunset had swallowed up the afternoon, and the grape vine lay ravaged beside them.

# FORTY-EIGHT

"I should have known," said Michael.

Sophia didn't say anything. She wore sweatpants and her husband's sweatshirt which had a sports logo on it that she didn't recognize. She had not slept in several days.

"I should have talked to him. I should have known. I've just been so damn busy with work lately, and..." Michael trailed off, waiting for some sign of sympathy.

It didn't come. Sophia stared at the wall, good as deaf.

"We should have had him change schools," said Michael, "or sent him to talk to someone. Something."

Sophia snapped out of her silence. "Fucking Christ, Michael, this is not the time."

"You need to talk about it, Sophia. You can't keep it bottled up like this."

"I'll let it out when he comes back," said Sophia. "I'll beat my chest and tear my clothes and think long and hard about all the ways I fucked up, and what a disappointment I am as a mother." She narrowed her eyes. "First, I'm going to beat him until he's blue, and then I'll cry until I can't stop. But right now, we don't have that luxury."

"The Valiant will find him," said Michael. "They've never let us down before."

Sophia didn't bother to answer. There was no point. There was nothing to do but wait until darkness fell and sleep came and dream dragged her to the March. The Harrows were the heroes but not the architects of their story. It was up to fate and whatever dim sentience was embodied in the March to choose when she would return.

Or at least, this was as Sophia then understood it.

Mary Ann and Constance sat listless on the porch. It was better to be outside then inside just then, better to be as far away from their frightened father and their mother waiting like a sore wound.

"How could he even have gotten out of the Tower?" Constance asked. "There are like, a million guards around all the time."

"John was always clever," said Mary Ann. "He'll be OK."

"Says who? Anything could have happened to him."

Mary Ann knew this was true, that John might be lying dead in a ditch somewhere, or carried off by a jubjub bird, or swallowed up by one of the nameless monsters which roamed the far reaches of the March, and also that these things should worry her, and also that they did not. She didn't have the energy to worry about John, or indeed to do much of anything except think of her love back in the forest. Thistle's dark eyes, his furrowed brow, the taught muscle in his chest. The way she could almost sometimes get him to laugh, the way his mouth had curled when she had sat on top of him. His smell like a budding leaf, his strong hands. Was this what love was, Mary Ann wondered? A narrowing of attention until you could only focus on one thing, one other, or not even that, on how you felt about that other? A form of devotion which was indistinguishable to those outside of it as anything but selfishness? Or was it just that there was something wrong with her, some essential flaw which kept her obsessed with her newfound romance even as her family warped themselves to despair fretting over her brother?

Mary Ann found that in truth she did not care. She had Thistle. Nothing else mattered. "I'm sure he'll turn up somewhere," she said. "You know how John is. You remember at the Christmas party two years ago, when he disappeared all night to read books in the basement?"

"Mary Ann, what the fuck is wrong with you? He's not hiding in the basement, he's lost and alone and he's probably scared and he might be dead."

There was nothing which could be said to this so Mary Ann said nothing. She plucked at a piece of string on her jacket and made sure to hold her frown.

"It's not a game in there," said Constance. "You ought to remember that as well."

"What's that supposed to mean?"

"It means that this thing with your boy has gone on long enough. He's not one of us. You understand that, right?"

"That's kind of rich, coming from you."

"Because I'm a lesbian?"

Constance had come out the summer before, in so far as you can declare a part of your personality which is as insuperable from your identity as the color of your eyes and nearly as obvious. It had changed nothing between them, though this was a mixed blessing. If Mary Ann had hoped, and she had, that her sister's revelation would spark new intimacy she had been disappointed. They remained as they had even as children, some great gulf of taste and judgment and personality standing between them, mocking their consanguinity and the best will in the world.

"I like women, Mary Ann. Women. You know, other humans? With two X chromosomes and breasts and the whole deal. What you're doing is like…kissing a sheep or something."

"Thistle isn't an animal!"

"He isn't a human either. He's part of the March. He's part of the story."

Mary Ann bared her teeth. "You're just as bad as Mom and Dad. You think because we rule the place it means we own it. They're people too, Constance. They have their own thoughts and their own lives and their own dreams."

"You're disgusting."

"Love is disgusting?"

"You aren't in love, you're just a child."

Mary Ann had grown twenty years in the last two days and did not need to take this from her sister. "I'm a woman," she announced.

Constance blanched. She opened her mouth, then closed it. She was worried she was going to say something awful. She went to the bathroom, locked the door, and stared at herself in the mirror – her broad forehead and thick shoulders and blunt, brown eyes. A thousand thoughts pressed through her mind, crushing over one another; that she might never see her brother again, that her mother and father might get a divorce, that Mary Ann had been the first to lose her virginity, that the March might go to war, that there were sometimes no good answers to anything. When she came outside, she found her father waiting aimlessly by the stairs.

"Dad," she began, "there's something I need to tell you."

# FORTY-NINE

John knew it was a mistake as soon as he hit the water, dropping down into the chilly depths and bobbing up again like a cork, gasping, flailing, thinking as the rapids carried him downstream "you're an idiot you're an idiot you're an idiot you're an idiot and now you're going to die."

He did not die, however. Cast about by the turbulent waters, nearly broken upon a jutting stone, but in the end he found himself upright in the shallows, white as a corpse but still breathing. The current had carried him far from Under the Mountain and the squall that still raged above it, and the afternoon sky was hyaline giving way to evening.

He got out finally, shivering and shaking. He had no idea where he was, or where he would go. He had no food, no tools or weapons, no money but then again there would be nowhere to spend it. He had more water than he needed. He considered trying to head back the way he came, along the banks of the river. Sir Floppy and Dame Delta would be out looking for him, hindered by the storm but they were Valiant after all, and would not give up easy on the search.

Instead, he draped himself in the late afternoon shadow and began to walk. He was in the hinterlands of the far north, past the last point of civilization. Ahead were only the compass points, the wards placed upon the borders by John's distant ancestors in a long-forgotten age. He moved through a trackless plain of wild grass, seeing no one nor even the remnants that anyone had ever passed this way before. He was cold and hungry but not frightened. What was the point? He had made his choice and despite everything he did not regret it.

When he saw the thing however, he did grow fearful, thought of his home and warm bed and his mother who loved him. A flatfish the size of a duplex slicked through the high weeds, long barbel wiggling from its gasping mouth, blind, skyward eyes staring upwards towards infinity. Its mouth was crowded with crooked teeth and a photophore extended from its forehead like a lantern pole, dull in the daylight but growing brighter. There were such things near the borders, where what was became what was not, strange blips of impossibility, monsters forgotten or unheard of in the comfortable confines of the Tower.

A dim mist kept the valley in a gray gloom free of shadow, though John thought-forged what wisps of darkness he could gather into a thick shell and long claws, watching as the creature drew close enough for him to make out the folds in its face, the mucousy membrane which served as its skin. He tried to be small, and quiet, but he could do nothing to hide his scent, the thing growing closer, blending in with the high grass, a slow squelching sound indicating its movement, choking the air with a sickening, saline stench. Its dangling luminescence threw the inside of its bristled mouth into stark relief, rows of crooked fangs and rancid particles of undigested flesh. John tightened the weak shadow around him until he felt like he might burst, preparing to loose himself in a single desperate instant, like an arrow from a bow, a suicidal attack but it was better than waiting to be swallowed.

Then the wind changed direction, the beast tarrying for a moment before gliding north in search of other game. The air seemed suddenly thick with pollen and humus, the breeze shifting once more to reveal a furrow in the grass which would serve as a track. John walked in a sea of green, a susurrus rustling through the weeds. It was still quiet, a deep and abiding silence, but it did not seem ominous any longer, only heavy, like a down blanket on a cold day. John let his feet lead him back towards the mountains and into the shadow of a low hill, where he found a small fire crackling in the gathering dark, though no other signs of habitation, no tents or bedrolls or cookware.

John took off his wet shirt and sat down beside the fire, felt the heat play across his skin. "Hello, Uncle Aaron," he said, after a while.

The fire swelled high, and bent as if to caress John in its warmth.

"We miss you, you know. Mom too. I don't suppose you've got anything to eat?"

The wind tilted its pitch flat in apology.

"No, of course not. Why would you?" John rubbed his hands together, then held them nearer to the flames. "What's it like, being dead?"

The fire did not answer, nor did the smoke or the breeze or anything else.

"It must be very quiet. So quiet that you can't even think. Just you alone, in all that quiet," John considered this dreamily for a moment. "But then again, I guess you aren't really dead, are you? You're just a ghost."

So far to the north the night fell with strange swiftness, cockshut following sunset without warning. A whip-poor-will offered its uncanny hymn, crickets providing background harmony. John sat with his head against his hand and watched the smoke grow over the fire until he could see visions within, battlements and barbicans and baileys, narrow machicolations, a single, twisting spire.

He shook his head. "I'm not going home."

The smoke became his sisters, his frantic father and then his mother, face fraught with worry.

"They'll be fine," said John. "They'll get over it."

The smoke burned loose and free, declining to respond to this absurdity.

"Do you remember what it's like, out there?" John asked,

angrily. "I have seven more years of school. They don't give seven years to people who rob banks! And what about after? College, a job? Why would I want to do that? Why should I have to? I won't," he said finally, firmly. "This is better."

Gloam turned to evening. A sly sliver of the new moon hung in a corner of the sky, so dim as to be nearly eclipsed by the stars. The wood burned. The smoke tightened, then began forming shapes once more. First it was a man, tall and broad shouldered, familiar though John had never seen him before, smiling a fierce, happy smile. Then it was that man at the head of an army, each tendril of smoke another soldier in his vast horde. That man with a crown atop his head, amid a kneeling crowd. The crowned man beside a Tower, the crowned man atop a throne, the crowned man with a wife beside him and a family surrounding him as once had his army. That family grown old, the wife old and the children old with her, holding their own children, then the wife gone, and the children gone and only the crowned man remaining. The crowned man alone, the crowned man wandering, the crowned man bent backed and beset with care, the crowned man laughing, the crowned man screaming, the crowned man sobbing. The crowned man tearing aside his crown and breaking it between his hands. The uncrowned man digging a hole, lying down in the earth but the earth refusing him, the old man alone, forever, bitter and maddened and vengeful in his pain.

A sprig of greenwood snapped in the fire, and the patterns turned to chaos, the smoke wafting off with the wind. John stared into the flames for a long time, as if waiting for more to be revealed, though nothing was, the fire was fire once more, and the smoke was smoke.

"I understand," he said finally.

John wept then, quietly, curling the shadows unconsciously around him. He would not cry again for many years. In time he fell asleep. When he woke the next morning, he was home in bed with the covers pulled high and the feeling of having lost something precious, of dream drifting tattered into day.

# FIFTY

Mary Ann woke in the March, alone in her tent. She stretched and yawned, flexed her fingertips, took careful notice of her heartbeat. In a few moments she would get up and put on her shirt and go outside to wash her face and then she would go find him, and then they would be together. She felt her heart beat faster in anticipation, glowed with postponed delight, the dream of the thing nearly as good as its reality.

The loud hoof beat of approaching yearling broke her out of her reverie. She dressed as quickly as she was able, pulling on her pants in the dark light of the tent and hurrying outside. She saw Constance helping her father down from his mount and knew everything that she needed.

"You rat," Mary Ann said. "You fucking rat."

"You wouldn't listen," Constance tried to explain, "I had to tell someone."

"Spiteful little bitch!"

"This is not the time," Michael said. A handful of Valiant remained mounted behind him, Sir Griseille and Dame Pontifax, clad in heavy armor and doing their best to notice nothing. Michael wore an unfamiliar scowl and Mary Ann did not care to think about the punishment which waited for her.

"Dad, you don't understand," she said, "you have to give me a chance to explain."

"Is it true?"

Mary Ann looked into her father's grim, heavy eyes. Then she hung her head.

Michael recoiled as if struck. "It's forbidden, Mary Ann," he said. "It's a thousand times forbidden. You don't have any idea what you're doing, what you're opening yourself up to."

"He's my boyfriend!"

"He's not a boy. He's not a human. He's a part of the March."

"So am I."

"And what do you think will happen if his father found out?" Michael hissed, looking around even as he said it. "As far as they're concerned, you're an outsider. That they even let you near the Heartwood is half a miracle. There would be war, Mary Ann, the whole March in flames, worse than anything your uncle ever did. Is that what you want? Are you really that selfish?"

Michael was bad at being angry. It hung heavy on him, profaned his face, set him to sweating. It was unhandsome and effective.

"I have to say goodbye," said Mary Ann.

"No."

"I can't just leave like this!"

"No."

"Please, Dad," said Mary Ann, her voice breaking, "please. You have to let me say goodbye."

Michael sighed and looked at his beautiful, miserable daughter, so much like Sophia but somehow so different. "Five minutes," he said, "but I'm serious, Mary Ann – if you aren't out by then I'm coming in for you."

Mary Ann nodded and brushed aside her tears. She was turning to leave when she caught on Constance once more, and her frown turned bitter. "I'll never forgive you," she hissed, "never. I'll die hating you."

"I said that's enough!" snapped her father. "It's not Constance's fault. It's yours." He shook his head back and forth, not angry anymore, only disappointed which of course was worse. "With your brother lost somewhere, and your mother sick with worry? This was all you could think about?"

There was no time to answer even if Mary Ann could have found one, and so she turned and ran off towards the Heartwood. Her father was right, she had been reckless and irresponsible and she did not care, weighing her family and her failure towards her family just then and finding both trivial against the love she felt for Thistle.

The border between the forest and the Heartwood was not firm, and it was only when she was already inside that Mary Ann realized she had reached it, coast redwoods and eucalyptus regnans and Douglas firs giving way to trees which had no names or only proper names, which bletted strange, spine-filled fruit, which blossomed in kaleidoscopic explosions of color, each a singular, unique creation. Some stood alone, preferring solitude in this quiet existence as they in their lives before. But others grew paired, wrapped tight around one another, evidence of the power of love to transcend even death.

Mary Ann found Thistle beneath one of those, two trees intertwined into the sky, one ebony, the other white as sycamore.

"This was my grandfather," Thistle said, leaning his hand against the darker of the two. "He died fighting against the End. My grandmother went soon after – of sorrow, or so they say. She ceased to eat and in time she ceased to drink, and one evening she went to rest here, and the next morning she was planted in the ground."

It was a lovely story and deserved more than the scan attention Mary Ann paid it. "My Dad's here," she said. "He wants to take me back to the Tower."

Thistle slumped against his grandmother's trunk. "Oh," he said.

"Do you love me?" Mary Ann asked.

Thistle blinked twice. "Yes."

"That's it?"

"Do you need more?"

"I'd take it."

"I love you," said Thistle, leaning forward to place the palm of his hand against her cheek. "I want you to stay in the forest and never go back to the Tower, to walk with you beneath the boughs, to wander and hunt and eat wild grapes, to have children and watch them grow, to die in time and to be planted beside one another, lost for eternity in the memories of our love, joined together until the end."

Mary Ann blushed red. Things seemed complete, in that moment, and also to waver on some razor's edge.

Thistle pulled his hand away. "Alas that none of those things will ever be. There's nowhere for us to go. Nowhere in the forest that my father would not find us, and nowhere beyond that your parents don't control."

"What if there was?"

Thistle cocked his head.

"You're right, we can't be together here even if our parents would allow it. But there are other lands, lands beyond the Harrow's reach."

"Where you took me? When…"

"Yes. It's nothing like the March. Nothing. Or only a little bit. It's more different than anything you can imagine, you'll be a stranger there, you won't know anybody or anything, you'll just know me. I don't know how we'd live or where we'd live or what we'd do, but we'd be together. The two of us." Mary Ann blushed. "If you wanted, I mean."

Thistle turned and looked out over the forest which was the only home that he had ever known, surrounded by his ancestors gone back to the dawn of time. "I will come with you."

"Even if it means giving up everything?"

"Yes."

"Are you sure?"

"Yes."

"That's good," said Mary Ann, "because we don't have a lot of time."

Indeed, Mary Ann could already tell her five minutes were up, the sounds of pursuit souring the stillness of the Heartwood. She would need to do it now, and she was not sure that she could do it, summon up whatever force was required to tear a hole through to another world and to carry Thistle off besides. She tried it like it had worked before, summoning up scraps of anger – at her sister for betraying her, at her parents for trying to control her – but she couldn't sustain it. Fear, likewise, was of no effect, though she ought to have been terrified, for the Aetheling Calyx entered the Heartwood just then, looking enormously displeased, and her father no doubt close behind. In the end it was love that did it, the memories of her time with Thistle in their secret grove, the thought of a future yet to be, one uncertain but full of light and promise, an entire life to build, until the thought of it grew so full and so bright within her chest that she felt as if she could no longer contain it, eyes prickly with energy, and then she let it bloom out of her and into the air, a door between the worlds.

Inside was an endless dark, black number one, a rent in the existence of the day itself, but the Aetheling Calyx in his unfathomable rage ignored it, grabbing Thistle by the shoulder and striking him fierce across the face.

"Locust!" he roared. "Weevil, blight-bringer, parasite, fool!" Thistle opened his mouth to protest but his father backhanded him to the ground. "You shame the seed that sprung you!"

Thistle was down on one knee and bled a thick sap from his nose and stared up at his father with fierce eyes. "I love her," he said simply.

His words served only to drive the Aetheling to further paroxysms, body trembling as if he could not contain his anger. He grabbed his son by the neck and lifted him off the ground, muscles straining. "Would that I had never sired you," he said, giving his son one fierce shake, like a dog with a rat, a loud *crack* echoing through the trees. "Would that I had carved you bloody from your mother's womb."

Mary Ann screamed. Thistle's legs kicked in his final spasms. The Aetheling tossed his son's near corpse through the portal, as if discarding rubbish.

"You killed him!" Mary Ann screamed.

Calyx shook his head. "You killed him," he said. "You and your family." Having murdered his son all the anger seemed to have drained out of him, body drooping like a drought-sick dahlia. "Why couldn't you have left us alone? All the March wasn't enough? You had to take him too?" He drew his bone knife from its sheath, long and sharp and inscribed with strange ruins. Sap hung from his dark eyes. "Curse you, Mary Ann Harrow," he said. "Curse you and all your line."

Mary Ann hung her head in shame, waiting for the blow.

But it didn't come, Michael arriving just in time, catching the Aetheling's hand and hurling him back against the ground. He was up again in an instant, no time for Michael to draw his weapon, the two circling each other, Calyx's long knife searching for a chink in Michael's heavy plate.

"Run, Mary Ann!" his father screamed, but Mary Ann did not listen, as if transfixed by her terrible guilt.

Then there was no time for words, Calyx feinting quickly before coming in under Michael's guard, planting his knife through a shoulder joint, blood splattering, but it slowed him down long enough for Michael to wrap him up and lift him off the ground. Calyx kicked and struggled but Michael's grasp did not weaken, tightened in fact, even as his life's blood painted his heavy armor, Calyx battering her father with the crown of his skull, snapping, biting, ripping away a bloody ear but Michael only roared and squeezed harder, a sudden sprint and he struck Calyx against the thick trunk of a distant ancestor, head rattling against the Heartwood. Calyx went suddenly limp, and Michael dropped him to the ground where he lay prone and motionless, staring blank eyed at the boughs above.

"Dad!" Mary Ann shrieked.

Michael opened his mouth as if to say something,

admonishment or absolution, Mary Ann would never know. The blood coming from his chest was coming from his mouth now also, and he had no strength to speak. Of course, it was in this moment that Constance arrived, just in time to see her father fall to the ground with a thump, dead as Mary Ann's foolish dreams.

# BOOK THREE

## 2023

# FIFTY-ONE

A sudden shift in weather had blessed the Harrow's annual Christmas party, December recalling its rightful place in the calendar, warm days giving way to a sudden snap of cold, gray clouds prophesying storm. But inside the house was bright with merriment, the return of the Harrow's children rejuvenating the traditional gathering. Old amusements mixed with pleasant novelties, the Santa statues sharing space with Julian's scraggly crayon portraits, and after decades of old Smoky Robinson LPs an AI-derived pop playlist blazed out from a voice-activated cylinder. Sophia was her charming self, exultant in blue, Julian wore a blazer of which he was just old enough to feel ashamed, and although no force on earth seemed sufficient to get Evie into anything other than sweatpants, she remained impossibly adorable. The punch was warm, the ice chest flourished with the brightly monikered labels of a dozen different artisan beers and John was amenable to playing bartender when he was not, with astonishing speed, pulling new dishes out from the kitchen.

"These oysters are amazing, John," said Mr Trevor.

"The trick is, you've got to fry them twice – once as a base, the second just before they're served."

"Is this what they teach you in your fancy New York restaurant?" asked Ms Alexievich, half-mockingly.

"This was my grandmother's recipe, actually," said John, turning the happy side of his face up to meet her, "a Harrow special, you might say."

Ms Alexievich dabbed at the corner of her eye, then ate another fried oyster.

Constance watched John from where she tended the fire, heavy gloves on her hands, Evie and Julian loud and cheery beside her.

"Mom, did you know Aunt Mary Ann lives in a bungalow?"

"Yes."

"What's a bungalow?"

"It's like a little house."

"Did you know that she has a palm tree growing in her yard? Right in her back yard!"

"There are a lot of palm trees in LA."

"Can we go visit her sometime?"

"We'll have to see."

"Can I have another piece of chocolate?" Evie asked.

"Ask your other mother," Constance grunted.

"Mommy A will say no."

"At least you'll have a few moments to hope," said Constance.

A lack of caution found Mary Ann pinned against a wall by a man with tufts of gray ear hair whose name, despite her best efforts, she could not recall.

"How's LA?" he asked. "Tell me everything."

"It's nice," said Mary Ann.

"Must be warmer than here!"

"It is. It's a lot warmer than here."

"I was telling Harriet – you remember Harriet? I was telling Harriet how much warmer it must be in Los Angeles than it is here in Maryland."

"They have different climates," Mary Ann agreed once more, looking for someone else to talk to, "you are not incorrect."

But it was slim pickings, the Harrow's Christmas party filled these days with aging neighbors and parents Mary Ann had never met and those parents' small children and, obviously, the Harrow themselves, potentially the least appealing conversational proposition. Mary Ann had gotten in that afternoon, after a two-hundred-dollar taxi ride from where she had appeared on the side of the highway a little ways north of D.C. She had arrived just as preparations for the party were getting frantic, barely enough time for a quick greeting and a shower and to force herself into one of her mother's old sun dresses, bright and strappy and seasonally inappropriate but it was the only thing that would fit.

"And what are you up to out there? Your mother told me you were working as an illustrator?"

"I was, for a while, but..." Mary Ann shrugged. "The crash."

"Oh," said the man confusedly, "which one?"

"Take your pick."

Constance found John in the kitchen, bent down over an open oven.

"You didn't need to do all this," said Constance. "That's why we got it catered."

John laid a tray of crab puffs to cool atop a trivet. "I tried the meatloaf," he said, "it was not good."

"You don't like meatloaf."

"But I know how it's supposed to taste."

Julian and Evie were in the living room, discussing their Christmas hopes with Hank Washington.

"...and a real big girl chemistry set, and a scooter, and this doll like my friend Owen has, and no clothes. But I'll probably get some clothes anyway," said Evie, making a sick face.

"Sounds rough," said Hank, smiling. "How about you, Jules?"

"Just some games for my Switch," said Julian, as if proud of his restraint. "What are you getting?"

Hank did not care to wonder. If this Christmas bore any resemblance to Christmases past it would be whatever money his mother had in her wallet at the time, or if he was very lucky a succulent purchased from a supermarket the night before. "We'll have to see what Santa brings me."

"Santa's not real," said Evie.

"Evie, hush!" said Julian.

"It's true. It doesn't even make sense. How could Santa make your Switch? Nintendo made your Switch."

"You don't know everything," said Julian firmly, an eight year-old idealist.

Back in the kitchen John was rattling a cocktail mixer and relaying a slightly lewd story to a too-jolly Mr Trevor, though it came to an abrupt end when Mary Ann arrived.

"Here we go," John said, pouring the contents of the shaker into a rocks glass, "a bit of Christmas cheer for you."

"Your brother makes a hell of a cocktail," Mr Trevor informed Mary Ann. The years had been unkind to Mr Trevor, now old and fat and unaccompanied, with red lines on his thickened nose.

"I always appreciate the enthusiasm of an expert," John said, winking, and Mr Trevor slapped him on the back and walked off.

"What are you auditioning for?" Mary Ann asked.

"I have absolutely no idea what you mean."

"You hate Mr Trevor. You used to call him Sir-Pukes-A-Lot, because he–"

"I like everybody, Mary Ann," John interrupted. "Besides, we wouldn't want any of our friends to get a bad impression of Harrow hospitality." He rinsed out the remains of his cocktail shaker and started on one for Mary Ann. "How was your trip?"

"Long."

"And where is your car, exactly?"

"You can probably take a guess."

"You always were the special one," said John.

"It's not me. Even back in LA, I'd started seeing things – you know what I mean. Things that don't belong here."

John exhaled slowly, as if released of some great tension. "Great," he said, pouring Mary Ann a martini, "that's great."

"How is that great?"

"I'm glad it's not just me," said John, "I was getting a little worried I was losing my mind."

"It's never been like this before."

"The walls are growing thin," agreed John, although with a certain mischievous grin, "be careful investigating old boudoirs."

"This is amusing?"

"I like a crisis. It keeps you sharp."

"I hear you've been using ours to your advantage."

"Word travels fast."

"When exactly did you start thinking of taking up the family business? I thought you hated it over there."

"Not hated, just saw it for what it was."

"And what's that?"

With John's face broken as it was, he could never manage a full smile or a true scowl; it was as if every feeling contained its opposite. "A game."

Something in this presumption so infuriated Mary Ann that she wanted to throw her drink into her brother's face, though she managed to restrain herself. "But whose rules? I saw one of us when I was in there."

John stopped smiling, or half-smiling, or whatever he was doing. "What do you mean, one of us?"

"I mean a Son of Adam, with eyelashes and fingernails and everything."

"There are no other humans there."

"There weren't," Mary Ann corrected. "I hope you've got everything as neatly figured out as you suppose, little brother. As for me, I'm not worried about falling through the wardrobe; I'm worried about what's going to come out of it."

Mary Ann looked worried and even John had stopped smiling when Evie appeared suddenly, tugging at his leg and peering up with John's own blue eyes.

"Uncle John, can I have some chocolate?"

"Knock yourself out," he said, handing over a box of almond bark.

With John's frustratingly excellent drink in her hand Mary Ann went and found her nephew in the living room, in enthusiastic consultation with a boy who looked vaguely familiar but whom she could not have ever met before.

He was kneeling beside the fire, breaking up embers with a poker. "Oak burns the longest," he explained, "but birch gets going easier. Best thing is to have a mix of both."

"Hi Aunt Mary Ann!" said Julian. "This is Hank. He's our next-door neighbor."

Hank closed the chain curtain on the fireplace and rose to meet her. "You're Mary Ann."

"I am," she said. His dress shirt was wrinkled, Sophia would never have allowed her children to go to someone's house without giving it a proper iron, but his muscles were taught beneath the cotton and his skin was the color of sweet coffee. "It's nice to meet you, Hank."

He took her hand with a strange sort of seriousness. "Charmed."

"Hank grows plants and he's going to show me how to shoot a three-pointer when the weather gets better," Julian explained.

"You're the one who did the arrangements," said Mary Ann. Hank smiled.

"They're beautiful," said Mary Ann. She realized that she was still holding on to his hand and let go of it quickly.

Adeline was in the kitchen, wondering why she had bothered to come, chalked it up to that universal human instinct for self-punishment, tonguing a sore tooth because it looms large in the jaw. Even under easier circumstances she had never liked the Harrow Christmas party, a display of familial unity of which she could never be a part, serving only to demonstrate the distance between her and the woman she loved.

"Freshen you up?" John was still serving his shift at the bar, a smile and a few drops of bitters and he was the most popular guy at the party.

"I'd best not," said Adeline, "I've got to drive the kids home."

"Safety first. That's my motto."

"Is it really?"

"How you been, Adeline?"

"Over the last five years?"

"Yeah."

"Peaks and valleys. I'm getting divorced."

"I think I might have heard that."

"How have you been?"

"Basically the same."

"How's work?"

"I quit," said John, "the night before I came."

"The same indeed," said Adeline.

John laughed.

Amid her duty as host Sophia had managed to find a moment of silence on a chair in the sun room, looking at the faces of her friends and family and acquaintances and thinking of who was absent; Aaron not drinking quietly in the side corner, her mother and father long gone and with them that confidence that things would turn out all right, that someone would take care of whatever it was that needed to be taken care of. There was Michael, of course, but then he was always there, his memory loyal as a shadow. The house seemed busy with ghosts that night, nor was it lost on Sophia that next year, if there was a party, another would be added to their number.

She saw Constance approach fretful from the corner of her eyes, tried not to sigh.

"Did Mary Ann tell you..."

"We talked," said Sophia.

"She says things are crossing between the borders."

"I heard."

"She says the bug are taking captives." Normally level-headed as a bomb disposal technician, there was something about her mother's equanimity that made Constance want to spoil it. "Not from their side, Mom, from ours."

This time Sophia did sigh. "I heard," she said a second time. "We'll talk about it tomorrow."

"You're pretty blasé about the end of the world."

"Everyone's world ends eventually," said Sophia.

Constance blanched but further discussion of her mother's mortality was mooted as Julian and Evie came sprinting in from the kitchen, in fight or play, it sometimes took a moment to discover and, in any case, often didn't matter, the sheer excess of energy sufficient to warrant reprimand. A sharp word from a following Adeline managed to still them, Mommy A back in her role as frustrated disciplinarian.

"You gave her chocolate?" Adeline asked.

"No," said Constance.

"She'll never sleep now."

"I didn't give her any chocolate," said Constance.

"Uncle John said it was OK," said Evie, a swirl of caramel on her cheek.

Adeline turned her eyes hard on her ex-spouse.

"Don't blame me for something my family did," said Constance.

"I try not to," said Adeline, "but sometimes it's hard. Julian, Evie, say goodnight to your mother and your grandmother and your aunt and your uncle and anyone else you feel like saying goodnight to. We're gone in five."

Protest gave way beneath Adeline's grim eyes, and the grandchildren went sullenly to offer their farewells, finding Mary Ann chatting with Hank Washington below a sprig of poisoned, crimson mistletoe.

"Goodnight, Hank," said Julian. "Goodnight, Aunt Mary Ann."

"Mommy A is making us go home," Evie huffed.

"It's time to go to bed," Julian explained obediently.

"Keep your head up, little man," said Hank.

Mary Ann noted the quality of their goodbye hugs, Julian's enthusiastic, Evie's brief and perfunctory, barely a touch, and then they were shuffled into their winter coats and mittens, an unsmiling Adeline hustling them off into the night. Most of the rest of the party were in the process of following them, venerable Mrs Dermout weighed down with leftovers, Mr Trevor still raving about John's oysters, the evening's merriment coming to an ebb.

"What's LA like?" Hank asked.

"It's warm."

Hank rolled his eyes. "That's all you got?"

"That's enough for most people. They're just asking so they can tell me they went there once to see their cousin Katherine who they had never really liked, and it's a nice enough place to visit but yadda, yadda autumnal foliage."

"Most people," Hank agreed, falling into expectant silence.

"It's beautiful," said Mary Ann. "There are hills everywhere, and they're mostly green. They're green a lot of the time, anyway. I can see mountains from my apartment, like actual, no shit mountains, with snow on top and everything. There are a thousand different kinds of flowers we don't have here, and the trees fruit in winter, I pick lemons from my neighbor's yard."

"It sounds wonderful," said Hank, eyes fixed on a verdant landscape which might as well have been a dream.

Constance came past. "Merry Christmas, Hank," she said distractedly, turning to Mary Ann. "I'm going to get started on the dishes. Would you take out the trash and come help me dry?"

"Can't wait," said Mary Ann, watching her sister stalk off. Her glass was empty. "You got any siblings, Hank?"

"No. Just me and Mom."

"That must be nice."

Hank thought for a moment of his cold, empty house. "It has its ups and down."

"Nobody to keep track of you, nobody to remind you of who you were or who you're supposed to be."

"Nobody," agreed Hank, or perhaps it was a lament.

Mary Ann took a look at the mess which awaited her, glasses and plastic cups everywhere, chairs left in all corners of the house, plates of half-eaten food rotting slowly, cold crab puffs sitting beside brown smears of remoulade.

"What kind of plants do you grow, exactly?" she asked.

John walked a riotously drunk Mr Trevor out the door, pointing him in the direction of an idling Uber even as Constance came to stand beside him.

"You got me in shit with Adeline."

"What do you mean?"

"Evie isn't allowed chocolate after eight."

"What can I tell you? It's the prerogative of an uncle to spoil their nieces. Remember when Aaron used to sneak us cake before dinner? It's tradition. And you do so love tradition!"

Sophia had, for the first time in remembered history, gone to bed early, and with John still charming out the last of the guests Constance found herself alone in the kitchen. She didn't altogether mind, priding herself as she did on her skills as a dishwasher. True, it lacked the glamour of creating the meal, a task at which Constance was a bare competent, taking after her father in this as she did in many other things – but cooking takes place with a glass of wine as accompaniment and the whole happy evening ahead, while washing dishes is a thankless task, begun as the punch turns to sugary sludge in your stomach, with no one around to applaud. Serving plates piled up on the rack, the sink water turned gray, her dish towels turned damp and grotty but still Constance fought even as her hands grew red and cracked and the hours ticked toward dawn. Finished, she still had the extraordinary if petty tenacity to wipe clean every countertop and taking out the trash – which Mary Ann, true to form, had not gotten around to emptying – before collapsing into bed and waking up in another world.

The anniversary of the coronation was an incongruous

celebration, meant to remind the Thousand People that while the March might be in chaos there was yet a Harrow on the throne. In the camps the refugees made their best attempt at merriment. Extra rations had been dispensed, and the newly arrived prosopon were staging plays in honor of the occasion, pompous melodramas filled with heroic princes and beautiful ladies and last stands which ended up, against all odds, in salvation. Below the endless fetters of the Gyved Throne the leaders of the Thousand People, those still living and at least nominally loyal to the Tower, attempted a simulacrum of their subjects' gaiety with mixed success. If superior knowledge offered a more desperate understanding of their circumstances, at least the booze was better.

"There you are," said John. He was dressed in black and silver damask, and he seemed taller than he had a few moments before.

"I was doing the dishes," said Constance.

"Do they give medals for that? Remind me."

"That's enough," said Sophia, arriving to squash the budding quarrel. Sophia had gone to sleep in the real world a sick, tired woman who had probably drunk one too many negronis, and had arisen at the top of the Tower reborn, a Queen without peer or competitor, the loving monarch of all the March. She stood high-necked and proud, the Bauble an encapsulated luminescence atop her forehead. "Remember," she added, bending down to offer Constance a kiss on her cheek, "this is for appearances."

"It always is," John said, smiling along with her.

Apart from being held in an enormous atrium and including among the revelers anthropomorphic children's toys and talking animals and creatures made of living water and many other things also it felt much the same as their Christmas Party. Sophia was her resplendent self and beside her John cut a fine contrast, the youngest Harrow returned to the March in its time of need. Already the Tower was ablaze with stories of his exploits; battles won, lands explored, improbable romances consummated. Even his scar served only to add to the mystique, evidence of some terrible and tragic misadventure. Anyway, it was difficult for most of the Thousand People to appreciate the extent of his deformity, humanity being, by common agreement, rather odd-looking.

Constance found herself relegated to a far corner with Dame Delta, drinking mulled wine and feeling envious.

"It's not the same," said Dame Delta.

"No," Constance agreed.

Dame Delta had recovered from the battle in the Proscenium, the frame of her wing hammered back into shape, the scales on her armor replaced, fresh blades added to her talons. She sipped black oil from a brass bowl and scowled at everything she saw. "Then again, there hasn't been a decent party in the Tower since Sir Reginald Fitzwillow died."

Constance smiled at the thought of the old bear, wondering what he would have made of his closest friend, grown fierce and bitter with age.

"By the Tower, that bear could put them back. I remember at one of these, before you were born, he and your father made a bet to see who could finish the most raisin mead. It took ten servants to carry him back to his quarters after."

"He lost?"

"Michael wasn't the Champion for nothing. They made them finer, in those days."

"It feels like it, sometimes."

Dame Delta tilted her mechanical eyes to where Citizen Anemometer stood clustered with Sophia and a handful of the March elite, her heavy eyelids closing halfway, claws sprouting unconsciously. "Heroes die young," she said, "and politicians live on forever."

"We're not young," said Constance sadly.

"But I doubt we'll live forever."

After some maneuvering Sophia managed to find herself

alone with Citizen Anemometer, a quick collogue amid the ongoing fete.

"My heart swells, Ambassador, to have you among us this evening."

"The very gears of my engine quicken likewise."

"I can only assume your presence means the rest of the anima have decided to join us here in the Tower?"

"Alas, there appears some confusion, for of course I am here only to offer you congratulations on the anniversary of your coronation. The Clockwork Republic remains prosperous and safe."

"And for how long, do you imagine? The Proscenium is not far from your borders."

"The anima, dear lady, are not the prosopon." An accordion-like bellows in his torso expanded, and he stretched a few inches in height. "Their misfortunes, lamentable and distressing, must nonetheless be regarded as, in some measure and degree, of their own making. The Clockwork Republic is well provisioned for any difficulty. This is not the first time the End has come."

"Never like this," said Sophia. "Never anything like this."

"A river may, after long deluge or according to the peculiarities of its tides, overflow its banks, and so in doing, wreak terrible ravage upon the unfortunates living in its catchment. And yet, no tide rises forever, and in time the flood recedes. The Clockwork Republic will withstand the coming assault, and without the grievous cost to its fortunes caused by a reckless retreat to the Tower. I daresay the Thousand Peoples have grown too used to the Harrow alleviating their difficulties. We must learn that even a parent cannot be expected to maintain their children indefinitely."

"I gather you have no issue?" Sophia asked.

"Alas, duty has forestalled the privilege."

"I thought not." Sophia looked out over the crowd to where Constance drank steadily, and John cavorted with a frowning turtle. "Had you been so blessed, you might have learned that a parent's task is never done."

John was now on hour six or seven of forced extroversion, if one counted from the first arrival at their Christmas Party, which perhaps one shouldn't, it having taken place in a different world. The mask had begun to tatter but he held to it gallantly, cosseting a margrave from the Palatinate, speaking quiet words of inspiration to a wavering widdershin, greeting the Toybox's new mayor, a googly-eyed blanket, with a mix of consolation and menace. It was a relief after so long surrounded by strangers and casual enemies and his own dear family to see an actual friend, albeit one it took John a moment to recognize, Pink having, in the years since they had last seen each other, grown ten times as large and ceased to walk upright and taken on an enormous biconic shell.

"Hello, Pink," said John.

"Your Highness," said Pink. He occupied most of one corner of the throne room, watching the festivities with heavy, thoughtful eyes.

"We're not really going to start on that, are we?"

"I could call you Will, if you'd prefer."

John smiled the way you smile when you think of something that has happened a very long time ago, even if that thing is painful, in simple wonder at the passing of the years. "John would be fine."

"I'll do my best."

"Your shell looks great," said John.

"Thanks," said Pink.

"Is that ivory?"

"I think it's more of a cream, actually."

"Cream it is, then. How are the clan?"

"Going stir crazy, stuck in the Tower for so long. The guards have been training some of the young with pikes, but it's slow going. The molluschite are not warriors."

John shrugged. "We're whatever we have to be."

Constance was very tired of being at a party. She wanted to be home in bed with a blanket wrapped up around her shoulders, and, for that matter, with Adeline beside her. In lieu of this she drank more wine.

"Refugees from the Hive report strange terrors," said Wisdom, having survived the retreat from the Proscenium though he had lost his books and had a long, thin crack through his mask. "Drones sent as slave-catchers, captives taken for unknown ends."

"Canard and calumny," said Anemometer, clicking his head sadly from side to side, "persiflage and tittle-tattle. The Hive are possessed of certain...peculiarities, but tolerance demands our sympathy towards cultural differences."

"Mass murder is a peculiarity?" Constance interrupted. "Captive sacrifice a difference in custom?"

Anemometer's various measuring instruments turned toward Constance, followed a moment later by his swiveling face plate. "I would hope that the Champion of the March would not be so swift to believe the wild rumors which pass about in these woeful times. Many are the virtues of the Thousand People, but we are quite addicted to bavardage."

"Gossip is preferable to denial."

"To foment reckless panic in these troubled times is folly."

"Who said it was reckless? The End rising, the Hive turned monstrous; a little fear might do us all some good."

"Even in these perilous times, dear sister," John said arriving suddenly, "we need have nothing to fear, so long as the Thousand People stand united. Alone, at odds, we are easy prey to our enemies. But standing together, fighting as one, there is nothing in the March or beyond which can match us." Every sentence was spoken a little louder, a little grander, and moving towards his peroration John swiveled slightly so that he was now no longer facing his sister or the nominal object of his conversation but the crowd which had come to gander. "The strength of the Harrow does not lie in the high walls of the Tower, but in the love of its subjects. Our bonds remain as tight as the day they were forged, and will remain adamant for a thousand years longer, and a thousand years again. United, we are indomitable."

The Thousand People seemed to agree, or at least their representatives erupted then in applause, the huzzah much the product of alcohol but loud and long nonetheless. Citizen Anemometer, clever enough to recognize a defeat, dipped his cup of oil and slunk away, though Constance found she could not muster his grace.

"Did you practice that in the mirror?" she asked quietly.

"Extemporaneous, but I cribbed from some movies. How'd I do?"

"I don't know how you can listen to that gasbag and not lose your temper. The sky is falling and all he can think about is his purse. How could anyone be so blind?"

John laughed and poured his sister more wine. "You think we're any better? It was sixty degrees last week, sixty degrees in December. People are idiots, doesn't matter what world they live in."

John was pulled away by a pair of faunae who needed him for some desperate consultation, and Constance found herself alone once more, eyes drawn to the network of chains ascending from her mother's seat. She found her father's link amid the enormous web, an infrangible chunk of burnished bronze, then her grandmother's, a filigreed masterwork which seemed almost too intricate to hold its weight. Constance had always found the Gyved Throne comforting, a tangible familial history offering reminder that she was not alone, only the latest in a long line of souls tasked with briefly carrying and then passing on a heavy burden. Lies, she could see now. There was nothing solid, nothing certain, she had spent her life wanting a home and a family and a crown only to see these dreams dissipate like mist come morning.

John said something funny, and the faunae broke out into

laughter. Constance watched Sophia watch him, her eyes, the blue eyes that they shared, bright and approving.

"After all those years sulking in the corner," Constance said, "who would have thought?"

"Some people don't know who they are until they get pushed to a wall."

"And some people don't wait for a crisis to be of use."

Sophia sighed. "Why don't you just say what you want to say to me?"

"I think I just said it. I've been here forever, Mom. I might not be a novelty, but I stayed."

"I know that, Constance. I appreciate that."

Constance felt flushed. She could see herself as she was acting just then and she didn't like it, an ugly, flustered woman harassing her dying mother, but somehow she couldn't stop herself. "And all this time, where was John? Or Mary Ann?"

Sophia went suddenly wide-eyed. "Where is Mary Ann?"

"Exactly," said Constance, "she's been gone forever, and now–"

"No, I'm serious. Where the hell is your sister?"


John found them beneath the patio, laughing and reeking of shag tobacco and skunk. Mary Ann shook a tangle of red hair out of her eyes. Hank Washington leaned against a post, smiling until he saw John.

"It smells like the parking lot of a Phish concert out here," said John.

Mary Ann laughed again, this time with some trace of embarrassment. "Just like old times, huh John?"

It was closer than he would have liked. Beneath the patio had always been the best place to do things you didn't want to be caught doing, John finding marijuana in ninth grade, smoking stemmy pot out of a pipe made from an old highlighter and some tinfoil, coughing his lungs out while his mother puttered around upstairs, their father dead, Constance gone to college, Mary Ann lost in isolation.

"John, this is–"

"We're acquainted," said John. "Merry Christmas, Hank."

"Merry Christmas, John."

"You want a hit?" Mary Ann asked.

"Thanks, I'm high on seasonal cheer."

Mary Ann snickered and flicked out the end of the joint.

"I'll be off, then. It was nice meeting you, Mary Ann Harrow," said Hank. The clouds had dissipated, and the moonlight played off his dark skin.

"It was nice to meet you, Hank Washington," said Mary Ann.

"John," said Hank.

"Hank," said John.

Hank crossed their backyard, hopping the small fence which separated their properties with an easy grace. The night loomed large and silent around the Harrow siblings.

"You got something you want to say?" Mary Ann asked.

"I'm collecting my thoughts."

"Will you get to it, already?"

"Can I just have a minute, Mary Ann? I'm not used to being on this end of things, I want to get it right."

"You're such an asshole."

"OK, I have it." John gave up his pensive pose and turned to face Mary Ann squarely. "What the fuck are you doing?"

"I'm just getting a little lit. When did you become this monument to sobriety?"

"That's a bit of a stretch, I've been drinking all night. But with like, Mom, or Constance, not unaccompanied minors."

"He's not that young."

"If you're arguing about their age, they're too young. You shouldn't be smoking pot with a high school student. I don't know why I even need to be telling you this. You shouldn't be doing anything with a high school student." John narrowed his eyes. "Especially not that one."

"You sound exactly like Mom right now."

"Believe me," said John, "I don't like it any more than you do."

# FIFTY-TWO

Leaving the hospital, they'd gotten caught in the busy pre-Christmas traffic, people rushing to the airport or to some desperate last-minute shopping, everything made worse with the steady, freezing rain. Sophia sat in the passenger's seat, staring out her window. Mary Ann was driving. She thought about putting something on the radio, but she wasn't sure what went best with terrible news. Maybe NPR.

"How are... things?" Sophia began.

"They're all right."

"How is Los Angeles?"

"It's nice. It's warm."

"How's work?"

"It's all right," said Mary Ann.

"And how was that boy you were seeing?"

"Jeffrey?" said Mary Ann, narrowing her eyes. "That's not really a thing anymore."

"Oh," said Sophia, with what Mary Ann took to be faint disappointment, "too bad."

"Why would you say it was too bad? Maybe he was a jerk and I'm better off without him."

"Was he?"

"That's not the point."

"I'm just making conversation, Mary Ann. You don't need to bite my head off."

Mary Ann found public radio on the dial, and they listened to a report on a drought in Zambia which was choking the veldt and had left Victoria Falls dry as a broken bone. In recent days Sophia had grown increasingly conscious of the fact that she was doing many things for the last time, or for the next to last time, or the second from last, or so on. Of course, this had always been true, time a constant if subtle thief, but she hadn't thought of it so much before. Now she was keenly aware of the weight of each passing moment, that she might never again sit beside her younger daughter, in a car, listening to bad news on the radio. It was a frustrating, stupid feeling, and pushed her to turn every conversation into a sermon.

"I just want you to be happy," Sophia said.

"I know that, Mom."

"I don't care if you have a boyfriend. I don't care if you stay single forever." This was a naked lie, of course, Sophia wanting for Mary Ann the same things she had wanted for herself, a house rich with family, grandchildren to carry on her name even if Sophia would never meet them.

"Thanks," said Mary Ann lamely. Traffic had slowed to a crawl, and they were stuck beside a late-model minivan, six seats and all filled, a smiling father and a compliant mother and a brood of freckled children and a chocolate Labrador retriever with a bandanna tied around its neck.

"Did anything ever happen with that greeting card company you were going to start? You seemed so excited about it."

Mary Ann had been extremely if briefly excited about the letter-press printing operation which she'd planned on starting with a friend, until said friend had gone to Burning Man and taken too much psilocybin and returned to the city determined to "just be, for a while, instead of doing", and Mary Ann had gone back to her freelance slog. "If it had turned into a million-dollar business, I'd have mentioned it."

"Just keep at it," said Sophia.

"Thanks."

"It'll happen."

"Yeah."

"You were always so talented," Sophia began, "so special–"

"I know, right? You'd figure something would have come from it."

"That's not what I meant."

Mary Ann laughed bitterly. "It's fine, Mom. Can we just drop it?"

They managed that for a bit, an expert on the radio informing them of the unprecedented loss of bird life in the previous year, gulps of swallows collapsing in mass graves, the surreal absence of song which was to be anticipated as the world grew inevitably hotter and more terrible. In compensation for this impending silence the family in the minivan had struck up a karaoke chorus, the leering father and servile mother and their obedient progeny caroling along in enthusiastic if muted harmony.

"I'm not though," said Mary Ann.

"What?"

"I'm not special. You and Dad always had exaggerated ideas about me. Fill a couple of sketchbooks when you're twelve and everyone thinks you're a budding Picasso."

"That's not fair," said Sophia. "You shone bright, Mary Ann. There was something about you, everyone could see it."

Which was worse, Mary Ann wondered; to lack talent, or to have betrayed the talent you had? The latter, she was pretty sure. Traffic crawled forward, the minivan keeping pace alongside, each passenger and now the dog as well barking in rhythm, mouths shuttering like chummed fish.

"Why didn't you come to the March last night?" Sophia asked.

"It didn't call me. You know how it is. The March takes who it wants."

"That might be true for the rest of us, but it isn't true for you."

They had never understood how Mary Ann was able to hijack the March's hand, to travel between the two lands independently of whatever whim determined the matter among the other Harrow. "It's not such an easy trick, Mom. It's dangerous. Anyway, I figured you'd have plenty to handle, with John and Constance jockeying for your approval."

Sophia grunted unhappily.

"Any idea which way you're leaning?" Mary Ann asked. In the van the family continued their uncanny canticle, arrangements as automated as a drum machine. The dog peered out the window with wide and ravenous eyes. "Just out of curiosity."

"Actually," Sophia said, "I always thought you would take over."

Mary Ann tore her eyes off the family in the minivan. "What?"

"I always thought, when the time came, you'd be the next Harrow."

"Bullshit. John is smarter than me."

"Smart isn't everything," said Sophia. "Your brother is looking for something to want, and right now he thinks it's the throne, but who know what he'll think tomorrow? And Constance...she isn't sure either. She just wants it because she thinks she always wanted it. Neither of them is any good alone. Maybe none of you are. But together, the three of you even out each other's edges. John's smarts, Constance's strength, and your.... well, heart, I guess."

A little blot of spittle had accumulated on Sophia's lip. Mary Ann felt disgusted staring at it, an ungracious feeling but there it was, shame at her mother's decay as much as her uncharacteristic turn towards mawkishness.

"I never wanted that," said Mary Ann.

"I know," said Sophia.

"To spend the rest of my time in the house, never leaving, never doing anything else. It wasn't for me."

"I understand that Mary Ann," said Sophia, more forcefully.

"I won't be the next link in the chain, Mom. My life in LA

might not seem like much to you, but it's *mine*. I made it, and I like it."

"Do you? You don't like your job, you don't like your boyfriend. You let life drift past rather than reaching out and taking hold of it." Sophia had wiped the saliva from her mouth and was her indomitable self once more. "You don't want to be the Harrow, fine. But for God's sake, you should be something."

Mary Ann turned back to the road. The minivan and the strange family were gone, lost amid the loosening traffic. Mary Ann got off at the next exit, driving past two fast food restaurants and a building which had once been a Blockbuster video and was now nothing, vacant and shuttered.

"Jesus, Mom," she said finally, "that was really mean."

Sophia shrugged. "I am dying."

It was a hell of a trump card. Mary Ann swallowed her response, and they finished the rest of the ride in silence.

# FIFTY-THREE

The End drew near.

The Lakelands were lost, the quetzal's mountaintop aeries had been abandoned. The endless fields of the arcimboldi were given over to rot and eternal night, the last desperate widdershin had arrived at the Tower from their distant deserts, hands and souls calloused by the thousand-mile-journey. A final flotilla had arrived from the southern oceans, caravel and drua and dhow crammed with zoeae and salt-water hydronese carrying tales of scum-tossed currents, of patches of dead sea miles in scope, of oceans silting to sediment and bone. The End drew near but then, the End was already here, festering in a wound or born abrupt from fear and despair, every refugee and for that matter even the most senior subjects of the Tower potential carriers.

Constance and Sir Szyylstyx and the Knight of the Veiled Countenance trudged up the long stairwell towards the Summer Gardens. Here in happier times the inhabitants of the Tower had promenaded amid the blossoms, pruned by arcimboldi and immigrant xerophile, a carefully manicured greensward blossoming daily. Then, like every other open space in the Tower, it had been turned to a refugee camp, displaced faunae pitching tents between the high hedges and fruit trees. Now word was that it had become something different, the End spreading rapidly, the guards forced to quarantine it off from the rest of the Tower and call in the Valiant to serve as exterminator.

They crossed over the Bridge of Sighs, ignoring the rain, and were met in the final gatehouse by a dozen members of the guard, scared souls with half-pikes and thin armor. John was there also, leaning lackadaisical within a shadow, smiling his half smile.

"What are you doing here?" Constance asked.

"I'm here for the same reason you are," said John. "The Harrow protect the March, and I am, after all, a Harrow."

"Kind of you to remember."

"Better late than never."

Constance was armored cap-a-pie. The sword-with-seven-locks was sheathed across her back, and she carried a gleaming, two-headed parashu, some minor treasure of the Harrow. John was clad only in his silhouette, but this seemed sharp edged and hungry, like a storm-tossed sea or a pack of winter wolves.

"Haven't I already demonstrated my willingness to kill for the Tower?"

"It's different when they know you're coming." Constance gestured and one of the guards started winding a side crank, the portcullis raising with a groan. "Close the door after us," she said, "but be ready with fire."

"At your command," said the guard, a saprophyte with dark eyes and a dotted pileus doing her best to look brave.

Inside the Summer Gardens were silent except for the heavy rain which muddied the earth and soaked the battered topiary and ricocheted off the stone path with a loud echo. It had been ruined even before the End had come, the desperate refugees trampling the carefully manicured lawns, eating the budding fruit, cutting down the trees for firewood, but now it seemed a wasteland. Constance led them cautiously forward, waiting for the inevitable attack. Her ax hung loose in her hands. John remained as insouciant as ever, pausing to pluck a bedraggled flower from a bush and place it behind his ear.

"Taking this real seriously, aren't you?"

"Light shines brightest in dark times."

"Can you do me a favor and not talk to me like I'm some lord you're trying to impress?"

"Isn't that the point of the Harrow? To inspire hope in our people?"

"You don't even like these people."

"I like some of them. I like Pink. Anyway, you think liking them would make you a better Queen?"

"I don't see how you can take care of people you don't care about."

"Caring is for kindergarten teachers. Leadership requires a bit more detachment."

There were lots that Constance might have said to this but she didn't have the chance, Sir Szyylstyx shouting warning and the End was on them, rats the size of teenagers, cats still larger with black eyes and pus-filled blisters erupting through their fur, a decomposing fox, a macerated badger. They came forward with talons extended and teeth gnashing but without further evidence of hate or rancor, springing up out of the darkness to offer their desperate dirge.

"Break in the chain!" screamed an End-ridden rodent, even as a sweep of Constance's axe severed its limb, black bile shooting out from the wound. "Knife in the gut!"

"Oil in the water!" roared the badger.

"Taint in the milk!" lamented the fox.

John launched clapperclaw into the mass of enemies, the sharpened edges of his penumbra slicing through the maddened faunae. Constance decapitated her rat, settling the matter and moving on to the next. Sir Szyylstyx was a whirl of motion, a dozen short spears twirling in his tentacles, and hidden beneath her hood the Knight of the Veiled Countenance managed similarly, a brooding, silent slayer.

Against them the End fought without plan or tactic, moved awkwardly and made no use of weapons, its only strength that it was everywhere and all but unkillable. A severed paw closed around Constance's greave, clambering past her knee and towards her cuisse before she crushed it and tossed it aside. A hamster, punctured by a thousand points of shadow, leaking ichor, still had life enough to toss itself against the Knight of the Veiled Countenance, who twisted aside before crushing its skill with the butt of her knobkerrie, head exploding like an overripe pomegranate.

"For the Harrow!" Constance yelled. "For the Tower!"

John offered no battle cry, springing deeper into the enemy, his defense lying in movement so rapid that the End could not follow or follow only in time to receive some sharp wound for their efforts. Constance came close in his wake, the curved blades of her parashu singing left and right, the ax not her preferred weapon but one she had attained long mastery of nonetheless. A badger half again the size of a man, muscles bulging beneath its balding fur, sprung out of a ruined rosebush and swung a blow at Constance, lost half a hand for his temerity but still struck hard enough to dent her breastplate and send her flying past where Sir Szyylstyx remained locked in mortal combat with a stoat.

"Canker on the leaf!" it howled. "Grit in the gears!"

Constance was up again in an instant, but it was too late, the badger bearing down on her, hands raised above its head – stopping, suddenly, caught in a tight web of shadows, a thousand tendrils of darkness wrapping around its body, even as it continued to press forward, singing its coronach.

"Bend in the steel! Worms in the fruit!"

"I hate this song," John said, then tensed his hands. The shadow turned razor-edged, contracting through flesh and bone, segmenting the badger's body into chunks of red meat though each bit retrained some grim mobility, sputtering like corn kernels on a skillet.

Sir Szyylstyx put one of his spears through the stoat's skull, out its throat and into the muck below. The Knight of the Veiled Countenance finished off the last of the rats beneath her thick-shod boots. They waited a while longer, but the End knew nothing of feigned retreat, coming forward in a mad rush until there were none left to fight. When Constance was sure it was over, she called for their fire-bearers, and while her back was turned John carefully picked up the badger's paw, wrapping it in a band of shadow and stuffing it into his cloak.

"Well fought," said Constance, to her Valiant and perhaps also to John. Sir Szyylstyx had a cut along his arm which would need to be branded with hot iron but other than that they had all survived unscathed. As the guards and the Knight of the Veiled Countenance doused the End-poisoned corpses with lamp oil and tried to coax them aflame, John and Constance stood over the still wriggling stoat, a length of metal through its windpipe and yet it begged for help.

"Damn whatever evil brought this upon us," said Constance.

John laughed bitterly.

"Something funny?"

"Like you said, Constance, we don't have an audience."

"What the hell is that supposed to mean?"

John looked at her cross-eyed. "You really don't know?"

"What?"

"Mom never told you?"

"Are you going to tell me what you're talking about, or I'm going to smack that smirk off your face?"

But it was already gone, replaced with uncharacteristic worry. "It's not my place – but the End isn't what you think, Constance, and we aren't either."

"I told you to knock it off with that enigmatic shit."

"Maybe you're better off not asking questions you don't really want the answer to. Just keep pretending this is a fairy tale and leave the hard decisions to the adults."

Constance was angry. She had been angry a lot lately, ever since John had gotten home, maybe long before. "What the hell would you know about the March? You've been back a week."

"And you never left." John looked wan in the hard rain, hair

matted against the top of his scar. "This world, our world…
it's all the same shit. There's nothing magic about the March
except that it's magic. It's not a better place, or a fairer one. The
strong eat, the weak get eaten. Over here we're at the top of
the heap," John started towards the gatehouse, leaving the rest
of them to deal with the clean up, offering one last sentence
as a parting shot, "and I aim to keep it that way, whatever it
takes."

# FIFTY-FOUR

Mary Ann did not really like kids. It was her terrible secret; one of them, anyway. By thirty-three she had gone to who knew how many baby showers and gender reveal parties, toddled living lumps of flush on her knee, watched women who had once backpacked through Asia and swallowed ecstasy in shady nightclubs pass into content middle-age, adopt a permanent pose of faint superiority as if possessed of some sterling secret they would be delighted to share, if only Mary Ann would listen.

Evie was all right, though, as uncannily self-sufficient as her uncle John. And it was impossible not to warm to Julian, an irrepressible bundle of optimistic energy, fascinated by every new development however banal or mundane. Early evening and they had just come back from the park, one of the half-dozen daily extracurriculars necessary to exhaust the children sufficient for slumber. They sat on the porch while John cooked dinner, Mary Ann maintaining a fatigued conversation.

"Do you surf?" Julian asked.

"No," said Mary Ann, "it's really, really hard. Also, I don't live by the ocean."

"I thought LA was by the ocean?"

"It is, but it's also by the mountains. It's big. It's a strange place."

"Oh," said Julian, fitting this information into the constantly expanding repository which made up his young mind. "Are you married?"

"Nope."

"Do you have a boyfriend?" asked Evie.

"I don't."

"Do you have a girlfriend?" asked Julian. "Some women love other women, you know."

"I was aware," said Mary Ann, "and no, I don't have a girlfriend either."

"Were you ever in love?" asked Evie.

"Once."

"What happened to him?"

"He died," said Mary Ann.

Julian's knowledge of death mostly came from Disney movies, beloved father figures fading just before the midway point. Evie, younger and smarter, thought of it like turning off a light switch, their goldfish in its bowl one evening and gone the next, Mommy C saying something about going back to the ocean, but Mommy C said lots of things.

"I'm sorry," said Julian.

"That's all right. It was a long time ago. I barely even think about it," Mary Ann lied.

Hank Washington dropped the trash in its bin and came over to the porch.

"Hank!" said Julian enthusiastically. Their next-door neighbor had rapidly risen to a prime position as the world's coolest person, though he faced stiff competition from John, who was very good at cooking, and Mary Ann, who lived in Hollywood and presumably knew all sorts of actors, Julian had forgotten to ask.

"Hey there, little man."

Evie busied herself in a coloring book and was no longer paying attention.

"How are you, Hank?" It occurred to Mary Ann that she was wearing her sister's saggy sweatpants and also that this shouldn't bother her.

"I'm doing all right. How's being home?"

"Strange," admitted Mary Ann. "Things look different after so long away."

"Smaller?"

"Kinda. But then again, there are a lot of things sized for children."

"What was it like, growing up here?"

"What do you mean?"

"The green lawn, the white picket fence. All that suburban Americana."

"You make it sound like a Spielberg movie," said Mary Ann.

"Shooting hoops with your siblings while Dad barbecues in the back yard."

"Dad did *not* cook," Mary Ann said. "He cleaned, but he didn't cook."

"Not even hamburgers?"

"Not even cereal."

"Mom, then, calling you all in for dinner, the table set, everyone in their spot."

"Do we say grace in this fantasy?"

"No," said Hank, smiling, "you're strictly secular. Except for Christmas."

"We stole Christmas from the Christians."

"I think I heard about that on the news."

Mary Ann laughed but he wasn't off entirely. Her earliest memories brimmed with joy, long Saturday afternoons exploring the woods behind their house, Constance strutting forward boldly, John following them on toddling legs; dim recollections of her grandfather who liked to embarrass them by singing in the supermarket, her grandmother so wise and generous as to seem almost saintly. Her mother and father had been the handsomest, smartest, best parents on the block, in the school, across the entire world, and she their proud seed. Then came the inevitable turn, Aaron disappearing and Joan dying and her mother retreating ever so slightly, quieter and crueler, Mary Ann bursting unceremoniously into adolescence, a rebellious and unruly child even before her father had died and everything had gone to shit. "I don't know, Hank. Things seem better from further off. It's like the Russian said – 'Every happy family is the same, but all unhappy families are unhappy in their own way.' And who's happy, really?"

"Yes," Hank agreed, his face long and handsome, "who?"

Hank was already heading home by the time John came outside to fetch the children for dinner, sparing them the trouble of another *tete-a-tete*.

"What did he want?" John asked. "Rake the yard? Clean the pool?"

"We don't have a pool," said Mary Ann.

"The two of you could go back and make sure."

"What's the matter, John? Jealous? Racist?"

"Are those my only options?"

"I'll hear a third."

"I'm concerned for you, Mary Ann. This isn't the people's republic of Cali. I think they still have laws on the books about deflowering a minor."

"You're an asshole."

"And you always had a bad instinct for men."

Mary Ann scowled. "You really are an asshole, John."

But all throughout the rest of the evening, over dinner and during Julian and Evie's bath time and amid passive-aggressive conversation with her elder sister, Mary Ann could still see his dark brown eyes.

# FIFTY-FIVE

By the time they got to the plane the flight attendants were getting ready to lock the doors and there weren't enough free seats for the whole family to sit together and so Daniel and David had to take an aisle and middle seat way in the back beside a man with a heavy roll of gauze wrapped around his forehead.

"Shotgun," said David.

"Shotgun doesn't work in a plane," said Daniel.

"Shotgun works everywhere," said David, "anyway, I'm older."

By three critical years, Daniel basically still a child who enjoyed action figures and occasionally wept in public, while David was a congealed mass of testosterone, all sweat and papule and indiscriminate body hair. A passing flight attendant offered them both a disapproving glance and Daniel shuffled subjugate into the center seat, after which David settled victorious in 54C, leaning his legs luxuriously into the aisle and taking out his portable video game system.

"Mom said I got to play for the first half of the flight," Daniel reminded him.

"I'm in the middle of a game."

"You can save it."

But David ignored him. Unwilling to accept this second reversal Daniel made a bold but ill-considered effort at appropriation, and David's response jostled him into the man with the bandaged head.

"You're such a jerk!" said Daniel.

"Why don't you cry about it, you little baby."

Daniel wanted to very much then, for no one feels as keenly the vast weight of injustice as a younger brother, but he knew it would only make things worse, and instead he took a dog-eared paperback out from his book bag. David played his video game, the flight attendants read their unnecessary safety protocols, and the 747 began its ascent out of LAX. The man with the bandaged forehead found a Christmas movie on his in-flight entertainment system.

By the time they had reached cruising altitude Daniel was deeply engrossed in *The Dragon Lords of Rigus,* following along with a rag-tag band of adventurers on a desperate quest to save their world from evil.

David's game was over or at least he had grown bored by it, even the most engaging electronic entertainment less fun that tormenting a sibling. "How many times are you going to read that?"

"Leave me alone."

"You know you're too old for it."

"No, I'm not. Adults read them too."

"Yeah, loser adults. Nerds."

"Can't you just watch something on the TV?"

"They're all the same."

"They're not all the same."

"They are all the same. Magic swords and princes and all that stupid shit." David burped loudly, a function for which he had developed impressive skill.

"Be quiet," hissed the man with the bandaged forehead, turning slowly to face them. A trickle of black blood had seeped out the edge of his bandage and streaked slowly towards his nose.

"What?" asked David.

It wasn't blood, Daniel could see that now, it was something like a slug or an inchworm and it crawled down the man's face, passing through the philtrum and pausing an instant to stare at them, the slug or the inchworm or whatever it was and the man also, two sets of veiny-red eyes. Then it crawled over the man's pink lips and disappeared into the back of his throat. "I said if you don't shut the fuck up, I'm going to snap your little brother's neck and make you watch."

When the flight attendant came by to take their drink orders a few moments later she found two boys staring pale-faced at the seats in front of them. "Anyone want anything to drink?" she asked.

"No Ma'am," said Daniel.

"No Ma'am," said David.

The man with the bandaged head had gone back to watching his Christmas movie and didn't want anything either.

# FIFTY-SIX

Below the gibbous moon and its attendant stars a shadow crept along the road, faster than a person could sprint or a yearling gallop or an owl manage even in its swiftest flight, moving in moments through rolling greenery and into the first foothills of the Low Mountains and towards the Hive itself, coming to rest finally on a narrow ledge high above the entrance as a thin man, dressed all in black. Mary Ann had been vague about her misadventures among the oothecan because she was not exactly sure what she had seen or because it was too terrible to allow clear description, and so John found himself unprepared for what lay below. But then he would have been unprepared irrespective, like the Soviets marching into Auschwitz, hardened killers left horror-struck and trembling.

The walls were mottled black and nearly as high as the battlements surrounding the Tower and dozens of feet thick and screaming, not in unison but piecemeal, like a xylophone struck by unseen hands, moans and shrieks and miserable pleas for mercy which would never arrive. The agony was like a physical force and even far distant John could feel its press, a bubble of energy with which the oothecan hoped to stave off the End, a work of flesh-magic of unprecedented scope and scale. Vast already and yet still it grew, the drones working day and night to expand it, without rest, until they dropped dead from exhaustion, the Hive caring no more for any individual specimen of its species than it did its captives. John could have hurried on, but he did not, forcing himself to gaze upon the

316

immense atrocity, one different in particularity but not in kind from any number that had marred his own realm, and supposing it some part of his duty as a Harrow and even as a human to bear witness to evil even if he could not end it.

But he did not tarry long, a gust of wind and he was night once more, slinking into the mouth of the hive, entering subsumed in the guttering shadows cast by the oothecan's torches, shifting silently over the heads of the knights which thronged the crooked passageways. Wary but not frantic, the soldiers and their drone attendants went about their business with brisk efficiency, despite the imminent arrival of the End and the horrifying, almost certainly useless measures they had taken to defend against it. As a shadow John passed an armory filled with pikes and crossbow bolts, then through a long passageway above a line of prisoners being taken up to join the walls, retracing false starts, wandering through the labyrinth until he came finally to a gigantic cavern deep below the earth.

Vats stretched throughout the room, tanks bubbling with the serpentine larvae of the oothecan, ready to be quickened by a few drops of the Queen's royal jelly. Knights busied about, making sure the breeding conditions remained correct, the work too important to be trusted to a drone. Curled high above along the chains of a hanging light, John waited until the room was momentarily empty, the attendants off on an errand. Then he was human once more, standing beside the breeding vats, staring for a moment at the larvae, restless in their torpor, hideous and innocent. From the pocket of night which surrounded him John pulled a shadowy bubble, the top dissipating to reveal the paw of the End-ridden badger which he had stolen days earlier, rotted with verruca, bloodless but still wriggling.

There was no dramatic moment of consideration, worried as John was that the attendant would return and having already decided upon his course of action. Careful to avoid its clasping, pointed nails, John tossed the hand into the vat of larvae. It lashed out as soon as it touched flesh, still motivated by some dim, menacing sentience, the End indefatigable in its efforts toward annihilation. John waited a moment longer, watching as it infected the last generation of oothecan, the poison spreading exponentially through the tanks, one larvae lashing out against the next. The vats began to bubble, to roil, the wormlike creatures maddened, set to continue their rapid expansion throughout the Hive, poisoning the attendant and the drones and the knights themselves and finally their queen, the oothecan helpless behind its wall of captives. John flickered away even as the insects burst through their tanks to wreak a terrible suicide on its haughty species, the Hive's last night an awful one, the end come early.

# FIFTY-SEVEN

Julian could tell there was something wrong as soon as he sat down at the dinner table. His mother was clipped and cruel, choking down Uncle John's roast even though it was really very good, and Julian didn't even like chicken. The chef himself sat with a deliberate if isolated merriness at one corner of the table, passing tabs of butter and boats of gravy, occasionally making unsuccessful attempts at conversation. Grandma looked wan and Aunt Mary Ann distracted, and outside a rising storm battered itself against their house.

"Mommy, is it too late to add something to my Christmas list?" Evie asked.

"Yes," said Constance, "Santa already started loading his sleigh."

"There is no Santa," said Evie.

"Santa or no Santa, the list has been finalized. Now eat your green beans."

"I don't like them," said Evie, "green beans taste weird."

"These are delicious green beans," said Constance, though her plate remained nearly as pristine as her daughters, "they're drowning in butter."

"That's all right, kid," said John, smiling, "I can fix you up a sandwich if you'd rather have that."

"She'll eat the dinner prepared for her."

"All right," said Aunt Mary Ann, turning to address the children, "why don't the two of you go into the TV room and watch something?"

319

"Like what?"

"I dunno, that cartoon show Evie loves where the dogs operate heavy machinery."

"I hate that show," said Julian.

"Another show then," said Mary Ann. "When I was your age, it was not this difficult to get me in front of the television."

And indeed, the children's reticence proved short lived, Julian and Evie slipping away from the table to occupy themselves with that device to which modernity has offloaded most of its of child-rearing.

John sopped up a bit of bread in chicken juice, chewed and swallowed gamely. "It must be this intangible bond between siblings, but I get the sense you're angry."

"You're a monster," said Constance.

"Let's not exaggerate. The Terminix guys do it all the time."

"The entire Hive given over to the End. What were you thinking?"

"They would have been overrun anyway," said John, "however many sacrifices they stuffed into their wall. They were a lost cause. The rest of the March, however, might learn from their misfortune. They know now that the fiercest among them could not last against the End. They know we're their only hope, however desperate that hope might me."

"And if they ever found out that you destroyed the Hive?"

"Who's going to tell them? You? Mom? Mary Ann?"

"It wasn't your decision to make." Constance very much wanted another beer and so she sat resolutely at the table. "You aren't the Harrow."

"No, I'm not, Mom is, and I notice she's been strangely silent. Feeling OK there, Mom? Want to weigh in on anything?"

Sophia sighed. "It's done. There's no point in lamenting it."

"That's all you've got to say?" Constance said, shocked. "Your son commits genocide, and that's all you've got to say?"

"Not like it's the first time. Remind me, what happened to

the verdurite? Are they still up north, arranging flowers and hugging trees or whatever?"

"The verdurite marched against us."

"Well, Dad did kill their king. It's been a while since I caught up on my just war theory, but I think that's a *casus belli*."

Mary Ann winced.

"Do you have anything to say?" John asked. "I mean, getting one back for my big sister and whatnot?"

"Leave me out of this," said Mary Ann.

"You're a Harrow," said Constance, "you're part of it."

"I didn't have a choice in that," said Mary Ann, getting up from the table to look in on the kids.

The TV was on, but they weren't in front of it, standing by the window watching frigid tufts of white slick against the roof and onto their patio.

"It's snowing!" said Evie.

"That's not snow," said Mary Ann, "it's freezing rain."

"What's the difference?"

"Snow is fun, freezing rain just kind of sucks. You can't sled in it, and they never cancel school because of it, but it still causes a lot of accidents. Also, it's colder than snow."

"How can it be colder than snow?"

"I don't know," Mary Ann admitted, "it just is."

"Why are Mommy and Uncle John fighting?" asked Evie.

Because Constance was resentful and John reckless. Because despite coming from the same womb, being raised in the same household, eating the same foods, hearing the same stories, they were as different as any two people could ever be. "They're not fighting, they're having a debate."

"It sounds like a fight to me," said Evie.

Back in the kitchen Constance had broken her commitment and gotten another bottle of beer. "The Hive going mad is no excuse for you doing the same."

"The Hive didn't go mad. The Hive did what they had to do. I did the same. You still think we're kids, playing make believe with Mommy and Daddy around to swoop in if anything goes wrong. You've seen the things I have. Walls slipping. Rents in the veil. It's the end of days here, chivalry's a luxury we can't afford."

"It's when you can't afford it that it matters most."

John groaned. "It's just adults in here, you can spare the sanctimony."

"You think I'm joking?"

"I think everyone's got a line."

"I'd die before I'd do what you did."

"How about your kids? Throw them under the guillotine likewise?"

Constance's eyes narrowed fiercely. "Don't talk about my fucking kids."

"See? Everybody's got a line."

"Fuck you," said Constance. "You don't give a shit about Julian and Evie. You don't give a shit about me and Mom and Mary Ann either, for that matter. You never gave a shit about anyone in your whole selfish, stupid life."

It was a terribly mean thing to say, and in fact Constance was not even really sure that she meant it, John sneering and set to respond in kind when the house went suddenly dark.

Evie screamed from the TV room.

"It's fine, it's fine," Mary Ann promised. "The storm knocked the power out. It's fine."

Constance appeared in the doorway. "Everything all right in here?"

"It's just the storm," Evie informed her didactically, "it knocked the power out."

"Glad you're on top of it," said Constance. "I'm going to go check on the circuit breakers. Mary Ann, can you keep an eye on the kids?"

"We'll be fine," Mary Ann promised.

There were candles everywhere, part of the holiday décor, but there were no lighters and John stubbed his toe trying to find one in the hallway cabinet, cursing unmanfully just as his frowning mother arrived.

"You should lay off your sister," said Sophia.

"Are you going to tell her that?"

"Yes. But I'm telling you first because you're meaner than she is."

"That's true," John agreed, "I am. It's part of why you should give me the throne."

"Shouldn't you wait until I'm dead before you start bickering over the inheritance?"

"I got dibs on the dinette set, I already told Constance and Mary Ann."

"It'll go great in your studio."

"Seriously, Mom, what's the problem? You know I'm the only choice. Is it that you just don't want to hurt Constance's feelings?" John smiled his nasty smile. "Such rank sentimentality ill befits a monarch."

"You sound like you've been reading CliffsNotes of *The Prince*."

"Who needs *The Prince* when your mom is the Queen? The Harrow do what's required of them, whatever that is. You taught me that. The verdurite, Uncle Aaron…"

It was too dark to see much but John could tell Sophia was scowling. "You're just pissing everyone off tonight, huh?"

"It seems the time for it, what with the weather and everything."

"All right, then. It's got nothing to do with Constance. I don't think you can handle it."

"No?"

"I don't think you're strong enough."

"I took care of the bugs," said John, "and without dragging you or Constance into it."

"But your sister was right, you didn't really care about the Hive, and so it didn't take anything for you to destroy it. I loved Aaron. I still love Aaron. I dream of my little brother more nights than I can count. Sometimes I'll be standing in the yard or playing with the kids, and I'll have to go inside and sit down in the bathroom because I can't stand to think about him gone. I carry what I did to him with me every morning and afternoon and evening of my life, for the last twenty years." Sophia narrowed her blue eyes, the same blue eyes as her mother and her son and her granddaughter, though harder than any of them. "And I'd do it again, if I had to, without hesitation. Don't compare that to kicking over an ant's nest."

Sophia left her son to simmer and headed to the basement, eschewing the aid of her dimmed flashlight, sixty-four years in the house and she knew it by rote instinct though experience offered no help when she nearly ran into Constance coming back from a failed expedition with the breakers.

"We need to talk," said Constance.

"You've been doing a lot of talking tonight, I'd have thought you'd be tired of it by now."

"What's the End?"

Sophia had the discomfiting memory of Aaron on the porch, thin and bedraggled and asking nearly the same question. "It's complicated."

"John knows, but I don't?"

"How does John know?"

"Who knows how John knows anything?"

"It's a secret."

"I'm your fucking heir, I deserve to know."

Sophia didn't say anything.

"I *am* your heir, right Mom?"

"This is not the time for this conversation."

"Jesus," said Constance. Her legs felt wobbly, and she was glad it was too dark for her mother to see her face. She very much regretting her last beer. "I've done everything," she said, making sure not to slur her words, "everything."

"Constance, it's been a long day, and you've been drinking."

"I stayed. They didn't. I sacrificed, Mom. The things I've

sacrificed for the March, for you… I gave up Adeline! I gave up my family."

"I never told you to do that."

"You wouldn't let her in! Grandpa let Dad in. What was so wrong with Adeline?"

In fact, Sophia couldn't really say, Adeline a bit snippy and cold and had her own ways, ways that were not the Harrow's, traditions she could never understand, customs she would never accept. If the other kids had brought anyone home perhaps Sophia would have managed better, but they hadn't, and so Adeline was left to bear the brunt of Sophia's scorn. "I'm sorry if I made things harder between you and Adeline. I truly, truly am. I'm sorry about a lot of things in my life, and that's high among them."

"That's it? You're sorry?"

"What else do you want?"

"I want what's mine!" Constance shouted, her voice cracking. "When Dad died, and the whole north was up in chaos, and we rode against the verdurite, I was there. And all those years since, the two of us alone, trying to keep the March from falling apart – I was there, Mom, I stayed. And after all that, after everything, he just gets to show up and take it?" Constance discovered she was crying. "I washed every dish after the party, Mom. Every fucking dish."

Sophia sighed and set the flashlight on the table and held her eldest daughter, feeling her breath come stuttering up from her chest and into her broad shoulders, remembering the countless thousands of times she had done the same, when Constance was a child with a scraped knee, when she was a forlorn adolescent, at the funeral after Michael had died, the two of them forming a living *pieta*.

"Your son can't draw," Sophia said finally.

"Excuse me?"

"Julian. He's a terrible artist."

Constance sniffled. "He's eight."

"And he's bad at drawing, even for an eight year-old. He'll never be any good at drawing. That doesn't mean you love him less, but it might mean you wouldn't buy him colored pencils for Christmas."

"What are you saying? I'm bad at being the Harrow?"

"It means you are who you are, Constance."

The bell rang throughout the house. Back in the TV room Evie screamed and this time Julian did too.

"It's OK," said Mary Ann, "I'm sure it's fine." Although she was not at all sure this was the case, hurrying to the door and checking through the keyhole before opening. "Hank?"

He stood on the stoop in a slicked down rain jacket, droplets of ice melting on his shaved head. "Sorry to disturb," he said, "our lights went out, and I saw yours did too, and I wanted to come by and make sure everyone was OK."

"We're fine!" said Julian, who had followed his aunt to the doorway, "we're lighting candles!"

"Candles are cool," Hank agreed.

"That's so lovely, Hank," said Mary Ann, "but actually, I think everything is OK here."

John came to the door then, saw Hank and sighed. "If it isn't the good Samaritan. Shouldn't you be looking after your Ma, in these times of woe and worry?"

Hank's mother was already asleep on the couch, a tab of Xanax and a bottle of red and she'd wake up unaware there had ever been a storm. "She's OK."

"That's good to hear, and we sure do appreciate you coming by, but we're pretty well-provisioned at the moment, and if anything happens there are several able-bodied adults around to handle it."

Mary Ann walked Hank back out onto the porch and closed the door.

"Don't worry about John," she said, "it's been kind of a long day."

But Hank didn't seem to be listening, uncharacteristically fretful. "I need to talk to you."

It had been Mary Ann's experience that this sort of preamble very rarely preceded anything positive. "All right."

But he didn't start, not for a long time, the two of them shivering beneath the awning as the freezing rain fell against their lawn and their driveway and the neighborhood beyond. Mary Ann was thinking that she wished she was wearing a sweater, and also of Hank's scent, sweet and subtle and huddled close beside her.

"Did you ever feel like...like you were born in the wrong place?" he began. "Not place like, place, but place like...like where you are in life."

"Oh yeah," said Mary Ann, "all the time."

"Like there was something else that you were supposed to be?"

"It's part of being a teenager. Actually, it's part of life all the time, but you don't talk about it as much when you stop being a teenager."

"I have these dreams, sometimes..."

"Dreams?"

"Since I was a little kid. Of trees," said Hank, continuing forward as if having gathered strength from this admission, "an endless forest of trees. Trees the names of which I don't know because we don't have names for them. Trees which stretch up forever."

Mary Ann could feel a buzzing in her fingertips, and in the ends of her hair, which, being nerveless dead skin was impossible. Then again, lots of things are impossible. "I think you should go home now, Hank."

"You're in them. We're there together, beneath the trees. Sometimes we..." he flushed and fell silent.

"That's flattering," said Mary Ann, "and you're a really special person, Hank, but I'm like twice your age."

"You don't understand. You've always been in them. You've

been in them before we ever met. For as long as I can remember, you've been there. Your hair. Your eyes. Your face." He reached out to touch her, and despite herself Mary Ann did not flinch back, or brush away his hand, leaning instead into his palm, warm and rough from long years of gardening. Her heart beat madly in her chest, that same strange sense of energy flooding from her torso into her extremities. "I think we were meant to meet. I think, maybe, we met already."

Headlights came up the driveway throwing the two of them into bright relief, Mary Ann caught in her moment of shame. Hank brought his hand away and held it up to his eyes, squinting as the car came to a stop in front of them.

"Expecting someone?" he asked.

Jeffrey stepped out of his rental car and into the frigid evening. He wore a wife-beater and seemed indifferent to the weather. Mary Ann felt like the one time she had taken Special K at a party in Venice Beach, a thunderous current passing through her body combined with a growing need to vomit.

"Who the hell is this?" asked Jeffrey.

"What are you doing here?" Mary Ann asked, trying to sound brave.

"Didn't even take you a week."

"You need to leave," said Mary Ann, "or I'm going to call the police."

But this threat held no weight for Jeffrey who walked through the rain and up onto the porch. The wound Mary Ann had made days earlier had grown worse, spreading down the length of his face, the flesh pocked, the veins thick and dark. "I didn't know you had a taste for jailbait." He was taller than Hank, a man standing over a boy. Mary Ann felt frightened and ashamed, of Jeffrey seeing Hank, of Hank seeing Jeffrey, of having warmed to the touch of a child some fifteen years her junior. "You faithless fucking cunt."

"Watch what you say," said Hank, stepping in between them, Mary Ann having the strangest sense of *deja vu*.

"Just can't keep your legs closed, is that it?" He was still staring at Mary Ann when his fist lashed out to catch Hank below the chin, striking with some unnatural force and sending the boy flying.

Mary Ann gasped, and Hank groaned and Jeffrey drew closer, eyes atramentous, hands filled with terrible strength. "I love you so much," he said. "Why won't you do what I fucking tell you?"

The front door opened and Julian and Evie, made mischievous by the excitement of the evening, slipped outside to investigate.

"Go back inside!" Hank yelled from where he lay on the ground.

It spread through Mary Ann's joints and her chest and the beat of her heart, her whole body cocked and loaded, and as Jeffrey let go of her and walked towards her nephew and niece who she did not really know but who were all the same *hers*, heirs to her blood and her name and her story she struck. Energy flowed from Mary Ann, severing an ink black aperture into existence just a little ways off from where she had intended, Julian and Evie and Hank Washington disappearing inside it. Mary Ann screamed and even Jeffrey seemed shocked, stumbling back down the porch and towards his car. The portal pulsed and shuddered and Constance appeared in the doorway, taking in the situation and then without a stutter in her movement or a moment's hesitation diving after her children. With her elder sister as example Mary Ann had no choice but to follow, the door between worlds closing even as she passed through.

# FIFTY-EIGHT

John laughed.

"What?" asked Sophia.

"I was thinking I know what you felt like," said John, "that time when I ran away."

But Sophia didn't smile. They were in the living room, on separate couches. The lights were still out, a single, sweetly-scented candle the only source of illumination. Sophia sat in silence. John was fidgety and distracted. It was not that he did not care, it was that there was so much to think about – how they would manage in the Tower, who would take charge of the Valiant, if there was some way to send his siblings aid – and all of it better than being afraid.

"They're together, at least," said Sophia, "that's something."

"That's something," John agreed.

Sophia felt a sense of despair which was alien to her, which she had not felt upon the death of her mother or the death of her husband or the news of her own impending demise, a swell of emptiness which leaked into every corner of her mind, which choked off all thought or feeling. She was, for the first time in her long life, utterly lost. "What do we do?" she asked. "What do we do?"

If John was not stronger than his mother, and indeed he was not, still he had closer experience with that absurd hopelessness which mocks all human effort and which can only be greeted with bitter humor. And so, he laughed again. "I would think the answer was obvious. We call up reinforcements."

# FIFTY-NINE

The first thing Constance had noticed upon arriving in the March was that she was still herself, that is to say the Constance she was in a suburb outside of Baltimore, Maryland, a square-shouldered, slightly plump woman who kept herself in good but not fabulous shape. She was not Constance of the March, Constance the Champion, densely muscled, reflexes honed to a razor's edge, expert with a dozen different weapons and her fists and knees besides. Her sweatshirt and jeans were muddied after long hours of travel and bending to check the track she was dizzy from the beer she'd drank at dinner.

"You sure we're going the right way?" Mary Ann asked.

"I can still read a trail. An adult, or near an adult, and two children. See? You can still the imprint from Evie's soles."

It was the most they had spoken since coming to the March, transitioning into a broad daylight amid a dry and ruined forest. In the real world only a few seconds had elapsed between the children disappearing and Constance and Mary Ann's pursuit but here that had been stretched out into hours, days maybe, it was impossible to say. They had followed the trail through to the afternoon and the sun now hung merciless in the sky, leering unforgiving on the remains of the ravaged forest. They had no water. There seemed to be no water anywhere, the trees desiccated and hollow where they had not been severed to a stump. Brittle branches covered the ground and cracked with every other step, left Mary Ann with the uncomfortable impression of walking through an endless bone yard or over the cracking carapaces of dead locusts.

"Where are we?" she asked.

"What do you mean?" Constance asked crossly. "We're in the March."

"I know we're in the fucking March, I just don't know where in the March we are. I never saw anywhere that looked like this."

A cruel smile spread across Constance's face. "Yes, you have."

Mary Ann looked about carefully, amid a growing sense of dread. "It couldn't be."

"What did you think happened, after the Heartwood? Did you think that wouldn't have repercussions?"

"I didn't know anything about this."

"Of course you didn't, you didn't have to. You went crazy, and then you never came back."

"I was sixteen! I spent a month in a padded cell and when I came out Dad was dead and everyone hated me."

"I was eighteen," Constance responded, "and I didn't have the luxury of insanity to hide behind. I took up Dad's sword and rode North. The verdurite were maddened by what had happened, warring on whomever they could find – the petrousian, the Hive, it didn't matter. We had to ruin the forest, bit by bit, chopping down the trees and leaving the wood to rot. They fought – all of them, you remember how they were, old men and young children with bone spears. Finally, we had the weather-witches bake them out, months and months with nothing but the hot sun above, until the woods were dry as kindling. Then we struck a fuse." Constance waved vaguely at the destruction she had wrought, so complete and so thorough that half a generation had failed to repair it. "The Matchbox War, they call it now. You think because you were too much of a coward to come back, things stopped? It just left us to clean up your mess."

They walked for a long time in silence. Mary Ann thought about the Kingdom of the Thorned Rose as it had been, as it remained potent if vague in her memory, the endless shade, the flowered boughs, the pool beside which she and Thistle had lain the day she had fed him grapes. She had never thought to revisit it, but the knowledge of its existence was at least some comfort. To see it ruined was to have even that torn from her, a shameful, hideous sadness, and rather than suffer it longer Mary Ann turned to Constance and sneered.

"You should thank me."

"You want to try that again?"

"You want to be honest, Constance? Let's be honest. You were thrilled when I wouldn't come back, it left you the starring role as savior. Mommy's little dearest, and all the attention you always wanted."

"Fuck you."

"It's like with the dishes, you pretend it's some terrible sacrifice you're making but it's just so you can feel superior. You liked being at home. You liked knowing who you were. You liked having your path laid out for you, never needing to wonder, never needing to struggle. You aren't angry that I ran away, you're jealous."

"Jealous?"

"You did everything they told you, and you're coming to realize the pat on the back wasn't worth the trouble."

"Mom needed me," said Constance, "the March needed me."

"And Adeline? And your kids?"

Constance's body was weak and stupid but still she felt pretty confident that she could beat the shit out of her younger sister if the situation called for it, which it seemed it well might. "Watch your mouth."

"You can wag your finger at me all you want, but at least I went for what I wanted."

"This was what you wanted?" Constance asked, nodding

at the dead forest, the graveyard of their father and many thousands of others, lost in the conflagration that flared from the ruins of Mary Ann's love.

"I wanted him," said Mary Ann. "I'm not ashamed of that. I loved him, and I was willing to sacrifice for that. You were too chickenshit to make a life with Adeline, not if it meant having to leave Mom. So, you blamed me and John for breaking free. Call me a coward, if you want – but I'm twice the woman you are."

Then there was a *thwack* and Constance screamed and bent double, a short stretch of fletched bone jutting out from below her knee. Mary Ann took one look at her sister and then went sprinting into the forest, pursued but not caught by a second arrow which missed her by a hairsbreadth even as she dodged into the rotting husk of trees.

"Pity," said the verdurite, coming out from cover, "but then, who would expect loyalty from one of your kind?"

In the park where Constance took Julian to play baseball there was a lover's tree, scarred oak attesting to generations of affairs forgotten or never forgotten by its inscribers. His skin looked like that, except that the symbols were not of love but hate, savage things, primitive in execution, like prison tattoos. He laid his bow on the ground and pulled a bone knife from the leather sheath on his chest, his only article of clothing, chest bared to the sun, member dangling naked between his legs.

"Nothing to say? No pleas for mercy, or oaths of vengeance?"

"Am I the first captive you've taken today?" Constance asked.

"A strange sort of question," said the verdurite, pausing for a moment in contemplation. "Meaning there are others, besides you and the one who ran off? Well, worry not – you won't be alone in your agony. Whomever it is you fear for, they too will water the Heartwood."

He bent over Constance, smiling savagely, turning back

around just in time to be struck by Mary Ann's makeshift cudgel, the branch breaking across his similarly arboraceous forearm and revealing a hard press of bone. A grievous injury but he did not scream, tackling Mary Ann, pinning her to the ground and raising his bone knife for the kill. Mary Ann held him back with desperate strength, certain it would not last long though in the end it did not need to, Constance plowing into him, the two rolling over one another and into the dirt. Whatever the weakness of her current form Constance had not forgotten the lessons taught by her father and Sir Floppy when she was just a child, slipping out of the verdurite's grip, pulling him into a choke hold even as she pinned his arms down with her legs, feeling the blood rush out from her wound. Mary Ann grabbed another club and battered at the immobilized enemy, thuggish and brutal, death-maddened, shattering his skull to reveal a pulpy green interior.

Constance rolled away from the corpse, caught her breath, pressed a hand against the arrow still in her calve. "Thanks."

"Don't mention it," said Mary Ann, dropping her blood-stained cudgel. "I'm think I'm going to throw up now."

"Me too," said Constance.

# SIXTY

Adeline and John stood on the battlements, looking down on an endless train of anima trudging towards the east gate, their lines extending out unto the horizon, the citizens of the Clockwork Republic come to seek late shelter. They chugged through the mud on winding cartwheels, they crawled ahead on metallic pincers, they were carried aloft by dirigible, sad and gray like low rain clouds. Each was different, each unique, self-constructing according to necessity and whim, *ad hoc* creations intended for a specific purpose, industry or music or war, living machines which violated the basic premises of the reality from which Adeline had come.

"Fuck," she said.

"Yeah," said John.

"Jesus."

"Yup."

"Fuck."

"Now you're just showing off."

"What is this? What am I looking at?"

"The March," John said simply.

"That's it?"

"Best I got."

Adeline gazed back over the precipice at the long train of living metal, creatures with iron treads and coal-powered pistons. She was dressed in a high-collared coat of Tyrian purple and fierce black boots, and she carried a staff of purple light which simmered and stretched in the air around her. "Why do I look like this?"

"You're a Harrow."

"No, I'm not. Constance and I are nearly divorced. Anyway, I never took her name."

John shrugged. "The March disagrees."

A ranine attendant came up the stairs just then, goitered green skin and a powdered white wig and billowy robes. "Your highnesses," he began, "the embassy from the anima are approaching."

"Thank you," said John, "we'll be down in a moment."

The toad bowed gracefully, then went back down the steps.

Adeline watched him descend, his reticella collar bobbing with each hop. "I didn't understand," she admitted. "Would you have understood?"

"No," John said, "that's why we have the book. Even then, it's pretty confusing."

"Did you find it? Make it?"

"The book? Or the March?"

"The March."

"I don't know," said John.

"How can you not know?"

"What was your father's name?"

"Saul."

"And his father's name?"

"David."

"And his?"

"I don't know," Adeline admitted.

"There you go. Three generations, that's as far as it goes back for any of us. Beyond that, you might as well be asking about the paleolithic."

They descended the walls to the bailey below where a team of servants, senseschals and administrators waited to help the refugees into the Tower.

"She loves you," said John.

"You haven't seen her in years."

"A brother knows. Anyway, Constance isn't the subtle one

in the family. It's like she's got someone walking behind her, writing all her thoughts down on a whiteboard."

Adeline smiled at the description, then frowned, thinking of her lover far away, and her children in circumstances yet more dire. "She'll find them?"

"She'll find them," John agreed, because there was no point in saying otherwise.

As the first of the anima entered the courtyard the herald announced them in a dignified croak. "Prince John and Princess Adeline wait to meet the representatives of the Clockwork Republic."

"Princess?" Adeline muttered.

"You look the part."

"What's that supposed to mean?"

"Nothing, it's just... purple. I wouldn't have thought it."

Citizen Anemometer rolled forward to offer homage, accompanied by the anima's elite; a mechanized counting desk with quills for fingers, artificial beauties with biceps of gold and faces of sterling silver, daedal creations of such vast wealth that they had given over their bodies to its worship, for even in the Republic equality was nominative. Anemometer himself wore a face plate that had remained hidden in his skull for long years, which he had supposed, in brighter days, he would never need to display, or to display only in false sympathy, a mask of lamentation and regret. His treads were worn from the long journey, his stainless-steel frame was spattered with mud, and when he saw John he lowered his jointed body in supplication.

"Allow me to... that is to say I would like to take this opportunity..." there was a small hole in his bellows, and he clamped one claw against it to force the words through, "the Clockwork Republic is grateful to the Harrow for their assistance in our time of need."

"What call for thanks between family?" John asked, assisting Citizen Anemometer upright once more. "The Tower is the home of the Thousand People, and inside we have space for all our wayward children."

Citizen Anemometer seemed little soothed by John's pronouncement. "We were pressed upon the road," he said, "our rear guard, by things that..."

"You need not fear," John promised. "The Harrow are in the Tower. The End will break upon our walls, and the land will be restored once more."

Anemometer's face plate did not shift, a despairing frown imprinted on the metal. "To think of how quickly it took the Hive." He had forgotten to depress the hole in his bellows, and his voice was weak and wavery. "All those thousands of soldiers, lost in one night."

"To foment reckless panic in these troubled times is folly," John said, returning Anemometer's words with a sly smile. "All will be safe within our walls. Now, you must be exhausted after your long journey. We have rooms prepared. Best retire."

Anemometer nodded and trudged off, escorted to the central donjon by the high chamberlain and his attendants. After the first ranks of the anima's aristocracy came the vastly larger swell of common machines, spinning Jennies and steam-engines, presses and pumps, less fortunate souls forced to make do with whatever quarters could be found for them amid the swarming city. Still, they were safe, or safer than they would have been in the Clockwork Republic, and John was feeling rather pleased with himself before Adeline cursed at him.

"You fucking Harrows," she said. "I thought it was just your mother, but you're twice as bad."

"Probably. What are you talking about?"

"You're all so goddamn arrogant it makes me want to scream. You've been staring at it for so long that you stopped seeing any of it. You just take all this impossibility for granted, like it was a dream, or something."

"It is a dream," John said.

"And if the Tower falls? What happens to our world? The real world?"

John shrugged, but he wasn't smiling anymore.

"Maybe it is a dream," Adeline said, "but what if it isn't yours? And what happens if it wakes up?"

# Sixty-One

Hank had made the fire with dried wood and the pocket Bic he used for lighting his joints. It was warmer here than it had been back in Maryland but not warm enough and they huddled close together, the three of them alone amid the endless desiccated forest, skeletal trees stretched into the tenebrous night. No bird songs interrupted the evening, nor even the hum of cicadas, the wood an arboreal necropolis stretching out indefinitely.

"This is fun, isn't it Evie?" Julian asked. "We're having a campfire."

Julian was being brave. Like when they had to remove one of his baby teeth because it was coming in crooked, and he hadn't cried until afterward, during the drive home..

"I'm hungry," said Evie.

"We'll find something soon," Hank promised. Hank was being brave also. He stared at his hands in the light of their flickering fire, thinking the skin looked darker and somehow harder. He might have wondered if he was going mad. He did not wonder, however, in fact everything that had happened since he had disappeared from outside the Harrow's house the night before had seemed *right*, somehow, natural. Which was, Hank Washington thought sadly, the sort of thing an insane person would probably think.

"We should tell a story," said Julian. "That's what you do when you're around a campfire."

"What kind of story?" asked Hank Washington.

341

"I don't know. Don't you have any stories from when you were a kid?"

But Hank did not, his father gone too young to remember, his mother a spectral presence little given to conversation. "Not really."

"That's OK," said Julian, "I'll start. Once upon a time in the March–"

"A march is a way to walk, and also a place you can live," Evie interjected.

"Got it," said Hank, "keep going."

"Once upon a time in the March," Julian continued, "a young prince and princess were lost alone in a ruined forest."

"Not *alone,* alone."

"No, not all alone," Julian agreed, "they had one brave knight with them. But they were all alone besides that. But it was OK, though, because they were on a big important adventure."

"To do what?" Evie asked.

"To get home, of course," said Julian.

Evie nodded in agreement.

"An evil wizard had cast a spell which took them to a different world," Julian continued, gaining momentum, "because he wanted to take them away from their mommies and their family. Because he was such a dumb mean jerk. And smelly, too. And anyway–"

But Evie was no longer listening, her head turned toward still silence of the dead wood, some precocious preternatural sense alerting her.

"Hank," she whispered, "there's someone here."

Hank's eyes shot up, too late to do anything but watch as they entered the clearing, coming to stand in a loose semi-circle around the fire. They were crooked and gray, like the trees which grow beside the highway, boughs warped from exhaust. Some carried bone spears, others bows, though the largest, a gnarled, graying elder, leaned on a staff made from the femur of some great beast.

There was something familiar about them, these mad minglings of man and tree. "Evening," said Hank Washington.

It was impossible to tell from their stern features if they didn't understand him or didn't care to respond.

"If we're trespassing or something, we're sorry," Hank continued. "We got lost. We need help."

The elder leaned on his stretch of marrow, staring for a long time at Hank before finally answering in a deep, oaken voice. "What are you?"

"I'm Hank Washington."

"No," the creature said, shaking his head slowly, "you aren't." His nostrils flared. His eyes went wider, in some hint of surprise. "Cousin?" he asked finally.

"What?"

"It is the end of days," said the elder, to the others or to Hank or perhaps to himself. "The dead come among us once more. And bearing gifts, no less."

"I don't know what you're talking about," said Hank, though this was not quite true. "Like I said, my name is Hank Washington, and I–"

"Whatever you are," the elder interrupted, "*they* aren't. They're outsiders. And outsiders water the Heartwood."

"They're just children," Hank objected.

"We were children, once. Wandering among our trees, gleeful and innocent. Then came the Harrow. Now we're ghosts. But even ghosts can remember. Even ghosts can dream, and cry for vengeance. Indeed, that's all that's left to us."

He made a gesture and one of his soldiers strode forward, Julian putting a protective if pointless hand around his sister even as Hank Washington with sudden speed ripped a branch from the fire and shoved it into the face of their attacker, who screamed and danced back.

"Run!" Hank yelled to the children, and not stopping to argue Julian grabbed his sister and sprinted off into the darkness, turning to see Hank flailing his torch but not waiting to see more, hurrying off as fast as their little legs could carry them, not stopping even when Hank began to scream.

They ran blindly through the rotting forest, the moon a distant circle obscured by the branches far above. Evie was crying and Julian was gasping and neither of them were paying very much attention to the path, stumbling ahead blindly until Evie tripped over a dead log and they both went tumbling into a long ravine, end over end through piles of wood chips until they reached the bottom.

It was darker there, and Julian had a splinter through his hand the length of a pencil. From the distant clearing Hank screamed one final time and then the night returned to its constant silence, quiet as a graveyard, interrupted only by the whistling wind.

"What's going to–"

"Shh!" Julian interrupted.

"But Hank–" Evie whispered.

"Be quiet, Evie!" Julian snapped, holding his sister as tight as he could and putting one hand over her mouth.

Julian was a brave child, but even brave men and brave woman, for that matter, still know fear, his heart beating so fast in his chest that he thought he might die, literally die, like Mr Manchette who had been their science teacher before collapsing during lunch one day, right into his bologna sandwich, according to popular rumor.

A voice from atop the gully called to them. "Come out, children."

Evie strained her head to look at the slender figure high above, standing on a fallen tree the width of a subway car. In the clearing beside the fire the wind had been light and almost friendly, but it had picked up during their escape, and now it seemed to whip through the forest, a howling tension like before a terrible storm.

"There's no point in running," continued the creature, "the end comes for everyone. It came for us. It has come now for you. Fighting only makes it worse."

She was naked except for a feathered headpiece which trailed behind her like the tail of a kite, pulled by the wind which grew abruptly to an impossible strength, a sudden squall, a localized harmattan, the huntress struggling against it, hands outstretched in defense even as she was flung from her perch to land awkwardly halfway down the side of the ravine, neck snapping like a twig in a fire, stunned body sliding slowly down the rest of the hill. Her eyes were still open, and her mouth still shuttered and she would be a long time dying though die she most surely would, Evie screaming and Julian screaming now likewise, holding her hand so tight that he thought he might break it, even as the air swirled madly, whirling about in the firmament, a living thing which, like the woods themselves, had turned savage.

# SIXTY-TWO

The Tower was in desperate straits, its citizens and refugees feverishly preparing their defenses. Scouts reported that the End had swallowed up the last of the Harvestlands and was coming forward swiftly, a day's march – though this was measuring by the standards of a faunae or an arcimboldi and not by the tireless End. John was everywhere. Not yet a king but he was, most assuredly, the Harrow, and all the Thousand People looked to him for leadership, to be their light in this darkest of days. He seemed never to sleep nor even to tarry, sprinting from one end of the Tower to the next, overseeing the defenses, finding room in an already overfilled city for the continuous waves of exiles, smoothing over the conflicts which inevitably rose from having all the Thousand Peoples stuffed into an ever-narrowing space. Already that day he had helped the anima place their heavy cannon on the outer battlements and settled a dispute between the Margravinate Fang and the Lord Rivermouth over their order of battle and found and killed a remnant of the End which had blossomed amid the apiaries. He hurried from one crisis to the next, listening quietly, coming to decisions which he expressed succinctly and about which he did not after worry, his time suddenly too precious to allow for anxiety.

John was watching the Tower's sorcerers prepare their battle-hexes, inscriptions along the walls and beside the moats, vast networks of scrawl done in cascarilla and oak ash and drawn blood, correcting a line here, suggesting an alteration there, when his mother appeared beside him.

346

"You weren't my first choice," Sophia said.

John looked shocked for a moment, and then he laughed, loud and long and honest. Sophia smiled along with him. John was the only one of her children who could have found any humor in her insult; Constance would have sulked, and Mary Ann would have yelled.

"Thanks," he said finally.

"Don't mention it."

"Not to be the bearer of bad tidings, but at the moment I'm all you've got."

"They'll come back," said Sophia, no longer smiling.

"We'll see. Even if they did, it won't matter. Constance is too soft, and Mary Ann won't do it."

"No," Sophia said, "Mary Ann won't."

"So, there you go."

"I know all of that. I still thought it was important to say."

"How come?"

"You're not as smart as you think."

"But I think I'm fucking brilliant, so even meeting in the middle I'd still be the cleverest person in the room."

"The gap between your ego and your ability is wide enough to drown in," Sophia said, suddenly serious, "and to carry us all down beside."

"All right," said John.

"Why do you want this?"

"What do you mean?"

"Why do you want the throne? Constance was right, you walked away from us a long time ago. Mary Ann I could understand, after what happened. But you?"

Already that day John had been asked many difficult questions, questions which meant life or death for the Thousand People. This was the first one he struggled to answer. "I don't know, Mom. What do you want me to tell you?"

"I want you to tell me the truth."

"People say that a lot, but they don't usually mean it."

"I'm not people."

John shrugged. "It mostly doesn't seem worth it."

"What?"

"Any of it. All of it. It's kind of pointless, if you think about it very long. Everyone's either sad or stupid, and the stupid ones are probably right to be stupid, at least they can pretend things might get better. But it never does, really, you just drag yourself through until you can't anymore."

"You haven't answered my question."

"Why do I want to be King?"

"Yes."

"It's a good distraction. I always liked a crisis. Keeps you focused."

In the courtyard below a group of non-combatants rushed to erect a field hospital, a massive tent to shelter the inevitable bloody casualties of the battle to come. A quetzal struggled to drag aloft a long stretch of tarp, colored wings straining against the air currents. A zoaea, spotted from age but still vital, wrestled a column into place, guided by an upside down widdershin. Below the half-finished portion a herd of adolescent aurochi set up beds, calves doing their best to be helpful. The rain fell in a steady demoralizing patter, muddying the ground and impeding all effort, but they continued on just the same.

"You should have had kids," Sophia said.

"I like to think there's still time."

"How can you be a King without an heir? Without someone you care more about than you do yourself? When I held Constance for the first time, when they brought her out to me and I could feel her body in my hands, her whole body. And then with you and Mary Ann... there's no way to explain it. Everyone's a kid until they have a kid."

"What about nuns?"

"You should talk less," said Sophia. "That's another piece of wisdom I wanted to impart to you before I die. You talk too fucking much."

"Fair enough."

"I wasn't a perfect mother."

"Perfect is a high bar."

"I asked too much of Constance – or maybe not enough. I should have sent her out of the house, made her find her own way."

"Probably, yeah."

"And I should have forgiven Mary Ann for being who she was."

"Spilled milk," said John. "If you see her again you can tell her you're sorry."

"I will," Sophia promised.

"And what about me? Got any last sins begging absolution?"

"You I did everything right with."

"And look how that turned out."

Sophia gazed a moment at her son's broken face and sad eyes. Then, without any further ceremony, she pulled the Bauble from her pocket, the single shining orb which was the greatest treasure of the Harrow, and settled it in his hands. It was like touching a live wire, but it was also like cradling a newborn, some strange mixture of strength and fragility, a power and responsibility which, deep down, John was not altogether sure he deserved or even wanted.

"You're right," Sophia said, "there's not really a purpose, but there is a reason, and you need to find yours. If this is a game for you John, you'll lose it. You'll give up when it gets too hard. If it's just you, if you're all you care about, it won't be enough. You need something else.

# Sixty-Three

They had followed the trail to an abandoned campfire, Constance noting the signs of struggle and the footprints which led away, a desperate scramble through the forest and then down into a ravine. From there the path had wound south, ending at a small cave in the hillside. With afternoon turning to evening and the last light of the sun heavy on the tree stumps and exsiccated vegetation, Mary Ann and Constance prepared to storm it.

"Are you sure you're up for this?" asked Mary Ann.

"My kids are in there," Constance said. "I'm up for it."

"All right. So, what exactly do we do?"

Constance's smile was full of teeth. "Go in hard and kill anything ain't kin."

"They teach you that in knight school?"

"More or less." The wound in Constance's leg was agonizing and almost surely infected but she could still walk, and she did not think it would hinder her from using the bow she had taken from the murdered verdurite. "We don't really have time for anything elaborate."

"I guess not," said Mary Ann. She pulled the bone knife from the pocket of her jacket, pricked her thumb on the point, watched the blood bubble up. "See you on the other side."

With that Mary Ann sprinted into the cave, Constance lagging behind on her injured leg, reaching the darkness a few seconds behind her sister, bow drawn, set to let fly even as she found Mary Ann confused and her children sitting in a corner, smiling at their arrival, by all appearances safe and well.

"Mom!" yelled Julian.

"Mom!" yelled Evie.

Constance dropped her bow and embraced her children, burying herself in Julian's hair, feeling Evie's arms wrap around her.

"The wind saved us!" said Evie.

"The what?" Constance, who was having trouble hearing over the rush of blood in her ears.

"The wind!" Julian repeated.

And indeed, although they were closed within the small tunnel and the day outside had been still the air seemed to swing back and forth, like a bird trilling greeting, offering an ineffable sense of comfort. Mary Ann felt it caress her skin, prickled her nose at some long-forgotten scent-memory.

"Uncle Aaron?"

Their reunion lasted into the evening. Julian relayed what had happened during their time in the March, Evie chiming in with some occasional revision. Mary Ann listened intently, divvying out the water and some pieces of dried meat they had taken from the verdurite. Constance could not let go of her children, patting Julian's arm or tugging Evie closer, feeling an enormous, exhausting sense of euphoria, for there is no joy so potent as the sudden absence of pain. Aaron swirled around them, the air imbued with his silent, smiling presence.

When the children were finally asleep, curled up beneath their aunt's jacket, Mary Ann and Constance sat by the mouth of the cave, talking quietly.

"I'm sorry," said Mary Ann.

"For what?"

"Basically, everything I said in the last conversation. And a lot of other things besides."

"Me too," said Constance.

"It was good, what you did, looking after Mom. I couldn't have done it. Neither could John. You're the best of us."

Constance shrugged. A day ago, this would have meant a lot

to her, but just then it was hard to care. "It's like you said. We are what we are."

"I shouldn't have disappeared."

"You had to figure things out for yourself, I guess."

"I didn't really do it though, did I? I just kept running."

"You're still a kid," Constance said, "you've got time."

Mary Ann crossed her eyes. "I'm three years younger than you."

"It's a big three years, though. A lot happens in those three years. You'll see."

Mary Ann laughed and put her arm around her sister's shoulders, mirror images of Julian and Evie in their quiet slumber. "I'm staying," she said.

Constance sighed. "Hank is dead, Mary Ann. He saved my kids' lives and I'm sorry and I'll always be grateful to him but he's dead. And even if he wasn't, what can you do about it? The way we are now..."

"I know," said Mary Ann. "I'm still staying."

To accept others as independent creations, whose decisions are as immutable as the revolutions of the heavenly spheres, is a lifelong process, never more than partially successful.

"All right," Constance finally managed.

"I'm done running from things," said Mary Ann.

"What happened to Dad wasn't your fault."

"It was kind of my fault. Anyway, it doesn't matter anymore. I can't do anything about that. But I can still save... Hank."

"All by yourself?"

The wind picked up as if in dispute.

"I'll have Uncle Aaron too," Mary Ann reminded her. "We'll manage it, whatever it takes. I won't lose him a second time."

# SIXTY-FOUR

Just before dawn, with rain clouds hanging heavy overhead, John went to the top of the Tower. Up the ascensors, through the hidden stairwell which led to the Harrow's secret room, then out a window onto the twisting turret, scrambling with the aid of spidery shadow-limbs till he had reached the highest point in existence. From this perch he gazed down at the last remnants of the Thousand People and the End beyond, a wave moving relentlessly towards its inevitable conclusion.

Were they worth saving? Any of them? Could one really say so? Life was a crass and desperate contest for a pool of resources always insufficient to meet the ever-sharpening desires of the most successful claimants, and morality only a cheap tinsel intended to obscure this rapacity. Short self-interest, petty greed and brute indifference were the throughlines to humanity and all that resembled it. It wasn't even anyone's fault – the scales were weighed against them from the beginning, the machinery operating in fundamental misalignment. Pain is more potent than pleasure, creation difficult but destruction effortless, and while kindness withers in the bud acts of cruelty blossom like kudzu. These bleak truths are written on every atom of existence, clear for all to see. That suicide had not universally followed the development of self-consciousness was, at bottom, a cheap biological trick, evolution ensuring an exaggerated sense of self-protection as it had opposable digits and a surplus kidney.

Alone atop creation, accountable to no one for his silent

thoughts, John gauged the leap, considered dooming existence in one final act of condemnation. Instead, he began to sing.

He sang of the sun; of a winter sun which offered light if little heat on long gray February afternoons while he trudged away to the sledding hill; of a summer sun which blistered asphalt and melted Popsicles and lasted long and late into the evening. He sang of a day in October when his father had taken him for a long hike, just the two of them, the sun as it had shown through the autumn foliage, the sun as it had warmed his father's smiling face. He sang of a day on the beach, *the* day on the beach, its abstract ideal, he and his sisters lost for long hours amid high dunes, fighting with driftwood swords, turning lobster-red in blissful carelessness then throwing themselves into the shallow breakwaters of the Atlantic. He sang of the sun's glare and the sun's heat, of the sheer joy of its rays, of its light which, despite everything, comes after dark.

It is the song that carries us along, unsure of the words and searching for harmony, futile and useless and beautiful despite or because of that fact. The sun rose for the first time in a long time over the Tower and the March beyond, on the Thousand People rising from uneasy slumber, on his family somewhere among them, and on John's tortured, smiling face.

# SIXTY-FIVE

They heard it first; a discordant threnody in countless competing registers, chattered through mandibles, bellowed past razored maws, hissed through forked tongues, intoned by animatronic speaker boxes, audible from a distance only as a continuous rumble, more vibration than sound.

"Lemme see!" Evie said, too small to see through the window.

Julian gave his sister an obliging boost.

They were high in the Tower, clustered together with the elite of the Thousand People too young or old or weak to play a part on the walls; the Gravinate Velvet, a doddering squirrel who had owned a third of the Palatinate before it had been lost to the End; Binky, the Mayor of the Toybox, his felt body faded and gray; hydronese ferik so old they left damp trails as if weeping. Ancient Wisdom and youthful Innocence made up the prosopon's contribution, and Citizen Anemometer was in quiet discussion with the first, his frame patched but his face still turned to its cast of despair.

"There are so many of them," he said nervously, "and we are so few."

"In times of darkness," said Wisdom from its mask of somber contemplation, "my nickname is courage."

"Facile apothegms, better fed to children."

"Stow that chatter!" roared Gravinate Velvet, his temper kept in check only by his doddering, ancient frame. "The Tower stands, and the Thousand People are united once more.

The Harrows have returned in our time of darkness, to lead us into the light. And they brought along some help," he said, nodding graciously towards Evie and Julian.

Julian returned it, and even Evie managed an unaccustomed curtsy.

The polyphony swelled deafening, breaking against the walls of the Tower like a strong wind, and soon the outriders of the End came into view.

"Crack in the glass!" screeched a sickened summer swallow.

"Hair in the mouth!" chittered an oothecan drone.

"Rust on the gears!" groaned a self-cycling anima.

"Flaw in the grain!"

"Flaw in the grain!"

They moved without plan or stratagem, an advance guard composed of the smallest and fleetest creatures. They had no instruments of siege and carried no weapons, not so much as a wooden club, as if they'd forgotten even the use of tools in their single-minded drive towards annihilation.

Strung along the battlements, clustered tightly in the courtyards, packing the barbicans, the Thousand People waited to meet them. Some cursed, some blustered. Some met their fate with stoic contempt, some broke and fled. An otter and a green-capped saprophyte, strangers the day previous, now brothers in arms, passed a skin of wine back and forth. A xerophile hidden in a sally port felt the sharp end of her ax and thought of her dead mate and lost blossoms, swore to sell her life at a terrible price. Below the canvas roof of the freshly-erected field hospital an anima medic with a bone saw for a hand waited anxiously for the first round of casualties, counted his small chest of demulcents and embrocations and tried not to despair. Parents kept their children busy with songs and games, even as their minds ran fretful to their partners on the walls. The Valiant and the Palatinate's cavalry and the zoaea with their halberds and all the others among the Thousand People who were bred or built or trained for war waited with quiet stillness, hazarding their strength for the coming fray.

Atop the battlements, dressed in fulgrinous brigantine, the Harrow's Bauble crowning his forehead, John waited to give the order to attack.

"Starting to sweat?" Constance wore the burnished plate of the Valiant, and the sword-with-seven-locks was slung across her back.

"Shouldn't you address me as his majesty, or something?"

"You'll be waiting on that till Armageddon."

"Couple hours, then?"

"I will throw you off this wall before I call you king, little brother."

Adeline found herself dressed once more in royal purple, holding her staff which was sometimes a spear and sometimes a scepter and sometimes a flickering serpent of light, depending on mood and inclination. "All right, now," she said, "let's not start playing Macbeth."

"Now that you mention it," Constance said, "I met these witches on the way over, and they were making some pretty compelling arguments for regime change."

"If you can't trust a group of crones screaming by the side of the road, who can you trust?" John asked.

Constance laughed. She should have been frightened, at the immensity of the coming host and the slim hopes of their desperate forces, but she found she was not. Adeline was beside her. Her family was whole once more. The End could do its worst. "They don't look like nothing," she said, spitting over the precipice.

"Don't spit," said Adeline. "Your mother raised you better than that."

"Where is Mom, by the way?" John asked.

Adeline shrugged and turned to stare at the great armies of the Harrow which manned the walls and filled the courtyards below. Still a stranger to the March, without the benefit of experience or even knowledge of the book, they seemed one impossibility after another; crab-creatures carrying edged spears, stoats in light armor with long rapiers, bristling bipedal cactus wielding executioner's axes, packs of scuttling sentient scrap metal, living mushrooms with billhooks, vegetable men with scythes fresh from harvest.

"How about you, champ?" John asked. "Any nerves?"

"Champion," Constance corrected.

"What?"

"Don't say champ, I feel like an old boxer."

"Champion sounds like the name of a dog."

"They both sound weird," Adeline decided.

The circumference of the End tightened, the Tower like a peak above a rising flood. They reached the first of the great network of traps which the defenders had prepared, falling into pits, caught by sharp snares and detonating mines, small scars on the great body which went all but unnoticed, the myriad multitude pacing forward. John lifted a fist and a dozen gyrfalcon flew signal flags around the battlements. An instant later the walls erupted, trebuchet flinging boulders, the anima's artillery booming, merriling launching fireworks with rubber-band guns into the fast-advancing foe. They tore pock marks in the ground, explosions of mud like fountains, reducing the oncoming wave to fur and bone and pig iron and hard stone.

"Wow!" said Julian, from far away.

In the air above the battlements the Tower's aeronauts met their counterparts, Dame Delta leading those of the Thousand Peoples who knew the joy of flight, eagles and goshawks, paper airplanes manned by merriling bombardiers, convocations of quetzal in beaded leathers with obsidian warclubs and leather atlatl, owls blinded by the bright sunlight but sworn to their bloody duty nonetheless. A dirigible shaped anima fired its culverin into an End-ridden pteranodon, a colony of bats fixed themselves on a mammoth dragonfly as if to drag it down by sheer weight of numbers. A nest of hornets followed after Dame

Delta in tight formation, buzzing fiercely, the Valiant turning to scatter them with a blow from her brass talons. A hundred bands of color flourished against the bright blue sky, jets of blood and oil and ichor falling in a hard rain, corpses careening onto the battlefield and against the ever-surging End.

"If you wouldn't mind, sister," said John, "I think it's nearly time."

"I'll see you when it's over," said Constance.

"Back at the house for milk and cookies?"

"Or a bottle of whiskey."

Constance turned to face Adeline, who was trying hard not to look anxious.

"Be careful," she said.

"I'm not sure that's really an option," said Constance.

"Then be brave."

Constance smiled and grabbed Adeline by the lower back and pulled her into a long kiss, the kind that lingers and makes onlookers uncomfortable.

"For luck," Constance said, pulling her great helm over her smile and calling for her spear and her mount and her knights, hurrying down into the courtyard, leaving John to smirk and Adeline's heartbeat to return slowly to normal.

"Don't say a fucking word," Adeline said finally.

"Wouldn't dream of it," John promised.

The End drew closer, indifferent if not unharmed by the cannonade of the Clockwork Republic, by the Catherine wheels which scintillated scalding in their midst, by spring-loaded spears erupting from the ground. John gave the next signal and the Tower's archers let fly. A mischief of mice in war paint released a volley of arrows from their short bows, strings echoing like the low note on some gigantic zither. A line of armipotent anima fired heavy lead from their ribauldequin bodies, sentient organ guns keeping up a steady volley. A platoon of petrousian peppered the besiegers with slings, stones the size of grapefruit shattering skull and bone.

Renegade arcimboldi hurled javelins over the parapets, having abandoned their native pacifism in light of the last, desperate days. The wave of missiles spread so fast and so thick that for a few moments they seemed to blot out John's sun, and below the battlements the day was dark as night.

The End died in obscene thousands – dismembered by gunfire, broken by boulder, skewered with arrow, but still their first wave reached the walls in maddening profusion. Those that could climb began their ascent without preamble, mucosal tentacles wrapping the walls, metal pins diviting into the azure stone. Those that remained land-bound pushed forward and kept pushing, as if to overcome the battlements by sheer weight, clamoring atop themselves in their mad rush for fresh flesh, inhuman ladders built by blind force.

"Nail in the tire!" cried a petrousian serving as steppingstone.

"Weevils in the flour!" claimed the etiolated arcimboldi climbing over him.

"Bugs in your mattress!" said a filth-matted squirrel scampering past both.

"Crack in the pane!" shrieked a shrike from yet higher.

The defenders met them as best as they were able, merriling unloading loud pop guns, Tower guards pushing at the top layer with their half pikes, widdershin peltasts hurling javelins from prehensile toes, all the mixed multitude of missilists renewing their efforts. Unexpected hollows, excavated by petrousian and saprophyte, gave way beneath the onrushing End, swarming crowds falling to their death. Unshelled molluschites, little given to war, dropped stones and hot ash from machicolations, watching their payloads descend on the ravenous horde. The sky itself remained rent with conflict, the Thousand People and their enemies whirling about in mad melee, so thick and so fast it was impossible to make out any particular engagement among the garboil.

Dame Delta divebombed into a net of climbing End, carrying a poisoned cat upward, great metal wings straining until she was high above the fray, her wriggling captive crying "Hole in your hat! Pebble in your shoe!" even as she let him fall a hundred yards to burst on the ground below.

She shrieked her furious war cry then wheeled back towards the Tower, landing with a loud thud in the courtyard where Constance and the other Valiant were gathered atop their mounts. "Were you thinking of doing any actual fighting today," she asked, "or was I supposed to do this all myself?"

"We await my brother's command," said Constance, "but I'd appreciate if you'd leave us a few, given that we went to all the trouble of getting dressed up."

"Shouldn't have any problem there," said Dame Delta. She had a long rent in her clothwork wing, and her frame was bent from where she had been struck by some strange grotesque.

Constance laughed through her great helm and shook her lance against the sky.

Everywhere the End rose, ladders made of flesh and scale and metal climbing higher even as the defenders stabbed and shot and cut at them. John gave the next signal, his avian messengers circling once more, and across the battlements the Tower's mages let loose their assault – salamanders in wizard hats, clockwork shamans festooned with fetishes, waterlogged witches leaning on crooked staves, a patchwork assemblage of sorcerers abandoning ancient feuds for the common good. Prepared hexes exploded off the walls, bolts of lightning streaked from the cloudless sky and waves of immolation rose to char the oncoming End like weenies dropped in a campfire. Drawn by forbidden necromancies long forgotten burial grounds disgorged skeletal soldiers to fight on behalf of their descendants, clawing their way up from the ground, silent save for their rattling. The earth turned to puddles and ponds and lakes of acid and the End dissolved within them, leaving bloody pink scum on the surface. A slick black patch appeared along the wall and a scaly tentacle the width and length of a telephone pole emerged from it, flailing wildly, leaving great bloody trails in its wake.

John roared and banged his fists against his chest and roared once more.

"What a shitty nihilist you turned out to be," said Adeline.

"Don't tell anyone," he said. "It'll ruin my rep."

A portcullis rose and the Valiant came charging, Constance in the vanguard with a long lance, skewering a corrupted widdershin and singing the Harrow's battle cry. Her comrades followed close beside her; Sir Szyylstyx with spears in every pedipalp, Dame Scarlet twanging her recurved bow, Dame Saguro pedaling furious on her velocipede, swinging her executioner's ax, a hundred others and each worth a thousand, riding down the End like a John Deere through a summer lawn.

"Get 'em, Mom!" Julian yelled from his place at the window, gazing jubilantly on Constance's heroics, on this turn in the battle which promised some hope of victory.

"That's my mom!" shouted Evie excitedly, "One of them! That's one of them!"

The Gravinate Velvet hooted approbation, squeezed his paw around the hilt of his sword and cursed that he was too old to fight. A drove of aurochi calves, young khagan in colored felts, raced to the windows to catch a sight of the mighty Valiant. Citizen Anemometer poured a long draught of lamp oil into a feeding tube, and his faceplate remained forlorn.

A gate opened and the heavy soldiers of the anima came to reinforce the Valiant's attack, creatures of brass and steel and iron, at once matross and artillery, mechanized war chariots with sharpened wheels spouting cannon fire from their bodies. A walking hydraulic press rambled across the battlefield, flattening the End beneath its enormous falling weight. Beings like buzz-saws rampaged through rotted flesh, legions of polished metal marching forward in robotic lockstep, the full might of the Clockwork Republic revealing itself in one terrible moment.

For Constance the battle had already narrowed down to

cut, thrust, and parry, too occupied in immediate conflict to have any sense of its larger development. Sir Szyylstyx was gone, lost somewhere amid the fray, and Dame Scarlet was long out of arrows, felling the enemy with a silvery scimitar. Constance had broken her lance against the stony skin of a petrousian, and now wielded a morning star that buzzed with a thick charge of electricity, rupturing the skull of a nonesuch, charring a rat. On her back her father's weapon was down to its last lock, and she could feel it buzzing through the heavy plate of her armor, begging to be unleashed.

The Valiant's charge slowed as the End was reinforced by a wave of new arrivals, slower and heavier than the first; blighted xerophile, shambling badger, ranks of oothecan knights, their exoskeletons cruddy and diseased, the whole vast Hive given over to the End. The rest of the Thousand People came streaming out onto the battlefield; schiltrons of zoaea carrying halberds in their feelers, claws clacking for combat; the caparisoned cavalry of the faunae, mixed ranks of woodland creatures with banners streaming; tin-soldiers releasing their pop-guns in stern volleys. A hooting herd of aurochi stampeded out from the East Gate, bovine sowar with sarissas sharp as their pronged horns. The peaceful sachems of the molluschite had been turned into mobile missile platforms, tails and snouts covered with sharpened metal as compliment to their shells, descendants firing stone bows from atop their backs. Shoals of hydronese in broigne armor with fencing blades danced across the battlefield, adding trails of living water to the streams of blood and viscera and oil which wet the ground. The few remaining petrousian came rolling out of the castle like boulders, carbanado children sacrificing their brief lives in hopes of halting the End's advance. Around the Tower and as far as the eye could see, the Thousand People flung themselves against their foe, the March united on its last desperate day.

# Sixty-Six

After she had finished tucking the little ones into bed, pulling the blanket up around Julian's shoulders, giving Evie a kiss on the forehead, Sophia went downstairs to watch the storm bruise itself against their house. Building all evening but it now approached crescendo, great gusts of wind and loud cracks of thunder, uncharacteristic for December, not that this meant much anymore. Sophia stared out the window a while, the night growing darker and darker, the occasional bolt of lightning illumining a front lawn and neighborhood which seemed like the surface of the moon, or somewhere even more distant.

Then she went to clean the kitchen. The world is often ending but the kitchen always needs cleaning. Sophia dried the last of the dishes and wiped down the kitchen counter and tidied up the pantry, even as she sensed dimly the disappearance of her family, some indefinable absence left behind. The storm grew fiercer, the lights flickered on and off. Sophia went about collecting discarded clothing from hampers and baskets and corners, John's room in particular a shameful mess, one she would be sure to speak to him about should they both live to see the morning. She was in the sunroom separating whites from darks and looking at their Christmas tree which sat in hopeful anticipation of the morning's festivities when she heard a window break, and the front door open, and watched as the intruder came through the mudroom with heavy, plodding steps.

If Sophia had not been a Harrow, not been witness in her second life to untold wonders and corresponding horrors, he would have been the most awful thing she had ever seen. Whatever was inside him had festered and would shortly blossom, his face and his neck and his shoulders and the flesh beneath his yellowed undershirt corrupted, a blackened, necrotic mass. Ganglia pulsed up and down his flesh, goiters fluttering like eyelids. His face was blank and addled, as if he could not quite remember why he had come.

"Jeffrey, I presume?" Sophia asked, assuming a fearlessness she did not quite feel.

"Used to be." He sat down in what had once been Joan's favorite comfy chair, abscesses squelching against the upholstery. "I always wanted to meet you," he said.

"Really? I'm surprised you know who I am. I didn't think Mary Ann would mention me much."

"She didn't, but I could tell she wanted to. You were always pulling at her peripherals." In the bay windows over Jeffrey's shoulder a face appeared, pale as skim milk or diseased flesh, leering a moment and then disappearing. "The people we love never really go away, do they?"

"No," Sophia agreed, "they don't. She isn't here, though."

"I know. I'm not here either. Only a little bit, and that's going quickly."

Sophia kept her hands busy with the laundry, stopping when she felt the weight in John's hoodie.

"I guess I'm not making a very good first impression," Jeffrey said. A pustule on the side of his neck split open, leaking a waxy effluvia down his chest. "Anyway, I'll find her soon enough."

"We'll see," said Sophia. She had returned to the laundry, but John's hoodie remained on the couch beside her.

Jeffrey went silent for a long time, though his body continued its unconscious movements and the plague continued to digest it, the canker spreading like some fast-moving leprosy. In the yard around Sophia's house things of darkness danced and gamboled, struck spiny tails against her siding, skittered across her shingles.

"She's special."

"She is special," Sophia agreed.

"I love her, you know."

"Does she love you?"

"What does that have to do with it?" Jeffrey asked, smiling a rotten row of teeth, his pink tongue like a mass of carrion. "It isn't a nice thing, love, it isn't a summer breeze, and it isn't chocolate ice cream. Love is madness. Love is *need*. Love doesn't care about reciprocity; it only demands satisfaction."

"You've got a very peculiar definition of love."

"No," said Jeffrey, "it's the same one we all have. The same one you have. We want the people we love to do the things we want them to do. We want to keep them where they are, as they are, and not to let them stray, and not to let them change."

"I think what you're talking about is obsession."

"They're synonyms. To love someone is to want them so bad that you would swallow them and carry them in your stomach rather than have them ever go away."

"Everything goes away," Sophia said sadly.

"Not for long," said Jeffrey. "I'm getting bigger, you know. Or it is. We are? No, *it*. *It* is. Soon it'll be everything, everywhere, where it is now and then here too. And then we'll be together again, forever. Just her and me. And everyone else. And it."

In her mother's chair Jeffrey loomed larger, swelling with bile, and outside all the monsters of Sophia's childhood gathered for a Black Mass, boggarts and barghests, shambling ghasts and nightgaunts, a black shuck howling its prophetic plaint, though Sophia did not need supernatural assistance to know that one way or another, she was not long for this world.

The thought steadied her, somehow. Her outcome was certain – there was no excuse not to meet it bravely. "You're about half right," she said.

"Am I?"

"Love *is* a form of madness – just not the sort you suppose. Love is sacrifice. A sort of...blissful martyrdom. It's to place another's value over your own to cherish their happiness even if it dooms yours."

With some difficulty, Jeffrey managed to force his mangled body out of the chair. "I disagree," it said, coming forward in a heavy shamble to end the conversation.

"Trust a mother," Sophia answered, pulling the pistol from out of John's hoodie, thumbing off the safety as her father had taught her one day many long years before, raising it and firing. The first shot winged across the side of Jeffrey's skull and the second went wide, but the third and fourth and fifth found center mass in his diseased flesh. He stared down at his wounds for a long moment, which spurted black blood onto Sophia's carpet. Then he fell back over the armchair, and gasped for a few seconds, and died.

# SIXTY-SEVEN

They fought the Endless unceasing, all through the long hours of the day as the sun turned high in the sky. Their sortie long abandoned, the Valiant and their armies had retreated within the shelter of the walls, leaving thousands behind to weep and die or turn and swell the enemy's numbers. The heavy infantry of the End had finally arrived, ranks of zoaea with rotted shells, lumbering petrousian with husks of lichen infecting their stony bodies, rumbling anima chugging noxious black smoke out their exhausts. Constance could be found wherever the fray seemed fiercest, storming along the parapets with her picked squad of Valiant. John played general as best he could, rushing reinforcements and distributing aid to their overstretched line. The defenders were pressed at every point, each moment seeing a thousand acts of desperate courage; suicidal charges, last stands, faceless heroics destined to disappear, to be forgotten should the Tower fall.

On a battered stretch of wall Adeline fought to defend a foreign land. The living light in her hands was whatever she needed it to be in any given instant, a lance skewering an onrushing boar, a massive press to force a wave of oothecan off the battlements, a violet scythe the length of a tall tree, swinging like a pendulum and slicing great swathes from the enemy below. In a brief moment of respite, it became a staff which Adeline leaned on for support, gasping heavily, more tired than she could ever remember being, even more tired than when Julian had baby colic and spent two straight months wailing.

Julian himself was safe within the central spire, as safe as anyone in the March could be; which, as Citizen Anemometer was reminding them just then, was not very safe at all.

"The walls won't hold," he said, "there are too many."

The calves had retreated to the far corner of the room, sitting nervously beside their nannies, though Julian and Evie still watched the battle from the high window, for all they could see the day was turning against them.

"There are moments," said weary Wisdom, "when I am best found in silence."

"What would you expect?" squeaked the Gravinate Velvet. "It's half his fault we're here in the first place. Maybe if the Republic had joined us earlier, given us more time to prepare—"

"What did it matter?" interrupted Anemometer, quaffing another can of oil. "What did we lose, with our blindness? Nothing we could have done would have changed anything."

Adeline had grown accustomed to the impossible in a surprisingly short period of time, a crash course in the fantastical and the grotesque but still there were limits, and the creature which came plowing towards the walls then strained them. It was far the largest living thing she had ever seen, bigger than a blue whale, bigger than a reconstructed Apatosaurus, and unlike these creatures it made no sense, stumpy legs and a truncated torso and withered arms and a cephalopodic skull half the size of its body. It pushed heedless through the other End, stomping its siblings or allies beneath its giant tread, getting closer and larger and larger and closer until it loomed even over the high walls of the Tower. "Worm in the apple!" it roared through its sharpened rostrum, the stench of its breath unfathomably foul. "Tear in the weft!"

Adeline's light flared forth, first an aegis to hold off the creature's tentacles, then lashing out in riposte, jagged spear like spines skewering its face and neck and flattened eyes. Still, it pushed onward, battering through Adeline's shields, pulling soldiers from off the walls and feeding them into its cavernous maw. The defenders fled in understandable terror and Adeline was left alone to meet it, dwarfed by its leering hideous face, her light condensing down tighter and tighter into a bowling ball and then a baseball and then a marble and then a single perfect point and then flaring out again into a widening prism which severed tentacles and carbonized flesh and exploded out the back of the creature's head. It shivered and groaned and then fell forward against the weakened walls, managing to accomplish its purpose even in death, the battlements shaking then collapsing, dropping thousand-ton slabs of blue stone onto the ground, a weight so heavy as to set the earth shuddering and halt, for a moment, the End's advance.

But only for a moment, the multitude as indifferent to the loss of one of its fellows as a human to a hair, swarming over the rubble in vast numbers. The armies of the Thousand People rushed desperately to meet them, Constance galloping her yearling along the walls, John's projected shadow carrying him towards the breach, but both too slow to make any difference. Adeline's light had flared into a protective shell, shielding her from the worst of the damage but sending her flying to the courtyard below. Ranks of End-maddened berserkers howled their battle cry and rushed into the breach, toward a final cordon of defenders and the vast civilian population beyond, a crack in the Tower's armor which was sure to prove fatal. As the enemy pressed forward to their final victory the air began to cool about them, a summer day turning to autumn turning to deepest winter turning to arctic frost turning to temperatures unseen on Earth outside of U.N.-funded laboratories studying sub-atomic particles. The metal bodies of anima shattered from the cold, the flesh of a hundred different races froze instantly, the water in the air pulled together into an iceberg which sprouted ten and then twenty and then hundreds of feet above the ground, filling the hole in the walls, an icy tomb encasing a thousand rigid bodies.

"It's grandma!" shouted Evie from her spot in the Tower. "It's grandma!"

"The Queen returns!" roared the Gravinate Velvet, forgetting his age in his excitement and leaping neatly atop a table to get a better view. "For the Harrow! For the Tower!"

Sophia Harrow hovered in the air over the glacier which she had willed into being, propelled by a stream of frigid air, coming to land lightly in the courtyard below. Across the Tower the Thousand People cheered their salvation and the return of their old Queen, even as her children came to meet her.

"You're late," said John.

"Sorry, yeah. I had to shoot a man in the chest."

It was some strange source of satisfaction to see that John could still be surprised. "What?"

"Mary Ann's boyfriend. Ex-boyfriend."

"You shot him?"

"Why do you have a gun?" Sophia asked her son.

"I was thinking of using it to kill myself," John admitted, "although, a lot's happened since then and I kind of forgot I had it."

Even amid the battle there was a moment for tenderness, Sophia's proud face filling with sorrow, and she set her hand on the shoulder of her youngest child. "You should have told me."

"You shouldn't be going through my pockets."

"You should do your own laundry."

"What about the police?" Constance asked from atop her yearling, armor spattered in black blood.

"I'll probably die before the arraignment," Sophia answered, "so it's not my main concern right now."

Adeline snickered.

"At the moment that's not actually that distinguished a condition," said John, frowning once more as he turned to face the End.

The massive monster proved only the first in a line of giants, lumbering, hundred-handed hecatoncheires, colossal nacreous anathema, an earthbound cuttlefish expanded a dozen orders of magnitude, a spumy spirochete the size of a minor league baseball stadium. How far had they come, these distant dreams of the March, these land-locked leviathan, these creatures of nightmare and myth? All the way from the distant borders, from where reality met with its opposite, waiting ages in isolation and despair even before the End had come to claim them.

In the growing dusk the Tower cast a long shadow into the multitudinous horde, dark and wide and rippling along the edges, and those edges began to move, limning into a gigantic avatar of the Harrow king. John was ensconced in the center of its chest, strutting hundreds of feet off the ground, only his Bauble visible from the shadowy depths in which he controlled his creation. Outside of his penumbra the land was piercingly bright, all the shade of the late afternoon pulled towards John's creation which stomped and kicked its way among the End like a cruel child amid a bed of ants. John reached the first of the behemoths, a saurian the size of a skyscraper, dodging over a sweep of its tail with surprising nimbleness. His hands turning to claws he caught the monster's open mouth, spreading wider until a *snap* could be heard across the length of the battlefield, John's shadow spreading into the creature's throat and running down its cavernous esophagus and filling its stomach and then bursting outward, a heavy rain of scale and flesh and gut lining and raw, pink meat.

"Gross," said Evie, watching from her window.

But Julian thought it was pretty cool.

# SIXTY-EIGHT

Evening had come quickly to what had once been the Kingdom of the Thorned Rose, Mary Ann unsure if this was some peculiarity of its latitude or a signal of the End's growing dominion, a night which would never give way to dawn. Uncle Aaron guided her through the ruined forest, a rustle of her hair telling her to be still, a gust of wind beckoning her forward, until they reached the boundaries of the Heartwood, the trees lying like ruined works of art, defaced tapestries and shattered porcelain.

They found Hank bloody but alive, fettered to a stump by strips of thick leather. His handsome face was battered, and there were long, shallow cuts on his chest from where the verdurite had tormented him. He did not look up until she was almost upon him, and then his swollen face stretched into a wide smile, honest despite the broken teeth.

"Come to save my life?" he asked.

"For the second time, actually," Mary Ann whispered, and began to cut his bonds with her bone knife. "But I think I also got you killed once, so I'm not sure how the math works out."

The twang of a bow and an arrow flew through the night, curving wide, Aaron's invisible hands at work. The next three ricocheted against the still evening air as if it were hard stone, but the fourth slipped her uncle's defenses and pierced through Mary Ann's hand and into Thistle's arm. A verdurite came sprinting into the clearing, spear raised; a sudden gust of wind and he was thrown against a far tree, but the next to arrive was a disfigured elder, self-made cicatrix running up and down his body, leaning on a crooked bone staff and incanting some strange curse. The air turned thick and heavy, as before a storm, then scattered into the night, carrying off what remained of her uncle and leaving Mary Ann and Hank alone amid their enemy.

"You don't remember me, do you?" asked the elder.

Mary Ann waved her bone knife in her free hand as if to ward him off, a futile gesture but the most she could manage.

"It *was* a long time ago. The forest was green, and I a sprout when you brought ruin to my people."

Mary Ann pulled desperately at where her hand remained skewered into Hank's arm but succeeded only in aggravating the wound further, blood dripping free and fast.

"It is right and just that you would come among us again, before the end of all things," the elder continued, "to water the Heartwood one last time."

"Hank has nothing to do with any of this," Mary Ann said. "Let him go, you can have me."

"Fuck that!" Hank began. "I'm not going anywhere."

"And where would he go? No one can be saved," said the elder, gesturing to one of his soldiers, who came forward then with a knife. "There is no salvation for any of us, only revenge."

Mary Ann's blood commingled with Hank's, running down his shoulder, gathering for a moment below his arm and then falling in a single thick droplet onto the ground below. Roots long dead, or thought long dead, stretched forth, the ancient magic of the verdurite holding despite everything. Hank's ancestors sprouted to greet him, Hank who was not Hank but Thistle, having always known it and coming to realize it just then, his skin turning oaken, his hair lengthening and thickening until it hung in long locks from off his scalp. Perhaps it was that she was a Harrow, perhaps it was only some ineffable magic of the March, but as their blood sunk into the earth Mary Ann found herself following Hank on his journey through time, caught in dreams of the distant past, for she carried, as do all of us, the gift and burden of a thousand ancestors, men and woman who lived and died and have only us to show for their passage. In one eternal instant Mary Ann was her mother, seeing her father for the first time in a college English class, and simultaneously she was her father, noticing the blue eyes of a beautiful woman resting on his face; and she was her grandmother, younger than Mary Ann could have imagined her ever being, running across beach sand on swift, certain feet; and her grandfather, bobbling his children on his knee; and countless other ancestors, a woman dancing in a smoky cabaret, a hard-faced laborer plowing a muddy field, a smiling sailor standing high atop a foremast. And amid and intertwined with all of this she was the First Harrow, who had found or forged a fairyland and then grown lost within it, an exile dying forever in a world which was not his own.

The ruined Heartwood sprouted in wild profusion, saplings stretching out of the ground, razed trees coming to flower, the verdurite fled or bowed in wonder at the sudden and impossible bloom.

# SiXTY-NiNE

The close of day signaled no respite for the Harrow or their Thousand People. The moats were filled with bodies, hills of corpses which reached nearly above the Tower walls and rustled with still animate chunks of flesh. Blasts of ice and darting pulses of violet light struck with increasing infrequency, left gaps in the wave of enemy which were all but immediately filled. Constance and the last of the Valiant rushed along the battlements, plugging the breaches with the exhausted forces still available, Dame Scarlet lost among a closing horde of corrupted zoaea, Dame Saguaro brought down while leading stout resistance, the Knight of the Veiled Countenance pierced by an allied missile, missing heroic doom by dint of cruel fate. Twice that afternoon Constance had seen Dame Delta leading their fliers in savage stoop upon the End's armies, but that was hours earlier and there had been no sign of her since.

John's avatar fought and kicked across the battlefield, grabbing great handfuls of the End and dashing them madly back against the ground, brought near to godhood by the Harrow's Bauble and his own fierce will. Monsters the height of mountains lumbered forth to meet him, incongruous abominations of bone and polyp and claw and mandible. A hagfish the length of a cargo train entangled John's legs and brought him to the ground, wrapping its mucosal body around his shadow. They wrestled back and forth, the earth tremulous from their movements, John coming upright and with one ferocious wrench pulling the thing into separate segments, splattering a torrent of slime across the battlefield.

"This is the end," Anemometer moaned, voice coming out his battered bellows in a sharp whine. "We're as good as dead."

"A coward to the last," cursed the Gravinate Velvet, shaking his furred arm in rage.

"Brave enough to recognize the truth when it stands before me," said Anemometer. "Brave enough not to shelter in the hopes of fools."

"Despair and I remain strangers," said Wisdom gravely, "nor have I wish for an introduction."

John's prodigious penumbra was frayed and tattered, the shadow loose, light leaking through, but from within its chest John fought on, squaring off against a four-headed giant with the face of a hydrophobic dog and the face of a bald buzzard and the face of a star-nosed mole and the face of a gibbous monkey, each roaring and snapping and spitting. John had formed his fading silhouette into a simulacrum of a knight, heavy armor and a long sword, and he circled around the beast, gauging out great chunks of its flesh. He caught a fist the size of a battering ram against a kite shield the size of a cliff face, severing the spindly neck of the buzzard but its siblings fought on furious, swiping a claw through John's shadow. It wavered and John found himself free-falling through his own embodiment, the shade flooding out like blood, John reforging it an instant before he struck the ground. Reduced and diminished and the monster still coming but John managed a final blow, shoving his sword through the giant's chest even as it knocked him backward in its dying rage, John falling against the top of the battlements with such force as to crater the stone.

"See how the Harrow protect you!!" Anemometer shouted. His frame began to shutter, a thermometer swelling with mercury, his eponymous wind gauge spinning madly. "Fools! Can't you see? We're doomed! Doomed from the beginning!" His face revolved through contrary emotions, joy and sadness and proud contempt, and his bellows inflated manically. A pulse of something black as oil but not oil bubbled out from his speaking horn, landing with a thick plop on the floor. "Sugar in the engine!" he cried. "Bend in the spokes!"

The nurses screamed and the Gravinate Velvet fumbled at his ceremonial sword, Anemometer still shaking though there could be no doubt any longer that he had been consumed by the enemy which even then pressed against their walls.

Atop one of these, battered and supine, John lay broken. His shadow was gone. He could not move his right arm and there was something wrong with his chest, breath coming weak and watery. He tried to rise but was forced to abandon the task as impossible. He had no strength left.

Constance found him amid the rubble, dismounting from her yearling and placing a hand against his forehead.

"I tried," he told her.

"You did great."

"I did my best."

"I got you, little brother," said Constance, rising, "I got you."

Constance reached for the final lock on her sword, thinking of the time that she had fought Louis Hambry and how little anything changes. Night was falling and in the growing dark the End seemed no longer an army but a single amebic blot spread to the far horizon and surging towards the Tower. Into the nothing of her not-sword Constance fed everything she did not want, every personal insult, cruel impulse, bitter memory, every moment of envy, every scrap of rage, resentment and guilt. Her weapon swathed across the battlefield, dissipating monsters and magical creatures and chunks of the earth and the air itself, an absence like the crisp blank white of fresh paper. The End writhed and reared, a vast serpent made of torn limbs and severed fingers and wriggling viscera, of scale and spine and marrow, rearing higher than the battlements, nearly as high as the Tower, rising still and Constance alone to meet it.

Her children did not witness her heroics, turned to the End-maddened Anemometer as he assaulted the others with blank fury. The Gravinate Velvet ripped his sword from its sheath and roaring "Harrow and the Tower, Harrow and the March!" came doddering forward to defend them, striking a glancing blow off Anemometer's frame, receiving for his pointless bravery a retort which snapped his neck and sent him tumbling. With single-minded madness Anemometer rushed on to the next victim, catching the watery flesh of a hydronese and crushing it between his metallic claws. "Leak in the raft!" he groaned. "Wilt on the vine!"

The calves screamed and young Innocence looked on in shocked horror even as Anemometer turned to dispose of Wisdom, who met his sad fate nobly and unflinching. Julian grabbed the dead squirrel's rapier from where it lay on the ground, the pommel a thick jewel, the blade light and thin. Julian had the same familiarity with the sword as did any other average eight-year-old, having extensively practiced waving plastic and wooden facsimiles in preparation for some similar situation. He planted himself between Anemometer and his sister, beating back the anima's attack. He looked like Constance just then, his eyes dark, the line of his face firm – but Evie looked like Sophia or John, her blue eyes flashing, the room warming rapidly, her skin sparking like struck flint.

"Get away from my brother!" she shouted, and a burst of great heat melted Anemometer's steel skin and bronze faceplate and clacking claws, smelting him down to a puddle on the floor.

On the battlements Constance swung her arc of annihilation in blind circles, the not-sword draining her of life even as it reduced the Endless to non-existence. Through now with the dross of despair she fed it whatever she could find; the taste of licorice, tasting licorice for the first time, watching Evie taste licorice for the first time, scowling at the taste, her Aunt's smile though she could not know it, Mary Ann at the dinner table, refusing to eat, Mary Ann in a coffee shop, refusing to speak, a coffee shop Constance had gone to in Paris during her gap year after college, a girl that she had seen there, the girl's tiny French flat, silk prints on the ceilings, Adeline, her skin and hair and eyes and fingers and lips and tongue, tasting sweet but bittersweet like something that Constance could no longer remember.

And still it was not enough, the End endless, all-consuming, a countless infinity which could lose half its force and remain unaware of the injury, all the efforts of the Harrow and the Thousand Peoples futile. In the central tower Anemometer was well-dead but had already spread his infection, the wounded hydronese turning an inky black, Evie exhausted from her magics. John remained in a crumbled heap atop the battlements, Sophia and Adeline were making their own last stands. The End had forced great gaps in the Tower's battlements, wounds through which they streamed, held off by the few remaining defenders, desperate souls, civilians holding spears bravely and without skill.

All hope seemed lost. It was time for a miracle.

In the courtyard amid the rushing armies of the End an aperture opened in existence and Mary Ann walked out of it. She looked stronger, firmer, red hair cascading down from her shoulders, neck proud and back unbent. She wore a gown of pure white light. Thistle, né Hank, né Thistle, stood quietly at her side. A spark in its collective consciousness and the End turned to face her, its nearest representative – a blind rat with festering flesh and a savage gut wound – shambled forward, claws outstretched but still lamenting. "Bend in the ruler! Grit in your eye! Flaw in the grain! Flaw in the grain!"

"It seems like that, sometimes," said Mary Ann, nodding sadly and waving the creature through the portal.


In the first light of Christmas Morning, beneath a cold, clear winter sun, while children waited fitfully for the start of the festivities and their parents hoped vainly for a few more hours of sleep, an old man stepped out onto the Harrow's front lawn. He felt the soft crunch of the hibernal grass below his feet, noticed a grackle perched on a tree branch, heard a dog bark. He smiled. Then he died.

*2024*

# SEVENTY

Sophia Harrow lay in her hospital bed, waiting for what was to come. It was past time for desperate measures, for experimental procedures and thousand-to-one-shots, nothing left but to go with dignity, or as much dignity as could be managed, plastic tubing piercing her veins, heart monitor bleeping arrhythmically. Her shoulders were thin, and her snowy white hair was patchy. Her eyes were still blue but would soon be shut forever.

"You want anything?" Constance asked. "Water, or something?"

"I'm fine," said Sophia. It took a great deal of energy even to mouth those two words, and still they were barely loud enough to be heard over the whir of the machines which were actively, perhaps pointlessly, prolonging her life. "How are the kids?"

"They're good, Mom. They're going to come see you tomorrow."

"And Adeline?"

"She's good too. She's going to bring them."

"That's good," Sophia said. "I'm glad."

Constance did her best to smile.

Being almost dead was like being nearly sleeping, and in her perpetual half-dream Sophia was a spectral presence, passing over a strange country in the early light of day. From high above a broken, azure palace she watched a menagerie of inexplicable creatures rebuilding the walls and battlements and their homes, some injured, all scarred, honoring the lost through labor and hope. There was pain but no despair, the past terrible and tragic and never altogether gone but worth carrying onward all the same. They had survived. They would survive a little longer. Sophia felt herself pulled forward, over a landscape scarred and pitted and lonely, roads overgrown with weeds and villages empty and great metropolises sitting like cenotaphs – but here too there were signs of life, refugees trickling back and exiles finding shelter amid the wreckage, making new homes to replace those they had lost. Sophia traveled farther, past ranging mountains and inshore oceans, a vast apocatastasis returning the land to its pristine state. Amid a ruined forest she saw the first shoots of green, young trees sprouting, a handful of survivors tending to them, life reasserting itself against death, death which is inevitable and certain and yet which is always and everywhere on the defensive, life exploding in boundless profusion, chaotic, painful, preferable to the alternative.

John sat on a bench in the hallway. His arm was out of its sling, but his leg was still encased in a tight-fitting plastic boot, and he held his cane loosely in his hands. He was very tired. If he thought hard, he could remember the last time he slept, a few hours snatched from an early morning the day previous. But he was not thinking very hard, or he was thinking very hard about many other things; about the funeral and what they would tell Julian and Evie and about clearing out his mother's room and about his life after Sophia had ended hers, all the long years that yet lay ahead, if he was lucky. At some point he realized he was crying. Not sobbing, his breath still even, but weeping nonetheless, tears streaming down his cheeks.

Mary Ann sat down beside him and cleared her throat.

John wiped his eyes. "Hey, sis."

"Hi, John."

"Do you want some water, or something?"

"That's OK," he said. "Do you have a tissue, maybe?"

"I can get one."

"That's OK," said John again. "It's good to see you."

"It's good to see you. How's it been?"

John smiled sadly. "I'm glad you came."

A doctor passed briskly. Somewhere someone coughed.

"How's your leg?"

"I've had to give up on my lifelong dream of becoming a Gaelic dancer."

"Heartbreaking," said Mary Ann, smiling. "How are the kids?"

"They're OK. Adeline moved in with us last week, to help out and everything. I'm back in the attic."

"For how long?"

John shrugged. "For the duration."

"All of you together?"

"It's a funny world," John admitted.

"Are you worried this will affect your louche hipster lifestyle?"

"I've been stealing Evie's baby aspirin; it's getting me by."

Mary Ann snickered. A nurse came out from one of the room's carrying a urine sample.

"How did you know?" John asked.

Mary Ann shrugged. "Out there by himself forever, inside his own head, lost and alone? I understand what that's like. I guess you do too."

"Yeah," said John. "Anyway, you did good."

"Thanks, John."

"Don't mention it."

John dried his eyes. He had not had a good cry for nearly twenty years, and hadn't realized how much he had missed it, that tranquility which arrives as breath returns to normal, exhaustion numbing the pain.

"We don't belong there," said Mary Ann. "Uncle Aaron was right. Whatever it is, it's not ours. We have to let it go."

"I think you're wrong," said John, because he did.

"Let's not fight about it," said Mary Ann.

"No," John agreed, "not tonight."

But tomorrow, certainly, and through who knew how many years to come. Likely this would be the last time that they would ever again meet in some common cause, perhaps the last time that kind words would be exchanged between them, perhaps the last time that they would see each other at all. John knew that and Mary Ann knew that and so there was no point in either of them saying it.

"I'm going to…" Mary Ann began.

"Right," said John, "sure."

"I love you, John," said Mary Ann, rising from the bench.

"I love you too, sis," said John, his face turning to its familiar crooked smile, "but you're not going to beat me."

Time would tell on that, as on everything, and Mary Ann was kind enough to allow her brother the last word.

Slipping into the hotel room she saw her sister and stifled a gasp. Constance looked ten years older, not just looked but *was*, having exhausted some quotient of her remaining years in those final few minutes holding off the End.

Constance pushed herself up from her chair. "It looks worse than it is," she promised, though in truth she still found herself grown tired easily, and there were occasions when she would sit for long moments failing to recall the capital of Ohio, or her father's middle name.

"You'd say that even if you were dying."

"Probably. How are you?"

"I'm OK."

"Safe?"

"Safe."

"The man?"

Mary Ann smiled.

"That's good. That's great." Constance wrapped her arms tight around Mary Ann's shoulders. She breathed in her sister's scent, felt her slender shoulders. Then she let her go. "I'll give you two a minute," she said, slipping out the doorway.

Mary Ann took the seat her sister had vacated. She held her mother's hand, the skin thin as wrapping paper, the flesh clammy beneath.

"It took you long enough," Sophia said.

Mary Ann burst into tears, burying her head against the hospital bed and her mother's fragile body.

"I was having the loveliest dream," Sophia said absently. "You were in it. So were your bother and your sister."

"All together?"

"No," said Sophia, "not all together. But it was nice just the same."

Mary Ann sobbed and gasped, gasped and sobbed.

"Enough, now," said Sophia, patting her daughter's hand. "That's enough. It'll be all right."

"I don't want to be alone," Mary Ann managed through her tears.

Sophia wanted to say that we were all always alone; that love is like a strike of lightning against a dark landscape, everything illuminated perfectly in an instant and then gone; that time is a ceaseless procession which marches forward indifferent to our sorrows and offers only memory as salve; and also that this was fine, this was enough; but she found she was too tired to form the words. Anyway, there was no good in trying to tell anyone anything. Thirty-seven years as a mother had taught her that much.

Mary Ann wiped her eyes. "I love you, Mom."

"I love you too," said Sophia Harrow, dying happily.

# ACKNOWLEDGEMENTS

Thanks owed to; Sam my agent, Paul my editor, Eleanor, Gemma, Desola and the rest of the crew at Angry Robot.

*Gracias a mis compas de Clark Street.*